**Sara** Orwig ... ... nds, dogs, books, lo... ... ees. She is married to and in love with the guy she met in college. They have three children and six grandchildren. Sara's one hundredth published novel was a July 2016 release. With a master's degree in English, Sara has written historical romance, mainstream fiction and con- porary romance. Sara welcomes readers on Facebook at www.saraorwig.com.

**Reese Ryan** writes sinfully sweet romance. She challenges characters with family and career drama and life-changing secrets while treating readers to an emotional love story filled with unexpected twists.

Born and raised in the Midwest, Reese has deep Tennessee roots. She endured many long, hot car trips to family reunions in Memphis via a tiny clown car loaded with cousins. Connect with Reese via Instagram, Facebook or www.reeseryan.com.

Discover more at millsandboon.co.uk

# MARRIED FOR HIS HEIR

SARA ORWIG

# SAVANNAH'S SECRETS

REESE RYAN

MILLS & BOON

First Published in Great Britain 2018
by Mills & Boon, an imprint of HarperCollinsPublishers,
1 London Bridge Street, London, SE1 9GF

*Married for His Heir* © 2018 Sara Orwig
*Savannah's Secrets* © 2018 Roxanne Ravenel

ISBN: 978-0-263-93593-6

51-0318

MIX
Paper from
responsible sources
FSC® C007454

This book is produced from independently certified FSC™ paper to ensure responsible forest management.

For more information visit: www.harpercollins.co.uk/green

Printed and bound in Spain
by CPI, Barcelona

# MARRIED FOR
# HIS HEIR

## SARA ORWIG

With thanks to Stacy Boyd,
who made this book possible.

Thank you to Tahra Seplowin
for fixing things and answering questions.

With thanks always to Maureen Walters.

Also, with love to my family,
who fill my days with joy.

# One

"Just remember, curiosity killed the cat." Nick Duncan shot his brother a narrow-eyed look, as if willing him to lay off.

But Stan didn't take the hint. He merely shook his head and continued. "What do you expect, Nick? A woman you don't know is coming by to tell you about an inheritance you didn't know you had. Of course I'm curious."

Nick had to agree, the man had a point.

He stepped off the porch into the front yard of his cattle ranch, the ND Ranch, taking a moment to let his gaze sweep over the landscaped front yard, green from the constant watering. But nothing could distract his thoughts. An inheritance?

"And you say our attorney told you to accept the appointment with her?" Stan asked, stepping up beside his oldest brother.

"Yeah. Apparently, she went to Horace and talked to him instead of calling me. How she found him, I don't know. That should be personal information." He swiped a hand across his neck. "I've been racking my brain, but heck, I don't know any Talia Barton, not in the oil business, not from ranching, not socially. And I'm sure I'd remember. Since I stepped down as CEO at Duncan Energy, I don't stay in Dallas. Only when I have to go to board meetings or something special. This ranch is where I live. I can't think of any woman named Talia. There have been so damn few women in my life since I became a widower."

"You mean no one that you've been interested in," Stan clarified. "You have a steady stream of women coming to see you, bringing you enough casseroles and desserts to open a restaurant out here. I'll bet you have a fridge filled with food in your Dallas house, too."

"Oh, yeah. The ladies don't want me to starve. They've got good intentions, but I'm not interested." He hadn't been interested in a woman in three years—and he didn't figure he ever would be again.

He took off his Stetson and swiped it across his jean-clad thigh, as if he could banish the memories as easily as he did the dust on his hat. All this time and thoughts of Regina could creep up on him at the oddest times.

He squared his shoulders and replaced the hat. "Well, no matter who she is, this Talia Barton can come out here to see me. I'm not driving to Dallas. I told Horace."

He'd also asked the attorney questions. Lots of them. But he hadn't gotten any answers. Whatever this mystery woman had told Horace, he wouldn't say. He'd merely insisted Nick make an appointment to meet her.

"Is Horace coming to the ranch?"

"No, I told him he didn't need to. Whatever she intends to do, this meeting should be short." Nick turned to his brother, looking into eyes that were as green as his own, and flecked with gold. "Come to think of it, Stan, you might as well stay. Whatever inheritance I'm getting, it may eventually involve you."

"Oh, no," Stan said, grinning. "I have my new horse loaded into my trailer and I'm taking him home. I'll hear later what the mysterious Ms. Barton is giving you. And, by the way, have you told Grandmother?"

Nick rolled his eyes. "Are you kidding? Of course not. At least not until I know why we're meeting."

Stan laughed. "No, I guess not. I sure as hell wouldn't tell her until I knew and maybe not even then."

Nick clapped his brother on the back. "Come on—let's go inside. I'm not waiting out here to greet Ms. Barton," he said, turning for his ranch home.

"No, no." Stan shook his head. "I told you, I'm leaving. This appointment is for you and it's private. You can call and tell me what the hell a woman you don't even know has for you."

"I'm still tempted to ignore Horace and refuse to see her."

"Horace has been our family attorney for years and your attorney since you turned twenty-one. You do what he says and meet with her. You know he's not giving you bad advice."

"I don't know. Any attorney who won't confide in his own client whom he has known since I was five years old is a damn poor attorney, if you ask me."

"You know Horace has to have a good reason for not

telling you what's involved." Stan started to leave, his wavy brown hair tangling in the breeze. "And it must be something good."

"If it isn't, I'm getting a new attorney," Nick grumbled, gazing down the long ranch drive that disappeared around a curve where a tall cottonwood's leaves fluttered in the wind.

Stan left, his boots clicking on the brick walk as he headed to his shiny black pickup with a horse trailer hitched to it.

While he rubbed the brown stubble covering his jaw, Nick watched the plume of gray dust Stan's truck stirred as he drove away. In minutes the dust settled and he went inside to wait in the study. He only wished his thoughts could settle just as easily. But he couldn't still the questions that swirled in his mind.

Talia Barton…

Since he had become a widower, he'd had a few one-nighters, all meaningless encounters, but not many of them and not in a long time. He had been working late hours to wear himself out, and working out before and after handling ranch tasks. He didn't date and he didn't want to. So how did he know Talia Barton?

It was fifteen anguishing minutes later when he heard a car pull up the ranch drive. He went to the window and watched as a black car slowed and stopped in front of the house.

In minutes the driver emerged from the car and Nick's interest increased a fraction as he viewed a tall, leggy blonde in high heels, a navy suit and a white blouse. Looking as if she had just stepped out of an office or a photo shoot, she would turn heads wherever

she went. If she had any persuasive abilities, he could
see why Horace had told him to meet her.

He forced himself to stand still. His house manager served as a butler, and since Royce knew she was
coming, he would bring her to the study. Instead, Nick
watched her come up the steps and his pulse jumped.
The woman was gorgeous.

He walked across the room to the open door. In
seconds he heard Royce talking to her, and when
they came into sight, Nick stepped forward. "Thanks,
Royce." He extended his hand to the woman. "Ms.
Barton, I'm Nick Duncan," he said as Royce left them.

The moment he wrapped his hand around her soft,
warm hand, he felt a sizzling jolt of awareness, something that hadn't happened since his wife. The reaction
startled him and he looked more closely at her.

He saw a flicker in her thickly lashed blue eyes that
caused his pulse to jump another notch. She felt something, too, and that knowledge fueled his reaction.

She cleared her throat and withdrew her hand. "I'm
Talia Barton. Please call me Talia," she said in a soft
voice. There was a directness about her that made him
feel she was a no-nonsense person, and once again,
he thought that people probably did what she wanted.

"Come have a seat where we can talk," he urged,
motioning her into the study. "I'm curious what it is
that you couldn't tell me about by phone," he said, his
interest growing because he was absolutely certain
he had never seen this woman in his life before now.
He would not forget her. "My attorney has urged me
to see you, so whatever it is, you've certainly convinced him."

"I think you'll agree after you hear me out," she

said, following him into the room. She took the leather chair he indicated and sat facing him.

Nick couldn't resist looking when she crossed her long, shapely legs. His reaction to her startled him again. He hadn't had this kind of response to a woman since his wife's death almost three years ago. The anniversary of the plane crash that had taken his wife and baby would be in August. Since his loss, it was as if he had become numb, half dead himself and oblivious of women, except for a few one-nighters at parties far from the ranch.

Why was he having this reaction to this mystery woman?

Talia looked into green eyes flecked with gold and realized there would be nothing easy about this meeting. To add to her jittery nerves, Nick Duncan was not only handsome and appealing, but there was some kind of vibrant chemistry between them.

In every way she possibly could, including hiring a private investigator to get information on Nick, Talia had checked into his life. To her relief, all sources reported that Nick Duncan was intelligent, reliable, capable, confident, successful and tough when he needed to be. From all that she could find out, he had been a good husband and father, even though he'd had his son for only a brief time.

Once he'd checked out, she'd gone ahead with her plans to meet him and lay out her problem for him. But she hadn't planned on this volatile chemistry that had simmered between them from the moment she had walked into the room.

When they had shaken hands the sizzle had startled her. So had the tingles when she'd met his gaze. It wouldn't matter, though, she told herself, because they would never mean anything to each other. Still, she had been surprised. Since her disastrous marriage while still in college and then divorce, she hadn't been drawn to any man. Besides, there was too much upheaval in her life now. But somehow, with a mere touch, Nick Duncan broke through all that. He was far more handsome and sexy in person than his pictures indicated. It wasn't even his personality because he was being polite, cautious and reserved. She knew he wondered why she was there and what she wanted. She might as well tell him and get this over with.

Nothing in her life—not the deaths in her family or her broken marriage—had hurt as much as this. Tears threatened, uncustomary for her, and she swallowed, looking around the room as she fought to get her emotions under control. She had rehearsed what she would say to him, but now that the moment had come and she was actually facing him, she wanted to run to her car and drive home.

And then what? she asked herself. If she didn't talk to him, the alternative was worse. Nick Duncan had checked out as a successful, intelligent, family-oriented man. A billionaire, owner of the ND Ranch, part owner of Duncan Energy, a company started by his father and now run by the two youngest Duncan brothers with Nick and his brother Stan on the board. Nick was a good rancher, a good businessman, a man who had had his own terrible loss. She had no choice but to do what she'd come here to do. She squared her shoulders and sat up straight, but before she could speak, he broke the awkward silence.

"Do you live around here?" he asked.

"I live in Dallas. I teach art in a two-year college."

He didn't know it, but his question gave her the opening she needed. She took a breath and gave him a faint smile.

"Mr. Duncan, I'm—"

"Nick, please," he prompted her.

"Yes, well, Nick, I'm sure you're curious as to why I wanted to see you…and there's no need to wait. I want your help about something belonging to you."

He leaned in closer, resting his hands on his knees as he looked at her intently.

"I've had a neighbor whose niece, Madeline Prentiss, inherited her house and Madeline and I became friends. Neither of us have any family, so we were drawn together. She had a degree and internship in landscape architecture. She worked for a landscape company and took a night art class I taught because she drew landscape plans for clients. We rode to class together that year and became even closer friends."

She related the facts, the history that he needed to know, but the whole time she spoke, all she wanted to do was leave. She didn't want to ask his help or ask him to do anything. She took a deep breath, looking into those curious green-gold eyes that made her heart beat faster, and suddenly she couldn't go on. They stared at each other.

"I had this all rehearsed," she said finally as she rose abruptly, "but it isn't easy. Just give me a minute."

"Sure. Take your time. Let me get you a glass of water," he said, getting up and leaving the room. She suspected he did it to give her a moment to get herself composed. She knew what she had to do. When he returned, he held a tray with a pitcher and two glasses of ice and water. He handed her one, and when their fingers brushed, for just an instant, she felt another flash of intense awareness of him as an appealing man. While she sipped the icy water, her gaze locked with his. The look in his eyes made her heartbeat quicken.

"Want to have a seat?" he said, setting the tray on a table. As they sat down again, she noticed his gaze on her as she crossed her legs. She placed her glass on a coaster on a small table beside her chair and adjusted her skirt.

"This is hard for me, Mr. Dunc—er, Nick—but it is definitely overdue. I was telling you about a friend of mine, Madeline Prentiss."

He nodded. "Is there a reason you're telling me all this about this particular person?"

"Yes. I'm here because of Madeline. You see, almost two years ago when Madeline was at a party in Austin, she had a romantic night with a man she met there but she never saw him again."

"I take it Madeline thinks I'm that man?"

"Yes. You were that man. That's definite, and in the past, she told me about the night you two had." She leaned in and had no choice but to gather her courage and blurt it out. "And there's a baby from that encounter."

Stunned, Nick felt as if ice water had been poured over him.

"You're saying that I fathered a baby with this woman? And I've never heard a word from her about it? Why did she wait until now and why send you? Where is Madeline now?" He couldn't stop the questions that spilled from his lips. Though part of him was in shock, the other part was in overdrive, and he wanted—no, needed—answers.

"Madeline didn't want to inform you of her pregnancy because that night, you spent a long time telling her how much you loved your wife. You told her about losing your little two-month-old son and your wife in a plane crash. You also convinced her that you missed your wife and you weren't ready to go out with anyone else. She told me you actually cried over your loss. Besides, she knew that you weren't in love with her and probably never would be."

"You're using the past tense." A chill skittered up his spine.

"That's right," Talia acknowledged. But she didn't elaborate. Instead she said, "Madeline had a talent. She could sing and she had gotten auditions and began to get bookings that paid more than the landscape business."

He suddenly remembered Madeline, because she had sung at the party the night he met her. Talia was right: she had talent.

"You remember her," Talia said, startling him that she guessed his thoughts so easily.

"It's a little blurry, but I do. I don't go out much, so there aren't many occasions to even try to recall, but I remember her because she was beautiful and talented. She sang for everyone that night."

"Madeline was on the way to a successful singing career, until several months ago when she was killed in a car wreck. She was young and she didn't leave a will. Since her death I've been caring for her baby, and now I'm in a fight with the state, which wants to take her precious baby away. I've pulled every string I can, but I'm not a relative nor the legal guardian of Madeline's baby. Madeline left no directive, nothing to indicate that she would want to appoint me guardian of her baby. She had no family, either. You, on the other hand, are her baby's blood father."

He barely heard what she went on to say to him. His mind was stuck on one phrase. ...*baby's blood father*...

He was the father of a baby.

A baby he didn't know with a deceased mother he barely remembered.

"Sorry, give me a second. This is a shock." He reached for his water and took a gulp. What he really needed was something far stronger. "When you said you needed to see me, I didn't dream it would be about a baby. My baby. A baby that's an orphan."

"Not really an orphan," Talia said, looking intently at him. "She has a living blood relative—her father. You. I've checked you out and you have high recommendations as to your character." She paused a second. Then her gaze seemed to deepen as she continued. "I need your help, Nick."

"How's that?" he asked, trying to pay attention and listen to what she was saying, but the shock of learning he had a baby still dominated his attention.

"You can keep the state from taking her."

"Her? A little girl?" he asked, his shock increasing. "I don't know one thing about little girls."

"There was a time you didn't know anything about running a ranch or about baby boys, either."

They stared at each other and he could feel an invisible ripple of conflict. He ignored it.

He had a baby girl whom he'd never seen. That was

the only thought that dominated his mind. "How old is she?" he asked her.

"Fourteen months."

"I had a baby boy for two months. He would be two years, nine months old now." Trying to push aside a familiar dull ache at the thought of Regina and Artie, Nick took a deep breath. "Beyond the two months with Artie, I have no experience being a father. It was different when I had a wife and we wanted a family, but… I don't know anything about babies. I don't know anything about little girls…"

His hand practically shook as he put his glass down on the table. The next thought struck him like a raging bull. "You're sure this is my baby?"

Talia showed no reaction. She maintained her composure as she replied. "Yes, Madeline was sure. You can get a DNA test if you'd like. Hattie is her name."

"Hattie's her name?" He liked the way it sounded.

She nodded. "I don't have any doubt about the outcome, but no doubt you'll be reassured when the DNA results prove that Hattie is your little girl."

For a moment they sat in silence as he gazed out the window at his land spreading off in the distance. Was this true? Was he a father again? Even though he had been a father for two months, he couldn't see himself as a dad to a little girl who was over one year old.

He looked back at Talia and met a cool, blue-eyed stare. She impressed him because in her quiet way, even when she didn't want to break the news, she had taken charge of this meeting, something that didn't happen to him with women, except for his grandmother.

"You've been caring for this baby?"

"Yes, I've been keeping Hattie since Madeline's

death. I watched Hattie often before Madeline died. As I said, she had no family and I was like a second mama for Hattie. Hattie has been in day care and I pick her up when I leave school. In a few weeks, the spring session will be over and I'm not teaching this summer. I'll take her out of day care and be home with her."

He sat quietly, mulling over all he had learned. How was he going to deal with this? He was a parent who didn't know anything about babies or little girls and he wanted solid proof that this was actually his child.

"I want the DNA test," he said. "Until I have proof, I don't want to do anything."

"I can understand that and I expected you to want confirmation. But you must understand, time is an issue here. However, if I tell the state agents that you're looking into gaining custody of your child, they'll probably back off for a while, especially long enough for you to get a DNA test."

"If they don't, I'll talk to my attorney and we'll deal with them."

She opened her purse, pulled out an envelope and handed it to him. "Here's the name, a number to call and the address for the DNA test. It takes time, but it will prove Hattie is your baby girl. My number is there also."

Nick took the envelope, turning it over in his hand.

"In the meantime," Talia added, "so we don't waste time, I think you should meet Hattie."

Maybe she was right.

He looked up at her. "You sound certain about my parentage. If I get this little child, if she is mine and the state backs off, where do you come in? You've been caring for her."

She shook her head and looked away, and to his shock it looked as if her eyes filled with tears. "I love Hattie like she's my own, but I know I have to give her up. She's your baby. You're young and you'll marry again. I'm realistic enough to know there won't be a place in her life for me once I turn her over to you."

She ran her fingers over her eyes and he knew she wiped away tears. He thought about his own loss. He only knew his son two months, but he had loved him beyond measure, so he could understand her feelings. She'd loved this baby for fourteen months and a lot of that time she had been the sole parent with only the help of the day care. He was sorry that she hurt and he knew the hurt would only grow.

"It's amazing how babies can wrap around your heart and steal it away," he said gently and she gave him a startled glance. "If you live in the area, perhaps we can work something out where you can see her. We'll talk about it after the DNA result is in," he added.

"Thank you. That's nice if it works out," she said, still staring at him as if reassessing her opinion about him. She brushed her fingers over her eyes again and took a deep breath before she spoke. "You're very doubtful this is your baby. I can understand that but—"

"You're certain that Madeline gave you the straight story?" he interrupted to ask her. "I mean, if I am the father, she had almost two years to tell me about the baby."

"I encouraged her to, but in the beginning, she worried that you might try to take Hattie from her. When her music career was beginning to take off she expected to leave Texas and move to New York or California or maybe Nashville, and she figured you'd never cross paths again."

And if that had come to pass, he'd never have known about Hattie. If she was indeed his.

Talia must have read his thoughts because she said, "You get your DNA test and we'll talk." As she stood, he came to his feet immediately. "Unless you have some questions, I think we're finished for now."

"You don't have a doubt, do you?" he asked and looked into her big blue eyes that made him draw a deep breath again and almost forget his question.

"No, I don't. I do want you to know the truth and the DNA should convince you. That and Hattie's looks."

Startled, he stopped thinking about Talia's blue eyes and stared at her. "You think Hattie looks like me?"

"You can decide when you see her," she said, smiling faintly.

Her smile couldn't hide the hurt that he saw in her eyes. She didn't want to give up the baby she'd come to love. He could see that. He also saw the toll this meeting was taking on her. It was time to end it.

"I'll get the DNA test and we'll get back together," he said as he led her out of the study. "I just can't fully accept this until I have some proof. I'm glad you understand that."

"Yes, I do." She stopped at the front door and turned to him. "You have my name, address and phone number in that envelope. I'll expect to hear from you."

There was authority in her tone that reminded him of his grandmother and he almost felt he should promptly answer, "Yes, ma'am." Instead, as he caught the scent of her perfume and looked into the depths of her eyes, he wanted to ask her out. The idea surprised him, and as fast as it came, he dismissed it. This woman had already complicated his life, and whatever happened, he needed to keep his wits about him and not get emotionally—or physically—involved with her. He wasn't going to consider dealing with Talia if Hattie turned out not to be his baby, either. Too bad, really. He suspected she was as strong-willed as he was, and under other circumstances he would have liked to get to know her.

Talia reached for the doorknob the instant he did, and instead of the cold metal handle, his hand touched the warm softness of her wrist. Instantly, his heartbeat sped up and he was aware that mere inches separated them. Her skin was smooth and flawless; her rosy mouth was as captivating as her gorgeous blue eyes. When he couldn't get his breath, the reaction she caused in him astonished him. Seconds after he'd lectured himself to resist her appeal, he reacted to it.

His eyes left her lips and traveled to her eyes when her voice broke the silence. "Nick," she said, "I may not have the right to ask you but…" He saw her throat tighten as she swallowed back tears. "If she is your baby and you don't want her, please don't abandon her and let her become a ward of the state. Surely there's room in your life and your heart for a child you've fathered."

"If this is my child, I'll take responsibility," Nick said. He couldn't help wondering if he was making a colossal mistake in committing himself, yet he wouldn't abandon a baby that was his own.

"I'll count on that. You won't regret it. She is an adorable, happy baby," she said, and he heard the wistful note in her voice.

Something hurt deep inside him as he once again thought of his own little boy, who came into his life and then went out too fast. Even though it was approaching three years since he last held Artie, he still hurt badly. "I'll get the DNA and contact you whatever the answer."

She nodded. "I'll be waiting and we can go from there. Thank you for telling me that Hattie can rely on you."

He opened the door and Talia stepped away, but he saw tears in her eyes again. "I'll wait to hear from you."

He watched her walk to her car, her hips swaying slightly with a poised, purposeful walk. She was one good-looking woman, but she had come into his life with potential news that would change it forever. So why the physical reaction to her? Maybe he was coming back to life and would have that reaction with any other attractive woman.

As fast as that thought came, he rejected it. He saw attractive women almost daily and had no such reaction. Not only attractive women, but friends, women who should stir the kind of response that this one had, but they didn't.

He headed to his kitchen to get a cold beer and get Talia Barton's big blue eyes and million-dollar legs out of his thoughts.

He opened his refrigerator and looked at all the casseroles, desserts and salads the local bachelorettes had brought. He wasn't aware he even knew this many women. With a sigh he retrieved a beer, sat at the table and opened the envelope Talia had given him. He read the notes she'd jotted in her neat teacher's handwriting.

Then he called to make an appointment for tomorrow with the DNA people.

He took a long pull on his beer and stared into space, thinking about Regina and little Arthur. He wondered if he would ever stop hurting, ever stop missing them. How was he going to love a little girl he didn't know when longing for Artie and Regina filled his heart?

Artie had been so tiny. Nick had rocked him, talked to him, sang to him, bathed and dressed him and carried him around when he cried. Occasionally, he gave him a bottle, but he hadn't been fully responsible for his son's care, and he never worried about what to do because if he had a question, Regina was there to answer it.

A fourteen-month-old baby girl would be another matter. She needed a mother who would shower her with love. The thought worried him until he shrugged it away. There was no reason to worry until he knew without any doubt that this little child was his.

And if Hattie was his child—how much would that bring Talia into his life?

# Two

Talia Barton drove away from Nick Duncan's ranch house. She could barely see for her tears, so she pulled over and tried to get a grip on her emotions. She loved Hattie and felt as if she was a second mother to the little girl. It had hurt terribly to try to get Nick to realize he had a responsibility to take Hattie. She had lived with a chilling panic since people from the state agency had stepped in and said Hattie should be a ward of the state because there was nothing official to indicate the mother had wanted Talia to raise Hattie.

Madeline's life had been filled with joy, excitement and the promise of a glittering future in the music world. She had talked about seeing an attorney and getting papers drawn up to make Talia Hattie's guardian, but hadn't gotten around to it. Madeline had been so busy with her career, so filled with a love of life and her baby, that she hadn't considered anything happening to take that life away. It hadn't occurred to Talia to worry about the possibility, either. The accident had been a painful, numbing shock that still was a raw hurt.

Thinking about parting with Hattie hurt and Talia cried quietly. Finally she dried her eyes. She prayed Nick would want his baby and would come forward to claim her. Talia knew that, whatever happened, she would not get to keep Hattie as her own. She had to accept that. If she couldn't raise Hattie herself, then she wanted the best possible outcome and right now there were only two solutions: Nick Duncan would claim his baby or the state would take Hattie. Talia didn't want the latter to happen.

Thinking about Hattie and wanting to get home to see her, Talia gripped the steering wheel tightly and pulled onto the road.

Her thoughts shifted to Nick and the moment she had first met him. The first time they had touched, the mere handshake had sent tingles radiating through her and made breathing difficult. What shocked her was that he had felt the electricity, too. She'd seen it in the look he gave her, felt it as he took her hand lightly, a slight, impersonal touch, yet it hadn't been impersonal. She had tingled to her toes, and she knew he reacted, as well. Another twist she couldn't worry about. Right now she was focused on getting him to become the dad for Hattie that he truly was, and as soon as possible. Hopefully, Nick would let her stay part of Hattie's life. Was that asking so much?

Yet she didn't know Nick and he didn't know her. What if someday he married again and his wife didn't want Talia in their lives? Would Nick keep Hattie from her?

She didn't want to think what would happen if Nick wouldn't claim Hattie. First he needed proof that he was her dad. The minute she'd seen him, Talia had noticed the family resemblance. Hattie had Nick's green eyes with little flecks of gold, his tangled brown hair and the same facial structure.

Talia shook her head. How was she going to go about work and keep focused on what she needed to do? All she could think about was Hattie every minute. She pulled into the day-care parking lot, climbed out of the car and went inside to find her little charge.

Hattie saw her coming and held out her arms. Talia picked her up, smiling at her and kissing her cheek as she squeezed her close. "Hi, sweetie," she said, smiling at the baby, feeling warmth and love pour over her. She loved this child with all her heart. If only Nick would love Hattie, too. She told herself he would, once he was certain she was his. Surely he wouldn't want the state to take her.

"How's my girl?" she asked, snuggling close and inhaling the sweet scent of baby powder. Then she leaned back to look at Hattie, who smiled and patted Talia's cheek. "I love you," Talia said.

"Wuv you," Hattie replied softly in her childish voice, but the words thrilled Talia even when it was *wuv* instead of *love*.

"I'm taking you home now," Talia said, getting Hattie's bag, gathering up her other things. She talked to two of the women who ran the day care and then signed out and left with Hattie.

"Once he sees you, I don't see how your daddy can

resist you," Talia said as she buckled the child into the car seat.

"Da," Hattie repeated.

"That's right," Talia said, brightening. "Daddy. We'll work on that one. Da-dee," she said, drawing out the word. Hattie giggled.

"I hope he makes you laugh. Da-dee," Talia repeated, hoping Hattie would pick up the sounds and learn the word.

"We'll keep trying. I want your daddy to be unable to resist you. I don't want him to take you from me, but if he doesn't, the state will, so better your daddy, who might let me see you occasionally."

The first week of May, Nick was in his office on the ranch, staring at the document in his hand. The results of the DNA test. Absolute proof that he was Hattie's father. He mulled over the news when Stan knocked and entered the open door.

"I needed to drive into town and thought I'd stop to see you. Are you doing okay with this?"

"That I'm a dad? Hell, no, I'm not." He'd told his brother the DNA test results as soon as they'd arrived. Over the last few hours he'd read them a dozen times. He dropped the report back on his desk. "Talia Barton is bringing Hattie to my Dallas house tomorrow so I can meet her. We're both trying to ease into this. Talia is hurting over losing her charge and I can't imagine becoming a parent to a fourteen-month-old little girl. I don't know how to cope with a baby girl."

Stan stared at him with his brow furrowed as he pushed his hat back on his head. "You want to let the state take her?"

Startled, Nick looked up at his brother, his brows rising.

"Sorry," Stan said. "I know you don't want to do that and I wouldn't want to, either. I'm sorry I even asked you a question like that."

"Forget it. She's mine and I'll take the responsibility that I should, though this deal just tears at me. I didn't even know the mother. I feel like every time I look at that little girl, I'll want her to be Artie."

"Sorry, Nick. You'll get used to her. I'll help any way I can."

Nick heard the earnest note in his brother's voice and he smiled. "Thanks, Stan. That offer means a lot," he said, suddenly feeling proud of his younger brother for volunteering to help.

"I've got to run. I just stopped for a minute. When tomorrow is Ms. Barton coming to see you and bringing the baby?"

"In the afternoon. In the morning I'll go to Dallas and she'll bring Hattie by after her last class."

"You're a dad and I'm an uncle to a baby girl. Wow. That does take some getting used to." His wistful look was replaced by a serious one. "I'm surprised the state hasn't already stepped in and taken the baby from Ms. Barton. She doesn't have legal rights."

"She's a teacher in a community college and she has a quiet, take-charge manner that probably makes people do what she wants."

"A battle-ax?"

Smiling, Nick shook his head. "Trust me, you'll never use those words again after you see her."

"A hottie?"

"She's stunning. You'll see. In addition, she has that

authoritative manner, in a quieter way, that our grandmother does."

"No kidding. I can't wait to meet her."

Nick didn't reply, but he looked forward to seeing
her again himself and that shocked him. He didn't want
to have that reaction to her because she had upended
his life.

He walked out with Stan. "I don't want to tell
Grandmother until I have everything lined up. I don't
want her trying to move into my house."

"What a thought. Of course, if you let Grandmother
move in, you won't ever have to make another decision. You can just drift."

"You know better than that. She'd make all the decisions but she'd keep me hopping every second. No,
she doesn't know until I'm ready. You go ahead and tell
Blake and Adam and I'll call them or text." He knew
he'd have better luck with his other two brothers than
his grandmother.

"Good deal."

"Talia said Hattie looks like me. We'll see."

Stan shot him a horrified look. "I'm afraid I can't
imagine a little baby girl looking like you." Then he
smiled.

"Frankly, I can't, either," Nick said, running his
hand over the brown stubble on his jaw.

"Even if you try to keep her out of your hair, Grandmother will want to approve of the nanny you hire. And
I'm sure you're hiring a nanny."

"I don't know what I'll do." Nick couldn't stop his
fears from surfacing again. He'd been fighting them for
the last few hours. "I don't even know this little girl,
much less love her. I keep thinking how she won't have

anyone who loves her here. Talia Barton adores her. She'll go from having love poured out to her to a bunch of strangers. That's not good and it's worrying me."

"We're not a bunch of ogres, Nick, but I see what you mean. She'll need someone to love her. It may not help her disposition, either," Stan said.

Nick had already thought of that, but he was more worried about having a little baby who wasn't loved.

"If she's that good-looking, marry this Talia person," Stan said, breaking into his thoughts.

"Stan!" Nick said, annoyed and amused at the same time.

"I'm kidding. I wouldn't worry, Nick. Babies adapt and we'll all be here to help. You know Grandmother is going to love this baby. She adored Artie. And pretty soon, we'll all love her, too."

"You're right, I suppose. Grandmother is going to have to cooperate on this one. I can't deal with a hassle from her."

"Send me a picture of the teacher," Stan said, going down the porch steps. He glanced over his shoulder. "I might want to propose. Then I'd be daddy and uncle to your little girl." He laughed at his own joke and Nick shook his head.

"You're hopeless, Stan. Take your suggestions and go," Nick said, laughing with his brother.

"Seriously, I'll help if you need me, although I don't know as much about babies as you do. My expertise ends with colts and calves."

"Thanks, Stan," Nick said, feeling a bond with his brother.

As Stan drove away, Nick returned to his office, but he couldn't get his mind to focus on the ranch work in front of him. He remembered Madeline. Since meeting Talia, he recalled everything about that night. He was sure he had used protection, yet here was this little baby and the DNA definitely made her *his* baby. He couldn't get accustomed to the idea, and guilt swamped him at the thought he would have to take her away from someone who poured out love to her and place her in a family of strangers.

Enough, he told himself. It'd work out. It had to.

He picked up the leather-bound ledger but the figures swam before his eyes. All he could think about was his new status as a daddy...and his electrifying attraction to Talia Barton.

Late the following sunny May afternoon Nick paced back and forth. He was in his mansion in a gated community of Dallas, waiting for Talia to arrive, and then he would meet his daughter. That still didn't seem possible. A night at a party—when he'd had too much to drink, been too long alone, hurting over his loss and trying to overcome the grief and desperation he felt— he'd had sex with a woman he'd barely known. Now he had a daughter for the rest of his life. A little girl who was going to move in with a father who was a total stranger. He knew that was better than the state and they would probably all grow to love her, but it was going to be rough for the little girl for a time and he hated that. And it was breaking Talia's heart, something he could understand all too well because of the loss of his son.

When he heard a car, he glanced at his watch. Talia was on time. He thought about seeing her again and that was one bit of this whole thing that he looked forward to, even though he shouldn't because she had already complicated his life beyond measure.

He hurried to the front door. When he reached for the door, he glanced out and saw Talia coming up the walk carrying a little girl in her arms. His pulse jumped as his glance swept over Talia's high heels and her deep blue sleeveless dress. Her hair was high, pinned on the sides of her head, and fell in spiral curls over her shoulders. The curls bounced slightly with each step she took. His gaze shifted to the baby in her arms. The little girl had one thin arm on Talia's shoulder with her fingers wound in Talia's long curls. Her other arm hung at her side. She had wispy, tangled brown hair, and from a distance she looked like a pretty child. He couldn't imagine that this was his baby, but she was. It was a shock each time he thought about it, and seeing her didn't make it any more real to him.

A little girl he didn't know in the arms of a woman he would like to know if circumstances were different. His life was going to change forever and he couldn't even imagine how.

He opened the door. "Come in. You and Hattie."

"Thank you," Talia said in a tight voice. From the sound of it, he was sure she was hurting. If she felt this bad just introducing him to his daughter, how much worse was it going to get for her?

He looked down at the baby in her arms, gazing into wide green eyes with gold flecks that were like his own and ran in his family. Hattie had the same color hair he did, the same facial features, but slightly darker skin. As if sensing something was wrong with the adults around her, she gazed solemnly up at him.

He stepped back so Talia could enter and closed the

door behind her, catching up with them, his gaze lingering briefly on the sexy sway of Talia's hips as she walked. Hattie twisted around to stare at him, studying him intently.

"Let's go to the family room. It's probably the most childproof room in the house. Arthur wasn't toddling around or even crawling, so we didn't get anything ready for a baby to explore."

"I'll watch her and she'll go home with me until you're ready to take her," Talia said. "Unless you have other plans."

"Plans? I'm just trying to get a grip on my new status."

She glanced up with worry in her big eyes.

"You're worrying about me taking her from you," he said.

She shook her head. "I'm worrying you won't take her and the state will get her."

He caught Talia's arm lightly, instantly having that startling awareness from the physical contact. He heard her breath catch and realized she felt something, too. Why did sparks fly between them when they didn't even know each other? Looking intently at her, he released her just as quickly. Standing so close, he was acutely aware of her while he tried to focus on the problem.

"Let's settle that one right now. I have the DNA and Hattie is my baby. I'm not giving my baby to the state to try to place in foster homes or wherever they can find. I'll take Hattie and you'll get to see her. You have my promise," he said, emotions tearing at him because he was making a huge commitment that he didn't even know if he could live up to. He had been tossed into fa-

therhood abruptly and it brought back memories of his
baby boy and of his wife, of being in love and happy
and filled with plans for a future that vanished in a
crushing blow when their private plane went down in
a storm. He hadn't ever expected to raise a little girl
he didn't even know, a child born to a mother he was
with for only a few hours. As he looked down into Talia's wide, frightened eyes, his insides churned and he
wondered if he could possibly keep the promise he was
making to her. This promise was monumental and a
life-changer. Along with tremendous responsibility, it
brought heartache. Every time he looked at this child
he'd be reminded of what he had lost in the past.

As she searched his gaze, tears filled Talia's eyes.
She brushed away her tears hastily. "You really mean
that, don't you?" she asked softly.

"Yes, I do," he said. "Don't cry. I'll take Hattie because she's my child and you'll get to see her. We'll
figure something out."

"I wanted so badly to adopt her and be her mother.
My attorney said I'd have to go through the state to
apply." Shaking her head, Talia turned away, carrying the baby to the window and talking softly to her.
He let her go so she could get herself pulled together
while he tried to calm his own nerves.

A few minutes later he glanced around and saw
Talia was standing a few feet behind him, holding out
Hattie to place her in his arms. As their hands brushed,
he felt a frisson of electricity shoot up his arm. He inhaled her perfume, an enticing scent. As he took Hattie, his gaze met Talia's, and if he let himself, he could
drown in the blue depths of her eyes.

His heart pounding, he forced himself to step back

slightly, and his gaze was captured by the baby, who stared at him with huge eyes.

She was soft, warm and smelled of soap and lotion. She wore a white blouse and a pink jumper.

"Hi, Hattie," he said quietly.

She touched a button on his shirt and then touched his chin.

He felt little fingers moving over the stubble on his chin while he gazed at her as solemnly as she looked at him. She ran her tiny fingers over his face. "I'll contact the state human services and let them know that I have my baby. I think that will take her name off any list they have."

"It will as soon as you've notified them that you're taking her permanently. My attorney checked and I can't just come calling and then take her home with me. I have a friend who is an attorney and he's been keeping up with this. When you step in and actually take care of her and she lives with you, they have to back off and leave you alone unless they get a complaint about the way she's being raised, which they won't. Since Madeline's death, Hattie hasn't had any family except me. There's no one else who cares about her except the women at the day care. They think she's sweet and adorable."

"So except for those ladies, you're her whole world. We'll definitely have to work something out so you can come see her."

Her blue eyes widened and he saw hope blossom in them. Then she turned them to the child he held.

"Hattie, this is your daddy. Daddy," she repeated distinctly and looked at Nick. He looked down at her, and for a few seconds all he could think about was Talia and how close she stood, how tempting she smelled. She looked back at Hattie. "Daddy," Talia repeated.

"Da," Hattie said, running her fingers on Nick's jaw again.

"God love the little children," Nick said softly and turned away. Emotions tore at him when she ran her tiny fingers over his chin because Hattie made him think about Artie. He would never hear Artie say "Daddy," and it hurt. He missed his son and felt conflicted over the little girl in his arms. He pulled out his handkerchief and wiped away tears, trying to get a better grip on his emotions.

"Do you want me to take her?" Talia asked.

"No. I'll pull myself together. Sometimes it just hits me out of the blue and I miss Artie."

"That's the way I'm going to feel about Hattie," Talia said so softly, he didn't think she was even talking to him.

He heard her and knew she was right, and that disturbed him. "At least you can come visit and I'll let her visit you," he said, making another commitment that might be difficult.

Hattie's little fingers ran over his cheek, her mouth turned down, and she looked worried by his tears. He smiled at her and she stared for a few seconds and then smiled.

"Da," she repeated. He looked into her big green eyes and they stared at each other. Could he be a real dad to her? Would he grow to love her the way he had loved Artie? Right now, he felt at a loss and he hurt. Guilt rocked him for missing Artie each time he looked at Hattie. It wasn't right, but he couldn't help himself because he longed for his little son. Hattie was a little girl he didn't know.

"One thing's for sure," he said. "She's related to me. She has the Duncan hair and eyes. I'm glad I have the DNA results, but this child is a Duncan."

Holding Hattie, Nick walked across the room with her. He wasn't sure what to do next. At a store specializing in babies, he had bought a small stuffed pink bunny for Hattie. The bunny was in a gift sack with pink tissue paper covering it and he had placed it on a game table.

He picked up the small sack and held it in front of her. "Hattie, this is for you from me. It's your present," he said quietly.

She looked up at him and then down at the sack. He held it closer in front of her. "This is for you."

She looked at the sack and at him in uncertainty, but then she pulled one of the pieces of tissue paper. As it came out of the sack, Nick smiled encouragement. "A bunny."

"Bun," she repeated and retrieved the small pink stuffed rabbit. He took the sack from her to set it on a table. "Mine," she said, hugging the bunny, making him smile.

"That was sweet, Nick," Talia said softly. "She likes you. She hasn't protested going to you or wanted me to take her. That's good."

He walked to Talia and held out Hattie. "I'll give her to you."

"Of course," she said, taking Hattie from him, their hands and arms brushing and bringing that same electric awareness of touching Talia that he felt each time they had contact. He glanced at her as he stood so close and she looked up, their gazes meeting. For another moment he was more aware of Talia than of Hattie. He couldn't understand the physical attraction, especially at a time when they both were torn up emotionally.

Moving away, he didn't want to pursue the feelings she stirred. His life was tangled enough already and he didn't need one more emotional pull. He suspected she wasn't any more enthused about the sparks flying between them than he was, but he couldn't figure how there could be one little glimmer of appeal under their current circumstances. She had brought him a monumental problem, changing his life, demolishing the little calm and peace he was beginning to get back after losing Regina and Artie. Talia was awakening feelings he hadn't experienced in a long time and he wasn't ready to deal with them. He didn't want to complicate his life with Talia as well as Hattie. Hattie was all he could deal with at present. A baby girl who needed two loving parents and siblings, but that wasn't possible.

He stared at her and thought about Stan telling him to marry Talia. "My brothers are filled with curiosity and eventually I'll have to tell my grandmother."

Talia's expression changed and she looked stricken. "You don't think your grandmother will like Hattie?"

"Talia, relax," he said patiently. "My brothers will be in awe because they're uncles now. My grandmother likes babies and was devastated by the loss of Regina and Artie. The reason I said I'd tell her eventually is because my grandmother is a take-charge person and she will be all over me with ideas about what I need to do. I can handle that, but it's tedious because I don't want to hurt her feelings."

Talia ran her hand across her forehead. "I know your mother is deceased and your dad lives in Palm Beach. You're the oldest son at thirty-four. Your brother Stan is thirty-three, Adam is thirty-one, and the youngest, Blake, is twenty-nine. Your dad started Duncan Energy. You took over later and then stepped down, and Adam is CEO. Blake works for him while you, as well as Stan, are on the board."

Startled, he looked up again. "How do you know all that?"

"I hired a PI to find out about you before I contacted you. I'm sorry that I pried into your life but I wanted to know what kind of person I would be dealing with."

He nodded. "I don't blame you. My dad will have no interest in Hattie one way or another. He's into his own life and we don't see him. He was a good dad and we loved him and everything was fine until Mom died when I was sixteen. Dad never has recovered. He drinks and he's married to his fifth wife. He doesn't come home to Texas, and when he does come back, my grandmother ties into him. She's my maternal grandmother and those two don't get along."

"I'm sorry. I don't have family, so family seems special and important to me, something valuable to be cherished."

He nodded. "That's a good outlook."

She blushed. "Well, again, I'm sorry for prying into your life. By the way, I know your age, so if you want to know mine, I'm twenty-nine. Madeline was twenty-eight when she was killed in the car wreck."

"She was beautiful and talented. I remember that much. Talia, forget hiring a PI. You had a good reason. That's how you found my attorney, isn't it?"

"Yes," she admitted.

"I wondered." Hattie chose that moment to let out a shrill giggle as she played with her bunny, eliciting a smile from Nick. "She is a happy little girl, isn't she?"

Talia put the baby on the floor so she could play. "She's a sweetheart. She's had a big loss in her life but she's still happy. I've tried to make up for the loss of her mother as best I can, which just means being there for her and showering her with love."

"You've done a good job and I'm grateful." He looked at Talia again. Her long blond curls framed her face and he realized he could spend the day looking at her. His gaze lowered to her mouth and he wondered what it would be like to kiss her. When he realized the drift of his thoughts, he tried to shift his focus. He reached down and ruffled Hattie's brown hair, which earned another giggle.

"She's been around a lot of kids at the day care and her mother used to take her to music tryouts and re-hearsals," Talia said, "so she's comfortable with people. You'll see."

"Artie was happy, too. He was so easy."

Hattie was busy with her new bunny, making sounds as she played with it. She was a beautiful baby but he couldn't feel like she was his yet. Nor could he keep from wanting Artie and Regina.

Talia watched Hattie, another of those concerned looks on her face. He knew what she was thinking about—that moment when she would have to give up little Hattie, when she would have to hand her over to Nick forever. He ached for her because he knew how she felt. He missed his own little boy, the baby he had rocked, kissed, fed and held. Hattie and Talia were bringing back memories that ripped him apart.

"Aw, hell, Talia, this is tearing us both up," he said, turning to her. "Let's figure where we'll go from here, what we'll do next and get this over with. I have to take her, but not today. We'll continue to send her to day care until we work out what we'll do. Then I'll take Hattie, so the state will have to back off and get the hell out of our lives."

He glanced at the child. "Thank goodness she doesn't know what's going on. She's going to miss you like hell." Talia had become mama to her. When they loved each other, a mother and child formed the tightest possible bond. Nick rubbed his forehead as he thought about what he was doing—taking a baby from the only mother she now knew. When Hattie woke crying in the night and he came to comfort her, would she be scared?

He looked intently at Talia and she stared at him.

"What?" she asked. "What's wrong?"

"As far as she knows now, you're her mother," he said.

"Yes, but you'll be her daddy before you know it," Talia answered solemnly. "And suddenly you'll be a family. You're bound to marry again and then she'll have a mama who loves her."

Talia looked away and he knew she was fighting tears again and he couldn't blame her.

He barely knew her, yet he ached for her. He wanted to put his arms around her and try to comfort her and to calm his own nerves and feelings of loss, but they had a fiery chemistry between them that he didn't want to ignite. He didn't know why sparks flared when they touched, but he didn't want the physical attraction to escalate. He didn't need that to complicate his thinking. He had to avoid crossing a line where they had more emotional problems between them to deal with, but it was a strain to keep from reaching out and comforting her. He fought the urge and stood facing her as he said, "Talia, you should raise her."

She turned her back to him and he suspected she lost the battle to try to avoid crying. "That was my biggest fantasy, that I was a stay-at-home mom and with her every day," she said in a soft voice as if talking to herself. After a moment she wiped her eyes while her back was still turned. "This is hard, Nick. It hurts because I love her as if she was my own baby. I've had two miscarriages, so I've lost two babies and I'm going to lose another one now—one that I love with all my heart."

This time he couldn't keep from stepping up close to her to pat her on the shoulder, and even that touch just made him want to pull her into his arms and hold her. "Shh, Talia," he whispered. He looked at the baby seated on the floor, still playing with her new bunny. She looked up at him and smiled, holding out her arms.

"Talia, she wants to be picked up," he said.

Glancing over her shoulder, Talia moved instantly, wiping away tears as she turned to get Hattie before he did. She scooped her into her arms and held her, hugging her and kissing her cheek. Hattie smiled and held Talia.

And Nick hurt for them and for himself.

Talia sat on the floor with her, doubling her long legs under her. He couldn't keep from letting his gaze sweep over her gorgeous, long shapely legs. As he watched them play, he couldn't deny his attraction. She was a beautiful woman.

Again, he thought Talia knew how to take care of Hattie better than anyone else on earth.

She stood and faced him while Hattie curled up on the floor and played with her bunny.

"She's getting sleepy, so we should go. You've got your DNA results and you've met your baby girl. I'll take her home with me tonight. You plan what you'll do, get baby equipment—and I will be happy to help with any or all of that if you want me to—and then I'll turn Hattie over to you. It really shouldn't take you long. I can give you a list of baby furniture she'll need. I don't want to give mine up because I hope you'll let her stay with me sometimes."

"Of course she can stay with you. She can stay a lot. Talia, she'll be lost without you," he said.

"She'll adapt. Children do adapt," she said and he heard the strain in her voice. "Whatever help you need, let me know."

"I'm letting you know right now," he said, suddenly wanting her help and knowing Hattie needed someone who loved her to be with her. If this were Artie, Nick absolutely wouldn't want him handed over to a house of strangers. Talia was the one person Hattie would know and love. And who would love Hattie with all her heart in return. Babies thrived on love. Talia would be the most possible help because she was already parenting Hattie.

The thought struck him like a lightning bolt. Suddenly he knew exactly what he had to do.

"I need your help," he said. "Move in here while we work this out. You don't have to tonight, but soon.

I can have someone drive you to school and pick up you and Hattie."

"In a limo?" she said, smiling and shaking her head. "I'm almost tempted to answer yes just to see everyone's reactions. I would be the most famous person in the school. No, Nick, thanks. I can't move in with you. We'll get this over and done with without me moving in because all too soon, I'd have to move out again. I'd cry over her every day."

"Okay. Come over for dinner tomorrow night, bring Hattie, and I'll have my first questions and problems lined up. And I will need the list of baby furniture. I got rid of the baby furniture that I had because I couldn't see any point in keeping it."

"If you want me to go shopping with you, I will."

He looked into wide eyes that made him momentarily forget baby furniture. "I won't go shopping," he said. "I'll hire someone to buy everything. You can earn some money on the side if you want to do it."

"I'll get it but you don't have to pay me. Just pay for the furniture. Where do you want it delivered? Here or the ranch?"

"I'll need it at both places. I live here and I live there. She's so little and yet she needs enough things to fill a big truck." He let out a deep sigh. "I need a wife."

"I'm sure you can find a wife easily enough," she said. "But please get one who really likes Hattie and means what she says."

He meant his comment as a joke, but he saw the sincerity in Talia's eyes. They were filled with worry and he was part of the problem. He stepped close, placing his hands on her shoulders, feeling her warm, smooth skin where her dress was sleeveless.

"I can't tell you to stop worrying because I know this hurts, but you'll always get to see Hattie. You'll get to be with her. She isn't going out of your life. Hang on to that. I'd give anything if I could see Artie."

She blinked and her eyebrows arched. "Oh, Nick. I'm sorry. I've probably been making things worse for you."

"We both hurt."

"Just love Hattie. She's going to need your love. She lost her mother, never knew her grandparents and now she's losing me. She'll need your love."

Her eyes filled with tears. "Sorry, Nick, sometimes I just can't avoid crying. I love her so much."

"I understand. I'll love her because she's my child. I only knew Artie two months, but I loved him beyond measure," he said so quietly, he didn't know whether she heard, but it didn't matter.

"There's just no way I can be her mother in the eyes of the state," Talia said, looking at Hattie. "Love doesn't even fit into their equation." Talia looked up to find Nick studying her intently.

He gazed at her in silence so long that she focused on him, frowning when she studied him. "What, Nick? What's wrong?"

Lost in his thoughts, he blinked. "I'm thinking. There's one way you can become her mother as far as the state is concerned. It would be legal and binding."

Frowning, she shook her head. "I don't think so. We don't have any—" She broke off to stare at him while her frown deepened.

"We can marry," he said.

# Three

"Excuse me—did I hear you propose marriage?" she asked, her heart thumping wildly. "Did you just propose to me?" Shocked, she stared at him and he gazed steadily back.

"Yes, I did," he replied, sounding surprised, as if he were telling himself as well as her.

"Oh, my heavens." Her head swam and she gulped for breath while she stared at him. "I may faint. I'm not going to," she added hastily. "I've never fainted."

"Hattie needs someone with her who loves her. I'm a stranger and so is my whole family. Anyone I'd hire would be even less concerned with her welfare. You love her and shower her with love and she loves you. Hattie needs someone to love her. You and I can have a marriage of convenience."

Talia couldn't believe what she was hearing. She would get to be with Hattie. She turned to look at the

baby playing on the floor. She would get to be Hattie's
real mother. "Nick, if we married, I could adopt Hattie.
She would really be my baby, my daughter. Actually,
our baby." Her hands flew to her chest. "I feel as if I'm
in a dream. A dream come true. Do you really mean
that? You're actually proposing marriage?"

"A marriage of convenience. We'll both benefit. I
know we're not in love. I can't love again and we don't
even know each other. But it'd be a legal marriage to
keep Hattie happy and help us both out." He grasped
her hands and asked her again. "Will you marry me in
a marriage of convenience?"

"I don't think you know what you're doing, Nick.
How happy I am." Excitement made her shake. "I can
adopt her legally and Hattie would really be my little
girl."

"That's right. You could adopt her."

She held back a gasp when it finally all sank in. "But
you're right, Nick. We don't even know each other.
Are you sure?"

"Yes, I am," he said quietly, looking as if he was
still giving it thought.

"Nick," she gushed and stepped closer to throw her
arms around him.

He caught her, slipping one strong arm around her
waist while he laughed softly.

Smiling at him, she felt light-headed and giddy.
"Oh, my. You just made my biggest, deepest wish come
true—to get to be Hattie's legal mother. I get to watch
her grow up. You just gave me the world." She leaned
back to look at him, gazing into green eyes that hid
whatever he was thinking or feeling. Then she hugged
him tightly.

"So… I take it your answer is—"

She stepped back to laugh. "Yes. My answer is yes. I'll marry you, Nick Duncan."

"You do realize I mean a legal marriage, but not a real marriage. That wasn't what I had in mind," he said. "You've heard of a marriage of convenience, right?" He didn't wait for her response. "We can marry and work out how we'll live. If we marry legally, the state can't touch us and you can legally adopt Hattie."

"I understand, Nick. Your proposal is still a dream come true. I love Hattie more than anyone or anything else and you are enabling me to keep her, to raise her, to love her and be with her. You have my forever thanks."

"There's no need to thank me," he said. "We'll be helping each other out." He gestured to the sofa and they both sat. "You'll have to get me up-to-date about your life and your history. You seem to know mine sufficiently."

That part was true, she silently acknowledged. She stared at him. She could easily see that Nick Duncan was a sexy, good-looking man, but her research had told her a lot about him. He was a billionaire oilman, rancher, widower with three brothers. He had a father he rarely saw and a grandmother living on his ranch. The Duncans were part of Texas history because it was a generations-old ranching family with immense wealth and political influence partially because his great-grandfather had been in the Texas Senate.

And here he was, offering her a marriage of convenience.

She looked at Hattie and couldn't get her breath. She hadn't imagined there was any way on earth to get to keep Hattie, and yet Nick was holding one out

to her. While she couldn't imagine marrying a man she
didn't know, that was what she was going to do. But
she wasn't worried. The PI hadn't turned up anything
bad about Nick. If she married him, she would always
have Hattie. She could barely think beyond that point.
She would become Hattie's legal mother, and as long
as they both lived, Hattie would be part of her life.

Her gaze went from Hattie to Nick and she was suddenly overwhelmed by emotion. "Nick—" She broke
off, placing her hands over her face.

In seconds, she felt his hands on her upper arms,
gently holding her. "Talia, don't cry."

"I can't keep from it. I'm sorry. It's just so overwhelming." She fumbled in a pocket to pull out a dainty
handkerchief and wipe her eyes.

"Talia, if you need them, I can give you references.
I promise you, I'm a good guy. I—"

She looked up at Nick, her brows knitted. Why was
he talking about references? Then it hit her, and she
smiled. "I don't need references, Nick. I'm crying for
joy. Because it's too miraculous to be possible that I
might get to keep Hattie."

"Oh." He smiled sheepishly.

"You just thought that up, didn't you? The whole
marriage-of-convenience idea."

"Yes, but the more I think about it, the more I think
it will work." He stood up, walked to Hattie and picked
her up.

"Talia, this is my child. I don't want to take her
from someone she loves and trusts and thrust her into
a houseful of strangers, most of us men. She needs a
loving mother. I couldn't bear to have had Artie put
into a home of strangers. She's only fourteen months

old and I know she'll adjust, but if we marry, she will go right along being the happy little child she is and she won't have a big adjustment to make. I'll have someone I think I'll like to love and take care of Hattie and help me raise her. And you'll be with Hattie and be her legal mother."

Her thoughts swirled and she looked at Hattie in the crook of his arm, which looked so natural.

Nick sat with her on his lap and Hattie immediately climbed down. Holding to his knee, she reached for a small table and then moved to plop down on the floor in front of a brass box filled with magazines. Hattie pulled one out to toss it behind her and Talia hurried toward her.

"Let her play with the magazines unless she'll get paper cuts," Nick said. "She's not going to hurt anything in that box. Those magazines will be recycled whenever Tina and her cleaning crew get to them."

"Cleaning crew, a limo, two mansions… Nick, I don't have that kind of life." Under normal circumstances she didn't think it would ever work out between her and someone like Nick. But this was a marriage of convenience. "But I can't get beyond the realization that now I get to keep Hattie and I'll become her mother. I can hardly sit still. I feel like dancing around the room. I feel as if I could dance all night and shout for joy."

He smiled. "I'm glad. I think this will be good for both of us. It lifts a ton of worries off my shoulders."

She sat down beside him. "The biggest thing is that we don't know each other at all."

"We'll get to know each other and you can adjust to the other stuff. Riding in a limo is not that different from riding in a car," he added and she shook her head. He sat back, placing one booted foot on his knee. He looked handsome, sexy, strong, and she realized she could easily fall in love with him, but he would never love her in return. They already had lightning streaking between them if they barely touched. How could she marry him, be around him constantly and keep from falling in love? She didn't think he ever would because all he had talked about since she met him was how much he missed his wife and baby. Was she willing to risk falling in love with him to get to be Hattie's mother? That was her fantasy, and now it was coming true. Yes, falling in love with Nick was worth the risk.

"Why don't you tell me about yourself," he suggested.

"I've had a very ordinary life in many ways. I don't have much family. I'm an only child and my mother died of breast cancer when I was a freshman in college. My father died suddenly from a heart attack when I was fifteen. He had insurance and he'd had a good job in the insurance business, so I was financially okay. I invested most of my inheritance and have done pretty well with it. I went to college on part of it, and I had scholarships for the rest of it." She stopped and stared at him. "I can't believe we're doing this, Nick."

"Go ahead. Tell me more about yourself."

She stared at him a moment, shrugged and continued, "I've always wanted to be a teacher. I love art and I like teaching. My senior year in college I married. His parents had money and provided generously for us. We were seniors, had money and neither of us worked. When we graduated, he still didn't want me to

SARA ORWIG                    53

work. He looked for a job, but it was a half-hearted hunt while he played golf and hung out at the country club."

"Who was he?"

"Quinton Smith from Houston."

Nick shook his head. "Not any family I know."

"Quinton is one of the reasons I hired a PI to check on you. Quinton was wealthy and he let it make a mess of his life, to my way of thinking. You're wealthy and I wanted to know you weren't anything like him. I also wanted to know some other things about you before I turned Hattie over to you."

"I don't mind the PI. I don't blame you. Go on about your life."

"Quinton couldn't find a job he liked and I never knew if he really got offers or not. After my first miscarriage I discovered that he didn't want children while I did. Also, I thought he should get a job. His mother provided abundantly for us and he didn't really see any reason to work if he didn't have to. By that time we were having arguments over his unemployment, and then I got pregnant again. When I miscarried the second time, I wanted a divorce and he did, too. The doctors couldn't find anything wrong. They said the stress was getting to me. Even so, I don't expect to ever have any children of my own. Does that matter to you?"

"No. You and I won't have a regular marriage. After I lost Artie I didn't expect to have any more children. Now I do have another child. That's enough. Under the circumstances, I don't want another child now. Can you accept that?"

"Of course. With my track record for miscarriages, I don't think I could give you any if you wanted more children. And I agree that children should come into a home filled with love. By the way, while I was in college with all the bills paid, I got my master's degree, so I'm qualified to teach in some colleges."

"You won't be teaching, Talia. I want you home with Hattie."

"Oh, Nick, that's my dream. I never, ever expected it to happen."

They were silent a moment and she returned to what she had been saying to him. "I only knew my husband two months before we married," she said, watching Hattie toss magazines behind her as she steadily removed them from the box. "I rushed into that marriage." She looked up at Nick. "I'm rushing into this marriage of convenience, too."

"This is different. We're not in love and we don't know each other. This is for convenience to get what we both want," he said. "Talia, if it doesn't work out and we get a divorce, you'll be Hattie's mother and we'll legally work it out to share her. As soon as we're married, you can start the adoption process so she will legally be your daughter. Is there anything else about your life, your past, I should know?"

Smiling at him, she shook her head. "No. I've led a quiet, uneventful life. You've heard all the highlights. I've told you about being friends with Madeline." Her gaze fluttered over him. And then it hit her. The handsome rancher facing her was going to marry her. Her heartbeat raced and she couldn't stop smiling. She would be a stay-at-home mother to Hattie, and she would be married to one of the most handsome, appealing men she had ever met. A man who had proposed for his baby's sake. That almost made her fall in love with him right then and there.

"Not that I need to know now, but I'm curious," she said when she gathered her thoughts. "Where will she go to school?"

He smiled and her heart fluttered again. How was she going to guard her heart against a smile like that? Against a body like his? She took a deep breath and released it slowly.

"You can move back to Dallas if you want her in school here. Otherwise, there is a country school she can attend if she lives on the ranch. My brothers and I went there. It's a good school. But that's in the future. Looking at the present, we'll need to childproof some rooms, keep her out of others until she understands the rules."

"The first thing I'd like to see you do is put a fence around that swimming pool."

"I'll get on it tomorrow. Also, tomorrow we can get an alarm that will go off if anyone falls into the pool."

Her gaze swept the large, casual family room with a game table on one side of the room, floor-to-ceiling sliding glass doors along the side opening to the patio and affording a view of his sparkling aqua pool with a waterfall and a fountain. The contemporary room held glass-and-steel tables and furniture in muted shades of brown to white. The room was two-story, with stairs on either side winding to the second level, where three walls of glass provided panoramic views. It was a stunning room, but the others on the ground floor that she had glimpsed through open doors had been equally impressive. Some had high-beamed ceilings with marble columns. Others had French eighteenth-century-style furniture with elegant antique satin and silk finishes. Oil paintings in gilded frames were on many walls.

As she looked around, she realized that when she became Mrs. Nick Duncan, she would live in this mansion with Hattie. She couldn't imagine that would be possible. Even more impossible to imagine, she would live here with Nick.

"Talia?"

She realized she was lost in thoughts about his proposal and him. "Sorry, Nick. This is all so fantastic. I keep getting carried away by the wonder of becoming Hattie's mother. What were we discussing? Oh, I remember. Childproofing the house. You'll need gates for the stairs, of course, and some things will have to be put away. This contemporary furniture looks durable and has no sharp corners… I'm assuming it's all unbreakable glass?"

He nodded. "See, you can deal with all that because you know what needs to be done. I haven't taken care of a toddler. Artie was a tiny baby."

"It doesn't take long to learn how to childproof a room."

"There's something else I have to do. I need to set up trusts for you and for Hattie."

"Nick, I have savings. As I said, my dad was in insurance and he had a big policy on Mom and on himself. I've got that money. I live a simple life and I've invested the insurance money. I don't need anything from you."

He looked amused. "You are one in a million, Talia, in a lot of ways. But I'd like to set up trusts for you and Hattie in case something happens to me. If you don't need or want yours, save it for Hattie."

"That's sweet, Nick, and if you want to do that, go ahead. But you've already given me my biggest wish."

"Speaking of Hattie, for now I'd like you to stay on the ranch most of the time. I really would like for us to be a family to whatever extent we could work it out. That would be the best thing for Hattie."

He was sitting there facing her, calmly fulfilling all her dreams and fantasies. She couldn't sit still any longer. "Ahh, Nick," she cried, standing up and flinging her arms in the air. "I can't sit still. It's the most fantastic thing possible. A stay-at-home mom on the ranch. You want us to be a family. It's wonderful."

He let out a laugh as he came to his feet. "You love her so much, Talia, I think this will work and we'll all be happy. A huge worry has lifted from me."

Overjoyed, Talia spun on her heels, but she must have slipped on one of the glossy magazines because the next thing she knew, Nick was steadying her, his hands on her waist. Instantly, she felt their heat singeing her through her clothes. She looked down at them, then up at him.

She expected him to pull his hands back, but he didn't. He just stood there, looking at her. For a moment, she had to admit she wished he'd never stop touching her. Then she realized the danger zone she was stepping into.

"I—I guess I should take Hattie home now and think about all we've talked about."

Was it her imagination, or did Nick actually look disappointed? He lowered his hands and stepped aside. "Okay." But before she could move, he reached out and grabbed her hand. "Talia, I think this is the best solution for all three of us."

That, she believed with all her heart. But as she looked into his green eyes, so like Hattie's only far more unfathomable, there was another part of her that acknowledged the danger in their plan. And it all started with the sexy man standing in front of her.

"I can't imagine marrying for convenience with love not any part of the equation, but I'll try my best to make it work." Had she really uttered those words, or had she merely thought them in her mind?

"It might not be easy, but nothing worthwhile is ever easy."

"What about having sex?" she asked, feeling heat flood her cheeks the minute the question was out.

His hand left hers and traveled up her arm in a slow, tantalizing path. His eyes blazed the trail till he looked up at her again and something flickered in their depths. Her heart pounded.

"Well, there's one way to find out," he said and slipped his arm around her waist, drawing her against him.

Her hands flew to his muscled arms as she looked into his eyes, and her heart thudded when she saw his intention. What she saw in his expression was personal, hot and demanding. That sizzling reaction they'd had each time there had been the barest physical contact sparked between them while awareness and desire ignited. Her lips tingled and her gaze shifted to his mouth and then she looked into his eyes again. When she did, she received a look that sent a tremor from her head to her toes. He intended to kiss her and she wanted him to.

His arms tightened around her, drawing her flush against his hard, muscled body, a masculine body that caused wild desire to shoot through her. Holding her tightly in his strong arms, he leaned closer and closer, until she yearned for his kiss. When his lips finally met hers, she was consumed by his dazzling kiss. A kiss like none she had ever experienced before. His kiss made her tremble as she wrapped her arms around him and opened her mouth to him, pouring herself, all her joy and excitement and enthusiasm, into her response.

A primal need enveloped her, and she wanted more of him, more than a kiss, no matter how passionate. His mouth stirred an irresistible, sizzling longing within her that she knew only hours in his bed would satisfy. She didn't know if her reaction was because of his fantastic marriage proposal or because he was the sexiest man she had ever met or if it was the fiery, spontaneous reaction they had to each other.

Now she was dazzled, tingling and wanting him. From mouth to thighs, her body was pressed against his. She felt his big Western belt buckle against her, but it was his lips and tongue that drew her attention. Touching, stroking in a demanding, passionate kiss that made her shake with need. With an effort, she broke away slightly, staring at him in shock. She wanted to wrap her arms around him and continue kissing him, while at the same time, she was stunned by her response to him. A fleeting thought made her wonder if she would ever see him the same way again.

"I think that kiss just answered your question," he said in a husky voice, looking intently at her. "I think we'll do all right together," he added. "And I'm sure sex will be part of the equation. I'm about to go up in flames," he added in a husky voice as he ran his hand across his brow that was beaded with sweat. They both were gasping for breath.

She barely heard him and it took a second to remember her question. *What about having sex?* Her pulse still raced and her mouth tingled; every inch down to her toes throbbed with desire. She had never been kissed like that and she stared at him, fighting the temptation to take the one step that would close the space between them and put her back into his arms.

His eyes narrowed as they stared at each other. She realized how he looked at her and how she probably appeared to him. "That was sort of…dazzling. I better go now," she whispered.

"I know you don't intend to, but I think you might bring me back to life," he said, still looking intently at her. He placed his fingers on her chin, tilting her head as he gazed into her eyes. "One thing, Talia. I have to be truthful. I loved Regina and I don't think I can ever love again. I miss her every day that goes by. Remember, this is a proposal for a marriage of convenience, not love."

"I understand that you still love your wife even though she's gone and I can cope with that. I don't expect us to fall in love." She said those words, but her thoughts went in a different direction. She couldn't stop thinking about his kiss. A kiss that made her want to step right back into his embrace, wrap her arms around him and kiss him again. If one kiss could do this to her, she thought, how would she be after a night of raging hot sex? Could she keep from falling in love with him?

His voice broke through her thoughts. "What we just conjured up between us wasn't love."

No, it was a raging inferno because of the sexiest kiss ever.

"Oh, Nick," she said, her heart pounding and her voice raspy, "it may not be smart to do, but I need to give you one more kiss of thanks for giving me my dream." Stepping closer, she flung her arms around his neck, and standing on tiptoe, she kissed him, again pouring all her gratitude, excitement and happiness into another kiss.

Instantly, his arms circled her waist and he pulled her up hard against his body as he leaned over her and kissed her in return, his tongue moving over hers, stroking hers, setting her ablaze once more. She moaned with pleasure, felt his hard erection press against her. She finally broke away to gasp for breath.

They stared in silence at each other as if they were just seeing each other for the first time.

"I think I might be getting a bonus in this marriage on top of becoming Hattie's mom," she whispered.

"We both are," he said.

With a little shake, she tried to get back to the moment and glanced down at Hattie to find the little girl happily tearing up the magazines.

"Oh, my goodness," Talia said, rushing to stop her.

"Don't worry about it," Nick urged. "That's all recycle stuff now. I've read everything there I'm going to read."

"She can't tear up magazines. Next thing you know she'll be tearing pages out of her books." She knelt beside her on the floor and pried the pages out of her little hands.

"Hattie, no, no, no," Talia said, shaking her head, while speaking gently. "We don't rip these up. Let's look at the pictures. See? Here's a little white dog," she said, showing Hattie a magazine with a dog picture.

Hattie pointed at it. "Doggy," she said, stabbing the picture with a small finger. "Doggy."

"Let's put the picture away in the box now."

Obediently, Hattie picked up the magazine and deposited it in the box.

In minutes they had the area cleaned up. Talia sat on the floor beside Hattie and glanced at Nick to find him sitting close at hand and watching her.

"We should get to know each other a little better as well as start making plans," he said. "Come over for dinner tomorrow night and bring Hattie. I'll get Kirby, my cook, to check with you about what Hattie can eat."

"Don't bother your cook about Hattie. I can bring what little she eats. And I'll bring her sippy cup. I'll take care of her."

"That's okay now, but Kirby will have to learn what Hattie needs."

She nodded. "Also, I'll make a list of the furniture she needs and we can talk about—" She broke off to stare at him. "I can't believe we're discussing marriage, even when I know it's a marriage of convenience."

"Talia, you're very appealing. I don't understand why you aren't taken, why men aren't lined up to take you out."

She laughed. "Thanks, but I never have dated a lot. As a teacher and now with Hattie, I'm not around single men very much and I don't really want to go out and I'm sure men can sense that." When Nick didn't look convinced, she added, "Maybe you and I just have some kind of weird chemistry between us. I figured that kiss was the norm for you."

"Our kiss a few minutes ago the norm? Oh, no. Regina and I were friends and then we fell in love and that makes a difference. Love changes everything. You and I are strangers."

"Does this change your feelings about the marriage of convenience?"

"Change my mind? Oh, no," he said, smiling at her. "Far from it. After the kiss we just shared, I'm still on fire and I'm more for this marriage of convenience than I was before. I think it's a workable idea. I want my child to have a mother who loves her. And the bedroom side of it may turn out to be a giant plus."

She felt tingles from the look in his eyes and the husky sexy tone in his voice. "I have to admit, those kisses just now were a giant bonus for me, too. I'm ready for some fun in my life." She smiled at him. "Just keep in mind the purpose in getting married."

Holding on to the nearest furniture, Hattie began to toddle away from Talia, who stood and picked her up. Talia gathered her things and put her purse and the big bag over her shoulder while she held Hattie with her other arm. "Wave bye-bye to Daddy," she instructed Hattie.

Hattie waved her chubby little hand.

"Very good," Talia said and smiled at Hattie.

"It's going to take me a bit of time to get used to being Daddy," Nick said. "Even though I was one, Artie was too little to talk or know what was going on. I didn't get called Dada or anything. I'll have to get accustomed to my new status."

"That's fine. She won't know you're adjusting to it. Good night, Nick."

"You're not going to kiss me good-night?" he asked and she saw the twinkle in his eyes and realized he was teasing.

"I think we did that sufficiently for tonight. On the other hand, I think it would make her happier to know she has parents who are compatible," she said, smiling at him. Still holding Hattie with one arm, she placed her other hand on his shoulder and leaned close to kiss him on the cheek, feeling the short stubble.

His arm circled her waist and he kissed her briefly on the mouth and released her to smile at her. "She looks happy, so I suppose you're right."

Nick walked to the car with her, opening the car door and watching while she fastened Hattie into the car seat.

Finally Talia was buckled in the driver's seat, ready to go, and Nick closed the door, leaning down to talk to her through the open window. "I'll send a car to pick you up for dinner tomorrow night. My butler has kids. He can go tomorrow with my chauffeur and they can get a car seat for Hattie and get it installed and then I'll send the limo for you. How's that?"

"It seems as if it would be easier for me to just drive to the ranch."

He shook his head. "If it's all right with you, I'll send the limo."

Startled, Talia nodded and realized life with Nick was going to be different from life as she had always known it. Limos, butlers, chauffeurs, trusts—her world was going to change drastically, thanks to Madeline and Hattie. It would change for the better because some things would be easier. She thought about Nick's kiss and felt hot all over, wanting his arms around her again. That was going to be a monumental difference. Would it work out without love between them? She didn't think he would get over his loss for a long time and she didn't expect him to fall in love.

Talia couldn't picture her life in the near future. She

couldn't imagine going from teaching to living on a ranch. Besides taking care of her precious little Hattie, she would get to paint and draw, something she'd never had time to do. And then there'd be the nights with Nick, sitting around the dinner table, sharing private time once Hattie had gone down for the night. Then…

"Talia?" he prompted.

Coming out of her daze, she nodded at him. "Sorry, this is a monumental change that never occurred to me and I got lost in my thoughts. I'm not going to argue about you sending a limo for us," she said, smiling and shaking her head.

"Let's get married soon, Talia. Hattie is my daughter. Frankly, I'd feel better if she had a little more security in her life than you're able to provide."

"That's true, Nick, but sending a limo isn't keeping a low profile."

"I know, but it's safer. If we're going to marry, let's go ahead and do so. You can have a small wedding, can't you?"

"Oh, yes. It's my second wedding. I don't want another fancy formal white wedding dress this time. I don't have family. I have a few close friends I'd like to invite. You're the one with family and heaven knows how many friends," she answered, thinking she was marrying an incredibly handsome man. He had looked handsome and appealing to her before he proposed and kissed her, but now she was dazzled by him. Looking at his mouth, his full lower lip, she wanted to kiss him again.

"I've had one big wedding. I'm not having another, especially when it's a marriage of convenience," he said. "We'll have a very small wedding, maybe a slightly larger reception because my friends might as well meet Hattie and you. Is that okay with you?"

"Yes, whatever you want," she said. "And about the honeymoon… I'm so excited over Hattie and my future, I don't think one is necessary."

"That's fine with me. One more thing you might think about… Hattie's name. I want to change it. You'll be a Duncan soon and Madeline is gone and so is her family. You'll be able to see to it that Hattie knows Madeline was her blood mother, but I would like her to have the Duncan name."

"I think that's a good idea. I'll always make sure she knows about Madeline, but you're her dad. I think she should be Hattie Duncan."

"What about a middle name?"

"She doesn't have one. Madeline couldn't think of one and said she didn't need it anyway. You could give her Madeline for a middle name. Or Madeline's last name—Prentiss."

Nick thought for a moment, obviously trying out the names in his head. "Not Madeline," he decreed. "Some kids might call her Hattie Maddie. So let's go with Prentiss. Hattie Prentiss Duncan. Has a good ring to it."

"That's fine with me, Nick."

"Talia, this is going to be good. You'll be good for my little girl. She'll be loved and it will be almost a seamless transition for her. It's an enormous relief."

"I hope you grow to love her, Nick."

"I will. I'll do my best to be a good dad." He stepped back from the car. "I'll see you tomorrow night," he said. Wind caught locks of his brown hair, tangling them above his forehead. He smiled at her and just his smile made her pulse race. It would be so easy to fall in love with her handsome future husband. She would have to constantly remind herself to guard her heart, even though she didn't think it was going to be possible.

But right now, she wouldn't worry. She wouldn't let anything negatively impact this wonderful night. She would be Hattie's legal mother. She would be a stay-at-home mom to the little girl she loved. Hattie was so adorable, she was certain Nick too would love his little girl just as he had loved his son. They'd have an amazing life together, the three of them. How could they not? Nick had fulfilled her deepest wish.

She thought about their kisses and her heart pounded, desire making her wish his arms were around her and his mouth on hers again. The man could kiss like no other she had known. He was the sexiest man she had ever met. Put that together with Nick giving her the deepest desire of her heart and he became the most appealing male on the globe.

She couldn't stop thinking about him as she drove back to her place. His kisses made her hot just thinking about them. What would it be like to make love? She tingled all over, and before she combusted, she told herself to wrangle her sexy thoughts and concentrate on her driving.

Easier said than done.

That night, long after she was in bed and Hattie was asleep, Talia lay awake, staring into the darkness, still remembering being in Nick's arms and kissing him. He had clearly warned her he would not fall in love. She needed to take sex the way Nick would—without getting emotionally involved.

"I can't do that," she whispered aloud in the dark

bedroom. She knew if she was intimate with Nick, gave him her body, her heart would go along with it. She was going to love him for giving her Hattie. She could try to keep a wall around her heart, but Nick was too appealing, too sexy, and he had given her the one thing in this world she wanted most.

She had to go into this marriage of convenience knowing that was all it was to Nick. A convenience. He had given her Hattie, and as long as he gave Hattie the love of a father for his child, Talia knew she shouldn't expect anything more.

She adjusted her pillow and turned on her side, but sleep was elusive. A half hour later, still wide-awake, she went to check on Hattie.

She stood beside her crib, watching Hattie sleep. "You'll have a daddy now," she whispered, looking at Hattie curled on her side, the pink bunny held tightly in the crook of her arm. "You'll have a daddy, a chauffeur and heaven knows who else—and you're going to take me into that world with you." Relief and joy filled her. At the same time, doubt pecked at her thoughts. Would she be able to adjust and get along with Nick? Keep Nick happy? She couldn't answer those questions. She was marrying a man who was a stranger.

"I'm going to marry your daddy and be your mommy forever," she said softly, focusing instead on the joy that welled up again in her heart. "Sweet baby, I get to be your mommy. I will love you all my life and take care of you the best I can. And your daddy? I'll just have to learn to live with your daddy, who doesn't love me. As long as he loves you—and he will—we'll be fine. As long as he kisses the way he did tonight, it should be a blast being married to him. He has to be the sexiest man on this earth. I'm going to try to keep my heart intact, but with kisses like tonight's, I don't think I can. Nick Duncan. Mrs. Nicholas Duncan with daughter Hattie Prentiss Duncan." The names sounded good on her lips.

"It seems impossible, doesn't it?" she asked the sleeping baby. "Only it is possible and it's going to happen. I'm going to marry Nick Duncan. He doesn't love me and he never will, but he's giving me my fantasy. Is he going to break my heart?" She shrugged. "Nothing would ever hurt like losing you, Hattie, and now you'll be my baby forever. And I will try to be the best mother possible. I will love you with all my heart."

She kissed the top of Hattie's head and slipped out before she stirred. As she moved through her small house, she felt dazed. Her life had changed in the past few hours, a change she hadn't expected. In a short while she would be marrying Nick Duncan and have a sprawling ranch and an elegant mansion to call home. Not to mention the sexiest man ever beside her.

But she knew their marriage would never involve love. Time might carry him away from the pain and loss he had suffered, but she didn't expect him to fall in love with her.

Talia knew loss, too. She had been hurt badly in her first marriage. She had lost her mother and her dad. She had suffered two miscarriages. Having endured all that, she knew they understood each other's pain.

Again, she smiled as she thought about the joyous, happy fact that she wouldn't lose Hattie. For that she would be forever grateful to Nick and she would do her best to help him be a daddy to Hattie. That was the best with Nick she could hope for and that had to be enough.

She returned to her bed, but knowing she was too wide-awake to sleep, she pulled a pen and paper from her nightstand and set about making her lists. One for the baby furniture and items she'd need to purchase, and another of the few people she'd like to invite to the wedding. Nick's guest list would no doubt be more plentiful, with his business contacts, friends and family.

What would his family think about her? The thought struck her out of the blue. And what would they think about Nick marrying to give Hattie a mother? His brothers and grandmother would know he wasn't in love. Would his family accept her?

More important, would they accept Hattie—a little girl whom Nick had known nothing about?

Doubt started creeping in, quietly but steadily, and by the time Talia shut off her light, she knew she'd lie awake till morning.

What was she thinking, marrying a man she barely knew with a family she didn't know? Marrying a man she didn't love and who didn't—wouldn't—love her? How could they make this marriage of convenience work?

# Four

$N$ick went up the walk to his grandmother's house, which was the original ranch house and much smaller than his home or Stan's palatial ranch house. His gaze ran over the house that was smaller than his. The original part was built pre–Civil War. Each Duncan to live in it added to the house and made changes. It had been repaired, improved and enlarged through the years, and Nick liked the old place, but he wouldn't live in it. He climbed the wooden steps to the porch, walked to the front door and rang the bell as he entered so they would know he was coming.

"Hello, Mr. Nick," Braden said as he walked toward the front door as Nick stepped inside.

"Hi, Braden," Nick said, greeting the man who served as cook and butler for Nick's grandmother. Braden Aldridge had worked for them since Nick was a kid. He wore his usual white shirt and black trousers and black boots.

A woman came down the hall and Nick smiled as he greeted the former nurse and now a companion for his grandmother. Her round face was framed by brown hair streaked with gray in a pixie cut. "Hi, Ida. The weather's good. I thought maybe Grandmother would be outside."

"She likes the air-conditioning a bit better," Ida said. "As always, she's looking forward to your visit."

"Something smells good, Braden."

"A pot roast. I'm sure you'll be asked to stay to eat with her."

"I can't today, but I hope I can get some to take with me. No one can beat your pot roast."

"She supervises. It's sort of 'our' pot roast."

"Grandmother has always been a good cook. We'll see if I get an invitation. Whether I do or I don't, I'll come by the kitchen before I leave anyway," Nick said, smiling at the cook, who was one of the best.

"How's she feeling?" he asked Ida as he walked beside her.

"She's fine and happy you're coming to see her."

"Good. I have some family news that she can tell you. I hope it doesn't upset her."

"Uh-oh. I was going to say that I can't wait to hear the news...unless it's bad news."

"No. Whatever she tells you, I think it's good news, and I think I'm doing what's best, but it'll give her a shock."

"Now I am curious," Ida said, smiling at him. "She's in the back and anxious to see you. Maybe I'll see you at dinner."

"Well, not tonight. I have company." He left her and walked down the hall to enter a large sunroom with a view of the patio to the south.

"Hello," he said, entering the room and crossing to his grandmother, who sat in her favorite recliner with her feet propped up. Switching off the television, she sat up as he leaned down to kiss her powdered cheek, getting a whiff of her usual lilac perfume. "You look comfortable," he said.

"I'm very comfortable. Now, this is not the usual time you come by for a visit, so what's up?"

He sat across from her, thinking how little she had changed over the years. Her gray hair was in its usual bun at the back of her head. She was tall and thin, but stronger than she looked. Her eyes were light brown, unlike his or his brothers'. Her glasses had slipped down her nose and she removed them, rubbing her eyes and looking at him.

"So what brings you visiting?" she asked. "You can't possibly smell that pot roast from your house, but I know it's one of your favorites."

"That it is," he said, wondering how she was going to take his news. He hoped they didn't have conflict over his marriage or over Hattie. "No, I didn't come calling because of the pot roast."

"Well, you might as well stay and eat some because I know how you like it and we have a lot."

"Thank you, but I can't stay because I'm having company and I'm going back to Dallas this afternoon."

"I'll send some home with you."

"I'd like that." They sat looking at each other and he knew he might as well tell her his news and get her reaction over with and go from there. He leaned forward, placing his arms on his knees and looking into her brown eyes. "I'm going to tell you two things that I think will shock you, so I'm just giving you warning now."

"Am I going to faint?"

He smiled. "I don't think so. You never have so far."

Her eyes twinkled and he wondered if she could take his next announcement as calmly. "Horace called and said a woman named Talia Barton wanted to see me and I should see her."

"Horace? Our attorney, Horace?"

"That's right. Here's why. A couple of years ago I was at a party and had an evening with a beautiful woman, Madeline Prentiss, who had a rising career in the music world. Talia Barton was her teacher and her friend. Fourteen months ago, this woman, Madeline Prentiss, gave birth to my daughter."

"Oh, my heavens, Nick. I'm a great-grandmother to a little girl?"

"Yes. Madeline didn't have family and Talia helped her care for the baby while Madeline pursued a singing career."

"Why didn't the mother tell you about the baby? Do you think it is actually yours?"

"She is definitely mine. I had a DNA test done. Talia Barton told me that Madeline thought I was still so in love with Regina and so torn over losing her and Artie that I wouldn't want to hear about the baby. Several months ago Madeline died in a car wreck. Talia has taken care of little Hattie and she's like a mother to Hattie. Now the state wants to take Hattie because Talia has no legal papers to show that Madeline wanted her to have Hattie."

"This baby is a Duncan. Your baby. You can't let the state take your baby. This woman came to tell you so the state won't get your baby?"

"That's correct. She wants me to be a dad to my daughter even though it means she will have to give up Hattie, a little girl she loves like her own. Talia will have to give up Hattie to the state or to me. She preferred me to take her. With Madeline gone, Talia is mama to Hattie." He took a deep breath and waited.

"You have a little girl," Myra said. "I am a great-grandmother to a little girl. How old is she?"

"Fourteen months," he repeated patiently, giving her time to absorb the first part of his news.

"Have you seen her?"

"Yes. She looks like the Duncans."

"Oh, my. You really think so? So you're going to raise a little girl. My goodness. I'm in shock, Nick."

"Grandmother, there's more. Talia Barton has been a mother to Hattie in every way except by blood and by law. She loves my daughter and takes good care of her." He swallowed hard. "I've proposed to Talia. She knows I'm not in love with her, but it is a way she can keep Hattie and Hattie will have the mama she loves."

"Nick, have you lost your senses? You can't marry a stranger because she knows how to take care of a baby. Mercy sakes. Don't tie your life up with some woman you don't know."

"I've already proposed. Hattie will have a mother who loves her."

"Nick, what is the matter with you?" she said, her voice getting louder. "You don't know this woman at all."

"I know Talia a little. She's an art teacher in a two-year college. That means the school system has checked her out to a certain extent. More important, I know she adores my daughter. She contacted me instead of letting the state just take Hattie away. If it weren't for Talia, I wouldn't even know I have a daughter."

"You know nothing about this woman except what you just told me and she knows nothing about you."

"She does know something about me. She had me checked out by a PI."

"She checked you out?" his grandmother shrieked. Nick merely nodded.

"Nick, our family is known by all Texans. We've been here since the battle at the Alamo."

He tried to hang on to his patience because he had expected her to react exactly the way she was. "Grandmother, not all Texans know who we are. Talia wanted to make sure I would be safe to leave Hattie with because if I didn't check out, she would have let the state take her."

"Oh, my word," she said, frowning and rubbing her hands together. "Don't be so foolish. Marrying a total stranger—that's asking for all sorts of trouble."

"I've invited Talia for dinner. I want you and my brothers to meet her and then you can tell me what you think. You'll meet Hattie, too.

"Talia is very nice. She's intelligent and she'll make a good mother. And now you have a little girl in the family," he said.

"A little child will adjust to someone else who is kind to her. Someone like you. We all will be good to her. She'll have a family and you do not need to marry a woman you just met. Don't get your life all tangled up. You know you won't be happy with her after Regina and little Arthur. Don't marry this Talia person."

"I think you'll like Talia."

"I can't imagine why you think that. And you don't know anything about little girls."

Nick ignored his grandmother's statement. He knew this would be difficult, so he simply forged ahead with his plan. "I'd like to have a family dinner Friday night. How's that? I'll send the limo to get you. We'll have dinner here on the ranch."

"Nick, oh, I'm so glad you have a little girl. What a joy she's going to be," she said, talking more to herself than to him. "We can take care of her. But you don't need to marry this woman. I do wish you hadn't committed yourself. Get out of it."

"Hold your opinion until after you meet her. See if you like her. I've got to run now. I'm going back to Dallas and I'll have Talia and Hattie for dinner tonight."

"You're not listening to me. Please don't do this in haste and regret it for years."

He brushed a kiss on her cheek. "I love you, Grandmother, and I know you want what's best for me. I know you'll love Hattie and I think you'll like Talia."

His grandmother shook her head. "Nick, I'll worry every day about you if you marry this woman."

He laughed. "Worrywart Grandmother is what you are. I know it's because you love me. You'll meet them Friday."

With that, he blew her a kiss and left her. His thoughts jumped ahead to tonight and seeing Talia again. In a lot of ways he was glad Talia had accepted his proposal for a marriage of convenience. She loved Hattie too much to miss this chance to become her legal mother forever. He also had mixed feelings and a streak of guilt because he still loved Regina and missed her and he missed little

Artie. He knew he would probably grow to love Hattie, too, but right now there were so many hurtful memories. Longing swamped him for his wife and baby and he knew no one would ever take their place.

He stopped by the kitchen, and before he could say anything, Braden held out a covered container. "Here's your pot roast."

Nick smiled. "Thanks, Braden. This is a super treat. The smell is killing me. I can't wait to sink my teeth into this. You're the best."

"Well, Miss Myra steps in here to stir every few hours."

Nick laughed. "I'll bet she does. And I bet she does a lot of taste testing."

Braden smiled. "Yes, she does."

"Thanks again," Nick said and left, forgetting the pot roast when he reached the car and thinking about his grandmother's warnings.

He was Hattie's father, so he would claim her and raise her, and it seemed the best solution to him to get Talia's help and keep her with Hattie.

He loved his grandmother, but this time she was worrying for nothing.

Late that afternoon as he worked in his Dallas office, Nick heard his phone buzz with a text. He looked at it and saw Talia had to cancel their dinner appointment because she needed to meet with two parents over a problem their son had at school. She hadn't found a sitter yet and it seemed best to cancel dinner.

He sent her a text to come eat pot roast before meeting with the parents and leave Hattie with him. Talia replied that it would be easier to grab a bite before she went and let him feed Hattie. She would bring everything for Hattie.

Nick remembered kissing her—something he thought about at least once every sixty minutes all his waking hours. He could get aroused just remembering holding and kissing her. Her kisses consumed him and made him want to carry her off to bed and forget the world. This marriage was going to be more than he had expected. He'd proposed knowing he wanted a loving mother for Hattie. Now he knew he was getting a woman whose kisses promised the hottest sex he had ever experienced. He wanted this marriage soon. He wanted her in his bed as a way to erase the hurt and loneliness he had lived with for too long now.

He'd looked forward to spending the evening with Talia. But now he would be taking care of Hattie all by himself. Nick rubbed his neck. He should be able to feed Hattie, but he didn't have a high chair for her yet.

Leaving his Dallas office, Nick went home, called his attorney and set up the trusts for Talia and for Hattie. When it was time for their arrival, he went outside to wait for them. As he paced, he was assailed by memories of times he'd spent waiting for Regina and Artie to come home from shopping or a doctor appointment. Would he ever stop longing for his beloved wife and son?

Even more worrisome, was he rushing headlong into a marriage that would be a giant mistake as his grandmother predicted?

Talia parked and got Hattie out of the car seat. Nick came bounding to the car, his long legs covering the distance quickly. Her heartbeat quickened when she saw him. In jeans, boots and a black short-sleeved knit shirt, he looked purposeful, seemingly filled with energy, sexy and appealing, and she wished she could spend the evening with him.

When Nick took Hattie from Talia, their hands brushed, and she had the same intense awareness of touching him as before, bringing back instant memories of his kiss. She looked up at him, and when their gazes met, it was as if they'd made a sexual contact.

He turned to look at Hattie and smiled. "Hi, Hattie."

"Ho," she said, smiling at him.

"That's her 'hello.'" Talia stood by him and patted his arm, feeling the solid muscle.

"I'm sorry, but this afternoon was hectic and I was late getting her and getting home. I would have fed her, but I was afraid that would make me late for my appointment."

"That's fine. Feeding her shouldn't be difficult."

"I brought a chair for her. It's in the trunk of the car. If you'll get it, I'll take Hattie."

"Sure, I'll get it. Don't worry about us because we'll get along just fine," he said.

"You can heat the chopped carrots for her and give her some milk. I brought her little sippy cup and lid. She loves strawberries and I've cut up some small bites. It's all in this bag plus some of her toys. I'm sorry, but I need to run. Phone me if you have a question."

He caught her arm and held it. "Talia, I'll take good care of her. Don't worry about her." They looked at each other intently and she got lost in his gaze, acutely aware that his hand still lightly held her arm. Her attention shifted to his mouth and then she remembered what he had said.

"I'm sure you'll be great with her," she stated, her voice sounding slightly hoarse. How could he cause such an intense reaction just by casually touching her or looking at her? She didn't think he was paying any more attention to their conversation than she was. All she could think about was kissing him. Was she going to fall in love with him if she was around him often? If they married and had sex, would she be able to avoid a broken heart? The question was becoming more important because her reactions to him were intensifying.

"I've got to run," she said, looking at him and still mesmerized by the way he gazed at her. She knew his thoughts were on their kiss, too, especially when his eyes lowered to her mouth.

With an effort she turned away and slipped behind the steering wheel. "I'll see you in a couple of hours. Call if you have a question or have difficulty."

"Sure. Don't worry. We won't have difficulty," he said, smiling at Hattie as she ran her fingers over his jaw. "She likes my whiskers."

"She's fascinated by you. You're the first man in her life and this is discovery for her. You'll be a good dad, Nick."

He smiled at Hattie. "I'm glad you have confidence in me. I hope it's contagious. I usually feel on top of challenges, but this one throws me. I don't know anything about baby girls. Do you care, Hattie?" he asked and she giggled while she still ran her fingers over his chin.

"I'm glad my face entertains her," he said.

"I'm going to be late," Talia said, more to herself than to Nick. "You might want to distract her so she doesn't see me leave. She's getting so she doesn't want me to leave her. I brought some toys in the bag, and if you'll take her inside and get them out, she'll forget about me."

She watched as Nick turned toward the house, talking to Hattie as he went. Then she drove away.

She tried to concentrate on the road, but it was impossible to avoid thinking about Nick. Since her disastrous marriage, she hadn't wanted to fall in love again with any man. And now she certainly didn't want to fall in love with Nick. It was obvious his heart was locked away. Sure, they had some hot chemistry between them, but that wasn't the bedrock of a solid marriage. Love was. And Nick was still in love with his late wife.

How many times would she have to remind herself of that?

As she turned at the green light, she forced her thoughts down a different path. Instead of worrying about guarding her heart against Nick, she reveled in the fact that Hattie would legally be her baby. She couldn't weigh the pros and cons of this convenient marriage. There was just one giant consideration—Hattie. Along with being her mother came the fun of going to bed with Nick.

Talia hoped this appointment didn't take too long because she wanted to get back to Nick and Hattie. Despite his reassuring words, he seemed nervous with the prospect of taking care of his daughter alone. Smiling, Talia shook her head. What was she thinking? Nick had been a dad. He was intelligent, capable, dealt with all sorts of situations and animals on that ranch. He would be fine with Hattie and Hattie would probably like being with Nick. How could he not cope with a little fourteen-month-old toddler?

* * *

"Darlin', here's a little bag all packed just for you. Let's see what's in it," Nick said, sitting on the floor in front of Hattie. He opened the bag and reached in to pull out a small white teddy bear. "Look, Hattie, here's your bear."

"Mine. Bear," she repeated, snatching it out of his hand and hugging it.

She tossed it aside and reached into the bag to pull out a small soft ball, which she threw across the room then turned to get the next toy. Nick held the bag and watched her, marveling that this was his child. He was still in shock from discovering this little girl who was going to become a major part of his life. Hattie pulled out another brightly colored box with a handle. When she turned the handle, it played a tune and she worked at turning the crank, her tiny fingers clinging to the small handle. "I should have known about you, little darlin', from the time you were born. I'm glad you're in my life now. I have a lot to learn about you."

She pulled out another toy and tossed it aside, reaching in to get another. Toys flew in various directions and he let her do what she wanted. She reached deep into the bag, pulled out a book and handed it to him.

"You want me to read *Peter Rabbit* to you? Come here, sweetie, and we'll read the book." Standing, he picked up her and her book and went to the rocker to sit and hold her, remembering holding Artie, who'd been so tiny compared to Hattie.

"Here's another bunny," he said, pointing to the rabbit on the cover.

"Bun," she said, sitting up and looking around. She got off his lap and held his knee as she reached for a chair. "Bun," she said again, more insistently as she clung to the chair and took a wobbly step, grabbing a table. She stretched out her arm and opened and closed her hand, and he spotted the pink bunny on the floor. He crossed the room to retrieve it, handing it to her.

"Here's your bunny. What you want, I think," he said, picking her up again as she hugged the bunny. Then she pointed to the chair.

"You seem to know what you want. We'll read about this bunny." He rocked her as he read. He hoped he could be a good dad. If he could rely on Talia, he thought they would get along fine.

After he read the book, he thought about Talia, who was bringing him back into the world. Her hot kisses ignited lust and thoughts of seduction. She was going to complicate his life more than it already had been. The minute they made love, emotions would come to life as well as physical desire, and right now he was struggling to get over mourning his losses and coping with the knowledge that he was the daddy of a little girl. A little girl who was pointing her finger at the book he held.

"Bun," she repeated.

He figured she wanted him to read the book again. "I'm guessing Talia reads to you a lot. Okay," he said, opening the cover. "Let's see about Peter Rabbit again."

It was almost 9:00 p.m. when Nick stood, carrying Hattie in his arms as he went to the door and opened it to greet Talia.

"I'm sorry I'm late," she said. She looked down at Hattie, curled against him as she slept. "How did she get along?" Talia asked.

"Don't ask about her. Ask if I survived. She was fine as long as I didn't get out of her sight and gave her one hundred percent of my attention. She's got the energy of the whole front line of a pro football team. For a little person who can barely toddle around, she's busy, and this house isn't set up for a baby. We may be babyproof in the family room now because she's thrown everything she could get her hands on if I didn't move it first. She's been asleep about five minutes—" He paused and his eyes narrowed. "You're laughing at me."

"I'm smiling because I'm glad you two have had a fun evening. I think you'll be a success as a dad," she said. "You'll get the kinks worked out and get the hang of having her in your house and in your life. It just takes a little time."

"I know you're laughing at me. I just couldn't keep up with her and there must be some trick to getting food down her instead of all over both of us. She wasn't thrilled with the carrots."

"Usually she likes carrots. I tried to bring what she really likes. She might not have been very hungry. Looks as if you have a bit of her dinner on you," she said, brushing tiny orange bits off his jaw. He was aware of her fingers touching him. She smelled wonderful with some exotic perfume and she looked gorgeous in a red dress with a straight skirt that clung to curves that made him forget the problems of the evening.

"Would my son have been like this? He seemed peaceful and easy except in the middle of the night when one of us had to walk with him. He didn't sleep too well through the night."

"Nick, he was two months old. That's a tiny baby. He couldn't toddle or crawl around the house. You would have gotten used to taking care of him. You'll get accustomed to Hattie. You're just starting," she said, taking out her handkerchief and wiping carrots off his shirt. "This will all come out in the laundry."

He caught another whiff of her perfume and was aware how close she stood, conscious of each brush of her fingers on his jaw. He wanted to put Hattie down and wrap Talia in his embrace.

"You really are laughing at me."

She looked up at him with twinkling blue eyes. "No, I'm not," she said as she smiled at him. "I'm happy all went well between the two of you." She glanced around the room that now had baby crackers scattered on the furniture and the floor. "You did a good job, but I can take her home now."

"Oh, no, you don't go now. I want some adult conversation. We still have some time. You sit with me and we'll talk. Want a glass of wine, a beer, pop, anything?"

"Sure. Sit and I'll get it. What would you like?"

"I'll wait. I have my hands full at the moment."

While Nick rocked Hattie, he watched Talia go to the bar and get a glass of ice water. She turned off all but one small lamp before she walked back to him. Nick watched Talia's every move, looking at her legs when she sat opposite him and crossed them. He wondered how soft they'd be if he ever got to touch them. The only sound in the room was the faint, rhythmic creak of the rocker. The one light brought out the highlights in Talia's long, silky-looking hair. Her thickly lashed eyes looked larger than ever. When his gaze lowered to her full red lips, he thought about their kiss. She was such a beautiful woman and again he wondered why no man had claimed her. She deserved the

love of a great guy who'd cherish her. He realized that
she would get cheated by agreeing to a loveless marriage of convenience. He drew a deep breath, reminding himself that she was getting what she desperately
wanted, just as he would get what he wanted from their
marriage agreement.

"Talia, spread her little blanket on the floor and let
me put her on it to sleep."

"Sure." He watched her skirt pull tightly, revealing a sexy ass. A slight slit in the skirt revealed more
of her long, gorgeous legs as she knelt and spread the
baby blanket.

He knelt beside her, placing Hattie on the blanket.
Still sleeping and holding her bunny close, she turned
on her side.

He walked over to take Talia's hand and pull her to
her feet. "Just a kiss. You look luscious and I want you
in my arms for a kiss."

His heartbeat raced and he was already hot thinking
about her and watching her move around. He wanted
her, and when her gaze went to his mouth, his heart
pounded. He slipped his arm around her tiny waist,
pulling her against him as he leaned down to kiss her,
brushing her velvety lips first with his and then coaxing her mouth open as he deepened the kiss. She was
soft, enticing and sexy, and he wanted to hold and kiss
her the rest of the night. He knew she wouldn't let
that happen, but he was desperate for even one kiss.
He brushed her mouth with his again. Her eyes were
closed, her fingers on the back of his neck, and she
was pressed tightly against him. As he gazed at her,
she opened her eyes to look up at him.

"You've brought me back to life," he whispered,

running one hand lightly over her breast. "I want you. I want you naked in my arms all night. I want to kiss you all over. Let's get on with this wedding so you can move in with me."

"That's fine with me," she whispered.

"Give me a date. How soon can we have the wedding?"

# Five

How could she think? With Nick showering light kisses on her ear and throat, she tingled from head to toe. Conscious thought was a distant memory, especially when his hands trailed down her back, over her derriere, pulling her up against him so that she could feel his arousal.

"When, Talia?" he whispered against her neck.

His prompt seemed to rouse her from her sensual stupor and she pulled back to look at him. She ignored the flare of gold in his green eyes and forced herself to focus instead on a mental calendar.

"How about the first Saturday in June? That way, school is out and I'll be through."

"That date is fine with me," he said in a raspy voice. He caught her chin with his fingers and gazed down at her.

"I want you, Talia. You're bringing me back to life."

"You're giving me my heart's desire, my fantasy dream, so I'm glad I'm doing something for you," she whispered, showering light kisses on his lips, the corner of his mouth, his throat.

"Stay here tonight," he whispered.

"I can't. I have school tomorrow and you don't own a crib. This is not the night. Wait for the wedding and then we'll have furniture—"

Her words stopped when his mouth covered hers and his arms tightened around her, drawing her against him. When his tongue slid past her lips and she opened to him in return, she forgot whatever she was about to say. She could only revel in the feel of him. His tongue stroked hers, stirring hot desire. His hard erection pressed against her, inviting her to thrust her hips against him.

Somehow she managed to pull away, and she opened her eyes to look up at him. He was breathing as hard as she was, and his eyes had darkened to a rich emerald green.

"Nick, I'll try my best to make all this work for the three of us," she managed to say. "This is going to be wonderful for Hattie."

"I agree. I want you to meet my family, so we'll plan dinner at the ranch. I can send the limo to pick you and Hattie up and you plan to stay the night. How's this Friday if I can round up my brothers?"

Any day was good for her. Right now all she wanted was to spend a night in his bed.

"Friday is fine," she said.

"Can you pick out a crib after school tomorrow? Call me when you find it and I'll buy it and I'll see to it that it's delivered and set up by Friday. Don't you worry about those arrangements at all. I can take care of that."

"Gladly. You're accustomed to getting things done the way you want them, aren't you?"

"A lot of things," he replied, "but I couldn't do one damn thing about Regina and Artie."

She expected to see sadness enter his eyes, as it usually did when he spoke of the family he'd lost. The flow of passion ebbed in their green depths, replaced by a wave of serious intent. But at least it wasn't sadness.

"Talia, I need to warn you. The first time you meet Grandmother, she'll be a grump because she doesn't want me to marry when I don't know you. But I think she's going to like having a great-granddaughter."

"I hope so. I love Hattie so much, I want everyone else to love her, too. Particularly the people in her family, all of you who are blood relatives. I'm the one who isn't."

"I'm sure they'll come round," he told her.

"It's getting late, Nick. I'd better take Hattie and go."

He shook his head. "Stay awhile and let's make some plans."

She couldn't say no to him, so she sat beside him in one of the two upholstered wing chairs that were close together and near Hattie.

He leaned over and took her hand. "You know, when I lost Artie, I got rid of his furniture. I just closed the door on the room and never went back in. You have free rein as far as the new furniture goes, and the decor. In fact, please do change it. I want the room to be Hattie's now. How fast can you get that done?"

"I can look at the room Friday night when we're on the ranch. Saturday, if I get right back to Dallas, I can pick out the furniture and make arrangements to have it delivered. I think I can get that much done very soon."

"Excellent," he said.

"I want it as soon as possible, too," she said, knowing the minute she became Mrs. Nick Duncan, she would become Hattie's stepmother. "If we have to, we can marry and have a crib or cradle in my bedroom while we get the nursery finished. Nick, as soon as we marry, I want to start the adoption process. I will always tell her about her mother, but I want everything tied up legally so she's my child."

"That suits me. So does having the wedding as soon as possible. The sooner we marry, the better. My attorney will deal with the state agency."

Talia looked at the child sleeping peacefully on the blanket and felt a rush of love. She had to be doing the right thing for Hattie. Nick would grow to love Hattie, she was sure. So would his family. But would they accept her—someone Nick was bringing into his family when he didn't love her and he barely knew her. How many of them had tried to talk him out of marrying her? What kind of future would she have with this marriage bargain?

Late Friday afternoon Nick sent a limo to Dallas to get Talia and Hattie. The chauffeur, Dusty Jones, carried their bags, and then with Hattie buckled into her new child seat in the limo, they left for the ranch.

As they slowed and stopped in front, Talia's gaze swept over the sprawling house that would soon be home for Hattie and her. Made of wood and stone, it was far less formal than the palatial mansion that was

Nick's Dallas home. But would she ever grow accustomed to it as her home?

Nick sat on the porch, and as the limo approached the house, he stood and walked to the top of the steps. Her pulse took the usual jump at the sight of him. In a long-sleeved blue Western-style shirt, jeans and boots, he kept her pulse racing. He didn't wear a hat and his light brown hair was blowing slightly with the breeze. Dusty stopped and came back to open the door for her, but Nick got there first. He reached out to take Hattie from her, his hands brushing hers. The instant they made the slight contact, her insides fluttered.

"Here's Daddy," she said as Nick held Hattie easily and reached out his hand to help Talia get out.

Hattie looked up at him. "Dada," she said, touching his jaw.

"I told you my face fascinates her," he said, smiling at Hattie, who smiled in return.

"Dada."

"That's right, sweet baby girl." He turned to Talia. "Come in. I'll take you to your suite. The new crib is set up, new sheets are washed and on your bed, and it's ready for you and Hattie."

"That's great, Nick. I'm anxious to meet your family and jittery, too."

"You meet—what? More than a hundred new students at the start of each semester? And I'll bet you're not jittery about them. My brothers are looking forward to meeting you. My grandmother is, too, even if she won't admit it. And they're all excited to meet Hattie."

"Meeting students at the start of the school year is entirely different. They have to accept me as their teacher and we're not going to live together. This is a relationship that's for better or for worse, one that'll have an effect on the rest of all our lives. Of course I'm jittery. Your grandmother sounds a little formidable because it's obvious she doesn't want me in the family."

"I do. End of argument. Grandmother will adjust." He led her into the house and up the wide staircase to the second floor. "And just wait until she meets Hattie. I know my grandmother and she's going to love Hattie. You'll get the fallout from that, so stop worrying. And my brothers?" he tossed over his shoulder at her. "Those guys will think you're wonderful."

She laughed. "I hope you're right."

He stopped in front of a door at the top of the stairs. "Here's your suite. Mine is next to it, right there," he said, pointing to the right. "And Hattie's nursery is next to it on the other side. In fact, the two rooms have a connecting door inside."

When he opened a door, she glimpsed Hattie's adjoining suite that was devoid of furniture with bare wood flooring. Her living area was spacious, filled with inviting, comfortable furnishings in primary colors. A sofa was upholstered in material with red and blue poppies against a white background, and there were red throw pillows. Dark blue wing chairs were on either side of the sofa and a circular glass table was in front of it.

"This is so pretty, Nick."

"You can change it if you want," he said. "I had a decorator change it last year," he added and she heard the harsh note in his voice. She also noticed that he didn't take her into the adjoining nursery. Instead, he turned to the opposite direction.

"There's your bedroom," he said, leading her into the space.

She moved ahead of him into another large room with a king-size bed covered in a comforter done in the same poppy motif. Near the bed stood a new white crib.

"This is wonderful, Nick. I think my whole house would easily fit into this suite and have room left over."

She ushered him to the door, knowing how difficult it must be for him to be near the nursery. Wanting to give him the out he no doubt desired, she said, "I need some time to get Hattie changed and get myself ready before your family arrives. So shoo." She smiled at him and couldn't help but notice how relieved he looked when he shut the door behind him.

Shortly before six Talia checked herself in a mirror again. She wore a conservative aqua dress with a scoop neckline, short sleeves and a straight skirt. Her hair fell in spiral curls that framed her face. She wore matching high heels and a silver bracelet, silver hoop earrings and a silver necklace. She felt jittery, an uncustomary nervousness, because she was uncertain about the evening. She hoped she could please Nick's grandmother and she certainly wanted all his family to love Hattie. She turned to survey Hattie again.

Wearing a pink dress with pink bows in her hair, Hattie sat on the floor, happily playing with a big clear plastic ball filled with plastic butterflies.

Talia heard Nick's boots on the oak floor of the hallway and her heart skipped a beat as he entered the room. He wore a white dress shirt, a silver-and-turquoise bolo tie, charcoal slacks and his black boots.

"Look. Here's your daddy," she said cheerfully as

she walked to meet Nick, wrapping her arms around him to hug him. "Hello, Daddy," she said, looking at Nick, knowing he was absolutely the most handsome man she had ever known. Definitely the sexiest.

"Well, hello, darlin'. The day just got better," he said, smiling at her and slipping his arms around her waist.

"I want her to learn to hug and be friendly with family," she said.

"I'm all for that," he said, squeezing her closer. He looked at her lips and she stepped away quickly, picking up Hattie before he could kiss her. She needed her wits about her tonight.

"Here's Daddy," she said, placing her hand on Nick's shoulder.

"Dada," Hattie said, smiling at him, and he took her from Talia.

"You look gorgeous," he told Talia, his gaze sweeping over her.

"Thank you," she said and smiled. "I'll admit that I'm nervous. I want them to like me."

"Stop worrying about my grandmother. As far as my brothers are concerned, they're going to love having you in the family and they'll all think you're gorgeous."

"I hope you're right about them. What about your grandmother's companion?"

"Ida Corwin? She's so quiet, you'll barely know she's here and usually she steps out of family events. She'll hang around with everyone after dinner to keep an eye on my grandmother."

He carried Hattie downstairs in one arm, while he held Talia's hand. She barely had time to get herself settled when his brothers arrived. Immediately, Talia saw the family resemblance. She met Stan, who was shorter than Nick and stockier. Adam, who looked the most like his oldest brother, and Blake, the only one with dark brown hair instead of lighter brown like the others. But they all had those Duncan signature green eyes flecked with gold.

When Nick tugged on her arm, Talia turned to face a tall, gray-haired woman. Nick introduced his grandmother, Myra Pierce. The woman didn't smile. She merely gave Talia a frosty greeting as she moved past her and sat in a wingback chair. Nick turned to a shorter woman, younger than his grandmother with friendly brown eyes and short hair streaked with gray. "This is Ida Corwin. Ida, I'd like you to meet Talia Barton.

"And here is the reason we're all together tonight," he said, picking up Hattie. "Grandmother, this is Hattie Prentiss. Of course, we'll have her name changed to Hattie Duncan as soon as we can process the paperwork." He held the baby toward Myra. "You've had a great-grandson. Hattie is your first great-granddaughter."

"This is my great-granddaughter," Myra repeated, sounding surprised as she gazed at Hattie. "She's a beautiful little girl. She looks like all the Duncans, too."

"I think so," Talia said as Nick handed Hattie to Talia.

"I'll talk to my brothers while you get Grandmother acquainted with Hattie," Nick said and left them before anyone could protest.

"I'll go speak to the others," Ida said and left them also.

Myra glanced at Talia. "You're very happy to marry Nick," Myra said in a cold voice.

"Yes. Marriage to Nick makes me Hattie's mother," she said, smiling at the baby.

Stan appeared at Talia's side. "I want to join this conversation, and actually, I'm supposed to tell you that Nick wants to show you something. Do you think Hattie will let me hold her?"

"I think she'd be delighted," Talia said, handing Hattie to Stan. "Hattie, meet your soon-to-be uncle Stan." She turned to Myra. "If you'll excuse me, I'll see what Nick wants and be back."

She left them, glancing back once to see Stan talking to Hattie.

She turned to see Nick standing by himself near a window and watching her approach. She tingled from the look in his green eyes.

He could set her on fire with just a look, and for a moment, she forgot everyone else. Nick's gaze held hers as she walked closer. She wanted to just walk into his embrace, but this wasn't the time to do so.

"Stan said you wanted to see me."

"Do I ever," he said in a husky voice. "You are even sexy just walking across the room."

Her pulse jumped and she drew a deep breath. He took her arm. "Come here. I want to show you something."

"We're leaving them?"

"Just for a minute. C'mon." They left the room, stepped across the hall into a formal living room, and he closed the door. Because of heavy pale blue silk drapes, less light came into the room. It was the east side of the house, so the late-afternoon sunlight did not spill into the room. She looked at Nick expectantly.

"Actually, I told Stan to go entertain Hattie and

Grandmother, and I told my other brothers to find something to do for a few minutes. I wanted to be alone with you because you look incredible."

"Nick," she said, laughing and tingling from his compliment, "thank you, but we need to get back. I just got introduced to your family. We can't disappear and— Don't you dare kiss me and get me all mussed up when I've just met them," she admonished when he came closer.

"You really don't want me to kiss you?" he asked in a husky tone while he lightly caressed her nape. All teasing had vanished, replaced by desire in his green eyes, and her heart thudded. She couldn't tell him she didn't want him to kiss her. Words failed her, and besides, she'd be lying if she said that. Right now, like always, all she wanted was to step into his arms and kiss him. Desire flared as she looked up and saw his hungry expression.

"Ah, Nick, I can't say no to you. Not when you look at me like that. You're going to—"

"Yeah, I am," he interrupted and pulled her tightly against him, his mouth coming down on hers.

Sensations rocked her, centering low inside her, hot and insistent, making her want him totally. She wanted his kisses, his caresses, his hands and body on her, his thick erection inside her. She wrapped her arms around him, stood on her toes and let her kiss tell him her desires.

She didn't know how long they kissed, but when she felt his hand at the back of her dress where her zipper started, she leaned away.

"Nick, wait. There's a family dinner out there. We need to go back and I need to pull myself together."

He stared at her while he took deep breaths. "You're right. I'll cool down. You make me forget everything else. Let's go back together. Hell, we're getting married soon. If we sneak off to kiss, that's not shocking."

"It is to me," she said and he smiled.

"I think that's my line. I didn't feel anything for a long time until I met you."

"Actually, while I haven't been bogged down in grief, I haven't felt anything for a long time, either. This is mutual," she said.

"It has been from the first moment we met and that's another shock," he replied. He took her hand and led her to the door. "Come on—let's see how Grandmother and Hattie are getting along."

"I think quite well or we'd hear Hattie."

He smiled and slipped his arm around her waist to give her a squeeze. "This marriage of convenience is the best idea I've had in a long time."

She wondered if he was reminding her so she wouldn't forget that it was a loveless marriage. She didn't care because this marriage made her Hattie's mother instantly. Stepmom at first, but he'd agreed about the adoption. She couldn't wait to get the process going.

Nick stopped and turned to her. He ran his finger back and forth on her wrist lightly, a casual touch, yet it made her pulse beat faster. "Before we join the others, can I get you something to drink? Wine, beer, mixed drink, margarita?"

"I'll take white wine," she said.

"Fine. Go ahead and join them. I'll get our drinks."

He walked her back to the room where she saw the brothers seated around Myra and Hattie. Stan sat close to his grandmother and held Hattie on his lap. She heard Hattie laughing and knew all was well.

"I think your grandmother is going to approve of Hattie," she whispered to Nick.

"I think she'll adore her. You just watch."

As Talia walked in to join the group, all the men came to their feet.

"Please be seated," Talia said, taking a chair offered by Adam. For a few moments she watched Nick's family interact with Hattie and felt herself begin to relax.

"You have a beautiful little girl who looks like the Duncans," Myra said to Nick as he joined them and handed a glass of white wine to Talia. He held a bottle of beer in his other hand.

"Her mother always said she was an easy baby, ready to smile and seldom fussy," Talia said. "She's stayed that way in spite of what she's been through."

"Ahh, we're going to get called to dinner," Nick said, looking up as his cook, Kirby, appeared at the door to announce dinner. Nick scooped up the pink bunny and picked up Hattie from his brother. "I'll put her in her chair."

At the dinner table, Nick sat at one end and Myra at another. Talia sat on Nick's right and Hattie sat between them in an old-fashioned wooden high chair that Nick said he and his brothers had used and their mother before them.

Throughout dinner she was constantly aware of Nick, laughing with him and with his brothers as they told stories of their antics on the ranch while growing up. It seemed he felt the same. His gaze never strayed far from her. Not for the first time, she thought about the night to come. She yearned for the kisses that were sure to come. No doubt there'd be more than kisses, and that thought made her want to be alone with him right now. Forever.

With a start she realized her biggest fear was coming true: she was in danger of falling in love with him, something that could only mean heartbreak. The minute that thought came, she pushed it aside. None of this marriage to Nick Duncan could be a mistake, she told herself. Because she would get to be Hattie's stepmom and then her legal mother if the adoption went through. That made this the most wonderful marriage possible.

Later in the evening Talia stood at the bar with Nick. "Your grandmother and your brothers have held Hattie all evening. Stan just put her in your grandmother's lap again. I better go see if she's okay with that."

Catching her wrist lightly, Nick drew Talia back. "The guys will watch Hattie, and Grandmother probably told them to put Hattie in her lap. My grandmother is so happy to finally have another little grandchild to dote on."

"She seems happy with Hattie and, surprisingly enough, she's been friendly to me and I'm glad."

"It's obvious she loves Hattie, so there is no battle there. I think my grandmother is going to love every minute you and Hattie are at the ranch. She's not the only one," he said and she smiled at him while her heart skipped a beat.

"I think this is going to be good, Nick. It's going to give me my dream, so I'll go into our marriage happier than I've ever been in my life."

"I'm glad. It may be a loveless marriage, but we're friends, and physically, we'll be lovers. That's a fantastic surprise," he said, his voice getting deeper while desire filled his green eyes. He took a step closer to her. "I'm ready for the others to go home so we can be alone. I've looked forward to tonight and not because of having the family visit."

His words made her tingle. Her gaze ran across his broad shoulders, then back to his mouth. Finally, she met his knowing gaze and she could feel the heat in her cheeks and knew she blushed.

"We better change the subject, Nick."

"This is the best possible subject, talking about kissing you and holding you in my arms. I may run them all off soon."

"Don't do that. It's my first visit and I need to go back and get to know them."

"You will. They think Hattie is fun or they wouldn't be hanging around her like they are. I know my brothers. They think you're gorgeous, so they'll come see you. You'll get to know them, I promise. Tonight I want your attention," he said in a husky voice that made her blood heat up and made her forget the others.

"Watch out, Nick. When you're being so appealing, so sexy, you may complicate our relationship. Neither of us wants that."

"No. I don't need another damn complication in my life or another big emotional upheaval. Not at all. But I think we can avoid that happening and still have a great married life," he said in a sexy, husky tone that played over her and made her tingle as much as if he had caressed her. She hadn't known Nick long, but she could tell he was intent on seduction.

"We better break this up," she said breathlessly, unable to hide her feelings. "We have company, and we need to give them attention."

He looked amused. "I will right now if you promise we can come back to this conversation."

She tilted her head to gaze up at him and ran her finger lightly over the back of his hand. "Of course we'll come back to the subject of seduction. You can count on that," she said in a soft, sultry voice.

He drew a deep breath, desire flashing in his expression. "Damn. I'd like to carry you off with me right now."

"Instead, let's go talk to your family," she said, walking past him, wondering if he guessed how fast her heart beat or how hot she felt. She wanted his kisses, wanted his hands on her, and knew that was what would happen after they got Hattie to bed. She could hardly wait.

Stan was the last to leave. At the door, he turned to Nick and glanced down at the baby asleep in his arms. "You have a sweet little daughter there, Nick. I think I'm going to like being an uncle again."

"I'm glad. She seems to like you."

Stan smiled. "She likes everybody. She won Grandmother over."

Stan turned to Talia. "We're happy to have you joining the family, Talia, and it was a good dinner, my brother."

"Thanks, Stan. For a bachelor, you do all right with little kids."

"What can I say? It's my experience with calves," Stan replied, grinning as he walked out the door.

The minute they were alone, Talia asked, "Want me to take Hattie?"

"No. I'll carry her to bed and then you can take over."

She followed him upstairs, treading softly so as to not wake the baby. "Thanks, Nick, for introducing me to your family. They were great and I'm so happy to get to know them."

"My brothers and I are close, so after we marry, you'll probably see them often. Grandmother will be good to Hattie and she'll shower her with too much stuff."

Talia laughed. "Says the man who has already given Hattie a pink bunny, her first present from a Duncan."

"I can promise you there will be more to come. Besides, you can't spoil a baby. You can a kid, but not a baby. To my way of thinking, a baby should be showered with love."

"Aw, Nick, that's nice," she said, thinking it might be even more difficult than she had thought to resist falling in love with him. "Don't get too nice. Even though you've given me Hattie, I don't want to fall in love because I know you never will."

"That's right," he said, suddenly sounding somber, his voice getting deeper. "I'm glad you're okay with that."

"I am," she replied. "I'm not looking for love, either. It didn't work out too well last time. I don't want a repeat of what I went through with my ex-husband. All I can hope for is that we're compatible. So far, so good," she said. Truthfully, they were more than compatible, she thought. His slightest touch set her heart pounding.

Right now she had a heart-racing awareness of him so close beside her. Since their kiss, she had been far more conscious of him when they were together. Now they were together, alone, late at night in his ranch house after a fun evening. She thought about the kiss they had shared and felt her pulse race.

She opened the door to her suite and Nick entered, placing Hattie in her crib. He settled her then turned to Talia. "At this point you take charge. Do what you need to do and come back down so we can talk awhile and maybe make a few plans about our wedding. The sooner we get married, the better."

"I agree with that. There's one thing, Nick… You're a wealthy man, but this is a marriage of convenience, so just a plain wedding band will suffice for me. I don't need an engagement ring because we're not going to be engaged more than a few days. I really mean it. A big ring won't be significant to either one of us. Let's let that one go."

He smiled at her. "Talia, I think there are few women in the world who would have made that speech to me. That's fine with me if you're good with it."

She nodded. "I won't be long. I just want to be sure she's down," she said, nodding at Hattie.

"Want something to drink?"

"Ice water would be nice, thank you."

"You've got it," he said and left.

She quickly changed into comfortable clothes and checked again on Hattie, who'd barely stirred. She looked down at her sleeping and smiled at the thought of how Hattie had been welcomed into a family who would love her. She and Hattie were both fortunate. She had one more week now until the semester ended. When that happened, she and Nick would marry.

A tingle went up her spine at the thought. Was it from anticipation…or apprehension?

She hoped she wasn't headed for more heartache.

Nick would not fall in love, and she didn't want to fall in love with a man who had no love in his heart for her. She simply had to guard her heart.

But living with an appealing, handsome Texas rancher who, based on his kiss, was the sexiest man she had ever known… Well, it might be easier said than done.

# Six

It seemed no time at all that it was June and she was standing at Nick's side, repeating vows. She wore a short pale blue linen dress with a V-neck and straight skirt. Her hair was gathered and fastened with clips high on the back of her head, long curls falling freely in back. Nick had sent her a corsage of white orchids pinned on one shoulder of her dress. They stood at the altar in a small chapel in Nick's large Dallas church with his family in attendance. There was a very small group for the service, and she was relieved that they hadn't planned a big reception afterward.

When Nick slipped the gold wedding band on her finger, she looked at the ring that signified she was Hattie's legal stepmother. A rush of gratitude and joy filled her.

When it came time for Nick to kiss her, she met

his gaze. His green eyes looked frosty and he barely glanced at her before he brushed his lips briefly against hers. Then they were introduced as Mr. and Mrs. Nicholas Duncan and the ceremony was over. One glance at him and she knew he hurt. This wedding was bringing back memories for him, making him miss his wife and baby son.

Nick had had his first wedding here, although it was in the sanctuary, not the little chapel. She was sure he was being bombarded by memories.

Today he wore a charcoal suit, a white dress shirt with French cuffs and gold links, his black boots and a sterling bolo tie. He looked incredibly handsome, but his somber countenance made her feel sad for him.

"Thank you, Nick," she said as she turned to him.

"I think I need to say thank you. You'll be good for Hattie and I won't have to worry constantly about her. In my family she will be showered with love."

"I'm glad she will be," Talia said, but she wondered if he even heard her. He seemed preoccupied, wrapped up in memories.

He took her arm and they turned for a picture. Originally they had agreed to skip the pictures, but then reconsidered so that Hattie would have them to look at someday and think they were happily married.

They went back to his Dallas house for a reception.

Even with just his family and a few very close Dallas friends of theirs, she guessed there were over twenty people at his house. Nick had carried Hattie almost the whole first hour they were there, showing her to people and introducing her. She couldn't keep her eyes from seeking him out across the room. What was it about him that drew her? From the very first moment, he had seemed sexy, exciting. Right now, in her view, Nick was the most handsome man in the room. Especially holding a baby.

Hattie had a pink dress with little embroidered rose-buds and a pale green matching sash. She wore a locket that had been Myra's when she was a child. Her hair was in ringlets with a pink bow that had two small rosebuds.

Inviting smells came from the kitchen and they welcomed their guests to a delicious buffet. There were small tables in the family room and on the patio, and extra staff had been hired to help serve. Nick had hired Paula Fletcher, Kirby's wife, to watch Hattie, wanting Talia to be free to enjoy her wedding day. Taking care of Hattie had never seemed a chore to her, especially today. She was Hattie's stepmom now and Nick had promised that Monday morning they would start the adoption process. They had already met with his at-torney, who had filed the petition for adoption. Nick's money would move the whole procedure along faster and she was giddy with joy.

In the afternoon a moment came when Talia finally sneaked away from the guests, standing alone by a table that held slices of wedding cake. She wasn't alone for long.

"We have a beautiful little girl," Nick said, appear-ing at her side.

His words thrilled her. "That sounds wonderful. I can't ever tell you how thrilled I am, Nick," she said, glancing around him. "I left Hattie with you, so who has her now?"

"Paula's watching her, but the family is entertain-ing her. None of us will let her toddle off."

"I'm glad you got a fence for your swimming pool," she said, glancing out the window to the backyard.

"Let's not worry about Hattie right now," he said, pulling her against him to kiss passionately.

Her heart thudded and all she could think about was Nick, her husband. She wrapped her arms around his neck and clung to him, kissing him in return, feeling as if she was on fire with longing.

"Did I tell you how beautiful you look today?" he asked in a husky voice when he broke the kiss.

She smiled at him. "You did."

"I'll say it again. You're a beautiful bride."

"Thank you. You're a very handsome groom," she said lightly. She would never tell him that when she first saw him waiting at the altar, he had taken her breath away. He'd looked like a celebrity, handsome, sexy and exciting.

Then she remembered how his look had changed.

"I'm sorry, Nick, if this is making you remember your first wedding and if it's stirring up old hurts."

"I live with those hurts on a daily basis, so this is nothing new. Life is filled with constant reminders of Regina and Artie. Each day, each month, I think how old Artie would be. And I won't lie. This has made me think about my wedding with Regina."

She felt her heart tighten in sympathy. But before she could offer him comfort, he changed the subject.

"But I'm more worried about you," he said. "You're getting cheated today. You should be marrying a man who loves you and who you love. I hope someday Hattie looks back and realizes how much you loved her and how much you sacrificed personally so you could be a mother to her. When she's old enough, I'll tell her, but right now that seems eons away. You've made a giant sacrifice to give her your love and be a mother to her."

"It's no sacrifice, Nick. To be her mother was my dream. She's so precious. I'll always be grateful to you," she said and meant it.

She put her hands on his chest, feeling the rock-hard muscles from his physical work on the ranch. "I want to give you something in return, Nick. I want to make you happy. I want us to be happy together and I want this marriage to be good for both of us," she said.

He looked down at her and she couldn't read the expression on his handsome face. For a moment she thought to ask him what he was thinking, but then he finally spoke.

"I don't think it's going to be a task to be happy together, Talia. And I'm sure the marriage will be good for both of us." The smile he gave her didn't quite reach his eyes, but she returned it anyway.

This was one of the happiest days of her life. She only wished Nick could feel the same way.

She could hardly believe how things had worked out. She was getting to raise Hattie as a stay-at-home mom, like she'd always wanted. Her resignation had already been accepted by the college. And despite her objections, Nick had set up her and Hattie with incredibly generous trusts that would ensure their financial safety for life.

Once again, as she had done at the altar hours ago, she vowed to make her new husband just as happy.

They rejoined their guests, and by midafternoon the only ones left were Nick's brothers. They sat on the patio and Nick seemed to be enjoying their time, so Talia slipped away to put Hattie down for a nap.

When she came down, Adam and Blake had gone and Stan was saying goodbye. As usual, he was the last to leave.

"Well, we did it," Nick said when he closed the door behind Stan. He placed his hands on her shoulders. "You're now Mrs. Duncan and the stepmother of a little fourteen-month-old toddler."

She was aware of his hands, lightly moving back and forth on her shoulders and setting fires in their paths.

She was his wife. And she was ready to love him tonight the way only a wife could.

Warning bells went off in her head, but she ignored them. A sexual relationship wouldn't sweep her into falling in love with him. Or was she fooling herself and already sliding down a slippery slope into being in love with her handsome, appealing new husband?

It was after ten when they finally tucked a sleeping Hattie into bed for the night. Because of her late nap, she hadn't been ready to go down at her usual bedtime. Once Talia placed her in the crib, Nick slipped his arm around her waist. "Come have a drink with me and let's sit and talk. I couldn't go to sleep now if I tried."

"Sure," she answered, smiling at him.

He walked her out of the suite, not taking his hands off her. He wanted Talia in his arms, wanted to carry her off to his bed. She excited him and enticed him. But guilt stopped him cold. It shook him because he felt all his loyalty and love should be with memories of the life he'd had with Regina, his best friend until her death. Talia and Hattie would never displace memories of Regina and Artie or replace his love for them, but he still felt guilty for wanting Talia.

He'd thought he was beginning to mend, but today had set him back. The loss of his first wife and son still hurt and it hurt badly.

While Talia knew there was no love between them, that theirs was strictly a marriage of convenience, she should have had a better day. He'd planned to make it so, but when this morning came, he didn't want to do anything except get through the ceremony and the day.

He was glad for Talia, who was happy because now there was no danger of losing Hattie. She deserved that and Hattie should be with Talia, someone who would pour out love and be a good mother. He was certain Talia would be that.

As they walked down the steps together, he couldn't get it off his conscience that he should have done better for her sake. She shouldn't be marrying out of convenience. She should have someone who loved her. A beautiful woman, Talia deserved a man who would shower her with love and attention. Nick felt guilty about Talia, and for other reasons, he felt guilty about Regina.

He and Talia had touched casually, lightly, off and on all day long. They'd held hands and repeated vows. But where was it leading? He glanced at Talia. She wasn't going to have a real marriage…but did she want a real wedding night? There was one way to find out.

"We've got the monitors in the family room to hear her if she should wake. Let's go have that drink."

The video monitor had been one of her earliest purchases. Talia had one in her small house, but here, in the Dallas mansion, it was a necessity.

"Fine, Nick, if you really want to. If you're doing

that because you feel you should for me, don't," she said. She knew he was hurting and still wrapped up in memories of when he had married the first time.

He smiled at her. "I'm doing it because I want to be with you."

"I won't argue with that, then."

As they went downstairs, she was intensely aware of his hand on the small of her back. She cast a glance at him. He had shed his jacket and tie, and the first couple of buttons on his shirt were unfastened. After the long day, his hair was tousled, begging her to reach out and smooth it. She had to admit he looked sexy, too appealing, and she could think of many things she'd rather be doing with him than talking.

When they went into the family room she saw a bucket of ice with a bottle in it. Surprised, she walked across the room with him, pulled it out and read the label. "Champagne? Where and when did this arrive?"

"I had Kirby put it out for us," Nick said, taking the bottle from her. When he popped the cork, he picked up a delicate crystal flute and poured the pale, bubbling champagne in first one flute to hand to her and then into the other flute. When he put the bottle back on ice, he turned to look at her and raised his glass.

"Here's to our marriage. Even though it is a marriage of convenience, may it be happy and may we be wed a long time." She touched her flute to his with a ring of crystal against crystal and they both sipped their champagne. When she looked at him, she realized he was paying attention to her now, gazing at her intently. Gone was the shuttered expression he'd had through the ceremony and most of the day.

She held up her flute. "May this marriage bring you the joy and happiness it's bringing to me."

He touched her flute and they sipped again. He turned to pick up the remote to turn on music and then he set his glass of champagne on the table and took hers from her. He stepped close to take her hand and draw her closer as he began to dance to the ballad with her.

"It was hard for me to get through today," he whispered against her ear. "You knew it was and you were so good about it."

He held her away to look into her eyes as they danced. "I should have made a bigger effort to hide those feelings," he told her. "I loved Regina with all my heart. I can't just shut that off. In some ways I feel as if I'm betraying her. Common sense makes me know that I'm not, but I can't stop feeling that way. And Arthur. I loved my son."

"You don't need to explain loving them," she said, feeling his pain, yet touched that he was trying to explain it. "I understand that." She'd certainly cried buckets of tears over losing her parents and her two unborn babies.

"I couldn't keep from getting carried back and thinking about my wedding with Regina."

"I really do understand."

"I know you do, Talia, and you were wonderful about it." He gestured to the champagne. "This is just my way of saying thank you." He twirled her around the family room in time to the soft music, then dipped her back over his arm when the love song ended. His gaze drifted over her, from her face down past her breasts, and it was as if he had lightly caressed her instead of giving her just a look.

Her heart thudded so hard, she thought he could hear it in the silence before the next song started.

His eyes settled on her lips and she thought he was about to kiss her. Instead, he whispered something she wasn't sure he intended her to hear. "You should have had more."

She straightened and framed his face with her hands. "Nick, stop worrying that we're not in love and I'm not marrying a man who loves me. Today you gave me what I wanted most in my whole life—that sweet child I love as if she were my own."

"No, I only partially did," he said, looking solemn. "I gave you what you wanted, but I've been in love, Talia. I married for love and had a baby we both loved. That's a whole lot more. It creates a world filled with joy and happiness during a wedding day and honeymoon. I couldn't give you that."

"But I'm happy, Nick, so stop worrying."

He opened his mouth to object, but she covered his lips with one finger. "Nick, life is filled with risks. We both took risks today. I took the risk of this 'convenient' marriage and I got what I wanted. You took the risk of marrying me and you got someone to care for Hattie. And I intend to do just that for the next eighteen years, give or take a year or two."

He gave her a searching stare as she lowered her hand. "How is it possible that I got so lucky finding you? Or rather that you found me. I'm so grateful for you, Talia." He took her hands in his and stepped back to sweep her with a glance, his eyes searing her flesh through her clothes. "Now that I can lay my conscience to rest, I want to say, you look stunning in your beautiful blue dress."

"Thank you," she said, smiling at him. "You look quite handsome yourself." She meant the compliment, despite the fact that at the same time she was trying to deny his appeal. She had to, because it'd be too easy to fall for this amazing, sexy, handsome man. She couldn't fool herself into thinking that he was happy about their arrangement. Surely he'd have preferred to go on his way, to live his life without including her in it. But she was part of it now, and as long as he was a good daddy for Hattie, Talia would be happy. She just hoped she could guard her heart enough so that she never lost it to Nick, because he was still in love with his late wife.

When the music started again, Nick stepped toward her. She thought he'd take her in his arms and resume the dance, but instead, his gaze settled on her lips. He inhaled deeply as his eyes met hers again—and she saw it.

Desire.

It blazed there in his green eyes, which had darkened to emerald.

While her heart began to drum, his arm tightened around her waist to draw her to him. "You're gorgeous, sexy and appealing, and it's time you know you're appreciated on more than one level," he said in a husky voice. As he held her tightly against his solid length, he leaned down, slowly, inch by inch, stealing her breath until finally his mouth covered hers. His tongue met hers in a slow dance, a tantalizing torment that made her tremble. Moaning, she wrapped her arms around his neck and kissed him in return.

She forgot all the reasons to be cautious with him. At the moment she just wanted his kisses, his hard body pressed against hers, his hands on her. She had danced with him today, laughed with him, married him, and now she finally could kiss him. And she did.

His kisses were sexier than she had ever experienced, this man who had made her biggest dream come true. It was a combination that was too enticing to resist. This handsome rancher had taken away her fears and worries about losing Hattie, had married her today. Tonight she wanted him—totally. She wanted his kisses, his body against hers, his hands on her. He must have read her mind, because as he continued to hold her close with one hand, his other hand trailed slowly down her back, over her bottom. Even through her clothes she could feel his caresses as he touched the backs of her thighs and then up her legs to her waist. While he kissed her, she felt his fingers at the buttons on the front of her dress. When she reached up to close her hand over his, he raised his head to give her a questioning look.

"We don't have to go to bed together tonight," she whispered. "There's a lot of time ahead of us. You've had an emotional day and I have, too, so if you're doing this out of a sense of duty, you don't need to do so."

He smiled as he unfastened a button. "Talia, I promise you, there is absolutely not one tiny shred of feeling that I have a duty to perform here," he remarked drily and she could hear the amusement in his voice. He unfastened another button, pushed the dress open and ran his warm finger lightly on the rise of her breast. "This isn't a chore for me," he said as his smile faded and his voice became hoarse, breathless.

"You'll complicate our lives from the first night we're together," she warned.

"I might do that," he said, his hungry gaze making her heart pound. "We complicated it when we married and we knew we had complicated it after that first kiss."

"Nick," she whispered, unaware of even moving as his arm wrapped around her waist and he drew her tightly against him. Her gaze flew to his mouth while her heart thudded. She couldn't deny it. She wanted his naked body against hers. They were married, man and wife, and she wanted it all with him, and at the moment she was reckless and eager enough to risk her heart.

"Nick, I want you, but I'm warning you, my body comes with a heart inside and emotions all tangled with sex. You're taking a risk here just as much as I am."

"After hearing your first words before your warning, I'm willing to take the risks," he whispered gruffly as he showered kisses on her throat and down her neck, onto her breasts.

"You've been warned," she whispered. "I'm not going to argue with you. I want you, and I have since that first kiss."

That may have been what Nick needed to hear, because he ran his tongue over her peaked nipple while he cupped her breast in his hand. Talia couldn't stifle the gasp that escaped her lips.

"You're so soft," he whispered. "Just to touch you is magic."

She framed his face with her hands, feeling the stubble on his jaw against her palms. "Nick, no one has ever kissed me the way you do. I suspect no one has ever made love to me the way you will. I want you to take all night," she said, certain that he was finally seeing her in the moment, that he was not lost in memories. He had come into the present and she was waiting, wanting him. "I want to kiss and touch you just as much as I want your hands and mouth on every inch of me."

"Sounds like the best possible plan," he whispered gruffly as he kissed her throat. Peeling away the top of her dress, he brushed more kisses down her slender neck. "Right now, I want you and I want to kiss and touch you for hours. We have all night to pleasure each other, to discover what we like." He straightened to gaze into her eyes and the desire she saw there sent delicious shivers up her spine. When his gaze lowered to her mouth, she couldn't get her breath. Then, finally, he tightened his arm around her waist and drew her to him to kiss her.

His mouth covered hers, his tongue heightening her desire while he kissed her. She wanted more of him, wanted him to make her forget everything else except their lovemaking. Passion spilled over her, setting her ablaze.

She unbuttoned his shirt and pushed it away to let it fall. As soon as it was gone, she showered kisses on his broad shoulder, running her fingers through the thick mat of curls on his chest. Her hands were at his belt, and in seconds, she pulled it free and dropped it while he continued to peel away her clothing until she was wearing only lacy bikini panties. He held her hips and stepped back a fraction to look at her.

"From the first moment I saw you, I knew you were beautiful. You're perfection," he said in a gruff voice, his gaze consuming her. "You make my heart race and my breathing difficult. You're gorgeous." He slid his hands down over her hips, pushing away the panties till they fell around her feet and she stepped out of

them. He ran his hands lightly over her, starting at her
throat, down over each breast, caressing her slowly,
cupping her breasts and circling each tip with his
tongue. He straightened, still watching her with half-
closed eyes, as his hands drifted down, one sliding
slowly over her belly while his other hand skimmed
over her bottom.

She gasped with pleasure and clung to his hips as
his hands drifted to her thighs.

"This is magic, Talia. You make me want you every
way possible."

He tossed aside the last of his clothes. His body
against hers was hot, hard and exciting, making her
tremble with eagerness and discovery as she ran her
hands and trailed her lips over him.

Her fingers explored lower, over his flat, muscled
stomach, down on his thighs, and then she stroked his
throbbing manhood that made her insides clench and
heat. She wanted him inside her. She wanted to give
herself, to feel that he was part of her, as close as they
could get.

"Nick, I want you—"

"Shh, just wait. We're just getting started. I want to
pleasure you, to stir you to heights, to discover what
you like best, to taste and thrill you," he whispered as
he filled his hands with her soft, full breasts. His fingers circled each taut peak slowly, deliberately, sending
showers of tingling sensations following the faintest
touch. Her breasts felt swollen, aching for his mouth,
and she yearned for him to come inside her, to move
together, to finally reach a climax together. She felt
driven, need building with each stroke of his fingers,
each slow lick of his wet tongue.

"Ahh, Nick," she gasped with pleasure, running her hands over his narrow hips, taking his thick rod in her hand to stroke and caress him. She rubbed against him and then ran her tongue slowly, intimately, where her hand had been.

He closed his eyes and wound his hand in her hair, holding her while he groaned with pleasure and desire. He pulled her up to him suddenly to kiss her hard, a demanding, possessive kiss that revealed he wanted her with an equally desperate urgency. His hungry kiss made her heart beat even faster. It was a kiss of possession that drove her wild with longing for all of him.

"Nick, the bed," she whispered.

"Soon," he answered, his hands drifting down to her silky inner thighs and then rubbing her intimately as she cried out and clung to him.

Kissing her, he scooped her up into his strong arms and carried her upstairs to his bedroom. He yanked away the covers and placed her on the bed. While he kissed her, he moved between her legs and then he looked down at her.

"You're beautiful. Every inch of you is so beautiful," he whispered.

She reached for him, but he pushed her hands away. He put her legs over his shoulders, giving him more access while he toyed with her, stroked her, set her on fire with longing.

Sensations bombarded her, driving her to move, to cry out for more of him as she shifted and knelt before him. She took his thick rod in her hand, exciting him as he had her.

He rolled her over on her stomach, running his hands over her and then his tongue while she writhed in pleasure and need beneath him. With a cry, she rolled over and sat up to kiss him, wrapping her long legs around him and pulling him down while she fell back on the bed. He retrieved a condom from the nightstand drawer and knelt between her legs to put it on.

"I want you now," she whispered, gazing into his eyes.

He entered her slowly, partially, pausing and then withdrawing and driving her wild.

"Nick, I want you now."

He entered her, filling her with his hot, thick manhood, then withdrawing while he kissed her. She arched beneath him, pulling at his firm butt, tightening her legs around him to draw him closer. "Nick, I want you, all of you," she whispered, pulling on him.

Finally he filled her, his manhood hot and thick. She moved her hips beneath him. "Love me," she gasped, wanting him desperately, tugging at him.

He kissed her, a kiss that made her breasts tingle and become more sensitive to the touch of his chest against them. She tried to pull him closer, arching her hips to meet his every thrust as he began to pump faster. With a cry of ecstasy and need, she met him and moved with him. His thrusts filled her, faster and more intense, until she shattered with a wild climax, arching beneath him, her cry muffled by his kiss. Seconds later he found his own release.

Still, he continued to thrust into her. She felt need build again inside her and clutched his broad shoulders, moving in perfect rhythm with him. In seconds he had her crying out while she shuddered in a powerful orgasm. Even in her ecstasy she felt him reach his climax, pounding into her with one final thrust.

SARA ORWIG                    125

"Ahh, Talia," he whispered on a ragged breath. "You have to be the sexiest woman on earth."

She held him tightly. Smiling, she couldn't answer. She was sunk in euphoria, satiated, enveloped in rapture, and she didn't want to speak or think or do anything except relish the moment and his body, his weight on her a reassurance that he was real and in her arms. He raised his head slightly to look at her. "You're not speaking. Are you all right?"

"I'm more than all right. I didn't know it could ever be that great. It's an effort to talk, an effort to think. I feel as if every bone in my body melted and I don't want to get out of this bed or let go of you ever."

He chuckled softly, a rumble in his chest causing her to feel the vibrations. "I hope you don't get out of this bed tonight. It was terribly shortsighted of me to think we wouldn't want any kind of wedding night to ourselves, not to mention dismissing all thoughts of a honeymoon."

"A honeymoon seemed a ridiculous thing to plan when we not only aren't in love, we didn't ever really plan to make love tonight. I feel too exhausted to talk about it."

He showered kisses on her face. "Well, it was shortsighted on my part because I knew what it was like to kiss you and I knew how beautiful and sexy you are. I guess I really have been numb to the world for a long time. Numb in all parts from my brain down."

She smiled. "You were far from numb tonight." She snuggled against his hot body. "Just stay here in my arms and hold me close and I'll be happy."

"That I can do, my dear."

She didn't know how long they lay in each other's

arms, but finally he spoke softly, his deep voice making vibrations in his chest. "Talia, tonight was spectacular, mind-blowing sex, hot and urgent, but I can't promise that it will be a buffer to keep away the hurt and pain of losses that I have. I'll still have moments. Hopefully, if I work at it, I can control my hurt and keep my low moments from dragging things down for you."

"Don't worry. I've told you how I feel. It's all worth it for what I get out of this marriage—Hattie as my daughter. And when you get to know her, you'll be a loving dad for her. I know you will. I can't ask for anything more. The rest is icing on the cake, and believe me, this hot, mind-boggling sex with you is better than the usual icing on the cake."

He rolled beside her, pulled her close and lay on his side to face her. He ran his fingers through her hair to comb it away from her face.

"The day will come, I'm sure, when I'll love little Hattie the way I loved Artie."

She heard the sorrow, as well as the hope, in his voice. "I'm so sorry for your losses, Nick. You probably thought you had everything in the world you wanted and it was all taken from you. If I had lost Hattie like I thought I was going to, I'd be far worse than you've been. When I thought the state might take her, I couldn't sleep or eat. Thanks to you that isn't going to happen, but believe me, I understand your hurt and can accept that."

He leaned down to kiss her forehead tenderly. "I'm lucky. Hattie can't ever take Artie's place, but she'll have her own place."

They lay in each other's arms quietly, till Nick spoke again. "This is good, Talia. Very good," he whispered against her. "Thank you again for being you and for understanding today."

"I told you—you've given me what I wanted the most. Few people can ever say that to someone else. You've made me a very happy woman, Nick."

"I'm glad."

They became silent and she realized there were no words of love, no easy banter after fantastic sex. The day had been an emotional roller coaster for him and somewhat for her, as well. But they had gotten through it better than she had expected.

They had gotten through it with his family welcoming her and now she was Mrs. Nicholas Duncan. Nick's wife and Hattie's mother. She turned to share her joy with Nick and saw that his eyes were closed, but she didn't think he was asleep. As if he knew what she was thinking, he reached out and slipped his arm around her, pulling her close against him and turning slightly so he could hug her.

"You've been great today," he said.

"Thanks," she whispered, wrapping her arms around him and wondering if she should leave right now and get in her own bed. She started to move away but he tightened his arm around her, so she settled back. The monitor for Hattie was right beside the bed, so she snuggled against Nick and closed her eyes.

The next thing she knew, she stirred because Nick was talking and holding her tightly. "Regina, Regina," he mumbled.

# Seven

Startled, Talia came fully awake. She realized Nick was dreaming and he must mean his late wife, Regina. "Nick," she whispered.

Sitting up suddenly and breathing heavily, he looked around the bedroom.

"Nick, you were dreaming."

He stared at her and she wondered if he even remembered that he had married only hours earlier.

He rubbed the back of his neck. "Sorry."

She slipped out of bed and grabbed up her dress. "I think I'll check on Hattie and stay in my room."

She left his bedroom, closing the door behind her, unable to deny the disappointment that enveloped her. He hadn't asked her to come back or to stay. Had he woken remembering his dream about his first wife? Or when tomorrow came, would he even remember dreaming?

Able to see because of a little night-light, she entered her suite and crossed the room to Hattie's crib.
As she looked at her, her heart filled with joy. She
loved Hattie and now she could be her mother. She
couldn't be angry with Nick for mourning the woman
he loved or the little baby boy he lost. Time would
help him heal to a point, but there would always be
memories that hurt, always be a void. If dreams came
about his first wife, he couldn't stop them. She could
understand his pain and regretted he was sad when
their wedding had showered her with happiness. She
felt as he got to know Hattie, the love for her would
help to alleviate his pain.

She climbed into her bed and hoped Nick slept
peacefully. The fantastic sex was one more thing that
would cause them to bond. She didn't expect Nick to
fall in love with her, but life could still be good if she
just didn't fall deeply in love with him and need his
love in her life. That was the one thing that could lead
to a broken heart. If she could just take the sex the
way he did, without emotional ties, without falling in
love, then they would have a good relationship. Could
she do that? Could she keep her feelings from getting
involved?

Common sense told her to keep up her guard, but the
way she reacted when he held her or when he kissed her
told her it wouldn't be easy. Nick was far too charming.
She sighed and shook her head. Could she keep him at
arm's length all the time? Did she even want to? They
were married, after all. Winning Nick's love might be
worth taking some risks.

Or was she just setting herself up for a huge heartbreak?

\* \* \*

Days later, on Monday, Myra asked her to come visit and bring Hattie. When Talia told Nick, he arranged for a limo, which seemed ridiculous to Talia, but she didn't argue with him. She had stayed out of his bedroom Sunday night and they'd had the brothers over in the evening, so she hadn't been alone with him. Earlier that day they had all gone to church together and then taken Ida and Myra to a local restaurant in the closest small town to have Sunday dinner together. The brothers had come back to Nick's and all of them had disappeared into the barn until evening.

Even though Talia hadn't been alone with Nick since their wedding night, she was acutely aware of him, feeling the same sizzling fires when he touched her lightly or when they exchanged glances. More so now than ever before because they had made love and it had been scalding, raging hot sex that she thought about constantly when she was with him or not.

Monday night the brothers were back and Nick went with them to look at some of his horses in the barn again. Later on, when she went upstairs to put Hattie to bed, she thought she was alone in the house. She had all the lights off except one, a small baby lamp with nursery-rhyme characters at the base. But in minutes Nick appeared. He knocked lightly on the door and came in.

"She's sound asleep, isn't she?"

"Yes," Talia said. "She had a big day. She's not used to all the attention, but she had a good time. She was good with your grandmother, sitting on her lap for as long as she did."

"You can't imagine how happy my grandmother is

over Hattie. All of us are amazed. I don't remember that kind of joy with Artie, but Artie was so little and he wasn't talking."

"I'm glad. Hattie must sense that because she seems to really like your grandmother."

His fingers closed lightly on her arm. "Come here," he said softly and shivers tickled her. "She's asleep." They walked out of the bedroom into the sitting room and he turned to her. He reached up to take a lock of her hair in his hand and she felt the contact through her whole body, a touch that would be nothing if done by anyone else, but with Nick, it was electrifying.

"I can't control my dreams," he told her without pre-amble. "I was dreaming about Regina the other night but that didn't have anything to do with us."

"I know that, Nick. I thought we'd both sleep better if I came back here with Hattie. These are new sur-roundings. I want to be here for her if she wakes up. I understand and it didn't upset me," she said.

"Okay. I just didn't want to hurt you, but I can't con-trol my dreams and I do dream about both of them. I haven't slept well since that plane crash."

"I'm sorry and I can imagine. You don't ever need to apologize where Regina and Artie are concerned. Not ever, not once. You had a devastating, terrible loss."

He looked away and was silent a moment. "Regina took him to see her folks in Montana. It was one of my planes, but not a small plane. It went down and all were killed. We had a pilot, copilot, Regina, her sis-ter and Artie."

"I'm so sorry for your loss. Don't ever apologize for dreaming about them or anything like that. You loved them."

He drew her into his arms and she went eagerly. She slipped her arms around his waist and held him tightly, hoping she was some comfort, some company for him, and that Hattie would bring him love and joy.

"I'm going to sleep in here tonight, Nick. I'll feel better and I don't want to rush into a lusty physical relationship that we both might regret."

"I won't ever have a regret about making love with you. Oh, Talia, you can't imagine what you do to me," he whispered, trailing kisses on her throat and then running his tongue over the curve of her ear as he caressed her nape and sent waves of fiery tingles that centered low in her.

She drew a deep breath and wound her arms around his neck. "Nick, aren't your brothers here?"

"I guess. I left them in the barn." He shrugged. "But I don't care really. They know we just got married."

"Nick," she said, starting to protest when his lips covered hers, his tongue stroking hers so slowly while he caressed her breast. She gasped with pleasure and couldn't stop him or say anything else to him. She was hopelessly lost in sensations that made her yearn for his thick, hard manhood inside her.

"I wasn't going to do this tonight," she whispered, tearing her mouth away from his.

"Neither was I, but now we are and I don't want to stop." His mouth covered hers, his tongue going over hers while he pulled her zipper down her back and then peeled away her dress.

"Nick, we should use some sense here—"

"Shh," he whispered, unfastening her bra and letting it fall. His hands cupped her bare breasts and he stroked her so lightly, slowly, his thumbs circling her taut nipples, and then his mouth covered them so he could lave them with his tongue. She gasped and thrust her hips against him, grinding against him, wanting him inside her, forgetting all her lectures to avoid making love with him anytime soon. She was lost in his kisses and caresses. She trembled, gasping for air and moaning with pleasure as his hands moved over her and more of her clothing fell away.

"I wasn't going to do this," she whispered again, as if she could convince herself.

Nick didn't respond. He merely picked her up and carried her to his bedroom.

Before she could utter a protest, he assured her, "The monitor is on and we can hear Hattie."

Once in his bedroom, he stood Talia on her feet and peeled away the rest of her clothes, tossing his own aside as he kissed her.

She ran one hand through his hair and the other over his broad shoulder, down his back, over his hip and then over his butt that was hard and muscular like the rest of him. Against her, she felt his erection, thick and hard, ready for her. He picked her up and she locked her legs around his waist as he took her breast in his mouth and ran his tongue over her nipple.

She clung to him while he lowered her down over his body, sliding her onto his throbbing rod. She cried out and locked her legs around him, moving in perfect rhythm with him as he pumped into her. She cried out again as her climax burst and made her shake, relief and ecstasy showering over her. He thrust hard and fast toward his own climax.

In seconds or minutes—she didn't know time—she

was aroused again, moving with him toward another shattering climax as she rode him.

When they were both sated, she had lost all track of time. Finally she slid down and placed her feet on the floor. He looked into her eyes and she felt as if a bond sprang to life between them, a tie that bound them together in rapturous intimacy. She knew it couldn't last, but for a moment, she felt something from him beyond pure lust. He pulled her to him to kiss her, another earth-shaking kiss. His kiss set her on fire as if they hadn't just made love, as if she hadn't reached more than one explosive climax that still took her breath away to think about.

She leaned away a fraction, placing her mouth at his ear. "I wasn't going to do that. I was going to be sensible, cautious, and get to know you."

"Oh, what you do to me," he whispered, trailing his tongue lightly behind her ear. "You've brought me to life. Sensible went out the window with our first kiss. Life is filled with hurt. When we find fireworks and rapture, I say go for it."

"I have to agree. Life is filled with risks, Nick. We both took big ones with this loveless convenient marriage. We didn't factor in kisses and more."

"We didn't factor in the hottest sex ever. Talia, you should come with caution signs on you."

"I don't think it's me. I think it's *us*."

"If it's 'us' we've complicated our lives."

"I hope we haven't," she said.

He picked her up again to place her in his big bed and then stretch out beside her. He drew her close against him, tangling his long legs with hers.

Wrapped in euphoria, she held him while she ran

her hand lightly over his shoulders and chest, marveling at his strong, masculine body. "You know, I could stay like this with you forever. In your arms, touching you and—" She broke off and gasped.

He opened his eyes and looked at her. "What is it?"

She sat up like a bolt. "Your brothers! We're lying here…like this, and for all we know they could be somewhere in this house waiting for you to return."

He smiled and patted her shoulder in a gesture meant to calm her nerves. "Trust me, Talia, they're not here. They have that much sense. They've gone and locked up and forgotten about us." He glanced at the monitor on his nightstand. "And Hattie is asleep and I have you here, naked in my arms against my naked body, and I'm going to want to make love to you again."

He pulled her back down to him, and the instant she felt the heat of his chest, she felt herself relax. "I think I want you to do just that," she whispered, sliding sensuously against him. At her touch his body came to life and she began stroking his manhood. As if she hadn't found ecstasy in his arms twice already, she needed him again.

"Oh, yes, Nick," she said, sliding over him and sitting up astride him.

"You're a sex-starved woman," he said, but she knew it wasn't a complaint. Nick needed no coaxing to participate in another round of lovemaking.

With one hand he toyed with her breasts while the other stroked her inner thighs, up and down, each time venturing closer to the apex of her womanhood but never giving her the satisfaction she craved. She undulated her lips, giving him access, letting her body tell him what it wanted, needed.

Gently he pushed her down so his thick erection was between her legs, hot and hard, and he shifted his thighs, closing her legs against him. She gasped with need and moved against him, rubbing against him, relishing the silky smooth feel of him as she heightened his pleasure. But it wasn't enough. She wanted him inside her until she cried out with a mind-blowing climax.

Taking the matter into her own hands, she led him where she wanted him. Nick needed no further instructions. In one fluid motion he entered her to the hilt, eliciting a long moan from deep in her throat. Then he thrust into her, and she rode him hard and fast, until she didn't think she could take another second of this insane pleasure. With one final movement, they both climaxed at the same second, and letting out a sigh, she collapsed on him.

He wrapped his arms around her and she lay against him, relishing the feel of him still inside her. She didn't think she'd ever felt so comfortable. She'd certainly never felt so satisfied. Burrowing her head against his chest, she gave herself over to the feeling of utter contentment.

Her eyes flew open and were captured by the only light in the room. His alarm clock. It was almost four in the morning and they had made wild, passionate love all through the night. She'd lost count of how many times but she'd loved each and every one of them.

And what about the man who'd taken her to those heights?

She looked over at Nick, sleeping beside her. How deep did her feelings run for him now? She couldn't say. All she knew was that each day together, each moment of lovemaking, was stealing her heart away. There in the darkness of his bedroom she finally admitted what she'd feared all along. Despite her caution, despite the warning, there was no way she was going to be able to resist falling in love with Nick Duncan.

She'd always be grateful that he had given her the chance to become Hattie's mother, and for that reason she was glad she'd married him. But in securing Hattie as her daughter, she'd set something else at risk. Her heart.

Nick stirred and his arms blindly reached out for her. She went into them and knew she was in big trouble.

For the second day that week, Nick's grandmother had invited Talia to bring over Hattie for a visit. Once again, she found herself in Myra's smaller ranch house, sipping coffee while Hattie played on the floor and Myra joined in.

She couldn't help but think the older woman seemed to become more animated and kind whenever she was in Hattie's presence. And Hattie, too, seemed to enjoy playing with her great-grandmother.

"I've been thinking, Myra," Talia said. "Would you mind if I painted a picture of you with Hattie? I like to do portraits and I think it would be fun to have one of the two of you."

With a little doll in hand, Myra looked up. "That's fine with me. I'd like it, but I don't see how you can get Hattie to sit for a portrait."

Talia smiled. "I don't expect her to sit for the painting. I'd take a picture and then paint from that. I do it a lot of the time. She'll have to be still only a few seconds while I take her picture and she's accustomed to doing that." Talia couldn't count the number of Hattie photos stored on her phone.

"I'd love that," Myra said, smiling and glancing back down at Hattie, who was busy with a small dollhouse and a set of tiny dolls. "Can you dress her the same way she was for your wedding? She looked adorable."

"Actually, I have a good picture of the two of you from the party. Here, let me show you," she said, scrolling through her phone till she found the shot she was looking for. She showed Myra.

"Ahh, I like that one." In the picture Hattie was sitting on Myra's lap and they were both smiling at the camera. Hattie had her pink bunny in her hands.

"Then I'll do a portrait of this. It'll be fun."

"I can't wait to see the result," Myra replied. Then she looked up at Talia. "You know, I've enjoyed having you here on the ranch. Both of you. I have a feeling now that you're here, I'll probably get to see Nick a lot more, too."

Hattie pulled herself up and stood holding on to Myra's leg. She gave a little giggle as she took the doll the older woman was holding.

"You're a beautiful little girl, Hattie," Myra said as she leaned over to kiss Hattie's cheek. "I had to wait a long time for another grandchild, but I couldn't ask for a more delightful one."

Talia knew all her concerns were unfounded. She needn't worry that Nick's family wouldn't accept and love Hattie. It was right in front of her eyes.

Myra sat up and looked at her. "You know, Talia, I'll be the first to admit I wasn't in accord with this wedding. But now I am so happy that you and Nick

married. You're good for him and Hattie is a joy. You
and Hattie are erasing his grief and for that I'm so
thankful."

Talia felt a surge of love for Nick's grandmother. Another of her concerns went by the wayside. It seemed
the Duncan family matriarch had accepted her, as well.

"Thank you, Myra. Nick has made it possible for
me to be Hattie's mother and for that I will forever be
grateful to him."

"Just be patient with him. You and Hattie are going
to take away his hurt."

That was the one thing she was still worried about.
That Nick still hurt over his late wife and son. She'd
never be able to erase his pain fully but maybe one day
she could make it more bearable.

She reached over and patted Myra's hand. "I hope
so."

Her hands were shaking.

As she twisted her hair and fastened it with a clip
at the back of her head, she could barely keep her fingers from trembling. She smoothed down the navy
suit and white silk blouse she'd chosen to wear and
gave herself a final once-over in the gilded mirror of
her suite in Dallas.

She could hardly believe this day had finally come.
She was scared and eager at the same time to go to
court for the adoption hearing. Taking a big deep
breath, she left her room and went to pick up Hattie.

She'd dressed Hattie as she had been for the wedding, in her best dress. The little girl had no idea what
was happening, the importance of this day. Talia figured it was just as well.

She carried Hattie downstairs to the library to meet Nick and Stan. Nick's brother had come to Dallas with them to help with Hattie while Talia and Nick were in court. Both men wore charcoal suits and black boots and hats. Stan's was Western style and he wore a bolo, while Nick's was a classic cut with a red tie. Stan was a handsome cowboy, but it was Nick who took her breath away. Just looking at him made her weak in the knees, made her think of the incredible pleasure he'd given her night after night.

But today she had other thoughts when she walked into the library and saw him. Today all she could think about was that he had made this moment possible. If all went well, she would be Hattie's legal mother by noon.

She walked to them, greeting Stan, who took Hattie from her and walked away to give her a moment with Nick.

"You look gorgeous," Nick said. "I'm sure the judge will take one look at you and give you whatever you want." He glanced down at his slim black watch. "We're right on time. Horace said he'll meet us at the courthouse and he said this won't take long." His hand at the small of her back urged her out the door, but she couldn't move.

"Nick, I am so scared."

"Don't be. Horace said everything will be fine. Believe me, he would know. Let's go get this done and you can relax and be happy," he said as he took her hands in his and led her to the car.

She felt as if she was in a daze when they walked into the empty courtroom with Nick's attorney. Stan sat on a front-row seat with Hattie with some toys in his pockets for her. Talia's nerves were prickly and she tried to breathe deeply and be calm. She glanced at Hattie, who sat looking at Stan's bolo and was quiet as if she, too, sensed this was a monumental moment in her life.

Looking official in his black robe, the judge appeared. Dazed, she went through questions she had to answer, listened as Nick answered questions. Fear enveloped her and she hoped she appeared calm. She told how she had known Hattie and how much care she had given her, how close she had been with Madeline, Hattie's mother. In addition, she had printed out all the pictures of her with Hattie and Madeline from her phone and iPad. The pictures started the day Hattie was born and chronicled her life until now, visible proof of Talia's presence and friendship with Madeline.

At one point Judge Wentworth wanted Hattie brought forward and Stan gave her to Talia. To her relief, Hattie was on her best behavior as she often was in new surroundings, and Judge Wentworth relaxed and smiled for the first time. When he spoke to Hattie, she turned to hug Talia and Talia held her close, glad Hattie had hugged her. She smiled at Judge Wentworth.

Time stretched, seeming endless, and Talia's nerves remained on edge. Shortly, she handed Hattie back to Stan while she and Nick signed papers. She had no idea how much time passed until she officially became Hattie's mother.

"Congratulations. You have a beautiful daughter," Judge Wentworth said when it was official.

Talia felt giddy with happiness. She looked at the official document in her hand, and tears of joy and relief stung her eyes as she smiled and looked at Nick. She hugged him.

"Thank you," she whispered in his ear.

He hugged her lightly in return, and when she stepped back, he smiled. "Thank you, Talia. She needs you." Nick's attorney congratulated her and gave her best wishes before doing the same to Nick.

She couldn't keep back tears of relief and joy as Stan came up with Hattie to congratulate her. Hastily wiping away her tears, she took Hattie into her arms and hugged her.

"I love you, my precious baby. You're my baby now," she whispered to Hattie, not even knowing if Hattie heard her or understood her. Hattie wiggled and Stan took her again. As soon as he did, Nick hugged Talia.

Tears came again while she held him. "Nick, thank you. I'll be forever grateful to you."

"You've always loved her like she's your child. Now I'm glad she's your child by law. We'll all be better off. This is what I wanted when I proposed this marriage of convenience. Hattie needs your love."

She looked at Stan holding Hattie and pointing to something out the window as he talked to her. She realized that when he was around Stan gave more attention to Hattie than Nick did, and she wondered when Nick would really treat her as his little girl.

Her gaze shifted to Hattie and joy made her smile. Hattie was really her daughter now. Nothing could mar the happiness she felt today.

She had another week lined up in Dallas. She needed to select wallpaper and decor for Hattie's rooms, as well as select the rest of the furniture for Hattie's nurseries in both Dallas and the ranch. Nick had said he would make arrangements for the contractor to get the work done on the suites. Whenever she had time and wanted to deal with it, she could make decisions about what she wanted for her art studio. Nick insisted she have a studio in Dallas as well as on the ranch, so she would. Nick's contractor would work on that, too, once he had Talia's input. That was something on her to-do list for this week.

She'd be in Dallas this week and Nick would be on the ranch. It was just as well that they were apart. It'd give them a chance to adjust to this new life they had. Sex was fantastic, but making love to Nick also meant she was becoming more emotionally involved with him. If they had too big an emotional conflict, it could hurt Hattie. And that was something she could never do.

At the end of the week, Nick waited on the porch for Talia and Hattie to get back from Dallas. He had on fresh jeans and a white cotton shirt that was open at the throat. He had missed them both—a surprise because he didn't think they had been in his life long enough to miss them at all. If he was truthful with himself, he'd admit that he missed Talia constantly, and he especially missed her at night. Their lovemaking had stunned him. She was hot, sexy, amazing in bed, though she'd given no indication of being that way until they were alone and began to touch and kiss. She had brought him back to life with an overwhelming burst of lust. At the oddest times throughout the day he was bowled over by thoughts of her, by the need to have her right there and then, naked in his bed.

After the loss of Regina and Artie, he had thrown himself into ranch work, which he had always enjoyed.

He'd worked late and then gone home to take care of paperwork regarding the ranch. Beyond being a board member, he wasn't active any longer in the family energy company in Dallas. Since marrying Talia, though, he had started work earlier and, whenever possible, cut out some of the late-night work. On those unavoidable late nights when he missed dinner with her, she would come join him and he looked forward to having her there, to just being with her. He didn't know what it meant, but Talia seemed to draw him to her, like a magnet.

Something else was strange. In the time since she'd been in his life, his dreams had diminished. Those horrible nightmares that made him wake up in a sweat and in pain over losing his wife and baby.

He paced the porch and looked down at his watch. Where were they?

All week he'd been counting the hours until tonight. He had missed her enough to be shocked at how important she had become in his life. Along with that, he felt nagging twinges of guilt, because he still loved Regina and Artie. He tried to reassure himself that Regina would want him to go on with his life, but that didn't assuage the guilt. In fact, it increased the more he was drawn to Talia. In some ways it was difficult for him to relate to a little girl, but Talia made up for any lack of love from him because she poured out her love on Hattie. So did his grandmother and brothers.

He squinted down the road, looking for any sign of kicked-up dust that would signal her arrival. Damn. He wished she'd get back soon. He'd carry her off to bed the minute she arrived.

Each day she'd been away they had talked several

times and for more than an hour each time. The text messages had flown back and forth, too. But it wasn't the same as having her beside him. And Hattie, too.

He drew a deep breath when the limo finally appeared. Nick was down the steps, running to meet them, when Talia stepped out. She wore a maroon dress that ended just above her knees, leaving her long, shapely legs bare. She unbuckled Hattie and then turned around to face him.

He hugged her lightly, catching a whiff of some exotic perfume, surprising himself again how glad he was they were home.

When he picked up Hattie to hug her, she put her slender little arm around his neck to hug him. She leaned away. "Wuv you," she said, smiling at him, and Nick felt a clinch to his heart.

"Oh, sweet baby, I love you," he said, feeling a knot in his throat as he looked into green eyes so like his own, only on a sweet little face that made him weak in the knees. It still hurt to know he would never hear Artie say those words to him, but he was hearing his little daughter say them.

"I'm glad you're both back," he said. "I have presents for you," he said to Hattie.

She giggled up at him and ran her chubby little hands across his cheeks.

"Let's go see what your presents are," he said and reached out to drape his arm across Talia's shoulders. "Hi."

"Hi, Nick," she said, smiling at him. The moment he looked into her eyes, he felt sparks fly between them. He couldn't understand the chemistry between them. All he knew was that it took his breath away and, as usual, made him want to rush her off to the bedroom as soon as possible.

"I couldn't keep from getting emotional over that greeting. It's a reminder I won't ever hear Artie say those words to me."

"No, but you are hearing Hattie say them to you. If you let her, she'll wrap herself around your heart and put it in her collection. She's a sweetie."

"I'm glad you two are back at the ranch and so is the rest of the family. Stan wants us all for Sunday dinner. Grandmother can't wait to see Hattie and I promised you two would come over today after you got in."

"That's good. I'll be happy to see her."

"I have all sorts of plans for later," he said, looking into her blue eyes that held his gaze.

"So do I," she said and his pulse raced.

They went to the family room and he picked up a box wrapped in red paper. Another present in blue paper was beside it.

"Here, Hattie, this is a present for you," Nick said, handing it to her.

She smiled and began to try to tear off the wrapping. She yanked free the stick-on bow and tossed it behind her. When she couldn't open the box, Nick helped.

"Dolly," she squealed, picking up a fancy doll with long blond hair and a pink satin dress. She hugged it to her chest.

"Thank you," Talia said to Nick, slowly and clearly so Hattie would hear and begin to learn the words. Hattie smiled at him and hugged her doll.

Nick watched her, happy because she was happy. Then he turned to Talia and took her hand, feeling her smooth, soft skin and wanting to run his hands all over her and lose himself in her softness. "Thank you for bringing her into my life. I could have so easily never known about her."

They exchanged a look and he didn't know exactly what she was thinking, but he suspected she was thinking how close she, too, had come to losing Hattie.

He shifted closer to put his arm around Talia as they watched Hattie. Nick gave his daughter the next present, which was a book that she immediately wanted Talia to read to her.

As he watched them huddle together as Talia read the story, Nick had only one thought: life was good.

It was almost nine by the time they put Hattie to bed. When they left Hattie's room, Nick took Talia's hand.

"Come here," he said.

"Nick—"

"Shh. Come with me," he said, leading her to his suite, where a lamp was turned low. "Hattie isn't the only one getting a present," he said, holding out a box wrapped in white paper and tied with a blue satin bow. She looked up at him with wide eyes.

"Mine? Are you aware this is June, not December? Why the presents, Nick?"

"I have presents for Hattie because she's my little girl. And presents for you because you're my wife now and you've been patient, understanding and kind. You got a raw deal in some ways even though you got what you wanted—Hattie. Anyway, here's a little token of my thanks."

She stepped close and put her arm around his neck,

pulling him closer as she brushed a light kiss on his mouth. Her lips were velvety soft, pure temptation.

"I didn't get a raw deal," she whispered. "I'm so happy, Nick. I've told you, that was my fantasy fulfilled, to get to keep her. You can't imagine how scared and worried I've been about Hattie, especially before I met you."

"Shh." His arm circled her waist. "That's all over. She's your daughter now and forever." He tightened his arm around her and really kissed her. It took only a startled second before she responded, her tongue meeting his, setting him ablaze. Then suddenly she pulled away.

"I have a present to open," she whispered, holding it up.

"I thought my kiss might make you forget the present," he teased and she smiled.

"I'll get back to you in a few minutes," she said in a sultry voice that made his pulse jump.

She untied the bow, tearing off the paper and opening the box. She gasped as the light caught the diamond pendant. "Nick, this pendant is absolutely gorgeous." She took it out of the box. "This is so beautiful. Put it on me, please," she said and turned so he could.

He lifted it over her head and fastened the catch, brushing light kisses on her nape as he did so. She turned to face him.

"It's so beautiful. Thank you," she said and kissed him again.

As they kissed, his hands went to her blouse to unbutton it. He wanted her with a hungry need so intense he was surprised.

"I'm so glad you're home," he whispered. He pushed

her blouse off her shoulders. "You're beautiful, so gorgeous."

He picked her up and carried her to his bed, yanking away the covers again. "Let me show you how much I've missed you."

Talia clung to him, wanting him yet holding back the words that she wanted to say, words that would tell him how much she cared for him, how important he had become to her. But now was not the time. Not when he was doing things to her body that drove away all conscious thought.

She could only moan in pleasure and longing as heat spread low in her belly and desire made her pulse race. His hand caressed her breasts and she felt them tighten. In another second she wouldn't be able to stop the sexual onslaught. She was torn between desiring him and protecting her heart. She was dallying with trouble, with seduction and heartbreak, yet his scalding kisses were fanning flames that wiped out all her half-hearted arguments.

For a few minutes or a long time, she didn't know, she kissed him in return. She wanted his loving, wanted all of him, wanted his body against hers and wanted more nights of his kisses. She had made her decision to take the risks with Nick. Life was filled with risks and it was worth taking a risk with her new husband, who had been so marvelous to Hattie and to her. They had repeated marriage vows that she felt they each would live by and that meant they would be together, for a lifetime. Even as she thought about it, his hands, his lips were driving all rational thought out of mind while a tiny, nagging voice still whispered warnings of a broken heart. Emotionally, she was torn. Physically, she desired him more than ever. When his hand slid over the curve of her hip and found the part of her that ached for him, she knew she couldn't deny her body what it craved.

Emboldened, she unbuttoned and pushed away his clothes and in seconds he was naked before her. When she reached out for his erection, grasping it in her palm, she heard his sharp intake of breath even as her heart thudded.

"You are so beautiful," he whispered as he cupped her breasts, pausing to look at her before he leaned forward to run his tongue over her nipple, circling it slowly, his tongue warm and wet. She gasped with pleasure, closing her eyes and letting him loose in order to cling to his hard biceps. He ran his tongue over her ear, down on her throat, then down over her breast while his fingers worried both nipples, slowly, featherlight.

She moaned softly with pleasure and desire, needing more, aching for him.

"I want you," she whispered. "Now. Inside me. I've missed you."

"We won't rush. I want to pleasure you. I want to take our time," he whispered, showering kisses between his words—words she barely heard over the drumming of her heart. She pressed against him and leaned away a fraction to rub her breasts against him.

"Ahh, Talia, what you do to me," he whispered as he picked her up. He placed her on his bed and then knelt between her legs, running his hands so lightly over her inner thighs, his fingers brushing her intimately. When he followed with his tongue, sensations bombarded her, but she was even more aware of the handsome, naked man caressing her, kneeling between her legs.

She gasped with pleasure, arching beneath him. His tongue drove her wild, yet she didn't want to end it that way. Instead, she pushed him back and sat up to straddle his legs. She leaned down and ran her tongue down his chest as her fingers danced over him.

"You have to be the sexiest man on this earth," she whispered and then ran the tip of her tongue beside the path of hair that arrowed to his impressive erection. She moved down, trailing wet kisses up his shaft, but when she opened her mouth to take him in, he stopped her. He grabbed her in his big hands and in a flash he was over her and she was beneath him and he was filling her as she arched to meet him.

Wrapping her long legs around him, she held him tightly. She cried out, raising her hips while he thrust slowly, taking time to heighten every pleasure, to build her needs.

When she lost control, she moved with him, both together as they strained to reach a pinnacle. His thick rod filled her, sensations rocking her. She cried out with release, her legs tight around him while she clung to him.

His release burst, spilling hotly inside her, giving her what she sought. Gasping for breath, she held him as he clung to her and they moved together, causing more waves of pleasure to pour over her.

His arms tightened around her, solid, reassuring as they pumped together and shared the moment. With a cry, ecstasy rippled through her when she climaxed again. Finally she was still, gasping for breath as much as he was.

He brushed long, damp strands of silken hair away from her face and caressed her cheek so lightly. "That had to be the sexiest climax I've ever reached," he said, looking down at her. "You're fantastic."

And so was he, she thought. And that was the problem. "Nick, we can't do this every night."

He shook his head and looked at her, as if he didn't believe what he heard. "We can't? Why not?"

"Because one of us might fall in love and the other one would not."

Her words obviously had no effect on him, because he didn't move off her. "I don't want this night to end. I want to kiss and touch and explore and hug straight through the weekend. Promise me you won't get out of bed or out of my arms."

"I'm afraid you're not getting that promise, but I'm here now." His body was hot, hard, muscled and masculine. As much as she shouldn't, she wanted nothing else but to run her fingers over him, discover every inch of him, memorize his body and everything about him that she could learn about him.

"Stay here with me tonight. I want you here in my arms. I want you close to me," he said, leaning down to kiss her tenderly. Then he turned, keeping her with him.

She slept with his arm around her. At one point during the night she turned to watch him as he slept and knew she was in love with him. It was too late to avoid that now.

She couldn't see him as an ordinary person. When he was around, she was excited, continually aware of him, still getting streaks of fire from the slightest physical contact with him. She was falling more in love with

SARA ORWIG    153

him with each day she spent around him. And it was
likely he would never be in love with her.

On the Fourth of July, Nick and his brothers had a
cookout on the ranch. All hands, their families, neighbors and friends were invited. Talia found it amazing
how well and smoothly the day went. She watched with
other moms while Hattie played with some of the little
kids who lived on the ranch, but her favorite part of the
day was when Nick had Hattie on his broad shoulders
and her fingers were wound in his thick hair while she
laughed. Talia wished Nick would spend more time like
this with Hattie. She knew they both needed to make
adjustments and they would, but he was still working
too late lots of nights, coming in too late to see Hattie.
He knew she poured love out to Hattie and he seemed
to feel that was sufficient, but Talia wanted Hattie to
have Nick's love, his attention. Whenever she worried
about how little he saw his daughter, she reminded
herself that he probably needed more time to adjust.

As she watched him play, she thought about being
with him later and excitement streaked through her like
a lightning bolt, burning up all her concerns.

The rest of the week, Talia spent most of her time
getting her art studio set up and checking on the prog-
ress of the nursery. She worked some on the portrait of
Myra and Hattie together. Friday night Nick came in
early. He cooked out and they ate on the patio. Afterward, they drove to his grandmother's house to visit
for a short time because she loved to see Hattie.

It was after one in the morning by the time Nick and
Talia were in bed with Talia pressed against his side.

He had his arm around her and she felt content, satiated, so happy after the day and night.

"Nick, I loved it that you came in early enough tonight for the three of us to eat together like a family and to give you time to play with Hattie."

"I liked it, too. I'll try to get in earlier more often. There are always things to do."

"There's a little girl who needs your love."

"She has that. You pour love out to her all day. She isn't going to lack for love. Neither are you," he said, turning to kiss her.

"Are you getting love mixed up with sex?"

"Is that a complaint?" he asked and she could hear the amusement in his voice.

"Absolutely not. I have no complaints," she said, knowing she would never admit to him that she often wished he showed more affection for Hattie.

Later, as she lay in his arms, she ran her fingers over his shoulder. "I need to get up and get my nightgown," she said, running her fingers over the stubble on his jaw. "You sexy man. And, oh, what muscles you have," she said, running her hand over his biceps and then across his shoulders and on his chest. "Oh, my."

"You keep that up and you'll start something again."

"Let me try and see if I can," she said, smiling at him. "I think I was going to get a nightgown."

"You definitely don't need one. I like you naked. You're warm and soft. I might wake and want to hold you. I don't want anything in the way."

She smiled at him. "I suspect you can get me out of that nightgown very quickly."

Before he could answer her, his phone rang.

"It's almost two in the morning—damn late for a

phone call. This isn't going to be good news." He retrieved his phone and looked at it and frowned, and she hoped it wasn't terrible news.

He sat up in bed. "This is Nick." He was quiet for a moment and then he drew a deep breath. "Oh, damn. I'll be there. I'll call Stan now. I'll talk to my brothers."

She let her fingers drift lazily over his bare back. "Go ahead," he said into the phone, but she noticed his voice had changed, gotten deeper. Chills broke out over her arms and she slipped out of bed to grab the nearest piece of clothing. She wrapped his white shirt around her, suddenly so cold.

# Eight

"I'll see you in about twenty minutes," he said right before he ended the call. Talia knew what that meant. Twenty minutes meant something had happened on the ranch. He couldn't get off the ranch and get somewhere else in twenty minutes.

He gulped deep breaths and suddenly threw his phone across the room, where it hit a chair and bounced onto the floor with a clatter.

"What's happened?" she asked, knowing it was really bad news.

"I have to go. I have to call my brothers first." But he didn't move. He sat at the side of the bed, his head down.

She waited quietly, giving him space, knowing he would talk to her when he was ready.

"My grandmother died tonight," he said softly without even moving. "She went to sleep and…died. She just quit breathing. Ida said she never heard a sound from her."

"Oh, Nick," Talia said, feeling a gut-wrenching pain inside. "I'm so sorry that's happened."

"When Ida went in to check on her, she realized Grandmother wasn't breathing. They called an ambulance and it should be here any minute now."

He turned to look at her then and his face was tight, his eyes dark. More than anything she wanted to reach out for him, but his posture told her to stay away.

"Just when she had something to live for and she was happy, filled with enthusiasm and energy to get to know Hattie. She loved Hattie and Hattie seems to have loved her. I wanted Hattie to know her." His eyes filled with tears and he wiped them with his fingers. "There's too much death in my life. Too damn many losses. We were all so happy. She was happy again. We haven't seen her like this in years." He slammed the mattress beside him and stood up. "Dammit to hell. One more death instead of life and joy."

Talia knew there wasn't anything she could say or do that would help him. She could just be there for him.

"I have to call my brothers and I want to go over there before they take her body to the funeral home. I'll probably have to call the sheriff since she died unexpectedly at home. I don't know. They'll tell me when the ambulance arrives."

"Can I do anything?" she asked quietly.

"Just watch Hattie." He got out of bed, yanked on his briefs and jeans before picking up his phone.

Talia quietly gathered her clothes that had been tossed in haste only a short while ago.

"Poor Hattie." He sighed as he pocketed his phone. "She lost her mother and now her grandmother. At least she has the two of us. Today she has us. Who knows who she'll have in a month?" He ground out the words and she knew he was hurting.

"I'll get dressed, Nick," she said, leaving him, feeling she couldn't comfort him and that he probably wanted to be alone.

She showered quickly and dressed. Then she crossed the bedroom to look in on Hattie. The little girl was on her side, holding her new doll. Her pink bunny was on her other side.

Talia went back to find Nick. He was on the phone with one of his brothers.

"I'll see you there, Blake. I'll call Mr. Morton at the funeral home."

She stood in the doorway, listening to him make his calls. Finally, he looked up and saw her. "I've talked to my brothers, also to the officials. I'll go over to Grandmother's now. Thanks for staying with Hattie."

"I live here, Nick." She crossed the room to him. "I'm sorry for your loss."

"Yeah, well, thanks. It's just too many, Talia. I feel like ripping my heart out and never loving again because it hurts to keep losing people I love. It hurts a damn lot. You might be a lot safer if you'd just stay the hell away from me."

She felt as if an invisible wall of anger surrounded him and shut her away. If he shut her away, he would Hattie, too.

"I'm here if you want me."

He drew her to him, pulling her down on his lap to hug her, sitting quietly holding her. "She was just so damn happy with Hattie and Hattie liked her. They would have had fun together," he said.

"Yes, they would have," she replied, stroking the back of his head. "At least, Nick, they got to know each other. Your grandmother got to give Hattie things that she wanted Hattie to have. We'll have pictures of them together to give Hattie and tell her about her great-grandmother."

"I'm glad, but that was too little, too late. There are too many losses, too many hurts. This just does it for me. I don't want to love another person because I lose them. I have to go. I'll talk to you tomorrow. You go on to bed."

"You know I'm not going to sleep. Go to your grandmother's. If you want me to come with you I can take Hattie. She'll sleep."

"No. There's no need in dragging you and Hattie over there, and if Hattie wakes, she'll just look for Grandmother. Aw, dammit." He ran a hand through his tousled hair. "She was bossy and gave me a hard time growing up, but I loved the old girl and I had to admire her because she was a strong woman. If my dad was drinking when we were growing up, she'd run him off." Nick shifted and Talia stood so he could get up.

"I better go," he said. "This is going to be a long night. Don't wait up. Tomorrow I'll get with my brothers and our pastor and we'll plan a service."

"I won't be asleep when you get back, so don't worry about waking me. If you want me, come to my room."

"Don't wait up for me. I might stay over there the rest of tonight with my brothers," he said as he picked up his wallet and keys from his dresser and turned to leave. Then he stopped and looked at her. "Somehow it's impossible to imagine life without her in it. She's been around the most and lasted the longest of any relative I've had."

Then he simply slipped out the door.

Four days later Nick stood by a window in the library on the ranch. They had their own cemetery and the grave had been opened and was ready for his grandmother's casket later today. He hurt and this loss brought back too many memories of the deaths of Regina and Arthur. He meant what he had told Talia. He intended to guard his heart, to keep from loving one more person because it hurt too badly to keep losing those he loved. He didn't want to get any closer to Hattie and Talia. Not at this point in his life. He and Talia were committed to a marriage of convenience, but love had never been part of the deal. And he intended to keep it that way.

He thought of the nights he'd spent making love with Talia. The sexiest nights he'd ever had. They could still have that. Love hadn't been part of it and no words of love had ever been uttered by either one of them. He just needed to keep love out of it.

What about Hattie? That little charmer could steal his heart away and make him as vulnerable to hurt as he had been over Arthur. That little son of his, who couldn't even talk, had wrapped around his heart. He had loved Artie so much. He could still shed tears over him and he felt he would the rest of his life. The same with Regina.

He wasn't going to give his heart to one more person, big or little. Today he better just worry about get-

ting through the ceremony and the graveside service
and then he could think clearly about those close to
him in his life. Talia and Hattie. His heart would be
hostage to them if he let go and loved them.

He heard voices and high heels and turned. His
breath caught when Talia came through the door. She
wore a black sleeveless dress with a straight skirt that
ended just below her knees. She was in high-heeled
black pumps. Her hair was fastened in a bun at the
back of her head. She wore very little makeup and she
looked gorgeous.

He missed her. Over the last few days they had
avoided each other, and he hadn't seen much of Hattie, either. She was in Talia's arms, and when she saw
him, she held out her hands and Nick took her. She
smiled at him, running her small fingers over his jaw.

His eyes met Talia's. "You look beautiful, even
today."

"Thank you," Talia said.

"If she were here, my grandmother would give me
a lecture. She'd tell me to be thankful I have you in
my life."

Gently she put her hand on his shoulder. "You're
going through a bad time, Nick. You're tough and you'll
get through it and then life will settle back more like
it was."

He just started walking to the door. "Let's go get
this service over with."

The service was held in the closest small town, and
then the family and friends went back for the burial in
the cemetery on the ranch where Nick's grandfather,
great-grandparents, an aunt and an uncle and two cousins, his mother, his first wife and his baby boy were

buried. The minister spoke and then the service was over and people filed by to give Nick and the rest of his family condolences.

Talia moved out of the way with Hattie and finally they got back in the limos to go to Nick's house for the repast. It seemed forever till everyone ate, shared memories of Myra and went on their way. Finally, long after Hattie had been put to bed, Nick's brothers left.

Nick closed the door and faced her. "Thanks, again, for being a help. Just being here. You and Hattie were bits of cheer in an otherwise hellish day."

She nodded in acknowledgment. "It was a nice service. Your relatives and Myra's friends all spoke so highly of her."

"You'll finish Grandmother's picture with Hattie, won't you?"

"Of course."

"I stopped in your studio and looked at it. It's good. I wish she could see it because it would have really pleased her. Talia, today has been another day of pain and loss. But I want to forget it now, to kiss and make love and feel alive." He embraced her and leaned down to kiss her, his tongue claiming hers as he held her tightly. In seconds, desperate need rose up in him and he picked her up and strode to his bedroom.

As soon as he stood her on her feet, he peeled away her black dress, running his hands over her silken skin, feeling her softness against him, wanting her with all his being. He wanted to lose himself in hot sex that drove the world away. And he could do that with her. He paused to look at her and she opened her eyes. Her lips were parted from his kiss. "You're beautiful and you're the sexiest woman I've ever known. I want all I can get of you tonight because you drive away my demons and make me feel alive."

"I want to make you feel that life is good because it is, Nick. You have to take some risks and we all get hurt, but life is good."

"Sex with you is what's good—more than good. I want you now."

Nick took her in his arms and kissed her hard, and she met his need with a passion of her own.

Unlike their other nights together, this time their lovemaking was fast. Talia let him set the pace, knowing what he needed tonight.

He shed his clothes and met her on the bed, already sheathed in protection. He moved between her legs, and as he claimed her mouth, he entered her. She wrapped her long legs around him and moved with him, holding him tightly, meeting his thrusts with her own. His hands were on her, touch making her want more, driving her closer to orgasm as she arched against him. With a hard thrust he sent her over the edge and she climaxed in a burst of ecstasy. Still, he pumped wildly, exciting her again, and in minutes she reached a second climax while he shuddered with his.

"Ahh, Nick, I love you."

The words were out. They were spoken in the throes of an orgasm that enveloped her in rapture and sensuous pleasure. But she couldn't take them back. Nor did she want to.

Dimly, she was aware that he hadn't made any responding declaration of love, but that thought was swiftly gone as she relished her spectacular sexual release.

He pulled her close in his arms. Their hot bodies were damp, legs tangled, arms holding each other while he showered light kisses on her and combed her hair away from her face. "You're beautiful, Talia. Fantastic to make love to," he whispered. "I want you in my bed every night."

That was as close to a declaration of love as she was going to get, she told herself. Not that she expected one, especially tonight.

Nick fell asleep quickly in her arms, and as she gazed into the darkness, she told herself that she had no one else to blame but herself. She'd cautioned herself to guard her heart, warned herself that he had a steel wall around him. But she hadn't heeded the warnings. She'd fallen in love…but Nick only wanted sex. She wanted to share her life, but he only wanted to share his bed.

She'd gone and done the unthinkable. Now could she settle for what he offered and be happy?

Nick woke and felt the empty bed. Talia had gone to her room sometime during the night. Before, she stayed in bed with him until they both got up. What he missed was seeing Hattie. He had gotten into the habit of tiptoeing in to look at her as she slept. She was never awake when he got up and left, so he would stand at her crib and look at her, amazed she was his little girl, thinking every morning how precious she was. He had stopped going in to see her. He hurt, and loving Talia and Hattie just made his heart a hostage. Hattie hadn't known he came in to see her in the mornings, so she wouldn't miss him now that he had stopped.

Sometimes he couldn't keep from thinking all through the day about Talia and their passionate, wild lovemaking, which made him long to go home and be with her.

At night he kept busy so he didn't come home until late. He wasn't going to get closer with Talia and Hattie. He had had so much pain and loss, he just wanted to get over the hurt and then pick up with life. Someday he might risk his heart again, but not yet. He'd heard Talia declare her love, but she had been in the throes of sex. He didn't think she was in love with him. After all, they had gone into this marriage knowing they weren't in love.

He wondered if he would lose Talia because of his lack of attention during the day. He hoped not. But he didn't think he would lose her because she needed him to be a father to Hattie.

Besides, they had their nights together.

Talia could no more resist making love with him than he could resist her. When he crawled into her bed late at night or picked her up and carried her to his room, he could kiss away any slight hesitation.

He had gone over and over everything in his mind and he always came up with the same answers. For a time, he intended to guard his heart from another terrible hurt. Hattie wouldn't miss him and he and Talia still had hot, sexy nights of passion that made them both forget everything else. Would he ever be able to let go again and love someone without fearing he would lose them, too?

Talia missed Nick—the Nick she had known before his grandmother's demise. Since then, Nick had thrown himself into work, leaving before dawn in the mornings and not getting in until late at night. When he wanted sex, he would pick her up from her bed to take her to his, kissing her the moment she stirred and started to speak to him. Any protest she had was gone the moment his mouth, his lips, his tongue were on hers.

During the day she lectured herself because their relationship wasn't what she wanted and he was avoiding Hattie and that hurt. But at night when he carried her to his bed, she would melt in his arms, all her arguments she had rehearsed blown to oblivion. She couldn't resist him, and sex was as fiery and spectacular as ever.

It was the second week of August when Nick came in at half past ten and found Talia sitting and waiting for him. He hadn't seen her for over a week and his first impression was she looked more gorgeous than he remembered. Her blond hair spilled in spiral curls around her face. She wore a plain blue cotton blouse with the first buttons unfastened, revealing the beginnings of full, soft curves and creamy skin, and he remembered exactly how it felt to fill his hands with her soft breasts.

"You're usually not up this late," he said. "I haven't seen you like this. You look great."

"No, you haven't seen me and thank you for the compliment. I'm not sure Hattie will know you now. You rarely see her, either, Nick. You really aren't a daddy to her any longer," she said softly.

"I pay her bills and I know you'll take care of her," he said.

Guilt filled him for avoiding them, but then he thought again about the losses in his life when he'd loved someone. "I'll come home earlier tomorrow and spend some time with her." He knew that was what he should do.

"We won't be here," she said coolly. "I'm taking her to Dallas for a few weeks."

Her words were like a knife to his gut.

He looked hurt, but she steeled herself. "I'll get a condo there," she told him. She'd already reached out to a Realtor she knew in the city.

"You don't need to get a condo. You can stay at my house. You can stay at a hotel and charge it to me if you want." He crossed the room to her, then reached down and pulled her to her feet. "Don't go, Talia. I want you here. Both of you. Nights with you are the best. They're special and keep me going."

"Nick, this isn't any way to live," she said, aware of his warm hands holding hers, of how close he stood. Every touch was sexy and made her want his kisses, but she couldn't live on sex alone. Outside of the bedroom he was moving out of her life. He had already gone out of Hattie's and that was what she couldn't take. She couldn't risk Hattie getting hurt.

"Nick, when we decided on this marriage of convenience, I knew what I was getting into because you were clear that you were not in love with me, but you said you would love and be a dad for Hattie. You're not being a daddy to her. You avoid her."

"I will be a dad to her. I can come home earlier and be with you and Hattie. I'll do that tomorrow night."

"I don't want just one night and then you're gone again for the next few weeks. I know you hurt badly over Regina, over Arthur, over Myra. But loss is a part of life. You've shut yourself off from life, from Hattie. Hattie no longer means anything to you."

"I feel if I give my love to anyone else, I'll lose them, too. I can't take any more loss. I can't just shut off all the heartaches I've had."

"No, I suppose you can't, but Hattie is out of your life. She's too precious for her to have that kind of father. I think for a little while we'll stay in Dallas and let you make some decisions about what you want and who you want in your life."

"I want the two of you. I thought I made that abundantly clear before you moved here." He placed his hand on her waist and his other hand slipped behind her neck to caress her nape lightly. She drew a deep breath and tried to keep on track, to avoid letting him touch and entice her until she forgot what she had planned to do.

"I don't want to keep on living this way, where she doesn't even see you. Nick, life is a risk, but most people think life is worth the risks. I do. You know what your grandmother would think about you withdrawing from Hattie. She'd tell you that's not living and it's not doing Hattie any good. She needs a daddy in her life who loves her and helps her. I know you've been generous financially, but she doesn't need your money. I'm able to take care of her without it. But it's your love she needs. The love, the living, the willingness to take some risks because you love someone enough to do so." She gazed into his stormy green eyes that had

darkened with anger, but she didn't care. She wasn't
going on this way and she wouldn't let him go on this
way with Hattie.

"I'll take the limo to Dallas. I need to work out the
future because I'm not coming back here to a life like
this. I'll be gone when you get home tomorrow night,
but you know where to find me. And I'm not going to
your room tonight. Thank you for all you did, Nick.
You gave me Hattie and I'll always be grateful for that,
and for getting to know your family."

He lowered his hands from her and for a moment
he said nothing. He just looked into her eyes. "Let me
know if you want or need anything."

Then he stood up and walked away and she felt as if
he were taking her heart with him. She thought about
Hattie, peacefully sleeping in her little bed, blissfully
unaware of the storm swirling around her and how her
life would be rearranged again.

Talia gave Nick time to get to his room, then put her
head in her hands and cried. She loved him and she
knew he hurt, but this way of life wasn't doing any of
them any good. Losing Myra had destroyed Nick but
her loss was ironic. Because his strong grandmother
would have been the first to tell Nick to pull himself
together and go on with living.

Talia wiped away her tears. Go on with living. That
was just what she had to do.

By the end of the following week her life had been
transformed again. She'd had interviews with two local
colleges to teach, and both looked like promising jobs
when the next school year started. Talia had enough of

her own money from her parents' insurance, and from her own savings, to care for Hattie without touching the funds Nick had provided. She used some to lease a condo near one of the colleges. She missed Nick and tried to keep busy so she wouldn't think about him, but everything reminded her of him. Nick was a forceful person and it was impossible to just forget him. She hurt and she missed him, and sometimes she was angry that he had shut himself off, especially from Hattie. The days were tough, but she busied herself with her daughter's care. But the nights... Nights were the worst when she wanted to be in his arms, wanted his kisses and his loving. Too many nights she cried herself to sleep, and at the same time, she hated that she couldn't forget him.

And then she missed a period.

Nick sat on his porch, trying to focus on the clock that he was trying to fix, but his thoughts kept wandering to the two females who were missing from his life. Talia and Hattie. He missed them constantly, especially in the evenings. Nights were hell, when he got into his big bed without Talia. And he missed Hattie's laughter, her little arms around his neck and her happy "Wuv you" declarations. He'd run them off by his total focus on his own pain and lost them just as much as he had lost Regina and Artie. Only this time it was due to his own stubbornness. Talia had hurt over the loss of his grandmother and then he had just hurt her more. And he hated to think he had hurt Hattie.

But what could he do?

He fumbled some more with the repair, but he couldn't reassemble the many clock pieces spread out on the table before him. It was kind of like his own life, he thought. All in pieces. Just as he probably wasn't going to get this clock working again, more than likely he wouldn't get his life in order, either.

He was miserable without Talia and Hattie. Really miserable. But what could he do?

He heard a motor and looked up from the repair to see Stan's pickup approaching. In minutes Stan stepped out of his truck and walked up on the porch. "Good morning, bro. What are you doing?"

"Trying to fix this old clock," Nick said.

"I have some things of Grandmother's that turned up in her attic. I brought them over for you and Talia to go through and see if you want anything for Hattie. They're in the truck."

"All right. Thanks. Set them on the table and I'll get them to her." He went back to work on the clock.

"Where's Hattie? I want to say hello. I haven't seen her for a couple of weeks now and that's way too long. She'll forget who I am."

With a long sigh, Nick pushed aside a screwdriver. "She's not here. She's in Dallas."

"Oh, okay. When will she be back? I'll come by. I've got a little toy for her. It's a windup kitty and it rolls around on the floor."

"That's nice, Stan. You'll have to go to Dallas to give it to her."

"How so?"

Nick looked up and saw his brother's eyes were narrowed. "Talia left and took Hattie with her. End of story."

"The hell you say. What did you do?"

"Look, what I do with my wife is my business."

"This sort of touches all of us, Nick. You had to have run them off because two days before Grandmother's death, Talia told me how wonderful it was for Hattie to be in this family. And at that time Talia sounded happy to be part of this family, too. So tell me, what have you done?"

"You sound just like Grandmother, only I can tell you that it's none of your dang business."

"You ran Talia off. Why? We can find out from her, so you might as well tell me. And I will go see her."

Nick stood up and faced his brother. "Look, I'm tired of people I love dying on me. My wife died. My baby died. Grandmother died. I just don't want to get deeply involved with anyone right now and that includes Hattie and Talia."

"I'll be damned. You're scared of life, Nick." He took off his hat and ran a hand through his hair as he sat beside his brother. "This time your fear is going to cost you something really precious and special. When did you get this way?"

"When those I love died on me."

"That's part of life. Grandmother had a good life and she was eighty-seven years old. It hurts, but you pick up and go on and you don't shut off an adorable kid like Hattie or a woman like Talia. Where is she?"

"I don't even know. She's in Dallas, but I don't know where or doing what. All I know is she isn't staying in my house."

"I hope she isn't already dating someone, because if she isn't, she will be soon. In fact, I just may go see her and tell her to divorce you and marry me. I'd treat her right. In fact, when I tell them, Blake and Adam might go after her and tell her to pick one of us. We won't even let you come see her or Hattie. It would serve you right."

Stan stood up and rushed down the steps, taking them two at a time. "Have a nice life by yourself."

"Where are you going?"

"To Dallas, you jerk. Get ready for a divorce."

He glared at the back of his younger brother's head. "You wouldn't dare propose to her and she wouldn't accept," he called out.

Stan didn't turn around. He just shot over his shoulder, "But someone else will."

Nick glared at Stan as he jumped in his truck. The wheels spun and he left, stirring up dust and speeding away.

"Dammit." Nick shook his head. Stan was hot-headed enough to propose to his wife, but Nick had to believe Talia had sense enough to turn him down. But his brother was right. There just might be one guy she wouldn't turn down.

The thought of her divorcing him and marrying someone else hurt.

He looked at the pieces of clock spread all over the table and knew what he had to do. He had to get his life back together.

He'd try calling her again, but she probably wouldn't answer, the same way she didn't take any of his dozens of calls before. He simply had to go find her.

The more he thought about it, the more he wanted her back. She was right. Life was filled with risks, but some of them were worth taking a chance on. He had hurt a whole lot more since she left and he wanted her back. He wanted his precious little girl back in his life. Because, as much as he hated to admit it, he loved his wife and daughter.

Talia glanced at her cell phone when a call came in. Nick had called more than a dozen times and twice today, but she didn't see any point in talking to him. She needed to make some decisions. She would have to talk to him someday, but she wasn't ready yet.

When her phone rang again, she glanced down at the screen and her stomach tightened when she saw it was a call from Stan. Something had to have happened for Stan to be calling her.

Suddenly chilled, she was scared something had happened to Nick or one of their other brothers.

"Talia, it's Stan," he said when she answered. "Can I come see you? I'm in Dallas."

"Of course. I'm in a condo. Let me give you the address. Is everything all right?"

"Oh, yeah. I have a present for Hattie."

She let out the breath she'd been holding and smiled. She missed Stan. Just as she missed Nick and all of them. "Sure. I'll be so glad to see you. Come on." She gave him her address and went to get Hattie ready for company.

She changed out of the yoga pants she wore to unpack boxes, dressing in red slacks, a red cotton blouse and red high-heeled sandals. She ran a brush through her curls and then turned to pick up Hattie and get her changed into a yellow playsuit. "Your uncle Stan is coming to see you. He has a surprise for you."

"Prize?"

"Oh, yes. Your uncles shower you with presents almost as much as your daddy did."

"Da," Hattie repeated as Talia's phone chimed again. But this time she saw Nick was calling. And this time she answered.

"Hi. I'm in Dallas and would like to come talk to you."

She closed her eyes, hurting, remembering the words that had passed between them and thinking about her pregnancy. She hadn't figured out yet when and how she would tell him. She remembered clearly that he'd said he didn't want any more children.

"Talia? Are you there? I really want to see you. Where are you?"

"Stan is on his way over. He'll be here any minute. Does he know you're coming?"

"No, he doesn't. Give me your address."

She did and he told her he would see her soon.

She stared into space. She couldn't tell him yet about the pregnancy. Not with Stan here.

It was another twenty minutes before her doorbell chimed, and she went to the door to open it and face Stan. He hugged her lightly and kissed her cheek. Hattie stood with her hand in Talia's and Stan knelt to pick her up.

"How's my pretty Hattie?"

She poked his chest with her finger and wrapped her arms around his neck.

"Hey, she remembers me."

Talia smiled. "Of course she does."

"Hattie, I brought you a present," he said, giving the little girl a pink sack with a pink silk bow with bells on it. She shook the sack, making the bells jingle, and she laughed. "Hattie, you have a present in the sack," Stan said.

"I think you've brought her a very fascinating sack. It'll take a while to get to the present." She led him into the living room, where they sat down. "Stan, Nick called after you did. He's on his way here. Did you know he was coming?"

"No. He didn't know he was coming earlier when I talked to him. Talia, I know he's hurt, but we had words. I told him I was going to come here and ask you to get a divorce and then propose to you. I'm sure my brothers will feel the same way." Before she could say anything, Stan continued. "Nick is just hurt and not thinking. I guess I shook him up if he's on his way to see you, so I'll get out of here. Just don't get out of the family too fast. We all want you back at the ranch and we miss Hattie."

She laughed and kissed his cheek. "You're great, Stan. I'm not leaving the family yet, but I don't know about Nick."

"Well, if you're not married to him, you can take your choice of me or Blake or Adam. But I'm the most fun," he said and she laughed again.

"That's an almost irresistible proposal, Stan. Thank you."

He stood up and handed Hattie to her. "I'm going to run. Show Hattie her present when she's through playing with the sack. I don't want to cross paths with Nick right now."

"Ahh, she has her new toy," Talia said, watching Hattie pull a furry toy kitten out of the sack and hug it. The child let out a squeal of delight.

"It's a windup toy, Hattie," Stan explained, reaching out to show her. But Hattie merely clutched it to her chest. "Looks like she'd rather hug it."

He went to the door to see himself out. "Good luck dealing with my brother, Talia. Remember, three more Duncans love you."

She smiled at him. "Thanks, Stan. That's sweet."

He smiled. "'Bye, Hattie. I love you."

He hadn't been gone twenty minutes when the doorbell rang, and she opened the door to face Nick.

# Nine

"Come in," she said, hating that she was breathless. He looked more handsome than ever in jeans, a long-sleeved tan Western shirt and his black boots. More than anything she just wanted to walk into his arms, but she wasn't going back to the life they'd had when she left him. Why was he here?

He came in, and Hattie hurried to him, holding out her thin arms. "Da."

"Hattie," he said, picking her up to hug her. "I love you," he said, closing his eyes, and Talia hurt for him even though she was upset with him. How could he not pour out his love to his baby girl?

Talia felt a dull ache. She wanted Nick's arms around her. She wanted him to hold her, to kiss her. She looked at his hands as he held Hattie. She could remember his hands too well, his fingers so light, so sexy, moving over her, caressing her.

"Talia." His voice penetrated her errant thoughts and she met his eyes.

He stood there holding Hattie, staring at her. He moved a step closer, holding Hattie with one arm, placing his other hand on her shoulder. "I want you and Hattie in my life. I love you, Talia, and I love Hattie."

She could hardly believe her ears. He was uttering the words she had dreamed of, longed to hear, fantasized about. Yet now she couldn't believe them.

"Nick, don't declare love until you're really certain. The last time we were together, you definitely were not in love. If you were, you didn't want to be and you didn't want to acknowledge it." She tried not to think about those nights when they had been together and she'd been in his arms in his bed with his body over hers, with him inside her, his hands taking her out of this world into bliss.

"I think Stan pushed you into this." She steeled herself and held her ground, ignoring the pull of his sexual magnetism. "I have two good teaching offers in colleges. I have a convenient place to live. I'm set here in Dallas and I think we need to step back and give each other some room. If next summer you still want us, we'll consider it."

"I didn't come because of Stan. I came because I've missed you and I've been miserable without you. You were right, Talia. You just have to live with risks. That's part of life. Loss is part of life, but hopefully, losses are balanced by gains. I need your love and Hattie's. I love you both. Your love and her love make up for the hurt from losses in my life."

"Da?" Hattie said and Nick smiled at her as she ran her fingers over his chin.

"I'm 'Da' to her."

Then he looked up at Talia and she could swear his eyes were glistening. "When she calls me 'Da,' I don't want to go home without both of you. I've missed you, Talia, and I've missed her more than I would have thought possible. I shouldn't have ever let either of you go."

Her heart drummed. She wanted to believe him, but she had to be sure before she went back and took Hattie, not only for Hattie, but for the child of Nick's she was carrying.

"We need to talk, Nick." Her voice echoed the seriousness she felt. "But we can't talk freely about anything important with Hattie here. Why don't you come in and play with her for a while. She'll take a nap soon and then we can talk."

She led Nick into the small living room of the condo.

"Can I take the two of you out to dinner?" he asked her as he followed.

She turned to him and shook her head. "Thank you, Nick, but no. I'm still getting settled here and I've got things to move around and unpack."

"I can send some guys from the ranch to help you, but I'd prefer you come home."

Talia didn't react to his offer. Either of them. Instead, she handed him one of Hattie's favorite toys. Hearing her unspoken answer, Nick sat on the floor and began to play with Hattie.

"I'll go get us cold drinks," she said. "What would you like?"

"A cold beer? Do you have any?"

"Sorry, I don't."

"I'll drink water."

It was an hour later, deep into the afternoon, before Hattie fell asleep. The whole time Talia sat there, watching Nick and his daughter, she felt her resolve weakening. Seeing him with Hattie was melting her. He was enraptured by the baby's every move, every sound, as she played with her doll and her bunny. Talia didn't want to admit it, but how could she fool herself? She was still in love with her husband.

By the time Nick carried Hattie to her crib and came back into the living room, Talia was like a firecracker with a short fuse. He went to her and reached down to take her hand and pull her to her feet. His arms went around her, and when she looked into his eyes, her heart thudded against her ribs.

Desire flashed in her, hot, insistent. She wanted his kisses, his hands on her, his body against hers. The last of her reserve and coolness vanished. One look from his green eyes and she was sizzling with longing, wanting him desperately.

"Talia, I've missed you. Come home," he whispered into her ear. "I want you."

And she wanted him. Right now every nerve ending in her body cried out for him. But it wasn't about what she wanted anymore. It was about what Hattie needed.

She stepped back so that she could look into his eyes. "What about Hattie? Are you really ready to give her your love, attention and time? To come in before she falls asleep at night? You have enough money that you could sit on your porch and rock for the rest of your life and never have to work, so when you work until nine or ten and your baby is sound asleep and you leave before sunup, you send the message that she isn't important to you. That you don't love her. I didn't expect love for me, but I did for your child."

"I am so sorry, Talia. I do love her and I miss her and every day is important with her because she grows so fast. I love her and I'll show her every day. I'll leave after her breakfast and come home for supper with her. How's that?"

"You really mean all that you're saying?" Talia asked, her heart beating faster.

"Yes, I do. I promise. I love Hattie and I'll spend my days proving it to you. And to her."

She stared at him, trying to decide if he would keep his promise.

"And I love you, Talia," he said softly, cupping her cheeks in his palms.

She gazed into his green-gold eyes and her heart beat faster. But she had to know…

"Nick, don't tell me that unless you're sure," she said.

"I'm very sure," he replied. "I almost lost you because of feeling sorry for myself and thinking too much about myself. But I've changed, Talia. I love you and I miss you. If you come home, I'll show you how much."

He stole her breath with a kiss. A passionate, possessive kiss that made her weak in the knees and intensified the ache for him low inside her. She wanted his hands and his mouth all over her.

He wanted her, too; she could feel his hardness pressed against her thigh. But would that change when he learned her news? Would he still want her to go home with him?

Struggling with her thoughts and fears, she pushed

him away. Her breath was ragged when she spoke. "Nick, I need to tell you something. Please sit."

He picked her up and sat in a chair with her on his lap.

She shook her head. "This isn't what I had in mind, because I don't think you're going to be happy. In a few minutes, I think you'll want to say goodbye and go home alone." Her heart ached as she said the words.

He shook his head and framed her face with his hands. "There's nothing you can tell me that can change the way I feel. I love you and I want you in my life always."

"I'll give you a chance to say that again and this first time won't count. Right after I give you my news." She drew a deep breath and blurted it out.

"Nick, I'm pregnant with your baby."

He stared at her as if he couldn't understand what she'd said.

"I'm carrying your baby now," she repeated. "I know that's not what you wanted. You told me you had enough and you didn't want any more children. Now, I've had two miscarriages, so I don't know what will happen with this third pregnancy. They couldn't find why I miscarried those first two times, but the doctor says so far everything looks fine this time. The baby's due next spring and—"

She realized she was babbling and she stopped herself. She looked deep in Nick's eyes and tried to read his thoughts. But failed. When he finally opened his mouth to speak, she steeled herself for his response, knowing he would rescind his offer, his declarations of forever love.

"I want you to come home with me and let me take

care of you and our baby. That's really what I want with all my heart."

She stared at him, not believing her own ears. He wanted the baby? He wanted her?

"Nick, don't tell me that if you don't mean it."

"I mean it." A smile broke out across his lips and he hugged her. "We're going to have a baby. Oh, Talia. I want you to come home with me. I want this baby."

"That's a complete turnaround from what you told me before."

"Yes, it is, but I've been around Hattie more and I've done without both of you in my life and that was worst of all. I'm willing to take those risks. I love you."

Her heart thundered so hard she thought it'd burst with joy. But before she could show him how happy she was, he stood up and put her carefully in the chair.

"I have to go out to my truck. I'll be back in a minute."

She went to the window, and she saw him in his truck looking down at something he must have in his hands. When he came back inside, she stood there waiting for him. "What are you doing?"

He crossed the room to her. "Talia Duncan, I love you with all my heart. And I love little Hattie. I want both of you to come back home so I can take care of you. And I want our baby. *Our baby*—that sounds wonderful. You'll carry this baby and Hattie will have a little brother or a little sister."

Tears stung her eyes and she slipped her arms around his neck. "Nick, you better mean what you say," she whispered before she kissed him.

His arm banded her waist tightly and he held her pressed against him. "Call your doctor tomorrow and see if we can have sex while you're pregnant."

She laughed. "That wasn't what caused my miscarriages and I can answer that. Yes, we can. This is very early in this pregnancy."

"I brought Hattie a present." He held up a small gift bag. "I got you one, too."

"Nick," she said, smiling. "Stop buying so much for Hattie. She'll be spoiled rotten."

"No, she won't. Impossible. She's way too sweet. Here's your present, Talia." He reached into the bag and pulled out a small box wrapped in white paper and tied with a big blue silk bow.

"Oh, Nick." From the size of the box, she guessed it was a bracelet to match the pendant he had given her. She tore the wrappings away and opened the box to see another fancy box, a much smaller one, that she opened. A dazzling diamond ring was nestled against black velvet.

"Nick, this is gorgeous."

He took it out of the box. "We married for convenience and I only gave you a wedding band. Now this is for love and this ring I got for you out of love. I want the world to know I love you and you're my bride." He took her hand and slipped the ring on her finger.

"Oh, Nick, I love it!" she said as she threw her arms around his neck and kissed him. His arms banded her waist again and he leaned over her to kiss her long and passionately, making her heart race and filling her with joy.

"Hey," he said, leaning back and looking down at her. "You're crying."

"They're tears of joy. I never thought I'd hear you say you loved me, but you did. I love you with all my heart and I know we're going to have a wonderful family. Nick, you will always miss Regina and Artie and your mom and your grandmother, but you're going to be showered with love by me, by Hattie and by our little baby."

He lowered his hand to her still-flat belly, as if to embrace their unborn baby. "I almost made the biggest mistake of my life, but I was already on my way to fixing it because I had that ring made for you two weeks ago."

She gazed into his green eyes and her heart pounded with joy. "Nick, I just know I won't miscarry this time. We'll have our babies, and Hattie will have a little brother or sister. You really did give me the world when you married me—your love, Hattie as my daughter, a new baby, your family's love. You have the money, sweetie, but I have the riches." She cradled his jaw and rained kisses over his face. "As long as we have each other's love and our little babies, we'll have everything. Everything worth risking your heart for." She set one last kiss on his lips. "I love you."

"And I love you, darlin', with all my being. Now I can tell those brothers of mine that not one of them is going to get you to leave me and marry him."

She laughed as she hugged him and leaned close again to kiss him. "I'm all yours. I love you, my handsome Texas rancher."

\* \* \* \* \*

# SAVANNAH'S SECRETS

**REESE RYAN**

To my parents, who instilled a love
of reading in me at an early age.

To the teachers who fostered that love.

To my childhood friends who felt reading
was as cool as I did—both then and now.

To my husband and family, who sacrifice
precious time with Babe/Mom/Nonni so that
I can share the stories in my head with the world.

And to the amazing readers who are kind
enough to come along for the ride.

Thank you, all.

# One

Blake Abbott rubbed his forehead and groaned. He'd rather be walking the floor of the distillery, preparing for their new product launch, instead of reviewing market research data. Out there on the floor was where the magic of making their world-renowned bourbon happened.

His assistant, Daisy, knocked on his open office door. "Blake, don't forget the interview for the new event manager position... It's in fifteen minutes."

Blake cursed under his breath. His brother Max had asked him to handle the interview. The new position fell under Max's charge as marketing VP. But he was at a trade show in Vegas. Probably partying and getting laid while Blake worked his ass off back at the office.

Their mother—who usually handled their special events—was in Florida helping her sister recover from surgery.

*Tag, I'm it.*

But Blake had more pressing matters to deal with. Production was two weeks behind on the limited-edition moonshines they were rolling out to commemorate the upcoming fiftieth anniversary of King's Finest Distillery. Once an illegal moonshine operation started by his great-grandfather in the hills of Tennessee, his grandfather had established the company as a legal distiller of premium spirits.

What better way to celebrate their golden anniversary as a legitimate enterprise than to reproduce the hooch that gave them their start?

Getting the project back on track took precedence over hiring an overpriced party planner.

Blake grunted, his eyes on the screen. "Too late to reschedule?"

"Technically? No," a slightly husky voice with an unfamiliar Southern drawl responded. "But then, I am already here."

Blake's attention snapped to the source of the voice. His temperature climbed instantly when he encountered the woman's sly smile and hazel eyes sparkling in the sunlight.

Her dark wavy hair was pulled into a low bun. If she'd worn the sensible gray suit to downplay her gorgeous features, it was a spectacular fail.

"Blake, I'm sorry." Daisy's cheeks flushed. Her gaze shifted from him to the woman. "I should've—"

"It's okay, Daisy." Blake held back a grin. He crossed the room, holding the woman's gaze. "I'll take it from here, thanks."

Daisy shoved a folder into his hands. "Her résumé. In case you can't find the copy I gave you earlier."

Blake thanked his assistant. She knew him well and was unbothered by his occasional testiness. It was one of the reasons he went to great lengths to keep her happy.

"Well, Miss—"

"Carlisle." The woman extended her hand. "But please, call me Savannah."

Blake shook her hand and was struck by the contrast of the softness of her skin against his rough palm. Electricity sparked on his fingertips. He withdrew his hand and shoved it in his pocket.

"Miss… Savannah, please, have a seat." He indicated the chair opposite his desk.

She complied. One side of her mouth pulled into a slight grin, drawing his attention to her pink lips.

Were they as soft and luscious as they looked? He swallowed hard, fighting back his curiosity about the flavor of her gloss.

Blake sank into the chair behind his desk, thankful for the solid expanse between them.

He was the one with the authority. So why did it seem that she was assessing him?

*Relax. Stay focused.*

He was behaving as if he hadn't seen a stunningly beautiful woman before.

"Tell me about yourself, Savannah."

It was a standard opening. But he genuinely wanted to learn everything there was to know about this woman.

Savannah crossed one long, lean leg over the other. Her skirt shifted higher, grazing the top of her knee and exposing more of her golden-brown skin.

"I'm from West Virginia. I've lived there my entire life. I spent the past ten years working my way up the ranks, first at a small family-owned banquet hall. Then at a midsize chain hotel. In both positions, I doubled the special events revenue. My recommendation letters will confirm that."

She was confident and matter-of-fact about her accomplishments.

"Impressive." Regardless of how attractive Savannah Carlisle was, he would only hire her if she was right for the job. "You're a long way from West Virginia. What brings you to our little town of Magnolia Lake?"

"Honestly? I moved here because of this opportunity."

When Blake narrowed his gaze in response, she laughed. It was a sweet sound he wouldn't mind hearing again. Preferably while they were in closer proximity than his desk would allow.

"That wasn't an attempt to sweet-talk you into hiring me. Unless, of course, it works," she added with a smile. "This position is the perfect intersection of my talents and interests."

"How so?" Blake was intrigued.

"I've been fascinated by distilleries and small breweries since I worked at a local craft brewery my senior year of college. I led group tours."

Blake leaned forward, hands pressed to the desk. "And if you don't get the position?"

"Then I'll work my way up to it."

Blake tried not to betray how pleased he was with her unwavering conviction. "There are lots of other distilleries. Why not apply for a similar position elsewhere?"

"I believe in your products. Not that I'm a huge drinker," she added with a nervous laugh. "But as an event professional, King's Finest is my go-to. I also happen to think you have one of the smoothest finishes out there."

He didn't respond. Instead, he allowed a bit of awkward silence to settle over them, which was a device he often employed. Give a candidate just enough rope to hog-tie themselves, and see what they'd do with it.

"That's only part of the reason I want to work for King's Finest. I like that you're family-owned. And I was drawn to the story of how your grandfather converted your great-grandfather's moonshine operation into a legitimate business to create a legacy for his family."

She wasn't the first job candidate to gush about the company history in an attempt to ingratiate herself with him. But something in her eyes indicated deep admiration. Perhaps even reverence.

"You've done your homework, and you know our history." Blake sat back in his leather chair. "But my primary concern is what's on the horizon. How will you impact the future of King's Finest?"

"Excellent question." Savannah produced a leather portfolio from her large tote. "One I'm prepared to answer. Let's talk about the upcoming jubilee celebration. It's the perfect convergence of the company's past and present."

"The event is a few months away. Most of the plans are set. We don't expect anyone to come in, at this late hour, and pull off a miracle. We just want the event to be special for our employees and the folks of Magnolia Lake. Something that'll make them proud of their role in our history. Get them excited about the future."

A wide grin spanned her lovely face. "Give me two months and I'll turn the jubilee into a marketing bonanza that'll get distributors and consumers excited about your brand."

An ambitious claim, but an intriguing one.

King's Finest award-winning bourbon sold well in the States and was making inroads overseas. However, they faced increased competition from small batch distilleries popping up across the country in recent years.

"You have my attention, Savannah Carlisle." Blake crossed one ankle over his knee. "Wow me."

Savannah laid out a compelling plan to revamp their jubilee celebration into an event that was as reflective of the company's simple roots as it was elegant and forward thinking.

"I love your plan, but do you honestly think you can pull this off in two months?"

"I can, and I will." She closed the portfolio and returned it to her bag. "If given the chance."

Blake studied the beautiful woman sitting before him. No wonder their HR manager had recommended the woman so highly. Impressed with her after a joint telephone interview, Max and their mother had authorized him to make her an offer if she was as impressive in person.

Savannah Carlisle was clever and resourceful, everything they needed for their newly minted event manager position. There was only one problem with hiring the woman.

He was attracted to her. More than he'd been to any woman in the two years since his last relationship imploded.

Blake was genuinely excited by the possibility of seeing Savannah every day. Of knowing she occupied an office down the hall from his. But there was the little matter of their family's unwritten rule.

*No dating employees.*

Problematic, since he'd spent the past half hour preoc-cupied with the desire to touch her skin again. But he had something far less innocent than a handshake in mind.

Blake wouldn't hire her simply because she was attrac-tive. And it wouldn't be right not to hire her because of her beauty, either.

His feelings were his problem, and he'd deal with them.

"All right, Savannah Carlisle. Let's see what you can do."

They negotiated her salary, and then Blake sent her off to complete the requisite paperwork. His gaze followed her curvy bottom and long legs as she sashayed out of the office.

Blake shook his head and groaned. This time, he may have gotten himself in over his head.

# Two

Savannah had never relied on sex appeal for a single, solitary thing in her life.

But today was different.

If her plan succeeded, it would correct the course of her family's lives. Money wouldn't be an issue. Not now, nor for generations to come.

Her grandfather would get justice and the recognition he deserved. Her sister wouldn't have to struggle under the crushing weight of student loans.

So failure wasn't an option. Even if it meant playing to the caveman instincts of a cretin like Blake Abbott.

He hadn't been obvious about it. She'd give him credit for that. But the smoldering intensity of his gaze and the sexy growl of his voice had made the interview feel a lot like a blind date.

His warm brown gaze penetrated her skin. Made her feel something she hadn't expected. Something she couldn't explain. Because despite the charm of the man she'd just met, she knew the truth about Blake Abbott and his family.

They were thieves, plain and simple.

The kind of folks who would cheat a man out of what was rightfully owed to him. Who didn't have the decency or compassion to feel an ounce of regret for leaving such a man and his family twisting in the wind, floundering in poverty.

So despite Blake's warm smile and surprisingly pleasing demeanor, she wouldn't forget the truth. The Abbotts were heartless and cruel.

She would expose them for the snakes they were and reclaim her grandfather's rightful share of the company.

Once she'd exited the parking lot in her crappy little car, she dialed her sister, Delaney, back in West Virginia.

"I'm in," Savannah blurted as soon as her sister answered the phone. "I got the job."

Laney hesitated before offering a one-word response. "Wow."

"I know you don't agree with what I'm doing, Laney, but I'm doing this for all of us. You and Harper especially."

"Vanna come home!" her two-year-old niece said in the background.

"Listen to your niece. If you're doing it for us, pack up and come home now. Because this isn't what we want."

"It's what Granddad deserves. What we all deserve." Savannah turned onto the road that led back to town. "This will alter our family's future. Make things better for you and Harper."

"This isn't about Harper or my student loans. You're playing to Grandpa's pride and yours."

Savannah silently counted to ten. Blowing up at Laney wouldn't get her sister on board. And deep down she wanted Laney's reassurance she was doing the right thing.

Their grandfather—Martin McDowell—had raised them after the deaths of their parents. He'd made sacrifices for them their entire lives. And now he was gravely ill, his kidneys failing.

"Grandpa's nearly ninety. Thanks to the Abbotts, his pride is all he has, besides us. So I say it's worth fighting for."

Laney didn't answer. Not surprising.

When they were kids, Savannah was mesmerized by her grandfather's stories about his days running moonshine in the Tennessee hills as a young man. But even as a child, Laney took a just-the-facts-please approach to life. She'd viewed their grandfather's stories as tall tales.

Their positions hadn't changed as adults. But Laney would come around when Savannah proved the truth.

Joseph Abbott, founder of the King's Finest Distillery, claimed to use recipes from his father's illegal moonshine business. But, in reality, he'd stolen their grandfather's hooch recipe and used it to parlay himself into a bourbon empire. And the tremendous fortune the Abbotts enjoyed.

"If the Abbotts are as heartless as you believe, does it seem wise to take them on alone? To get a job with them under false pretenses and snoop around in search of...what? Do you think there's a vault with a big card in it that says, 'I stole my famous bourbon recipe from Martin McDowell'?"

"I didn't get this job under false pretenses. I'm extremely qualified. I'm going to do everything I can to help grow the company. We're going to be part owners of it, after all." Savannah navigated the one-lane bridge that crossed the river dividing the small town.

"You're risking jail or maybe worse. If something were to happen to Granddad..." Her sister's voice trailed. "You're all Harper and I would have left. We can't risk losing you. So, please, let it go and come home."

She didn't want to worry Laney. School, work, taking care of a two-year-old and seeing after their grandfather was strain enough. But this was something she had to do.

If she succeeded, it would be well worth the risk.

"I love you and Harper, Laney. But you need to trust that I'm acting in all of our best interest. And please don't rat me out to Grandpa."

"Great. I have to lie to him about it, too." Laney huffed. "Fine, but be careful. Remember, there's no shame in throwing in the towel and coming to your senses. Love you."

"Love you, too."

After hanging up, Savannah sighed heavily and focused on the road as the colorful shops of the quaint little town of Magnolia Lake came into view.

She parked behind the small building where she was staying. It housed a consignment and handmade jewelry shop downstairs and two apartments upstairs. The shop and building were owned by Kayleigh Jemison, who was also her neighbor.

Inside her furnished, one-bedroom apartment, Savannah kicked off her heels and stripped off her jacket. Her thoughts drifted back to Blake Abbott. He was nothing like the cutthroat, ambitious jerk her grandfather had described. Blake was tall and handsome. His warm brown skin was smooth and practically glowed from within. He was charming with a welcoming smile and liquid brown eyes that made her stomach flip when they met hers.

Her grandfather had only known Joseph Abbott personally. The rest of the Abbotts he knew only by reputation. Maybe he was wrong about Blake.

"You are *not* attracted to him. Not even a little bit," Savannah mumbled under her breath. "He's the enemy. A means to an end."

But Blake was obviously attracted to her. A weakness she could exploit, if it came to it.

An uncomfortable feeling settled over her as she imagined Laney's thoughts on that.

The solution was simple. Avoid Blake Abbott, at all costs.

# Three

Savannah signed her name on the final new hire form and slid it across the table.

Daisy was filling in for the HR manager, who was out sick. She studied the document and gave it a stamp of approval. Her thin lips spread in a big smile, her blue eyes sparkling. "You're officially a King's Finest employee. Welcome to the team."

"Fantastic." Savannah returned the smile. "So, what's next?"

The conference room door burst open.

*Blake Abbott.*

He was even more handsome than she remembered. The five o'clock shadow crawling along his square jaw made him look rugged and infinitely sexier. Uneasiness stirred low in her belly.

"Daisy, Savannah… I didn't realize you were using the conference room." His hair, grown out a bit since their initial meeting, had a slight curl to it.

"We're just leaving anyway." Daisy collected her things. "Did I forget there was a meeting scheduled in here?"

"No, we decided to have an impromptu meeting about the changes Savannah proposed for the jubilee celebration. We can all fit in here more comfortably. Come to think of it—" he shifted his attention to Savannah "—this would be a great opportunity for you to meet my family…that is… our executive team."

She wasn't in a position to refuse his request. Still, there was something endearing about how he'd asked.

It took her by surprise.

"I've been looking forward to meeting the company's founder." Savannah forced a smile, unnerved about meeting the entire Abbott clan. Especially Joseph Abbott—the man who'd betrayed her grandfather.

"I'm afraid you'll have to wait a bit longer." He sounded apologetic. "We want the changes to be a surprise. Speaking of which... I know it's last-minute, and I hate to throw you into the fire on your first day, but do you think you could present your ideas to the rest of our team?"

Savannah's eyes went wide. "Now?"

"They're all really sweet." Daisy patted her arm and smiled. "You're going to love them. I'm just sorry I can't stay to hear your presentation. Got another new hire to process. Good luck!" Daisy called over her shoulder as she hurried from the room.

"I've been telling everyone about your proposal. Got a feeling my father and brother will be more easily persuaded if you wow them the way you did me."

Savannah had anticipated meeting every member of the Abbott family, eventually. But meeting them all at once on her first day was intimidating. Particularly since she had to refrain from saying what she wanted.

That they were liars and thieves who'd built their fortune by depriving her family of theirs. But she couldn't say that. Not yet, anyway. Not until she had proof.

"I've got my notes right here." Savannah opened her portfolio. "But with a little more time, I can create a formal presentation."

"What you presented to me is fine. They'll love it." Blake slid into the seat across from her.

Her belly did a flip.

"Hey, Blake, did you eat all of the...? Oh, I'm sorry. I didn't realize you were meeting with someone," came a voice from the doorway.

"It's all right." Blake waved in the woman Savannah recognized as his sister. "Zora, this is our new event manager, Savannah Carlisle. Savannah, this is our sales VP, Zora Abbott—the baby of the family."

"And they never let me forget it." Zora sat beside her older brother and elbowed him. The woman leaned across the table and shook her hand. "Welcome aboard, Savannah. We need you desperately. You've certainly impressed my big brother here. Not an easy feat."

A deep blush of pink bloomed across Blake's cheeks. He seemed relieved when another member of the Abbott clan stepped into the room.

"Max, this is your new event manager, Savannah Carlisle," Zora informed the handsome newcomer, then turned to Savannah. "Max is our marketing VP. You'll be working for him and with our mother—who isn't here."

There was no mistaking that Max and Blake were brothers. They had the same square jaw capped by a cleft chin. The same narrow, brooding dark eyes. And the same nose—with a narrow bridge and slightly flared nostrils.

Max wore his curly hair longer than Blake's. And where Blake's skin was the color of terra-cotta tiles, his brother's skin was a deeper russet brown. Max was a little taller than his brother, with a leaner frame.

"I look forward to working with you, Savannah." Max sat beside her and shook her hand, his grip firm and warm. His smile seemed genuine. "I'm excited to hear more of your ideas for the anniversary celebration."

"That's why I invited her to join us. She can relay them much better than I can."

Two more men walked into the room. "Didn't realize we were having guests," the younger of the two said, his voice gruff.

"My brother Parker." Zora rolled her eyes. "Chief financial officer and resident cheapskate."

Parker was not amused, but the older man—whom Zora introduced as their father, Duke—chuckled and gave Savannah a warm greeting.

Parker offered a cursory greeting, then shifted his narrowed gaze to Blake.

"I thought we were going to discuss the proposal honestly." Parker sat at one end of the table. Duke sat at the other.

"We will." The intensity of Blake's tone matched his brother's. He nodded toward Savannah. "No one is asking you to pull any punches. She might as well get accustomed to how we do business around here. Besides, she can best respond to your questions about the kind of return on investment we should expect."

"Welcome, then." Parker tapped something on his phone. "I've been described as…no-nonsense. Don't take it personally."

"I won't, if you promise not to take my tendency to shoot straight personally, either." Savannah met his gaze.

Parker nodded his agreement and the other siblings exchanged amused glances.

"You found someone Parker can't intimidate." Zora grinned. "Good job, Blake."

The Abbotts continued to tease each other while Zora or Blake filled her in on the inside jokes. Savannah smiled politely, laughing when they did. But an uneasiness crawled up her spine.

The Abbotts weren't what she'd expected.

Her grandfather had portrayed them as wild grizzly bears. Vicious and capable of devouring their own young.

*Don't be fooled by their charm.*

"Ready to make your presentation?" Blake asked.

Parker drummed his fingers on the table and glanced at his watch.

*Don't show fear.*

"Absolutely." Savannah stood, clutching her portfolio.

Blake's warm smile immediately eased the tightness in her chest. Her lungs expanded and she took a deep breath.

Savannah opened her portfolio and glanced around the room.

"All right, here's what I'm proposing…"

* * *

Blake typed notes into his phone as Savannah recapped her presentation. She'd won over everyone in the room. They were all on board with her plan—even penny-pinching Parker.

The event had graduated from the "little shindig" his mother had envisioned to a full gala. One that would retain a rustic charm that paid homage to the company's history. Savannah had also suggested holding anniversary events in other key cities.

The upgrades Savannah proposed to the old barn on his parents' property to prepare for the gala would significantly increase its rental income. They could charge more per event and would draw business from corporations and folks in nearby towns. All of which made Parker exceedingly happy.

"There's one thing I'm still not sold on," he interjected. "The majority of our market share is here in the South. Why invest in events elsewhere?"

"It's the perfect opportunity to deepen our reach outside of our comfort zone," Savannah said.

Parker folded his arms, unconvinced.

"She's right." Blake set his phone on the table and leveled his gaze on his brother. "I've floated the idea with a few distributors in the UK, California and New York. They love our products and they're eager to introduce them to more of their customers. I'm telling you, Parker, this could be a big win for us."

Savannah gave him a quick, grateful smile. A knot formed low in his gut.

"Savannah and Blake have done their homework," his father said. "I'm ready to move forward with Savannah's proposal. Any objections?"

Parker shook his head, but scowled.

"Excellent. Savannah, would you mind typing up your notes and sending them to the executive email list so my wife can get a look at them?"

"I'll do my best to get them out by the end of the day, Mr. Abbott."

"Duke will do just fine. Now, I'm late for a date with a five iron."

"The gala is going to be sensational." Zora grinned. "Right, Max?"

"It will be," Max agreed. "I wasn't sure that turning Mom's low-key, local event into something more elaborate and—"

"Expensive," Parker interrupted.

"Relax, El Cheapo." Zora's stony expression was a silent reminder that she wasn't just their baby sister. She was sales VP and an equal member of the executive team. "The additional sales will far exceed the additional expenses."

"Don't worry, lil' sis. I'm in." Parker tapped his pen on the table. "I'm obviously outnumbered. I'm as thrilled as you are to expand our market and rake in more cash. I just hope Savannah's projections are on target."

"I look forward to surprising you with the results." Savannah seemed unfazed by Parker's subtle intimidation.

"C'mon, Savannah." Max stood. "I'll show you to your office. It isn't far from mine."

Blake swallowed back his disappointment as she left with Max, Zora and their father. So much for his plan to give Savannah a tour of the place.

"Watch yourself," Parker warned.

"What do you mean?" Blake stuffed his phone in his pocket and headed for the door.

"You know *exactly* what I mean. You've been stealing glances at Savannah when you think no one is looking. Like just now." Parker followed him.

"You're exaggerating."

"No, I'm your brother." Parker fell in step beside him. "I know the signs."

"Of what?" Blake turned to face his brother. "A man very impressed with his new hire?"

"It's worse than I thought." Parker shook his head. "Look all you want, just don't touch. She's our employee. A subordinate. Don't cross the line with her. And for God's sake, don't get caught up in your feelings for this woman."

"Good advice." Blake resumed the walk to his office. "Too bad you haven't been good at following it."

"That's why I know what a horrible idea it is."

"Don't worry, Parker. I won't do anything you wouldn't." Blake went into his office and shut the door.

He didn't need Parker to remind him that Savannah Carlisle was off-limits.

# Four

Savannah surveyed the gleaming copper stills and the pipes running between them that filled the distillation room. "They're beautiful."

She was home. Exactly where she was meant to be, had it not been for Joseph Abbott's treachery.

"I guess they are." Daisy checked her watch again.

Blake's assistant was a nice enough woman, but her limited knowledge wasn't helpful to Savannah's cause. If she was going to take on the powerful Abbott family and prove they'd stolen her grandfather's bourbon recipe and his process for making it, she needed to learn everything there was to know about the making of their signature bourbon.

Daisy gave the stills a cursory glance. "I never really thought of them as beautiful."

"I do. I just didn't think anyone else did," a familiar, velvety voice chimed in.

*Blake again.*

The man seemed to pop up everywhere. Hopefully, it wouldn't be a daily occurrence.

"Didn't mean to scare you, Dais." Blake held up a hand. "Just met with Klaus—our master distiller," he added for Savannah's benefit. "I'm surprised you're still here. Doesn't Daphne's softball game start in an hour?"

"It does." Daisy turned to Savannah. "Daphne's my ten-year-old daughter. She's pitching as a starter for the first time."

"I'm sorry." No wonder Daisy had tried to rush her through the tour. "I didn't realize you had somewhere to be."

"Get out of here before you're late." Blake nodded toward the exit. "Tell Daph I'm rooting for her."

"What about the tour? We're nowhere near finished. Sa-

vannah has so many questions. I haven't done a very good
job of answering them."

"You were great, Daisy," Savannah lied, not wanting to
make her feel bad. "Your daughter's pitching debut is more
important. We can finish the tour another day."

"Go." Blake pointed toward the exit. "I'll finish up here.
In fact, I'll give Savannah the deluxe tour."

Daisy thanked them and hurried off.

"So you want to know all about the whiskey-making
process." Blake turned to Savannah. He hadn't advanced a
step, yet the space between them contracted.

"I mentioned that in my interview." She met his gaze,
acutely aware of their height difference and the broadness
of his shoulders.

His fresh, woodsy scent made her want to plant her palms
on his well-defined chest and press her nose to the vein visible on his neck.

"Thought that was just a clever bit to impress me." The
edge of his generous mouth pulled into a lopsided grin that
made her heart beat faster.

"Now, you know that isn't true." Savannah held his gaze
despite the violent fluttering in her belly.

She was reacting like a hormonal high-school girl with
a crush on the captain of the football team.

Blake was pleasant enough on the surface, and certainly
nice to look at. Okay, that was the understatement of the
year. His chiseled features and well-maintained body were
the stuff dreams were made of.

But he wasn't just any pretty face and hard physique.
He was an Abbott.

*E-N-E-M-Y.*

Her interest in this man—regardless of how good-looking he was or the sinful visions his mouth conjured—needed
to stay purely professional. The only thing she wanted from
Blake Abbott was insight into the history between their
grandfathers.

"So you promised me the deluxe tour."

"I did." His appraising stare caused a contraction of muscles she hadn't employed in far longer than she cared to admit. "Let's go back to the beginning."

"Are you sure?" Savannah scrambled to keep up with his long, smooth strides. "I've nearly caused one family crisis already. I don't intend to start another today. So if you have a wife or kids who are expecting you—"

"That your not-so-subtle way of asking if I'm married?" He quickly pressed his lips into a harsh line. "I mean… I'm not. None of my siblings are. Our mother is sure she's failed us somehow because we haven't produced any grandchildren."

"Why aren't you married? Not you specifically," Savannah added quickly, her cheeks hot.

"We're all married to this place. Committed to building the empire my granddad envisioned nearly half a century ago."

Blake held the door open and they stepped into the late-afternoon sunlight. Gravel crunched beneath their feet, forcing her to tread carefully in her tall spike heels.

They walked past the grain silos and onto a trail that led away from the warehouse. The property extended as far as she could see, a picturesque natural landscape that belonged on a postcard.

"Someone in town mentioned that you have another brother who isn't in the business."

"Cole runs the largest construction company in the area. With the explosion of high-end real estate around here, he's got the least time on his hands."

"Doesn't bode well for those grandchildren your mother wants."

"No, it doesn't," Blake agreed. "But she's convinced that if one of us finally takes the plunge, the rest will fall like dominoes."

"So then love is kind of like the plague?"

Blake's deep belly laugh made her grin so hard her cheeks ached.

"I can't disagree with that." He was smiling, but there was sadness in his eyes. There was a story there he wasn't willing to tell, but she suddenly wanted to hear.

The gravel gave way to a dirt path that was soft and squishy due to the recent rain. Her heels sank into the mud. "I thought we were going to start at the beginning of the tour."

"We are."

"But we already passed the grain silos." She pointed in the opposite direction.

He stopped, turning to face her. "Do you know why most of the storied whiskey distilleries are based in Kentucky or here in Tennessee?"

Savannah shook her head. She'd noticed that the industry was concentrated in those two states, but hadn't given much thought to why.

"A whiskey with a smooth finish begins with the right water source." He pointed toward a creek and the hills that rose along the edge of the property. "See that limestone shelf? Springs deep in these limestone layers feed King's Lake—our sole source of water. The limestone adds calcium to the water and filters out impurities like iron that would make the whiskey bitter."

She studied the veins in the limestone shelf. "So it wouldn't be possible to produce bourbon from another water source with the same composition and flavor?"

"Not even if you used our exact recipe." He stood beside her, gazing reverently at the stony mountain and the waters that trickled from it. "Then there's the matter of the yeast we use for fermentation. It's a proprietary strain that dates back to when my great-grandfather was running his moonshine business seventy-five years ago."

"Most distilleries openly share their grain recipe. King's Finest doesn't. Why?"

"My grandfather tweaked the grain mixture his father used. He's pretty territorial about it." Blake smiled. "So we keep our mash bill and yeast strain under tight control."

The fact that Blake's grandfather had stolen the recipe from her grandfather was the more likely reason.

"I'm boring you, aren't I?"

"No. This is all extremely fascinating."

"It's a subject I can get carried away with. Believe me, no other woman has ever used the word *fascinating* to describe it."

"You still think I'm feigning interest." Something in his stare made her cheeks warm and her chest heavy.

His lips parted and his hands clenched at his sides, but he didn't acknowledge her statement. "We'd better head back."

They visited the vats of corn, rye and malted barley. Next, they visited the large metal vat where the grain was cooked, creating the mash. In the fermentation room there were large, open tubs fashioned of cypress planks, filled with fermenting whiskey. The air was heavy with a scent similar to sourdough bread baking.

In the distillation room, he gave her a taste of the bourbon after it passed through the towering copper still and then again after it had made another pass through the doubler.

"It's clear." Savannah handed Blake back the metal cup with a long metal handle he'd used to draw a sample of the "high wine."

Her fingers brushed his and he nearly dropped the cup, but recovered quickly.

"The rich amber color happens during the aging process." He returned the cup to its hook, then led her through the area where the high wine was transferred to new, charred white oak barrels.

They walked through the rackhouse. Five levels of whiskey casks towered above them. Savannah fanned herself, her brow damp with perspiration, as Blake lowered his voice, speaking in a hushed, reverent tone.

"How long is the bourbon aged?"

"The signature label? Five years. Then we have the top-shelf labels aged for ten or more years." Blake surveyed the upper racks before returning his gaze to hers. "My grandfather made so many sacrifices to create this legacy for us. I'm reminded of that whenever I come out here."

Blake spoke of Joseph Abbott as if he were a self-sacrificing saint. But the man was a liar and a cheat. He'd sacrificed his friendship with her grandfather and deprived him of his legacy, leaving their family with nothing but hardship and pain.

Tears stung her eyes and it suddenly hurt to breathe in the overheated rackhouse. It felt as if a cask of whiskey was sitting on her chest. She gasped, the air burning her lungs.

"Are you all right?" Blake narrowed his brown eyes, stepping closer. He placed a gentle hand on her shoulder.

"I'm fine." Her breath came in short bursts and her back was damp with sweat.

"It's hot in here. Let's get you back in the air-conditioning. Our last stop is the bottling area." His hand low on her back, he guided her toward the exit.

"No." The word came out sharper than she'd intended. "I mean, I promised your father I'd get that presentation out today."

"You told him you'd try. Do it first thing tomorrow. It'll be fine."

"That's not the first impression I want to make with the company's CEO. Or with his wife, who's eagerly awaiting the information." Savannah wiped the dampness from her forehead with the back of her hand. "I gave my word, and to me, that means something."

# Five

It was clear Blake had offended Savannah.

*But how?*

He replayed the conversation in his head. Before she'd looked at him as if he'd kicked a kitten.

They'd been talking about how his grandfather had built the company. The sacrifices he'd made for their family. How could she possibly be offended by that? Especially when she'd already expressed her admiration for his grandfather's entrepreneurial spirit.

"If sending the presentation out tonight is that important to you, I won't stop you. All I'm saying is…no one will hold it against you if we receive it tomorrow."

Savannah turned on her heels, caked in dry mud from their earlier walk. She headed back toward the main building.

Even with his longer strides, he had to hurry to catch up with her. "You'd tell me if I upset you?"

"You didn't. I'm just—" Her spiked heel got caught in the gravel, and she stumbled into his arms.

He held her for a moment, his gaze studying hers, enjoying the feel of her soft curves pressed against his hard body.

Her eyes widened and she stepped out of his grasp, muttering a quick thank-you.

"I'm angry with myself for not remembering the presentation earlier."

"You've been busy all day. That's my fault."

"It's no one's fault." She seemed to force a smile. "I appreciate the deluxe tour. What I've learned will be useful as I prepare my presentation. It's given me a few other ideas."

"That's good, then." Blake kneaded the back of his neck. "I'll walk you back to your office."

"I'd like to find it on my own. Test my sense of direction." Savannah's tepid smile barely turned up one corner of her mouth. She headed back to the building, calling over her shoulder. "See you tomorrow."

When she was too far away to hear it, Blake released a noisy sigh. He returned to his office by a different route.

Despite what Savannah said, he'd clearly upset her. He couldn't shake the gnawing need to learn why. Or the deep-seated desire to fix it so he could see the genuine smile that lit her lovely eyes, illuminating the flecks of gold.

Blake gritted his teeth.

*You do not feel anything for her.*

He said the words over and over in his head as he trekked back inside, past her office and straight to his.

*You're full of shit, and you know it.*

Why couldn't his stupid subconscious just cooperate and buy into the load of crock he was trying to sell himself?

There were a million reasons why he shouldn't be thinking of Savannah Carlisle right now. Long-legged, smooth-skinned, caramel-complexioned goddess that she was.

He shouldn't be thinking of her throaty voice. Her husky laugh. Her penetrating stare. Or the way she sank her teeth into her lower lip while in deep thought.

Blake shut his office door and loosened his tie. He dropped into the chair behind his desk, trying not to focus on the tension in his gut and the tightening of his shaft at the thought of Savannah Carlisle…naked. Sprawled across his desk.

He opened his laptop and studied spreadsheets and graphs, ignoring the most disconcerting aspect of his growing attraction for Savannah. What scared him…what was terrifying…was how Savannah Carlisle made him feel. That she'd made him feel anything at all.

Especially the kind of feelings he'd carefully avoided in the two years since Gavrilla had walked out of his life.

Since then he'd satisfied his urges with the occasional

one-night stand while traveling for business. Far away from this too-small town, where every single person knew the private affairs of every other damned person.

In painful detail.

He hadn't been looking for anything serious. Just a couple of nights in the sack. No feelings. No obligations beyond having safe, responsible sex and being gentlemanly enough never to speak of it.

But from their first meeting, he'd been drawn to Savannah. She was bold and confident. And she hadn't begged for a shot with the company. She'd simply laid out a solid case.

He would've been a fool to not hire her.

Her indomitable spirit and latent sex appeal called to something deep inside him. In a way that felt significant. The feelings were completely foreign and yet deeply familiar.

He didn't believe in love at first sight or soul mates. But if he had, he'd have sworn that Cupid had shot him the second Savannah Carlisle sashayed her curvy ass into his office.

Blake loosened the top two buttons of his shirt. Parker's admonition played on a loop in his head. It could be summed up in five words: *Don't think with your dick.*

If Parker recognized how perilous Blake's attraction to Savannah was, he was in big trouble. He needed to slam the lid on those feelings. Seal them in an indestructible steel box fastened with iron rivets and guarded by flaming swords and a den of rattlesnakes.

Because he could never go back there again. To the pain he'd felt two years ago when Gavrilla had walked out. She'd left him for someone else. Without warning or the slightest indication she'd been unhappy.

Without giving him a chance to fix things.

In retrospect, she'd done him a favor. Their stark differences—so exciting in the beginning—had been flashing red lights warning of their incompatibility.

Blake sighed. It'd been a while since he'd taken a business-meets-pleasure excursion. Experienced the adrenaline of tumbling into bed with a stranger.

He'd have Daisy schedule a meeting with a vendor in Nashville or maybe Atlanta. Somewhere he could blend in with the nameless, faceless masses.

*Anywhere but Magnolia Lake.*

Blake hit Send on his final email of the night—a response to a vendor in the UK. He checked his watch. It was well after seven and Savannah's proposal hadn't pinged his inbox.

She'd been determined to send it before she left for the night. That meant she was still in her office working on it.

Blake rubbed his unshaved chin. Perhaps she'd encountered a problem. After all, it was her first day. He should see if she needed help.

Blake packed up his laptop, locked his office door and headed down the hall. He almost kept walking. Almost pretended he didn't hear the tapping of computer keys.

He groaned, knowing he was acting against his better judgment.

"Hey." He gently knocked on Savannah's open office door. "Still at it?"

"Finished just now." Her earlier uneasiness appeared to be gone. "You didn't wait for me, did you?" She seemed perturbed by the possibility.

"No. Just finished up myself. But since I'm here, I'll walk you to your car."

"I thought small towns like Magnolia Lake were idyllic bastions of safety and neighborliness." Savannah barely contained a sarcastic grin as she grabbed her bags.

"Doesn't mean we shouldn't practice courtesy and good old-fashioned common sense." He opened the door wider to let her out, then locked it behind them.

They made the trip to her small car in near silence. She stopped abruptly, just shy of her door.

"About earlier." She turned to him, but her eyes didn't meet his. "Sorry if I seemed rude. I wasn't trying to be. I just…" She shook her head. "It wasn't anything you did."

"But it was something I said." He hiked his computer bag higher on his shoulder when her eyes widened.

"It won't happen again."

"Good night, Savannah." Blake opened her car door. He wouldn't press, if she didn't want to talk about it.

They weren't lovers, and they needn't be friends. As long as Savannah did her job well and played nice with others, everything would be just fine.

He stepped away from the car and she drove away.

Blake made his way back to his truck, thankful Savannah Carlisle had saved him from himself.

Savannah let herself into her apartment, glad the day was finally over.

When she got to the bedroom, she pulled a black leather journal from her nightstand. It held her notes about the Abbotts.

Savannah did a quick review of what she'd learned on the job today and jotted down everything she could remember.

Their processes. The grains used in their bourbon composition with a question mark and percentage sign by each one. The industry jargon she'd learned. Next, she outlined her impressions of each member of the Abbott family—starting with Blake.

Finished with the brain dump, she was starving and mentally exhausted. She scarfed down a frozen dinner while watching TV.

Her cell phone rang. *Laney*.

"Hey, sis." Savannah smiled. "How's my niece? And how is Granddad doing?"

"They're both fine. How was your first day?"

"Long. I just got home." Savannah shoved the last bite of processed macaroni and cheese into her mouth, then dumped the plastic tray into the recycle bin. "I made my proposal to the entire family—"

"You met all the Abbotts?"

"Everyone except their mother, Iris, and Joseph Abbott." Savannah was both angry and relieved she hadn't had the chance to look into the eyes of the coldhearted bastard who'd ruined her grandfather's life.

"What were they like?"

Savannah sank onto the sofa. Blake's dreamy eyes and kind smile danced in her head. The vision had come to her in her sleep more than once since they'd met.

In her dreams, they weren't from opposing families. They'd been increasingly intimate, holding hands, embracing. And last night she'd awakened in a cold sweat after they'd shared a passionate kiss.

She'd struggled to drive those images from her head while spending a good portion of her day in his company.

"The Abbotts aren't the ogres you expected, are they?" There was a hint of vindication in Laney's question.

"No, but I met most of them for the first time today. They were trying to make a good first impression. After all, even a serial killer can have a charming facade."

Laney didn't acknowledge her logic. "Tell me about them, based on what you observed today. Not on what you thought you knew about them."

Savannah removed her ponytail holder and shook her head. Her curly hair tumbled to her shoulders in loose waves from being pulled tight.

"It was hard to get a read on their dad—Duke. He's personable, but all business."

"What about the rest of them?"

"I met Blake, Parker, Max and Zora—the four siblings who run the distillery. There's a fifth—Cole. He has his own construction company."

"Why didn't he go into the family business?"

"Don't know." Savannah had wondered, too.

"Quit stalling and tell me more."

"Zora is sweet. Max is funny. Parker is kind of an ass-hole."

"And what about Blake Abbott? This was your second encounter. Did your impression of him improve?"

"Yes." She hated to admit that it was true. But Blake's genuinely warm interactions with his employees during the tour made him appear to be an ideal boss.

"So now that you see you were wrong about the Abbotts, will you please let this thing go?"

So much for Laney being on board with the plan.

"The congeniality of Joseph Abbott's grandchildren isn't the issue here."

"Savannah—"

"If they're genuinely innocent in all of this…well, I'm sorry their grandfather was such a bastard. It isn't like I plan to steal the company from under them the way he did from Granddad."

"Then what exactly do you want, honey? What's your grand plan here?"

"Our family deserves half the company. That's what I want. And if they don't want to share, they can buy us out. Plain and simple."

Laney made a strangled sound of frustration. A sound she made whenever they discussed their grandfather's claims regarding King's Finest.

"I couldn't do what you're doing." Laney's voice was quiet. "Getting to know people. Having them come to like and trust you. Then turning on them."

Savannah winced at the implication of her sister's words. "I'm not 'turning' on them. I'm just standing up for my family. As any of them would for theirs. Besides, I'm not harming their business in any way."

"You're spying on them."

"But I'm not taking that information to a competitor. I'm just gathering evidence to support Granddad's ownership claim." Savannah tamped down the defensiveness in her tone.

"And what about Blake?"

"What about him?"

"You like him. I can tell. What happens when he learns the truth?"

A knot twisted in Savannah's belly. "If he's as good a man as everyone seems to think, he should want to make this right. In fact, I'm counting on it."

# Six

Savannah smiled in response to the email she'd just received from Max, who was away at another trade show. They'd secured the endorsement of a local boy who'd become a world-famous actor. With his rugged good looks and down-home, boyish charm, he was perfect.

Her plans for the jubilee were in full swing. The rustic gala, to be held in the Abbotts' old country barn, would celebrate the company, its employees and distributors and attract plenty of media coverage. The renovated barn would provide King's Finest with an additional revenue stream and create jobs in the small town.

Savannah had been working at the distillery for nearly a month. The residents of the small town had done their best to make her feel welcome—despite her desire to hang in the shadows and lie low.

Every Friday she turned down no less than two invitations to the local watering hole for drinks after work. One of those invitations always came from Blake.

An involuntary shudder rippled down Savannah's spine when she thought of Blake with his generous smile and warm brown eyes. Savannah shook her head.

She would *not* think of how good Blake Abbott looked in the checkered dress shirts and athletic-fit slacks he typically wore. Each piece highlighted the finer points of his physique. A broad chest. Well-defined pecs. Strong arms. An ass that made it evident he was no stranger to lunges and squats.

His clothing was designed to torture her and every other woman with a working libido and functioning set of eyes. It tormented her with visions of what his strong body must look like beneath that fabric.

A crack of thunder drew her attention to the window. She checked the time on her phone. It was barely after seven, but dark clouds and a steady downpour darkened the sky, making it feel later.

Savannah worked late most nights. The gala was quickly approaching and there was so much to do.

Plus, being the last member of the administrative team to leave each night gave her a chance to do some reconnaissance. She could access files she didn't feel comfortable perusing when Max, Blake or Zora might pop into her office at any minute.

Then there was the surprising fact that she thoroughly enjoyed the work she was doing. She was often so engrossed in a task that time got away from her.

Like tonight.

Outside the window, increasingly dark clouds loomed overhead. The steady, gentle rain that had fallen throughout the day was now a raging downpour.

Another flash of light illuminated the sky. It was quickly followed by a peal of thunder that made Savannah's heart race.

It was lightning that posed the real danger. Savannah knew that better than most. The thunder was just sound and fury.

She loathed driving in inclement weather. Tack on the steep hills, narrow roads, one-lane bridge and her vague familiarity with the area, and it was a recipe for disaster.

One wrong turn, and she could end up in a ditch, lost in the woods, undiscovered for months.

*Stop being a drama queen. Everything will be fine. Just take a deep breath.*

Savannah took a long, deep breath.

She'd hoped to wait out the storm. Her plan had backfired. Engrossed in her work, she hadn't noticed that the rain had gotten much heavier. And it didn't appear to be letting up anytime soon.

After composing and sending one final email, Savannah signed off her computer. She gathered her things and headed for the parking lot, as fast as her high-heeled feet could carry her.

*Shit.*

She was without an umbrella, and it was raining so hard the parking lot had flooded. No wonder the lot was empty except for her car.

If it stalled out, she'd be screwed.

A flash of lightning lit the sky like a neon sign over a Vegas hotel.

Jaw clenched, Savannah sucked in a generous breath, as if she were about to dive into the deep end of the pool. She made a mad dash for her car before the next bolt struck.

Despite the warm temperatures, the rain pelted her in cold sheets as she waded through the standing water. Her clothing was wet and heavy. Her feet slid as she ran in her soaking-wet shoes.

Savannah dropped into the driver's seat and caught her breath. Her eyes stung as she wiped water from her face with the back of her hand, which was just as wet.

She turned her key and gave the car some gas, grateful the engine turned over.

There was another flash of lightning, then a rumble of thunder, followed by a heavy knock on the window.

She screamed, her heart nearly beating out of her chest.

A large man in a hooded green rain slicker hovered outside her window.

She was cold, wet, alone and about to be murdered.

*But not without a fight.*

Savannah popped open her glove compartment and searched for something…anything…she could use as a weapon. She dug out the heavy tactical flashlight her grandfather had given her one Christmas. She beamed the bright light in the intruder's face.

"Blake?" Savannah pressed a hand to her chest, her heart

still thudding against her breastbone. She partially lowered the window.

Even with his eyes hidden by the hood, she recognized the mouth and stubbled chin she'd spent too much time studying.

"You were expecting someone else?"

*Smart-ass.*

If she didn't work for the Abbotts, and she wasn't so damned glad not to be alone in the middle of a monsoon, she would have told Blake exactly what she thought of his smart-assery.

"What are you doing here? And where'd you come from?"

"I'm parked under the carport over there." He pointed in the opposite direction. "Came to check on the building. Didn't expect to see anyone here at this time of night in the storm."

"I didn't realize how late it was, or that the rain had gotten so bad. I'm headed home now."

"In this?" He sized up her small car.

She lifted a brow. "My flying saucer is in the shop."

Savannah knew she shouldn't have said it, but the words slipped out of her mouth before she could reel them back in.

Blake wasn't angry. He smirked instead.

"Too bad. Because that's the only way you're gonna make it over the bridge."

"What are you talking about?"

"You're renting from Kayleigh Jemison in town, right?"

"How did you know—"

"It's Magnolia Lake. Everyone knows everyone in this town," he said matter-of-factly. "And there are flash-flood warnings everywhere. No way will this small car make it through the low-lying areas between here and town."

"Flash floods?" Panic spread through her chest. "Isn't there another route I can take?"

"There's only one way back to town." He pointed toward

the carport. "The ground is higher there. Park behind my truck, and I'll give you a ride home. I'll bring you back to get your car when the roads clear."

"Just leave my car here?" She stared at him dumbly.

"If I could fit it into the bed of my truck, I would." One side of his mouth curved in an impatient smile. "And if there was any other option, I'd tell you."

Savannah groaned as she returned her flashlight to the glove compartment. Then she pulled into the carport as Blake instructed.

"Got everything you need from your car?" Blake removed his hood and opened her car door.

"You act as if I won't see my car again anytime soon."

"Depends on how long it takes the river to go down."

"Seriously?" Savannah grabbed a few items from the middle console and shoved them in her bag before securing her vehicle. She followed Blake to the passenger side of his huge black truck.

She gasped, taken by surprise when Blake helped her up into the truck.

"I have a couple more things to check before we go. Sit tight. I'll be back before you can miss me."

*Doubt it.*

Blake shut her door and disappeared around the building.

Savannah waited for her heartbeat to slow down. She secured her seat belt and surveyed the interior of Blake's pickup truck. The satellite radio was set to an old-school hip-hop channel. The truck was tricked out with all the toys. High-end luxury meets Bo and Luke Duke with a refined hip-hop sensibility.

*Perfectly Blake.*

A clean citrus scent wafted from the air vents. The black leather seats she was dripping all over were inlaid with a tan design.

A fierce gust of wind blew the rain sideways and swayed

the large truck. Her much smaller car rocked violently, as if it might blow over.

Another blinding flash of lightning was quickly followed by a rumble of thunder. Savannah gritted her teeth.

She'd give anything to be home in bed with the covers pulled over her head.

*Everything will be fine. Don't freak out.*

Savannah squeezed her eyes shut. Counted backward from ten, then forward again. When she opened them, Blake was spreading a yellow tarp over her small car.

*Damn you, Blake Abbott.*

She'd arrived in Magnolia Lake regarding every last one of the Abbotts as a villain. Blake's insistence on behaving like a knight in shining armor while looking like black Thor made it difficult to maintain that position.

He was being kind and considerate, doing what nearly any man would under the circumstances. Particularly one who regarded himself a Southern gentleman.

That didn't make him Gandhi.

And it sure as hell didn't prove the Abbotts weren't capable of cruelty. Especially when it came to their business.

But as he approached the truck, looking tall, handsome and delicious despite the rain, it was impossible not to like him.

*Relax. It's just a ride home.*

The storm had Savannah on edge. Nothing a little shoo-fly punch wouldn't soothe. She just needed to endure the next twenty minutes with Blake Abbott.

Blake stood outside the truck with the wind whipping against his back and his soaking-wet clothing sticking to his skin. He forced a stream of air through his nostrils.

Parker's warning replayed in his head.

*Don't think of her that way. It'll only get you into trouble.*

He'd come back to the plant after dinner with his father to make sure everything was okay. But he'd also come back looking for her, worried she'd spent another night working late, not recognizing the dangers of a hard, long rain like this. Something any local would know.

He would have done this for any of his employees—male or female. But he wasn't a convincing enough liar to persuade himself that what he was doing tonight…for her… wasn't different. More personal.

Something about Savannah Carlisle roused a fiercely protective instinct.

*Keep your shit together and your hands to yourself.*

Blake took one more cleansing breath and released it, hoping his inappropriate thoughts about Savannah went right along with it.

When he yanked the door open, Savannah's widened eyes met his. Shivering, she wrapped her arms around herself.

"You're freezing." Blake climbed inside the truck and turned on the heat to warm her, wishing he could take her in his arms. Transferring his body heat to hers would be a better use of the steam building under his collar. "Is that better?"

Savannah rubbed her hands together and blew on them. "Yes, thank you."

Blake grabbed a jacket off the back seat and handed it to her. "Put this on."

There was the briefest hesitance in her eyes before Savannah accepted the jacket with a grateful nod. It was heavy, and she struggled to put it on.

Blake helped her into it. Somehow, even that basic gesture felt too intimate.

"Let's get you home." Blake put the truck into gear and turned onto the road that led across the river and into town.

They traveled in comfortable silence. It was just as well. The low visibility created by the blowing rain required his complete focus.

They were almost there. Savannah's apartment was just beyond the bridge and around the bend.

*Shit.*

They were greeted by a roadblock and yellow warning signs. The water had risen to the level of the bridge.

"There's another way into town, right?" Savannah asked nervously.

Blake didn't acknowledge the alarm in her brown eyes. If he didn't panic, maybe she wouldn't, either, when he broke the bad news. "That bridge is the only route between here and your place."

"I can't get home?" Her voice was shaky and its pitch rose.

"Not tonight. Maybe not tomorrow. The bridge is in danger of washing out. I could possibly make it across in my truck, but the weight of this thing could compromise the bridge and send us downriver."

"So what do I do for the next couple of days? Camp out in my office until the bridge is safe again?"

"That won't be necessary." Blake groaned internally. Savannah wasn't going to like the alternative. "My house is up the hill a little ways back."

"You think I'm staying at your house? Overnight?" She narrowed her gaze at him. As if he'd orchestrated the rain, her staying late and the bridge threatening to wash out.

"You don't really have another choice, Savannah." He studied her as she weighed the options.

She pulled the jacket around her tightly as she assessed the road in front of them, then the road behind them. "Seems I don't have much of a choice."

A knot tightened in the pit of Blake's stomach. He'd hoped that she would be stubborn enough to insist on returning to the office. That he wouldn't be tortured by Savannah Carlisle being off-limits *and* sleeping under his roof.

"Okay then." He shifted the truck into Reverse, turned

around and headed back to the narrow road that led to the exclusive community where he and Zora owned homes.

As they ascended the hill, the handful of houses around the lake came into view. A bolt of lightning arced in the sky.

Savannah flinched once, then again at the deafening thunder. She was trying to play it cool, but her hands were clenched into fists. She probably had nail prints on her palms.

Why was she so frightened by the storm?

He wanted to know, but the question felt too personal. And everything about Savannah Carlisle indicated she didn't do personal. She kept people at a safe distance.

She'd politely refused every social invitation extended to her since she'd joined the company. Some of his employees hadn't taken her repeated rejections so well.

He'd tried not to do the same. After all, distance from her was exactly what he needed.

When they arrived at his house, he pulled inside the garage.

"You're sure this won't cause trouble? I mean, if anyone found out…" A fresh wave of panic bloomed across her beautiful face. "It wouldn't look good for either of us."

"No one else knows. Besides, any decent human being would do the same," he assured her. "Would you prefer I'd left you in the parking lot on your own?"

"I'm grateful you didn't." Her warm gaze met his. "I just don't want to cause trouble…for either of us."

"It's no trouble," Blake lied. He hopped down from the cab of the truck, then opened her door.

She regarded his extended hand reluctantly. Finally, she placed her palm in his and allowed him to help her down.

Blake stilled for a moment, his brain refusing to function properly. Savannah was sopping wet. Her makeup was washed away by the rain, with the exception of the black mascara running down her face. Yet she looked no worse for the wear.

Her tawny skin was punctuated by a series of freckles splashed across her nose and cheeks.

Something about the discovery of that small detail she'd hidden from the world thrilled him.

His gaze dropped to her lips, and a single, inappropriate thought filled his brain.

*Kiss her. Now.*

She slipped her icy hand from his, slid the jacket from her shoulders and returned it to him.

"Thank you." He tossed it into the back seat and shut the door.

When he turned to Savannah she was shivering again.

He rubbed his hands up and down her arms to warm her before his brain could remind him that was an inappropriate gesture, too.

Her searing gaze made the point clear.

"Sorry... I..." Blake stepped away, his face heated. He ran a hand through his wet hair.

"I appreciate the gesture. But what I'd really love is a hot shower and a place to sleep."

"Of course." Blake shrugged off his wet rain slicker. He hung it on a hook, then closed the garage door. "Hope you're not afraid of dogs."

"Not particularly."

"Good." Blake dropped his waterlogged shoes by the door to the house. When he opened it, his two dogs surrounded him, yapping until he petted each of their heads. They quickly turned their attention to Savannah.

"Savannah Carlisle, meet Sam—" He indicated the lean Italian greyhound who, while peering intently at Savannah, hadn't left his side. "He's a retired racing greyhound I rescued about five years ago."

"Hello, Sam."

"And that nosy fella there is Benny the labradoodle." Blake indicated the rust-and-beige dog yapping at her feet, demanding her attention.

"Hi, Benny." Savannah leaned down and let the dog sniff her hand, then petted his head. "Pleasure to meet you."

Benny seemed satisfied with her greeting. He ran back inside with Sam on his heels.

"Did you rescue Benny, too?"

"No." Blake swallowed past the knot that formed in his throat when he remembered the day he'd brought Benny home as a pup.

He'd bought Benny as a surprise for his ex. Only she'd had a surprise of her own. She was leaving him for someone else.

"Oh." Savannah didn't inquire any further, for which he was grateful.

Blake turned on the lights and gestured inside. "After you."

# Seven

*Stop behaving like the poor girl who grew up on the wrong side of the tracks. Even if you are.*

Savannah's wide eyes and slack mouth were a dead give-away as Blake gave her an informal tour of his beautiful home.

She realized the Abbotts were wealthy. Still, she'd expected a log cabin with simple country decor. Maybe even a luxurious bachelor pad filled with gaming tables and the latest sound equipment.

She certainly hadn't expected this gorgeous, timber-built home overlooking a picturesque lake and offering breathtaking mountain vistas. The wall of windows made the pastoral setting as much a feature of the home as the wide plank floors and shiplap walls.

Rustic charm with a modern twist.

It was the kind of place she could imagine herself living in. The kind of home she would be living in, if not for the greed and betrayal of Joseph Abbott.

Her shoulders tensed and her hands balled into fists at her sides.

"You must be tired." Blake seemed to sense the shift in her demeanor. "I'll show you to your room. We can finish the tour another time."

Blake always seemed attuned to how she was feeling. A trait that would be endearing if they were a couple. Or even friends.

But they weren't. It was a reality she couldn't lose sight of, no matter how kind and generous Blake Abbott appeared on the surface.

She was here for one reason. But she'd learned little about Joseph Abbott and nothing of his history with her grandfather. If she opened up a little with Blake, perhaps he'd do the same, and reveal something useful about his family.

Maybe Blake didn't know exactly what his grandfather had done. But he might still provide some small clue that could direct her to someone who did know and was willing to talk.

But none of that would happen if she couldn't keep her temper in check. She had to swallow the bitterness and pain that bubbled to the surface whenever she thought of Joseph Abbott's cruel betrayal.

At least for now.

"I'm tired. And wet. And cold. So I'm sorry if I'm cranky." Her explanation seemed to put him at ease.

"Of course." He led the way through the house and up an open staircase to the second floor. Sam and Benny were on his heels.

"I hate to ask this, but do you think I could borrow a T-shirt and some shorts?"

"Don't think I have anything that'll fit you." Blake stopped in front of a closed door. His gaze raked over her body-conscious, black rayon dress. Soaked through, the material shrank, making it fit like a second skin. Blake made a valiant effort to hold back a smirk.

He failed miserably.

"I'll see what I can find."

He opened the door to a spacious guest room with a terrace. The crisp, white bedding made the queen-size bed look inviting, and the room's neutral colors were warm and soothing. The angle of the windows provided a better view of a docked boat and an amphibious plane.

*Maybe being a guest chez Blake won't be so bad after all.*

"Thanks, Blake. I'll be out of your hair as soon as I can, I promise."

Her words drew his attention to her hair, which was soaking wet. A few loose strands clung to her face.

He reached out, as if to tuck a strand behind her ear. Then he shoved his hand into his pocket.

"It's no trouble. I'm just glad I came back to check on you... I mean, the plant." His voice was rough as he nodded toward a sliding barn door. "The bathroom is there. It's stocked with everything you need, including an unopened toothbrush."

"Thank you, again." Savannah set her purse and bag on the floor beside the bed.

Neither of them said anything for a moment. Blake dragged his stare from hers. "I'll find something you can sleep in and leave it on the bed. Then I'll rustle up something for us to eat."

With the violent storm crackling around them, she hadn't thought about food. But now that he mentioned it, she was starving. She hadn't eaten since lunch.

"All right, cowboy." She couldn't help teasing him. She hadn't ever heard the word *rustle* used outside of a cowboy movie.

Blake grinned, then slapped his thigh. "C'mon, boys. Let's give Savannah some space."

The dogs rushed out into the hall and Blake left, too, closing the door behind him.

Savannah exhaled, thankful for a moment of solitude. Yet, thinking of him, she couldn't help smiling.

She shook her head, as if the move would jostle loose the rogue thoughts of Blake Abbott that had lodged themselves there.

*Don't you dare think about it. Blake Abbott is definitely off-limits.*

"Hey." Blake was sure Savannah could hear the thump of his heart, even from where she stood across the room.

She padded toward him wearing his oversize University of Tennessee T-shirt as gracefully as if it was a Versace ball gown. Her black hair was chestnut brown on the ends.

Ombre, his sister had called it when she'd gotten a similar dye job the year before.

Savannah's hair hung down to her shoulders in loose ringlets that made him want to run the silky strands between his fingers. To wrap them around his fist as he tugged her mouth to his.

Absent cosmetics, Savannah's freshly-scrubbed, freckled skin took center stage. She was the kind of beautiful that couldn't be achieved with a rack of designer dresses or an expensive makeup palette.

Her natural glow was refreshing.

Seeing Savannah barefaced and fresh out of the shower felt intimate. She'd let down her guard and bared a little of her soul to him.

Blake's heart raced and his skin tingled with a growing desire for this woman. His hands clenched at his sides, aching to touch her.

He fought back the need to taste the skin just below her ear. To nip at her full lower lip. To nibble on the spot where her neck and shoulder met.

Blake snapped his mouth shut when he realized he must look like a guppy in search of water.

"Hey." Savannah's eyes twinkled as she tried to hold back a grin. "Where are Sam and Benny?"

"I put them downstairs in the den. Didn't want to torture them with the food or annoy you with Benny's begging. One look at that sad face and I'm a goner." He nodded toward the orange-and-white University of Tennessee shirt she was wearing. "I see the shirt fit. Kind of."

Savannah held her arms out wide and turned in a circle, modeling his alma mater gear. "It's a little big, but I think I made it work."

*That's for damn sure.*

The hem of the shirt skimmed the tops of her thighs and hugged her curvy breasts and hips like a warm caress.

Blake was incredibly jealous of that T-shirt. He'd give

just about anything to be the one caressing those undulating curves. For his body to be the only thing covering hers.

The too-long sleeves hung past her fingertips. Savannah shoved them up her forearms. She lifted one foot, then the other, as she pulled the socks higher up her calves. Each time, she unwittingly offered a generous peek of her inner thigh.

Blake swallowed hard. The words he formed in his head wouldn't leave his mouth.

"Smells good. What's for dinner?" She didn't remark on his odd behavior, for which he was grateful.

"I had some leftover ham and rice." He turned back to the stove and stirred the food that was beginning to stick to the pan. "So I fried an egg and sautéed a few vegetables to make some ham-fried rice."

"You made ham-fried rice?"

There was the look he'd often seen on her face. Like a war was being waged inside her head and she wasn't sure which side to root for.

"Yep." Blake plated servings for each of them and set them on the dining room table, where he'd already set out a beer for himself and a glass of wine for her. He pulled out her chair.

She thanked him and took her seat. "I didn't realize you cooked. Did your mom teach you?"

Blake chuckled. "There were too many of us to be underfoot in the kitchen."

"Not even your sister?"

Blake remembered the day his mother decided to teach Zora to cook.

"My sister was a feminist at the age of ten. When she discovered Mom hadn't taught any of us to cook, she staged a protest, complete with hand-painted signs. Something about equal treatment for sisters and brothers, if I remember correctly."

"Your mother didn't get upset?"

"She wanted to be, but she and my dad were too busy trying not to laugh. Besides, she was proud my sister stuck up for herself."

"A lesson your sister obviously took to heart." Savannah smiled. "So if your mother didn't teach you to cook, who did?"

"I became a cookbook addict a few years back." A dark cloud gathered over Blake's head, transporting him back to a place he didn't want to go.

"Why the sudden interest?" She studied him. The question felt like more than just small talk.

Blake shrugged and shoveled a forkful of fried rice into his mouth. "Got tired of fast food."

"I would think there's always a place for you all at Duke and Iris's dinner table." Savannah took a bite, then sighed with appreciation.

What he wouldn't give to hear her utter that sound in a very different setting: her body beneath his as he gripped her generous curves and joined their bodies.

"There is an open invitation to dinner at my parents' home," he confirmed. "But at the time I was seeing someone who didn't get along with my mother and sister." He grunted as he chewed another bite of food. "One of the many red flags I barreled past."

"You're all so close. I'm surprised this woman made the cut if she didn't get along with Zora or Iris."

This was not the dinner conversation Blake hoped to have. He'd planned to use the opportunity to learn more about Savannah. Instead, she was giving him the third degree.

"We met in college. By the time she met any of my family… I was already in too deep. A mistake I've been careful not to repeat," he added under his breath, though she clearly heard him.

"Is that why things didn't work out? Because your family didn't like her?"

He responded with a hollow, humorless laugh. "She left me. For someone else."

The wound in his chest reopened. Not because he missed his ex or wanted her back. Because he hadn't forgiven himself for choosing her over his family.

Though, at the time, he hadn't seen it that way.

After college, he'd moved back home and worked at the distillery, and he and Gavrilla had a long-distance relationship. But when he'd been promoted to VP of operations, he'd asked her to move to Magnolia Lake with him.

The beginning of the end.

Up till then, his ex, his mother and sister had politely endured one another during Gavrilla's visits to town. Once she lived there full-time, the thin veneer of niceties had quickly chipped away.

Blake had risked his relationship with his family because he loved her. She'd repaid his loyalty with callous betrayal.

She'd taught him a hard lesson he'd learned well. It was the reason he was so reluctant to give his heart to anyone again.

"I'm sorry. I wouldn't have brought it up if I'd known it would stir up bad memories." Savannah frowned.

"You couldn't have known. It's not something I talk about." Blake gulped his icy beer, unsure why he'd told Savannah.

"Then I'm glad you felt comfortable enough to talk about it."

"That surprises me." He narrowed his gaze.

"Why?"

"You go out of your way not to form attachments at work."

Savannah's cheeks and forehead turned crimson. She lowered her gaze and slowly chewed her food. "I don't mean to be—"

"Standoffish?" He did his best to hold back a grin. "Their words, not mine."

"Whose words?"

"You don't actually think I'm going to throw a member of my team under the bus like that, do you?" Blake chuckled. "But that fence you work so hard to put around yourself… It's working."

"I don't come to work for social hour. I'm there to do the job you hired me to do." Savannah's tone was defensive. She took a sip of her wine and set it on the table with a thud.

"That's too bad." Blake studied her. Tension rolled off her lean shoulders. "At King's Finest, we treat our employees like family. After all, we spend most of our waking hours at the distillery. Seems less like work when you enjoy what you do and like the people you do it with."

"Am I not doing my job well?" Savannah pursed her adorable lips.

"You're doing a magnificent job." He hadn't intended to upset her. "I doubt anyone could do it better."

She tipped up her chin slightly, as if vindicated by his statement. "Has anyone accused me of being rude or unprofessional?"

"No, nor did I mean to imply that." He leaned forward. "All I'm saying is…you're new to town. So you probably don't have many friends here. But maybe if you'd—"

"I didn't come to Magnolia Lake to make friends, Blake. And I already have a family."

Savannah had given him a clear signal that she didn't want to discuss the topic any further, but she hadn't shut the conversation down completely. There was something deep inside him that needed to know more about her.

"So tell me about your family."

# Eight

They'd talked so much about his family. Savannah shouldn't be surprised he'd want to know about hers.

Not in a getting-to-know-you, we're-on-a-date kind of way. In the way that was customary in Magnolia Lake. One part Southern hospitality. One part nosy-as-hell.

Had she not been determined to keep her personal life under wraps, she might've appreciated their interest.

She didn't want to discuss her family with Blake or any Abbott. But she hadn't gotten anywhere in her investigation. If she didn't want to spend the rest of her natural life in this one-horse town, she needed to change her approach.

If the quickest route to getting answers was charming the handsome Blake Abbott, she'd have to swallow her pride, put on her biggest smile and do it. At the very least, that meant opening up about her life.

"I have a sister that's a few years younger than me."

"That your only sibling?"

"Yes."

"What's she like?"

"Laney's brilliant. She's been accepted as a PhD candidate at two different Ivy League schools. All of that despite being the mother of a rambunctious two-year-old." A smile tightened Savannah's cheeks whenever she talked about Laney or Harper. "Someday my sister is going to change the world. I just know it."

"Sounds like Parker." Blake grinned. "While the rest of us were outside running amok, he had his nose in a book. For him, being forced to go outside was his punishment."

"Seems like his book obsession paid off."

"A fact he doesn't let any of us forget. Especially my mother." Blake chuckled. "You and your sister…"

"Delaney." No point in lying about her sister's name. He could find that out easily enough.

"Are you close?"

"Very. Though with our age difference and the fact that we lost our parents when we were young, I sometimes act more like her mother than her sister. Something she doesn't appreciate much these days."

"Sorry to hear about your parents. How'd you lose them, if you don't mind me asking?"

She did mind. But this wasn't about what she wanted. She needed Blake to trust her.

"The crappy little tenement we lived in burned down to the ground. Lightning hit the building and the whole thing went up in no time." She could feel the heat and smell the smoke. That night forever etched in her brain. "A lot of the families we knew growing up lost their lives that night."

"How'd you and your sister get out?" There was a pained expression on Blake's face. It was more empathy than pity.

A distinction she appreciated.

"My dad worked second shift. When he arrived home the building was in flames. He saved me and my sister and a bunch of our neighbors, but he went back to save my mother and…" A tightness gripped her chest and tears stung her eyes. She inhaled deeply and refused to let them fall. "He didn't make it back out."

"Savannah." Blake's large hand covered her smaller one. "I'm sorry."

The small gesture consoled her. Yet if not for what Blake's grandfather had done, her life would be very different.

She couldn't know for sure if her parents would still be with her. But they wouldn't have been living in a run-down housing project that had been cited for countless violations. And they wouldn't have lost their lives that stormy night.

"Thank you." Savannah slipped her hand from beneath

his. "But it was such a long time ago. I was only nine. My sister was barely four. She hardly remembers our parents."

"Who raised you two?"

"My grandfather." She couldn't help smiling. "I didn't want to go live with him. When my parents were alive he'd always seemed so grumpy. He didn't approve of my dad. He'd hoped my mother would marry someone who had more to offer financially. But after my dad gave his life trying to save my mom… He realized too late what a good guy my father was." She shoved the last of her food around her plate. "He's been trying to make it up to them ever since."

They ate in silence, the mood notably somber.

"Sorry you asked, huh?" She took her plate to the kitchen.

"No." Blake followed her. "I understand now why you don't like to talk about yourself or your family."

"I'd rather be seen as polite but aloof than as Debbie Downer or the poor little orphan people feel sorry for."

A peal of thunder rocked the house, startling Savannah. The storm had abated for the past hour only to reassert itself with a vengeance.

"It's raining again." Blake peered out the large kitchen window. When he looked back at her, a spark of realization lit his eyes. "Your parents… That night… That's why you're so freaked out by thunderstorms."

Savannah considered asking if he wanted a cookie for his brilliant deduction. The flash of light across the night sky turned her attention to a more pressing issue.

"Where do you keep the bourbon around here?"

Blake chuckled. "I was saving it for after dinner."

"It's after dinner." Savannah folded her arms. "After that trip down memory lane, I could use something that packs a punch."

"You've got it."

She followed him down to the den. Sam and Benny greeted them, their tails wagging.

*This* was the game room she'd anticipated. But instead

of having a frat-house quality, it was simple and elegant. There was a billiards table, three huge televisions mounted on the walls, a game table in one corner and groupings of chairs and sofas throughout the large room.

One bank of windows faced the mountains. The other faced the lake with more mountains in the distance.

Savannah sat on a stool at the bar. "This place is stunning. It isn't what I expected." She studied him as he stepped behind the bar. "Neither are you."

A slow grin curled one corner of his generous mouth. Her tongue darted out involuntarily to lick her lips in response. There was something incredibly sexy about Blake's smile.

He was confident, bordering on cocky. Yet there was something sweet and almost vulnerable about him. When he grinned at her like that, she felt an unexpected heaviness low in her belly. Her nipples tightened, and she mused about the taste of his lips. How they would feel against hers.

Blake produced a bottle of King's Finest top-shelf bourbon. Something she'd only splurged on for high-end, no-expenses-spared affairs when she'd planned events at the hotel.

"If you're trying to impress me, it won't work." She lowered her voice to a whisper. "I happen to know you get it for free."

"Not the premium stuff. I buy that just like everyone else." He chuckled. "Except for the bottle we give employees every year at Christmas. But I did use my employee discount at the gift shop."

Savannah couldn't help laughing. She honestly didn't want to like Blake or any of the Abbotts. She'd only intended to give the appearance of liking and admiring them. But then, she hadn't expected that Blake would be funny and charming in a self-deprecating way. Or that he'd be sweet and thoughtful.

Blake was all of that wrapped in a handsome package that felt like Christmas and her birthday rolled into one.

*And that smile.*

It should be registered as a panty-obliterating weapon.

"How do you take your bourbon?" Blake set two wide-mouth glasses on the counter.

"Neat." She usually preferred it in an Old Fashioned cocktail. But with the sky lighting up and rumbling around her, drinking bourbon straight, with no fuss or muss, was the quickest way to get a shot of courage into her system.

Before the next lightning strike.

Blake poured them both a fourth of a glass and capped the bottle.

Savannah parted her lips as she tipped the glass, inhaling the scent of buttery vanilla, cherries and a hint of apple. She took a sip, rolling the liquor on her tongue. Savoring its smooth taste.

Light and crisp. Bursting with fruit. A finish that had a slow, spicy burn with a hint of cinnamon, dark cherries and barrel char absorbed during the aging of the bourbon.

Savannah inhaled through both her nose and mouth, allowing the scent and flavors of the twelve-year-old bourbon to permeate her senses. She relished the burn of the liquor sliding down her throat.

"You approve, I take it." Blake sat beside her and sipped his bourbon.

"Worth every cent." She raised her glass.

"My grandfather would be pleased."

Savannah winced at the mention of Joseph Abbott. It was like being doused with a bucket of ice water.

She took another sip of the bourbon that had catapulted King's Finest to success. Their King's Reserve label had quickly become a must-have for the rich and famous.

Her grandfather's recipe.

"I look forward to telling him in person." Savannah smiled slyly as Blake sipped his bourbon. Her grandfather always said liquor loosened lips. She couldn't think of a more suitable way to induce Blake to reveal his family's secrets.

"Up to watching a movie or playing a game of cards? We could play—"

"If you say 'strip poker,' I swear I'll—"

"I was thinking gin rummy." The amusement that danced in his dark eyes made her wonder if the thought hadn't crossed his mind.

"Since you, and the entire town, are hell-bent on getting to know me, I have another idea." She traced the rim of her glass as she studied him. "'Truth or dare?'"

Blake laughed. "I haven't played that since college."

"Neither have I, so this should be fun." She moved to the sofa. Benny sprawled across her feet and rolled over for a belly rub. Savannah happily complied.

Blake studied her as he sipped his bourbon. He still hadn't responded.

"If 'truth or dare?' is too risqué for you, I completely understand." Having satisfied Benny's demands, Savannah crossed one leg over the other, her foot bouncing. Blake's gaze followed the motion, giving her an unexpected sense of satisfaction.

He sat beside her on the couch, and Sam settled at his feet.

"My life is an open book. Makes me fairly invincible at this game." He rubbed Sam's ears.

"A challenge. I like it." The bourbon spread warmth through Savannah's limbs and loosened the tension in her muscles. She was less anxious, despite the intense flashes of light that charged the night sky.

Thunder boomed and both dogs whined. Benny shielded his face with his paw.

Savannah stroked the dog's head. "By all means, you go first, Mr. Invincible. I'll take truth."

A grin lit Blake's dark eyes. "Tell me about your first kiss."

# Nine

Blake had always considered himself a sensible person. Sure, he took risks, but they were usually calculated ones. Risks that would either result in a crash and burn that would teach him one hell of a lesson or pay off in spades.

Sitting on his favorite leather sofa, drinking his granddaddy's finest bourbon and playing "truth or dare?" with the sexiest woman who'd ever donned one of his shirts was the equivalent of playing with fire while wearing a kerosene-soaked flak jacket.

Or in this case, a bourbon-soaked one. They'd both had their share of the nearly empty bottle of bourbon.

Their questions started off innocently enough. His were aimed at getting to know everything there was to know about Savannah Carlisle. Hers mostly dealt with character—his and his family's. But as the game went on—and the bourbon bottle inched closer to empty—their questions grew more intimate.

Too intimate.

Savannah was an employee and he was part owner of King's Finest. He shouldn't be sitting so close to her, well after midnight, when they'd both been drinking. While she was wearing his shirt, her skin smelling of his soap.

Savannah folded her legs underneath her, drawing his eyes to her smooth skin.

They were playing Russian roulette. Only the six-shooter was loaded with five bullets instead of one.

Neither of them was drunk, but they were sure as hell dancing along its blurry edge.

"What's your favorite thing to eat?" he asked.

"Strawberry rhubarb pie. My sister makes it for my birthday every year in lieu of a cake." She grinned. "Your turn. Truth or dare?"

"Truth."

Savannah leaned closer, her gaze holding his, as if she were daring him instead. "Tell me something you really wanted, but you're glad you didn't get."

The question felt like a sword puncturing his chest. His expression must have indicated his discomfort. "Married."

Savannah's cheeks turned crimson and she grimaced. "If it's something you'd rather not talk about—"

"I wanted to surprise my ex with a labradoodle for her birthday." He got the words out quickly before he lost his nerve. "Instead, she surprised me. Told me she'd fallen for someone else, and that it was the best thing for both of us."

"That's awful. I'm sorry."

"I'm not." He rubbed Sam's ears, then took another sip of bourbon, welcoming the warmth. "She was right. It was the best thing for both of us. Marrying her would've been a mistake."

They were both quiet, the storm crackling around them.

He divided the remainder of the bottle between their two glasses and took another pull of his bourbon. "Truth or dare?"

"Truth." Her gaze was soft, apologetic.

"Why'd you *really* come to Magnolia Lake?" It was a question he'd wanted to ask since he'd learned she moved to town prior to being offered the position.

He couldn't shake the feeling there was more to the story than she'd told him that day. Savannah Carlisle was an organized planner. And too sensible a person to move to an area with very few employment options on the hope she'd be hired by them.

"Because I belong at King's Finest." Something resembling anger flashed in her eyes. "It's like I told you—I was compelled by the company's origin story. I want to be part of its future." She shifted on the sofa. "Now you. Truth or dare?"

"Truth." He studied her expression and tried to ignore

the shadow of anger or perhaps pain she was trying desperately to hide.

"If you could be doing anything in the world right now, what would it be?"

*"This."* Blake leaned in and pressed his mouth to hers. Swallowed her little gasp of surprise. Tasted the bourbon on her warm, soft lips.

A soft sigh escaped her mouth and she parted her lips, inviting his tongue inside. It glided along hers as Savannah wrapped her arms around him. She clutched his shirt, pulling him closer.

Blake cradled her face in his hands as he claimed her mouth. He kissed her harder and deeper, his fingers slipping into her soft curls. He'd wanted to do this since he'd first seen the silky strands loose, grazing her shoulders.

He reveled in the sensation of her soft curves pressed against his hard chest and was eager to taste the beaded tips straining against the cotton.

Blake tore his mouth from hers, trailing kisses along her jaw and down her long, graceful neck.

"Blake." She breathed his name.

His shaft, already straining against his zipper, tightened in response. He'd wanted her in his arms, in his bed, nearly since the moment he'd laid eyes on her.

He wanted to rip the orange shirt off. Strip her down to nothing but her bare, freckled skin and a smile. Take her right there on the sofa as the storm raged around them.

But even in the fog of lust that had overtaken him, his bourbon-addled brain knew this was wrong. He shouldn't be kissing Savannah within an inch of her life. Shouldn't be preparing to take her to his bed. Not like this. Not when they were both two glasses of bourbon away from being in a complete haze.

He wouldn't take advantage of her or any woman. His parents had raised him better than that.

Blake pulled away, his chest heaving. "Savannah, I'm sorry. I can't… I mean…we shouldn't—"

"No, of course not." She swiped a hand across her kiss-swollen lips, her eyes not meeting his. She stood abruptly, taking Benny by surprise. "I…uh… Well, thank you for dinner and drinks. I should turn in for the night."

Blake grasped her hand before he could stop himself. "You don't need to go. We were having a good time. I just got carried away."

"Me, too. But that's all the more reason I should go to bed. Besides, it's late." She rushed from the room, tossing a good-night over her shoulder.

"Benny, stay," Blake called to the dog, who whimpered as Savannah closed the door softly behind her. "Come." The dog trotted over and Blake petted his head. "Give her some space, okay, boy?"

The dog clearly didn't agree with his approach to the situation. Neither did certain parts of Blake's anatomy.

"Way to go," he whispered beneath his breath as he moved about the room, gathering the glasses and the empty bottle.

*I shouldn't have kissed her. Or brought her here. Or given her that damn shirt to wear.*

He could list countless mistakes he'd made that evening. Missteps that had inevitably led them to the moment when his mouth had crashed against hers. When he'd stopped fighting temptation.

Blake shouldn't have kissed her, but he wished like hell that he hadn't stopped kissing her. That Savannah Carlisle was lying in bed next to him right now.

Sam's howl and Benny's incessant barking woke Blake from his fitful sleep at nearly three in the morning.

"What the hell, guys? Some of us are trying to sleep." Blake rolled over and pulled the pillow over his head.

A clap of thunder rattled the windows and the dogs intensified their howls of distress.

Benny hated thunderstorms, but Sam usually remained pretty calm. Blake sat up in bed and rubbed his eyes, allowing them to adjust to the darkness.

"Guys, calm down!" he shouted.

Benny stopped barking, but he whimpered, bumping his nose against the closed door.

Blake strained to listen for what might be bothering the dogs. Maybe Savannah had gone to the kitchen.

He got out of bed, his boxers sitting low on his hips, and cracked open his bedroom door.

No lights. No footsteps. No running water. Aside from the storm and the rain beating against the house, everything was quiet.

"No! No! Please! You have to save them."

"Savannah?" Blake ran toward her room at the other end of the hall. He banged on the guest bedroom door. "It's me—Blake. Are you okay?"

There was no response. Only mumbling and whimpering.

"Savannah, honey, I'm coming in."

He tried the knob, but the door was locked. He searched over the door frame for the emergency key left by his brother's building crew.

Blake snatched down the hex key, glad he hadn't gotten around to removing it. He fiddled with the lock before it finally clicked and the knob turned.

He turned on the light and scanned the room.

Savannah was thrashing in the bed, her eyes screwed shut, tears leaking from them.

"Savannah, honey, you're okay." He touched her arm gently, afraid of frightening her. "You're right here with me. And you're perfectly fine."

"Blake?" Her eyes shot open and she sat up quickly, nearly head-butting him. She flattened her back against the headboard. "What are you doing here?" She looked around, as if piecing everything together. "In my room."

"You were having a bad dream. The dogs went nuts. So did I." He sat on the edge of the bed, his heart still racing from the jog to her room. "I thought you were hurt."

Her voice broke and her breathing was ragged. "Sorry I woke you, but I'm fine."

"No, you're not. Your hands are shaking, and you're pale."

"Thank you for checking on me." She wiped at the corners of her eyes. "I didn't intend to be so much trouble tonight."

"I'm glad you're here." Blake lifted her chin so their eyes met. "I'd hate to think of what might've happened if you'd been out there alone on that road tonight. Or home alone in this storm." He dropped his hand from her face. "Do you always have these nightmares during a storm?"

"Not in a really long time." She tucked her hair behind her ear. "Talking about what happened that night probably triggered it." Savannah pressed a hand to her forehead.

"I shouldn't have pushed you to talk about your family. I just wanted to…" Blake sighed, rubbing Benny's ears.

"What were you going to say?" For the first time since he'd entered the room, her hands weren't trembling. Instead of being preoccupied with the storm, she was focused on him.

"There's this deep sadness behind those brown eyes."

Savannah dropped her gaze from his.

"You try to mask it by throwing yourself into your work. And you ward off anyone who gets too close with that biting wit. But it's there. Even when you laugh."

"Let's say you're right." She met his gaze. "Why do you care? I'm just another employee."

"I would think that kiss earlier proved otherwise."

"So what…are you my self-appointed guardian angel?" Savannah frowned.

"If that's what you need." He shrugged.

Silence stretched between them. Conflicting emotions played out on her face. There was something she was hesitant to say.

Blake recognized her turmoil. He'd been struggling with it all night. Wanting her, but knowing he shouldn't. He struggled with it even now.

"Thank you, for everything, Blake. For coming to check on me." She scanned his bare chest.

Blake was suddenly conscious that he was sitting on her bed. In nothing but his underwear.

Good thing he wore boxers.

"Sorry. You sounded like you were in distress, so I bolted down here after Benny woke me up."

Savannah turned her attention to Benny's wide brown eyes and smiled for the first time since Blake had entered the room. She kissed the top of the dog's furry head.

"Were you worried about me, boy?" She laughed when Benny wagged his tail in response.

Blake chuckled softly. Benny was a sociable dog, but he'd never been as taken with anyone as he seemed to be with Savannah.

"You've earned at least one fan here." Blake's face grew hot when Savannah's gaze met his.

"Thank you both." She gave Benny one last kiss on his snout. "I won't keep you two up any longer. Good night."

"Good night." Blake turned out the light.

Savannah flinched in response to the lightning that flashed outside the window.

"Look, why don't Benny and I sleep in here tonight?"

"With me?" The pitch of her voice rose and her eyes widened.

"I'll sleep in the chair by the window."

She scanned the chair, then his large frame. "I don't think you'd be very comfortable contorting yourself into that little chair all night. Don't worry about me. Seriously, I'll be fine."

A bolt of lightning flashed through the sky, followed by a loud cracking sound.

Savannah screamed and Benny whimpered and howled, hiding underneath the bed.

"It's all right." Blake put a hand on Savannah's trembling shoulder. He went to the window and surveyed the property.

Lightning had hit a tree just outside the bedroom window. A huge section had split off. The bark was charred, but the tree wasn't on fire.

Blake turned back to Savannah. Her eyes were filled with tears, and she was shaking.

"It's okay." He sat beside her on the bed. "There was no real damage, and no one was hurt."

Blake wrapped an arm around her shoulders. He pulled her to his chest, tucked her head beneath his chin and rocked her in his arms when she wouldn't stop crying.

"You're fine, honey. Nothing's going to happen to you, I promise."

"What if I want something to happen?" She lifted her head. Her eyes met his, and suddenly he was very conscious of the position of her hand on his bare chest.

The backs of her fingertips brushed lightly over his right nipple. "What if I want to finish what we started earlier?"

Electricity skittered along his skin and the muscles low in his abdomen tensed as his shaft tightened.

He let out a low groan, wishing he could just comply with her request and give in to their desire. He cradled her face in his hand.

"Honey, you're just scared. Fear makes us do crazy things."

"Wanting to sleep with you is crazy?" She frowned.

"No, but getting into a relationship with a member of the management team is ill-advised."

"I'm not talking about a relationship." She seemed perturbed by the suggestion. "I'm just talking about sex. We're adults, and it's what we both obviously want. I'm not looking for anything more with you."

He grimaced at the indication that it was him specifically she didn't want more with. For once in his life, he longed for a good *It's not you, it's me.*

"That won't work for me." He sighed heavily. "Not with you."

They were way past the possibility of meaningless sex. He felt something for her. Something he hadn't allowed himself to feel in so long.

"Why not with me? I'm here, and I'm willing." She indicated his noticeable erection. "And unless you're hiding a gun in your boxers, it's what you want, too."

"Savannah…" Blake gripped her wrists, holding her hands away from his body. "You aren't making this easy for me."

"I thought I was." She grabbed the hem of the shirt and tugged it over her head, baring her perfect breasts. The brown peaks were stiff. Begging for his mouth. Her eyes twinkled. "Can't get much easier than this."

Blake's heart raced as the storm raged around them. He wanted to take the high road. But right now, it wasn't his moral compass that was pointing north.

Blake tightened his grip on Savannah's neck and something about it sent a thrill down her spine. Her core pulsed like her heartbeat.

The cool air tightened the beaded tips of her breasts. His gaze drifted from the hardened peaks back to her.

"You're scared. You've been drinking. You're not thinking clearly right now. Neither am I."

"We slept off the bourbon hours ago," she reminded him, pressing a kiss to his jaw. His body stiffened in response. "Besides, you kissed me last night." She kissed his neck, then whispered in his ear, "And don't pretend you haven't thought about us being together before tonight."

Savannah relished Blake's sharp intake of breath when she nipped at his neck. She wanted his strong, rough hands to caress her skin. And she longed to trail her hands over the hard muscles that rippled beneath his brown skin.

Adrenaline rushed through her veins, her body hummed with energy and her brain buzzed with all of the reasons she shouldn't be here doing this.

Just for tonight, she wanted to let go of her fear and allow herself the thing she wanted so badly.

Blake Abbott.

Sleeping with him would complicate her plans, but weren't things between them complicated anyway? Whether they slept together tonight or not, things would never be the same between them.

Maybe she didn't want them to be.

If it turned out her grandfather was confused about what had transpired all those years ago, she need never tell Blake why she'd really come to Magnolia Lake. And if her grandfather was right...and Blake's family had used him cruelly... why should she feel the slightest ounce of guilt? The Abbotts certainly hadn't.

Either way, she wanted him. And she had no intention of taking no for an answer when it was clear he wanted her, too.

Savannah wriggled her wrists free from Blake's loose grip. She looped her arms around his neck, her eyes drifting shut, and kissed him.

Blake hesitated at first, but then he kissed her back. He held her in his arms, his fingertips pressed to her back.

The hair on his chest scraped against her sensitive nipples. She parted her lips and Blake slipped his tongue between them, gliding it along hers.

Savannah relished the strangled moan that escaped his mouth. The way it vibrated in her throat. That small sound made her feel in control in a moment when she'd normally have felt so powerless.

As helpless as she'd felt when she'd watched the building burn. Unable to save her parents.

Her parents. Her grandfather. Laney.

What would they think of what she was doing right now? Giving herself to the grandson of the man who had taken everything from them?

Savannah's heart pounded in her chest as she tried to push the disquieting thoughts from her head.

They wouldn't understand, but she did. She wasn't giving herself to Blake Abbott. She was taking what she wanted... what she needed...from him.

She'd gotten lost in her thoughts. Blake was the one driving the kiss now. Both of them murmured with pleasure as his tongue danced with hers. Then he laid her back and deepened the kiss.

Savannah glided her hands down Blake's back and gripped his firm, muscular bottom.

His length hardened against her belly and he groaned, his mouth moving against hers.

Savannah kept her eyes shut, blocking out the lightning that periodically illuminated the room, and the thunder that made poor Benny whimper. Instead, she focused on the beating of her own heart. The insistent throb and dampness between her thighs.

Savannah couldn't control what was happening outside. But she could control this. How he felt. How he made her feel.

Powerful. Alive. In control.

She slipped a hand beneath his waistband and wrapped her fingers around the width of his thick shaft. Blake moaned against her open mouth, intensifying the heat spreading through her limbs. She circled the head with her thumb, spreading the wetness she found there, relishing the way his breathing became harder and faster in response.

He grabbed her wrist, halting her movement as she glided her fist up and down his erection.

"Neither of us is ready for what happens next if you keep doing that, sweetheart." His voice was low and gruff.

"Then we should stop wasting time and get down to business."

Blake shooed the dogs from the room and locked the door behind them before returning to bed. He cradled her cheek.

"Savannah, you know I want you. But I don't want you to do this for the wrong reasons."

"Does it matter why?"

"Yeah, baby. In this case, it does." He swept her hair from her face. "Because this isn't a typical one-night stand for me."

"Why not? I'm sure you've done this lots of times before." She tried to rein in her frustration. In her limited experience, it had never been this difficult to get a guy to have sex with her.

"Not with someone who works for me."

*Suddenly an Abbott is worried about being ethical?*

"It'll be our little secret. And it'll be just this once." She hated that an Abbott had reduced her to groveling.

"I can't promise that, because I'm already addicted to your kiss." He kissed her mouth. "Your taste." He ran his tongue along the seam of her lips. "And if I get more…and make no mistake about this—I do want more…there is the definite risk of becoming addicted to having you in my bed."

It was the sweetest, sexiest thing any man had ever said to her.

She wanted to hear more of it while Blake Abbott moved inside her, making her forget her worries and fears and replacing the tragic memory associated with thunderstorms with a pleasurable one.

"I can't promise what's going to happen tomorrow." She kissed him again, trying to convince him to let go of his worries, too. "I can only tell you that this is what I want.

It isn't the liquor or my fear talking. It's me. I want you. Period."

His body tensed, and his eyes studied hers there in the dark. Then he claimed her mouth in a kiss that shot fireworks down her spine, exploding in her belly. Her core throbbed with a desire so intense she ached with the emptiness between her thighs.

An emptiness only he could fill.

Blake trailed kisses down her neck and ran his rough tongue over one sensitive nipple. He gripped the flesh there and sucked the hardened nub. Softly at first, then harder. She moaned as he licked and sucked, the sensation tugging at her core.

"Oh, Blake. Yes." She arched her back, giving him better access. His eyes met hers and he smiled briefly before moving on to the other hardened peak, making it as swollen and distended as its counterpart.

He trailed kisses down her belly and along the edge of the waistband of her panties. Suddenly, he pulled aside the fabric soaked with her desire for him and tasted her there.

Gripping a handful of his short, dark curls, Savannah gasped and called out his name. She spread her thighs, allowing her knees to fall open and providing Blake with better access to her swollen folds and the hardened bundle of nerves he was assaulting with that heavenly tongue.

He reached up, pinching one of her nipples as she rode his tongue. Every muscle in her body tightened as a wave of pleasure rolled through her hard and fast.

She was shivering and trembling again. This time, it wasn't because of the storm. It was because Blake Abbott had given her an orgasm that had struck her like a lightning bolt.

And left her wanting more.

# Ten

Blake groaned as the sunlight filtered through the window of the guest bedroom. He peeked one eye open and lifted his arm, which had been draped across Savannah as she slept. He looked at his watch.

It was well after seven. Normally he would've worked out and walked the dogs by now. He was surprised Sam and Benny weren't already...

His thoughts were interrupted by Benny's moaning and scratching at the door.

Savannah sighed softly, her naked bottom nestled against the morning wood he was sporting.

Hell, his erection had probably never gone away after his night with Savannah. A night in which he'd brought her to pleasure with his mouth and fingers so many times that her throat was probably raw from calling his name.

He hadn't made love to her, and he hadn't allowed her to give him so much as a good hand job. A decision his body—strung tight as a piano wire—bemoaned. But he had to be sure her head was in the right place. That she wasn't just acting out of fear.

Blake sucked in a deep breath, inhaling the scent of her hair. He wanted to run his fingers through the silky curls again, brush her hair back so he could see her lovely face.

But he didn't want to wake her. He wasn't ready to burst the bubble they'd been floating in.

He couldn't bear for her to wake and regret their night together. A night he didn't regret in the least.

Blake slipped out of the room, got dressed, fed the dogs and took them for their usual walk, avoiding all the water-logged areas. He surveyed the damage to his property and the neighborhood. There were a few downed branches and lots of upended lawn furniture. A tree had fallen through one neighbor's roof. Shingles littered their front lawn, and a yellow tarp, draped over the roof, billowed in the wind.

But for Blake, the storm hadn't been a bad thing. It'd brought Savannah to his home and into his bed.

Blake hoped she hadn't been serious about making this a one-off. He liked her. A lot.

Dating Savannah would ruffle his family's feathers. He wouldn't tell them right away. Not until he knew whether this was serious. If it was, he'd just have to deal with the consequences of breaking their unwritten rule.

Blake opened the side garage door and let the dogs in, wiping their muddy paws on a rag. As they went back into the house, he paused to listen.

The house was silent. Savannah was evidently still sleeping. He washed his hands and checked the kitchen for breakfast food. He cursed under his breath for putting off grocery shopping.

Every Southerner knew you stocked up on basic goods when there was an impending storm of any kind.

Luckily, there were his mother's and sister's refrigerators to raid. Both of them kept their pantries and deep freezers well stocked. His mother's deep freezer likely contained a side of beef and enough chicken to feed the entire company. Zora's would be filled with frozen meals and store-bought goodies.

Right now, he'd settle for either. But since Zora lived closest, he'd start with her.

"You two be good." He patted Sam's and Benny's heads. "I'll be back before you know it. And don't bother Savannah. She's sleeping." He headed back toward the garage. "That means you, Benny."

Benny whimpered, dropping on the floor in the corner and resting his head on his paws.

Blake hopped in his truck and drove the five minutes to

his sister's home on the other side of the lake. She was outside gathering broken tree limbs.

"If you came to help, you're too late. I'm just about done here." Zora stepped on a long branch, snapping it in two. Then she snapped each piece in half again.

Blake hugged his sister. It didn't surprise him that she hadn't asked for assistance. Since she was a kid, Zora had been determined to prove her independence.

"Well, since you've already got everything under control, maybe you can help me out. I don't have anything for breakfast back at the house. I was gonna go grocery shopping this weekend but the bridge is out." He shoved his hands in his pockets, hoping to avoid his sister's usual forty questions.

Zora stopped breaking branches and eyed him. "Why don't you fix breakfast here for both of us?"

"Because."

"I'm not twelve, Blake. That doesn't work anymore." Zora propped a hand on her hip.

Blake sighed. "Okay, fine. I have company."

Zora stepped closer. "Female company?"

Blake tried to keep his expression neutral.

"You don't have women over to the house. Ever. Not since you broke up with Godzilla."

"Gavrilla." But he didn't correct the part about him initiating the breakup. They both knew it wasn't true, but saying it seemed to make his family feel better.

"Whatever." She waved her hand. "This must be serious if you brought one of your out-of-town hookups home."

"How did you—"

"I didn't, but I always suspected that's why you never take Daisy when you travel." Zora looked more proud of herself than she had when her team had posted record sales numbers the previous quarter.

"Don't you have anything better to do than to worry about who I'm sleeping with?"

"People around here talk. If they're not talking, nothing's

happening. I haven't heard about you hooking up with any-one around here and...well...you are a guy."

"Zora, *enough*."

He was *not* going to have a conversation with his sister about his sex life. Though Zora was an adult, she'd always be his baby sister.

"I can't help it if I'm smarter than you." She shoved him playfully.

"You're the Jessica Fletcher of who is doing who in this town. Congratulations, Brat." He dug up her childhood nick-name. "Now, can we get back to my request?"

"Right. You need to shop my pantry."

Zora removed her work gloves and headed toward the ga-rage of her colonial. The place was newer than his, though a bit smaller and far more traditional-looking.

"Let's find something you and your girlfriend can eat for breakfast."

"Didn't say she was my girlfriend." Blake gritted his teeth.

Zora turned to him. "She woke up at your house, presum-ably in your bed. Just let that sink in for a minute."

"I'm seriously starting to wish I'd gone to Mom and Dad's house. Besides, they have real food. Not just crap that comes out of a box."

"That hurts." Zora punched his arm. "Besides, that's no way to talk to someone you want a favor from, big brother."

Zora opened her well-stocked fridge. She cut an egg car-ton in half and gave him half a dozen eggs. Then she took out a mostly full package of thick-cut maple bacon and an unopened jug of orange juice. She arranged everything in a reusable shopping bag.

"Please tell me you at least have the basics...cheese, milk, maybe an onion and some mushrooms."

"I'm the one who actually cooks for myself," Blake re-minded her. "But I think I used my last onion making fried rice last night."

"You cooked dinner for her, too?" Zora's eyes lit up like a Christmas tree that had just been plugged in. "After you left Mom and Dad's last night?"

Ignoring her question, Blake accepted two sweet onions from his sister and dropped them in the bag, careful not to crack the eggs. "Thanks, Brat."

"You're not even going to give me a hint who I'm feeding?" She leaned one hip against the fridge.

"I don't kiss and tell." He hoisted the bag. "And I didn't sleep with her."

"Then why won't you tell me who it is?"

"Because it's none of your business."

"Speaking of business...your mystery guest wouldn't happen to be a certain not-so-Chatty-Cathy employee who you can't seem to keep your eyes off, would it?"

Blake froze momentarily, but recovered quickly. Zora was fishing, hoping to get a reaction out of him. If he played it cool, she'd move on to another theory.

"Thanks for the food," he called over his shoulder. "Holler if you need help with the yard."

"Only if you'll bring your girlfriend over."

Blake shook his head and climbed back in his truck.

*Brat.*

He waved and backed out of his sister's drive. As he headed toward home, his neck tensed in anticipation of seeing Savannah.

Savannah's eyes fluttered open. She was floating on a warm cloud of indescribable bliss, and her entire body tingled with satisfaction. Her mouth stretched in an involuntary smile.

Last night, Blake had given her mind-blowing pleasure, and he'd done it without removing his boxers.

He'd focused on making their encounter special for her. Even if it meant denying himself.

No one had ever given her such intense pleasure or focused solely on her needs. Savannah groaned. She'd finally met a man who made her want *things*. Things she hadn't allowed herself the luxury of wanting.

*God, why does he have to be an Abbott?*

Because apparently the universe hated her.

As she'd given in to her desire for him, she'd convinced herself she could remain detached and keep their encounter impersonal. Transactional.

But when he looked into her eyes, all she'd seen was Blake. Not his family versus hers. Not the history of their grandfathers. Nothing but him.

For a few hours, she'd allowed herself to buy into the delusion that she could have him and still get justice for her family.

But she couldn't have both. At some point, she'd have to choose. And her allegiance was to her own family.

Savannah sighed and rolled over. Blake wasn't in bed. She got dressed and went down to the kitchen.

*No Blake.*

She walked through the house, calling him without response. His truck wasn't in the garage. When she returned to the kitchen, she saw his note.

*Gone to rustle us up some breakfast.*

She couldn't help smiling. *Smart-ass.*

Why couldn't he stop being funny and thoughtful and all-around adorable? He was making it difficult to focus on her mission. Which was the only thing that mattered.

She was alone in Blake Abbott's house. She'd never get a better opportunity to see if there was anything there that could shed light on what had happened between their grandfathers.

She went to Blake's office. The door was unlocked, but the moment she opened it, the dogs ran down the hall and greeted her.

Savannah shut the door and stooped in front of the dogs, petting them and giving Benny a peck on his nose.

"Stay here. I just need to take a quick peek." Savannah slipped inside, shutting the door behind her. The dogs yipped in protest.

A loud thump nearly made her jump out of her skin. One of the dogs had jumped against the door.

*Benny.* The thud was too heavy to be Sam.

She glanced around. The neat, organized room was flooded with sunlight.

She had no idea how long it would be before his return. There was no time to waste.

Savannah searched the bookshelves. She looked through drawers and scanned files for anything related to the company's origin. She sifted through his desk drawers, hoping to find something...anything.

There was nothing out of the ordinary.

She spotted his laptop. The same one he used at work.

Frustrated, Savannah sat down at the large oak desk and groaned. She bumped the mouse and the screen woke.

It was unlocked.

He'd obviously used it that morning and hadn't been gone long. Savannah rummaged through the computer directories. All she found were the same files she accessed at work.

Savannah pulled open the desk drawer again and lifted the organizer tray. A photo of Blake, Sam and a woman was wedged in back.

*The ex.*

She was pretty, but something about her didn't feel real.

*Hypocrite.*

She was under Blake's roof, sleeping in his bed and trying to stage a coup at his family's company.

At least his ex had been up-front with her treachery.

Guilt gnawed at Savannah's gut. She replaced the photo and then put the drawer back in order.

There were few personal photos elsewhere in the house,

but the office walls and shelves were filled with family pictures and photos of King's Finest employees—many of whom had worked for the Abbotts for decades.

Savannah was struck with deep, painful longing for her own family. The parents she'd never see again. The ailing grandfather who'd raised her. Her sister and young niece. They were the reasons she was doing this.

She had no desire to hurt Blake, but this was war. And in war, there were always casualties.

Her family hadn't started it. But she sure as hell would finish it.

Even if it meant hurting Blake.

She was a spy working on the side of right. Sometimes trickery and deceit were required. And sometimes people got hurt. Good people. People you liked. But wasn't getting justice for her family more important than hurting Blake Abbott's pride?

He was a big boy. He'd get over it. Just as he'd gotten over his ex.

Or had he?

Savannah glanced at the drawer where the woman's photo was hidden.

She sighed softly. He'd never forgive her once he learned that she was the granddaughter of his grandfather's enemy.

But maybe he'd eventually understand.

Joseph Abbott hadn't given her a choice. This was what she had to do, even if what she really wanted now was Blake Abbott.

The garage door creaked. Savannah peeked through the window. Blake's big black pickup truck was approaching.

Savannah made a quick sweep of the room, ensuring everything was as she'd found it. She hurried into the hall past the dogs.

"Stay." She held up a hand when they tried to follow her. Benny's paw prints were all over the door, but there was no time to clean them.

Savannah hurried upstairs and got into the shower. She pressed her back against the cool tiles and reminded herself she'd done what she had to do.

So why was her chest heavy with guilt? And why did her eyes sting with tears?

Because she couldn't stop wishing last night had been real and that she could have Blake Abbott for herself.

# Eleven

Their tails wagging, Sam and Benny ambushed Blake when he stepped through the garage door.

"Calm down, you two." Blake set the grocery bag on the counter and unloaded it.

The house was quiet, but the note he'd left for Savannah had been moved, so she'd been downstairs.

Blake put the bacon in the oven and set up an impromptu omelet bar. When the bacon was done, he grabbed another shirt for Savannah and headed toward the guest room. The room where he'd awakened with her in his arms.

He knocked on the door. "Savannah, you up?"

She opened the door wearing a bath towel wrapped around her curvy frame. Her hair was wrapped in another. "Sorry. I just hopped out of the shower."

"Then you'll be needing this." He handed her another shirt, this one a gray short-sleeve T-shirt.

"Thanks." She clutched the garment to her chest. "That was thoughtful of you."

"Breakfast is set." He shoved his hands into his pockets, feeling awkward, as if they were strangers who hadn't been intimate the night before. "Hope you like omelets and bacon."

"I love them." Her smile was polite. Distant. "Be down in a sec."

"Okay then." Blake rubbed the back of his neck. He wasn't sure where things stood between them, but their awkward morning-after conversation didn't bode well.

He jogged down the steps and paused, head tilted, noticing paw marks on the office door. He obviously hadn't done a thorough job of cleaning Benny after their walk.

Blake grabbed a rag and some wood cleaner and wiped

the door down. Then he cleaned Benny's paws again and tossed the rags into the laundry room.

Why was Benny trying to get into the office?

He wouldn't unless someone was in there. The muddy prints weren't on the door when Blake left. That meant Savannah had been inside.

But why?

Blake returned to his office. Everything was exactly as it had been that morning. Still, she'd been there. He was sure of it.

He returned to the kitchen and cut up some fruit, his mind turning.

"Smells delicious." Savannah stood at the entrance of the kitchen with Sam and Benny at her feet.

Traitors.

They dropped him like a bad habit whenever Savannah was around, Benny more so than Sam.

"Thanks. I made bacon, set up an omelet bar and made a fruit salad." Blake poured himself a glass of orange juice. He lifted the container. "Juice?"

"Please." She sat at the breakfast bar. "But let me make the omelets. I insist."

"The stove is all yours." He handed her a glass.

Savannah sipped her juice, then melted butter in a pan and sautéed vegetables.

"I hope you were able to get some sleep," Blake said finally. He wanted to ask why she'd been in his office.

"Didn't get much sleep." She flashed a shy smile. "But I certainly have no complaints."

"Glad to hear it." The tension in Blake's shoulders eased. He parked himself on a stool.

"One other thing…" Savannah pulled an ink pen from the breast pocket of her T-shirt and handed it to him. "I borrowed a pen from your office. Hope you don't mind."

"Of course not." Blake breathed a sigh of relief. Savannah did have an innocent reason for being in his office. It was good he hadn't accused her of snooping. "Glad you found what you were looking for."

He tapped a finger on the counter after an awkward silence fell over them. "About what happened last night," he began.

Her posture stiffened. She didn't turn around. "What about last night?"

"It was amazing."

"For me, too. Believe me." Savannah's cheeks were flushed but she seemed relieved. She moved to the counter and cracked eggs into a bowl.

"I like you, Savannah. I have since the day you walked into my office and called bullshit on me for trying to reschedule your interview."

She looked at him briefly and smiled before washing her hands at the sink with her back to him. "But?"

"But I shouldn't have kissed you or let things get as far as they did."

She turned off the pan with the vegetables, then heated butter in another pan.

"I get it. I work for your family. Last night was my fault. You tried to show restraint. I should apologize to you." She glanced over her shoulder at him. "It won't happen again."

"That's the thing." Blake stood, shoving his hands into his jean pockets. "I don't want it to be over. I don't think you do, either."

Savannah turned to him slowly. She worried her lower lip with her teeth.

"It doesn't matter what we want. You're an Abbott, and I'm…" She sighed. There was something she wouldn't allow herself to say. "I'm your subordinate. If anyone knew about what happened last night…it wouldn't look very good for either of us."

She wasn't wrong.

Blake groaned, leaning against the counter. "I've never been in this position before."

"You've never been attracted to one of your employees before?" she asked incredulously.

"Not enough to risk it."

Her teasing expression turned more serious. She returned to her task. "You're worried I'll kiss and tell, like everyone else in this gossipy little town."

"That isn't it at all."

"Then there's no problem. Once the bridge opens, you'll take me back to my car and we'll pretend this never happened."

Blake wanted to object. But Savannah was right. It would be best if they pretended last night never happened.

But that was the last thing he wanted to do.

"Thanks for breakfast," Savannah said as she ate the final bite of her omelet. "Everything was delicious."

They'd endured the awkward meal, both acting as if walking away from each other was no big deal. The heaviness in the air between them indicated otherwise.

"Your omelet especially." Blake gathered their plates and took them to the sink. "Good thing I raided my sister's refrigerator."

"You told Zora I was here?"

"Of course not." He turned to scrape the plates. "She hinted that she thought it was you, but she was just fishing. Trust me."

Savannah joined him at the sink. "What did she say *exactly*?"

"I don't recall her exact words."

Savannah was supposed to be a fly on the wall. Working in the background, hardly noticed. Now she had the full attention of Blake and she'd be on Zora's radar, too.

And if Zora suspected, did that mean she'd already told the rest of his family?

"But your sister asked specifically if it was me you were entertaining for breakfast?"

"She didn't mention your name. And if she had any real reason to believe it was you, she would've told me. There's nothing to worry about."

"Maybe for you. Your family won't fire you over this."

"No one is getting fired. I promise." He dried his hands on a towel and gripped Savannah's shoulders. "Look at me."

She did, reluctantly.

"I'd never let you get fired because of me. Trust me. All right?"

Savannah nodded, her breath coming in quick, short bursts. She'd come so far, and she was so close. She wouldn't let anything derail her plans—not even Blake Abbott.

"When do you think I'll be able to leave?"

"Got a weather alert on my phone." Blake pulled it out of his pocket. "The bridge is still closed. According to the alert, it'll be a couple of days. My dad already emailed us to say that if the bridge isn't open by tomorrow, the plant will be closed on Monday."

"I can't stay here all weekend."

"You don't really have a choice." He held her hand. His voice was quiet and calm.

"I don't want to complicate things for either of us."

"And I don't want you to leave." Blake lifted her chin. He dragged a thumb across her lower lip, his gaze locked with hers.

"I don't want to, either." The truth of her admission shocked her. They weren't just words, and she wasn't simply playing a role. "But we've discussed all the reasons I should."

"I know." He stepped closer. His clean, masculine scent surrounded her. "But I don't care."

"I do." She stepped beyond his reach. "And one of us needs to be the adult here."

"You walking away right now won't resolve our feelings for each other."

"What do you expect me to say, Blake?"

"Say you'll stay. That you'll spend another night in my bed." He slipped his arms around her waist and hauled her against him. "This time, I know you're making the decision with a clear head. So I won't hold back."

Her belly fluttered and her knees were so weak she could barely stand. She held on to him. Got lost in those dark eyes.

"Say it." Blake pressed a gentle kiss to one edge of her mouth, then the other. Then he kissed the space where her neck and shoulder met. "Say you'll stay."

Savannah wanted Blake so badly she ached with it. Despite who his family was. Despite what she'd come there to do.

Blake Abbott was the last man in the world she should want. Yet she'd never wanted anyone more.

"Yes." Her response was a whisper.

"Yes, what?" His gaze followed his hand as it trailed down her arm.

Her skin tingled wherever he touched it. "Yes, I'll stay with you."

"Where?"

It wasn't a question. It was a demand issued in a low growl that caused a trembling in her core. Her knees wavered slightly.

"In your bed." Her eyes met his.

Blake's pull was as strong as the earth's gravity. She was too close to escape its effects. And she wouldn't want to, even if she could.

He grinned. "Good girl."

Even as she gave in to him, she needed to prove she wasn't a pushover. "But I'll only stay until—"

He covered her mouth with his, swallowing her objection as if it were a morsel that had been offered to him. Blake tugged her hard against him as he laid claim to her mouth.

Savannah gasped at the sensation of his erection pressed to her belly. She had zero willpower where this man was concerned. The dampness between her thighs and hardening of her nipples were evidence of that.

Blake tugged the T-shirt up over her hips, planted his large hands on her waist and set her on the cold quartz countertop. She shivered in response. He stepped between her legs, spreading them. Blake stripped off her shirt and dispensed with her bra. He assessed her with his heated gaze.

"Beautiful," he murmured.

He'd seen her naked the night before. So why did she feel so exposed? As if she was standing on a stage naked?

He surveyed her full breasts and tight, sensitive nipples that were hungry for his mouth, his touch. Her belly knotted and electricity skipped along her spine, ending in a steady pulse between her thighs.

Blake stepped as close as the countertop would allow him. He kissed her neck and gently nipped the skin, as if marking his territory.

He palmed the heavy mounds. Sucked a beaded tip into his warm mouth.

A soft gasp escaped her lips. She slipped her fingers into his short, dark curls as he sucked, then laved the hypersensitive nub with his rough tongue.

Her mind flashed back to how delicious it had felt to have that tongue attending to more sensitive areas of her body. How it had felt inside her.

"Blake, please." She hardly recognized her own voice as she made the urgent plea for him to relieve the deep ache between her thighs. "I want you."

He trailed kisses down her belly as he laid her back on the cool surface. "Don't worry, babe. I know exactly what you want."

Blake slid her back on the counter and pulled her legs up so that her heels pressed against the countertop. Starting inside her knee, he kissed his way down her inner thigh to her panties.

He tugged the damp fabric to one side and kissed the

slick, swollen flesh. Each kiss sent her soaring higher, making her want him more. In any way he wanted to take her.

She arched her back, lifting her hips off the cool quartz. Blake cupped her bottom and sucked on her distended clit, bringing her close to the edge. Then he backed off, lavishing the surrounding flesh with slow, deliberate licks before sucking on it again.

Savannah was falling. Hurtling toward her release. She covered her mouth and tried to hold back the scream building in her throat.

"No." He lifted his head, leaving her aching for his mouth. His hooded gaze locked with hers. "Don't hold back. Whatever you're feeling… I want to hear it. Every murmur. Every scream."

He slowly licked the swollen flesh again, his tongue moving in a circular motion, hitting everywhere but where she needed him most.

Teasing her.

"Understand?" His eyes met hers again.

She nodded. "Yes."

He went back to sucking on her slick bud. She trembled, bucking her hips and clutching his hair.

She let go of embarrassment and fear. Of her worries about what would happen next. Instead, she floated on the sea of bliss surrounding her.

She let go of every moan. Every curse.

Until she couldn't hold back the river of pleasure that flooded her senses, shattering any remaining control.

She called his name. Her back arched as she rode his tongue until she'd shattered into a million tiny, glittering pieces.

Savannah lay there afterward, her breathing rapid and shallow. Her chest heaving. Feeling both satisfied and desperate for more.

Blake placed delicate kisses on her sensitive flesh. Each kiss caused another explosion of sensation.

He kissed his way up her belly and through the valley between her rising and falling breasts, as he pulled her into a seated position. His eyes met hers momentarily, as if seeking permission. Then he pressed a kiss to her open mouth. The taste of her was on his tongue.

Blake lifted her from the counter and led her up the stairs and to the opposite end of the hall.

His bedroom.

The decor was rustic, but elegant, in keeping with the style of the house. A king-size bed dominated the space. Large windows flooded the room with light and provided a nearly unobstructed view of the lake and the mountains in the distance.

Before Savannah could admire the space, he'd taken her in his arms and kissed her again. His tongue delved into her mouth. His hands drifted over her body. Her hands explored his body, too, and traced the thick ridge beneath his jeans.

Savannah loosened his belt, eager to touch the silky head of his velvety shaft again. She slipped her hand inside his pants, gripping the warm, veiny flesh. He grunted and shuddered at her touch before breaking their kiss.

Blake turned her around abruptly and nestled her bottom tight against him. His groan of pleasure elicited a sigh from her.

Pinning her in place with one strong forearm slung low across her stomach, Blake kissed her neck and shoulder. He glided the backs of his fingers up and down her side. The featherlight touch made her knees shake. Her sex pulsed with need.

Had the few men she'd been with before been doing it all wrong?

Blake hadn't entered her. Yet he'd found countless ways to bring her such intense pleasure she wanted to give him everything.

All of her.

He slid his fingers into the hair at the nape of her neck,

turning her head. His mouth crashed into hers. She gasped when Blake grazed one painfully hard nipple with his palm.

The contact was so slight. A whisper against her skin. But it made her want to drop to her knees and beg for more.

She considered doing just that, but Blake pinched her nipple, sending a bolt of pleasure to her core. She cried out, though she wasn't sure if it was from the pain or the pleasure.

He toyed with her nipple—so sensitive she could barely stand it. Then he glided his hand down her belly, dipping it beneath her waistband.

She gasped against his hungry mouth when he slipped two fingers through her wetness. He massaged the sensitive, swollen flesh, avoiding her needy clit.

Savannah moaned, moving against his hand. He swallowed her cries, intensified them with his movements.

His long fingers drifted from the back of her neck and lightly gripped her throat. Not enough to cause constriction or bruising. Just enough to let her know he was in control.

There was something about his grip there that was primal and erotic. A surprising turn-on that brought her closer to the edge.

"You like that, don't you?" His warm lips brushed her ear as he whispered into it, his voice tinged with deep satisfaction. "I knew you would."

"Blake, please, I'm so close." Her words were clipped, her tone breathy.

He used four fingers, massaging her clit and the sensitive flesh around it. His hand moved faster, until she shattered, her knees buckling as she cried out his name.

Savannah Carlisle coming apart in his arms was probably one of the most erotic things Blake had ever seen.

Her caramel skin glistened with sweat. Her small, brown nipples had grown puffy and rock-hard after his ministrations. So sensitive that the slightest touch had her ready to fall apart.

Savannah's body was perfect. Womanly curves in all the right places. Smooth, creamy skin. Long, shapely legs.

Her responsiveness to him was a thing of beauty. The way her skin flushed, from head to toe. The slow grinding of her hips against him. The little murmurs that grew louder as she became more aroused. How wet she'd gotten for him—even before he'd laid a hand on her.

Then there was the air of mystery about her. Something Blake appreciated after living most of his life in this tiny town.

He liked that he knew very little about this woman. That he had to earn every bit of knowledge he'd gathered about her. Savannah Carlisle was an enigma he'd enjoy unraveling.

Bit by bit.

They moved to his bed, where Blake lay on his side, his head propped on his fist as he stroked her skin.

Savannah had given him her trust. Something he didn't take lightly.

Until now, he'd focused on her satisfaction. It was no selfless act. He'd relished the control. But he ached with his desire for her. His body was taut with need.

Savannah released a long, slow breath and opened her hazel eyes. Her lopsided smile was adorably sexy.

One look at her kiss-swollen lips and the vivid image of Savannah on her knees flashed through his brain. He groaned, his shaft stretching painfully.

"That was amazing. I can't wait to find out what comes next."

He dragged a thumb across her lower lip. "And I can't wait to give you what comes next."

Savannah's eyes danced. She accepted the digit, sucking it between her soft lips, her gaze locked with his.

Blake pulled his thumb from her mouth with a pop. He

kissed her as Savannah removed his shirt, and he shed his remaining clothing.

The widening of her eyes, followed by an impish grin as she glided her tongue across her upper lip, made his erection swell. He swallowed hard, needing to be inside her.

Blake rummaged through his nightstand, praying he'd find at least a handful of condoms. He didn't stock them at home.

Hookups were something that happened elsewhere. Outside of this tiny town.

Blake wasn't sure how to categorize what was happening between them. But it definitely wasn't a one-off, meaningless hookup.

Finally, he found a strip of three condoms. He took one and tossed the others on the nightstand.

He fumbled with the foil packet, finally ripping it open and sheathing himself as quickly as his fingers would allow.

Blake knelt on the bed. Savannah's mouth curved in a smile, but her eyes held a hint of sadness.

Whatever it was…a painful memory, a bad experience… he wanted to wipe it away. He'd make her forget whoever had come before him. Men who probably hadn't shown her the sincerity and respect he would.

He dragged the lacy panties down her legs and pitched them on the floor. He admired her glistening pink center as she spread her thighs for him.

Blake groaned. A delicious sensation rippled through him as he slipped the head of his erection through her wetness. He pushed his hips forward, then drew his shaft back over her firm clit.

Savannah's belly tensed and she made a low keening moan. The sound became more pronounced with each movement of his hips.

He needed to be inside her. Now.

Blake pressed his shaft to her entrance. Inched his way inside her warm, tight walls.

They both murmured at the incredible sensation. He cursed as he moved inside her, his motions measured, controlled.

*So. Fucking. Good.*

He went deep. Hit bottom. Then slowly withdrew. Beads of sweat formed on his brow and trickled down his back as he tried to maintain control.

He refused to give in until he'd brought her to pleasure once more with him deep inside her.

Blake took her by surprise when he flipped their positions so he was lying on his back. She dug her knees into the mattress on either side of him and leaned backward, bracing her hands on his thighs. Her gaze locked with his as she moved her hips furiously, her breasts bouncing.

The sight of this beautiful woman grinding her hips against him was almost too much for him to take.

Suddenly, she leaned forward and planted her hands on his chest. Blake reached up and slipped the tie from her ponytail. Her loose curls cascaded forward, shielding her face like a dark curtain.

He gripped a handful of her hair, flipping it out of the way so he could watch as she got closer. He gritted his teeth, tried to slow his ascent as her mouth formed an O, euphoria building on her face.

She was close, and he was ready.

He rolled her onto her back again. Kneeling on the mattress, he leaned forward, increasing the friction against her hardened nub as he moved between her thighs.

Savannah cried out. Digging her heels into the mattress, she arched her back and clutched the bedding. With her eyes screwed shut, her head lolled back as she gave in to sweet ecstasy.

Pleasure rolled up his spine as her inner walls spasmed. He continued to move his hips. A few more strokes and Blake cursed and moaned as he came hard inside her. He shuddered, then kissed her softly, still catching his breath.

Savannah looped her arms around him. He settled the weight of his lower body on her and supported himself on his elbows as he kissed her. Slowly. Passionately.

It was something he'd never do with a hookup. Something he hadn't realized he missed...until now.

Blake pulled away, but Savannah tightened her grip on him.

"Can't we stay like this just a little while longer?"

Blake lay on his side and pulled Savannah against him, cradling her in his arms. He tucked her head beneath his chin and pulled the cover over them.

They lay in silence, enjoying the warmth and comfort of each other's bodies. Savoring everything they'd just shared.

As he drifted to sleep, his only thought was the need to keep Savannah in his bed.

# Twelve

Savannah had awakened in Blake's arms for the second morning in a row. At least last night they hadn't made the mistake of falling asleep without discarding the condom, as they had the night before. To make matters worse, her birth control pills were at her apartment. She hadn't taken them for the past three days.

*What if you're...?*

Her heart beat furiously whenever she considered the possibility. So she couldn't allow herself to consider it. Not even for a moment.

When Blake received notice that the bridge had re-opened, she was relieved. Blake had taken her to pick up her car, and she'd followed him in his truck back across the river.

Her time with Blake had been amazing, but it was a weekend fling. Two people confined together in a storm.

Shit happened.

That didn't make them a couple.

Yet Blake believed they could be more than a fling.

Savannah pulled into the parking lot behind her apartment building and got out of her car, wishing the circumstances were different.

She tugged down the hem of the too-tight, wrinkled rayon dress, ruined the night of the storm. She approached Blake, who leaned against the truck, waiting for her.

"I appreciate your insistence on seeing me home." She scanned the parking lot and a nearby street, which was a main thoroughfare in town. "But I think I'm good now."

"Don't worry. I'm maintaining my distance." His tone was laced with irritation. "But I know the history of this building." He nodded toward it. "It flooded during storms like this a few times before. Kayleigh needs a new roof, but she can't afford one and she's too damned stubborn to let my brother Cole fix it for her."

"Fine." She glanced around again. "But remember—"

"You're just an employee. Got it." He narrowed his gaze, his jaw tight. Blake headed toward the back entrance that led to her apartment, without letting her finish.

If he wanted to be that way…fine. It would absolve her of the guilt she might have felt when she finally exposed the Abbotts for who they really were.

She unlocked the main door, and Blake trailed her up the stairs to her apartment.

"Kayleigh's done a good job with the place." He glanced around the small space. The entire apartment was probably smaller than his great room.

"It's not a house on the lake with mountain views, but it's home." Savannah closed the door behind him and dropped her bags on the sofa.

"You think I'd look down on you because you have a smaller place?" Blake's brows furrowed. "Is that why you keep trying to push me away?"

Savannah didn't respond.

"You can't convince me this weekend didn't mean anything to you."

Savannah's throat tightened and her lungs constricted. "I thought I'd been clear. I'm not looking for a relationship. That would cause problems for both of us."

"I'm not saying we should run out and tell the world."

"You don't want your family and friends to know you're slumming it."

"I never said that." The vein in his neck pulsed. He raked his fingers through his hair. "You're purposely being combative."

"But it's the truth." She sank onto the sofa. "Besides, I doubt that Iris Abbott would want any of her precious boys to fall under the spell of some poor girl from the wrong side of the river."

Blake shoved aside the magazines on the coffee table and sat in front of her. He lifted her chin, forcing her gaze to meet his. "You don't really believe that."

"Because you know me so well." She pulled free of his grip.

"I know you better than you think. I know your fears, what turns you on..." He leaned in closer, his voice low. "I know how to satisfy you in ways no one else has."

Blake was too close. He was taking up all of the air in the room, making it difficult for her to breathe.

"So what?" She shrugged. "You haven't known me long. Maybe you wouldn't like me if you really knew me."

He leaned in closer, his gaze softer. "That's something I'd like to find out for myself."

She swallowed the lump in her throat. "Why is getting to know me so important to you? Most men would be content with a no-strings weekend." She forced a laugh. "You don't even have to pretend you're going to call."

"I'm not most men. Not when it comes to you." Blake kissed her.

She held back, at first. But when he took her face in his hands, Savannah parted her lips to him and pulled him closer, needing more of the connection they'd shared.

When he pulled away, one edge of his mouth curled in a smirk. "Is that your way of admitting that this weekend meant something to you, too?"

"If I say yes, will you take me to bed?"

"No." He stood, the ridge apparent beneath his zipper. "But it does mean I'm asking you on a date."

"Around here? Are you crazy?" She stood, too. "Everyone will know before dessert."

He sighed heavily. "True."

"Then where do you propose we have this date?"

"My place for starters." He tucked her hair behind her

ear. "But pack for the weekend. I've got something special in mind."

He kissed her, made a quick inspection of the apartment, as promised, and left.

Savannah closed the door behind him and exhaled.

*What have I gotten myself into?*

She needed to vindicate her grandfather and get the hell out of Magnolia Lake before she fell any deeper under Blake's spell.

She'd barely sat down when there was a knock at her door.

Had Blake changed his mind?

"Savannah, it's me—Kayleigh." A wall separated their apartments, though there were separate staircases leading to each.

Savannah opened the door. "Hi, Kayleigh. Is everything okay?"

"I bought too much food and I thought you might be hungry."

"Starving." She let the woman in. "Thanks for thinking of me."

"Haven't seen you around since the storm. I was worried." Kayleigh set containers of barbecue chicken, wedge fries and coleslaw on the table.

"Got caught on the other side of the river." Savannah gathered plates, napkins and silverware.

"I hope someone put you up during the storm." Kayleigh was trying to figure out where she'd spent the past few days.

"Thankfully, yes." Savannah put the dishes on the table and sat across from her landlord and neighbor.

"Well, that's a relief."

Savannah was eager to change the subject and avoid the question she knew would come next. "Everything smells delicious. Thanks for sharing."

"My pleasure." Kayleigh spooned coleslaw onto her plate.

Savannah fixed a plate for herself, hoping the other shoe didn't drop.

"I noticed that Blake Abbott followed you home today."

The other shoe dropped.

Savannah couldn't deny what Kayleigh had seen with her own eyes. But she could spin it.

"I'm about the only person in town who doesn't have a truck or SUV. Blake was nice enough to make sure I made it back across the river safely."

"And it was kind of him to see you inside."

Didn't the people in this town have anything else to do with their time?

"He mentioned that the building's roof has leaked in previous storms."

"Damn Abbotts think they're better than everyone else."

"He mentioned that you won't let his brother fix the roof."

"I'm not one of their charity cases." Kayleigh opened a jar of preserves and spread it onto her biscuit. "I can afford to get my own roof repaired...eventually."

They ate in companionable silence. But even the delicious food wasn't enough to keep Kayleigh quiet for long.

"It's none of my business what you do and who you do it with." The woman took a sip of her sweet tea. "But getting involved with an Abbott isn't too smart, if you ask me."

Savannah chewed her food. She had no intention of confirming her involvement with Blake Abbott, but she didn't bother denying it, either.

"You've made it clear you don't like them," Savannah said. "But you've never said why."

Kayleigh's scowl briefly shifted to a pained expression. Then her mask of anger slipped back in place.

"They're always throwing their money around like they can buy anyone they want."

"Did they do something to you specifically?"

Maybe the Abbotts had a pattern of cheating business partners. If she could prove that, it would go a long way toward supporting her grandfather's claim that Joseph Abbott had done the same to him.

"I went to school with Parker." She groaned. "That one is a piece of work."

Savannah couldn't disagree with that. Parker was smart, but his people skills were nonexistent. Everyone at the distillery seemed to understand that was simply who Parker was. No one took his overly direct approach personally. She'd learned to do the same.

"Is Parker the reason you don't like the entire family?"

"Parker is only part of the reason." Kayleigh's mouth twisted. She dropped her fork, as if she'd lost her appetite. "The other reason has to do with my father."

"What happened?"

The fire that always seemed to blaze in Kayleigh's eyes faded. "When I was growing up, my dad was the town drunk. In and out of the local jail all the time. Generally horrible to my mother, my sister and me."

"That must've been difficult for you. Especially in a small town like this one."

"There wasn't a week that went by when I wasn't humiliated by some kid talking shit about my dad's latest antics."

"Kids like Parker?"

"Not at first. At first, he and his brothers were about the only kids who didn't tease me. But then Parker started hanging with a different crowd… He wanted so badly to fit in back then."

"Doesn't sound like the Parker Abbott I know." Savannah tried to imagine the abrasive man as an impressionable kid who just wanted to fit in. She couldn't. "The guy I know doesn't care much what anyone thinks of him."

"It's true. Parker was different from the other kids. Smarter. More direct. Way too honest." Kayleigh shook her head and sighed. "So he tried to be part of the crowd. That meant embarrassing me, like all the other 'cool' kids." She used air quotes to emphasize the word.

"I see why you dislike Parker, but why don't you like the rest of the Abbotts?"

"Because Duke Abbott is a liar and a thief." The fire was back in Kayleigh's eyes. The icy tone returned to her voice.

*Now we're getting somewhere.*

Savannah leaned forward. "What did Duke Abbott steal from you?"

"We didn't have much, but my grandfather had left my mom a ton of property adjacent to the distillery. The old house and barn were dilapidated, but when my dad was sober we'd take a ride out there and walk around. He wanted to fix the place up. Make it a working farm again." She swiped angrily at the corner of her eye.

"In those moments when my dad was completely hammered, those walks on my grandfather's property were the one good memory I held on to. The only hope I had that one day he'd finally come through and be a real father to us."

"What happened to the farm?" Savannah knew the answer before she asked the question. Why else would Kayleigh hate the Abbotts when everyone else in town fawned over them?

"While my sister and I were away at college, Dad got really sick. Sicker than he or my mother were telling us. His liver couldn't take any more. My mother didn't want to burden us with their financial problems. So she sold the property to Duke Abbott for a fraction of what it was worth to pay hospital bills and help with our tuition."

"Must've been a tough decision for your mother."

"Selling her dad's property for a song broke her heart. She died not a year later. That's when I learned that greedy bastard Duke Abbott had bought it." Kayleigh paced the floor. "He'd already torn down the old house and put new buildings up."

*Like father, like son.*

The sound of her own heartbeat filled Savannah's ears. She was getting closer to establishing a pattern of the Ab-

botts cheating neighbors and friends. It evidently hadn't
been much consolation to Kayleigh, but at least her family
had received *something* for their property. That was more
than her family could say.

"Sorry—I don't want to dump my issues on you. And I
don't mean to be the kind of petty person who doesn't want
her friends to have any other friends." Kayleigh returned
to her chair and nibbled on a wedge fry. "But I had to warn
you. The Abbotts seem like sunshine and roses. But when
it comes to something they want, they'd as soon stab you
in the back as smile in your face."

Savannah was surprised Kayleigh had referred to her as
a friend. She hadn't thought of the woman that way. Kayleigh always seemed closed off, and Savannah hadn't been
eager to make new friends, either. But maybe together they
could form an alliance against the Abbotts.

She opened her mouth to tell Kayleigh who her grandfather was, and the reason she loathed Joseph Abbott. But
the truth was, she didn't really know Kayleigh.

What she did know was that Kayleigh was part of the
town's gossip circle. If she told her the truth it would be all
over town by morning. She'd lose her one advantage over
the Abbotts: the element of surprise.

Blowing her cover wasn't worth the risk.

Instead, she thanked the woman for her advice and
turned the conversation elsewhere, while her grandfather's
advice played on repeat in her head.

*Never trust an Abbott farther than you can throw one.*

Not even Blake.

But that didn't mean she couldn't enjoy whatever it was
that they had. For now.

# Thirteen

"Hello, darlin'. Miss me?"

Blake glanced up from his laptop to find the whirlwind that was Iris Abbott in his office.

"Mama." He met her in the middle of the room so she could give him one of her trademark bear hugs. "Dad didn't tell me you were back."

"I wanted to surprise you."

"How's Aunt Constance?" Blake straightened his collar and sat behind his desk.

"Much better." She sat in one of the chairs across from him. "She'll only need me for a few more weeks. Then I'll be home for good."

"How long are you staying?" Blake studied his mother's face. Iris Abbott considered flying a necessary evil. If she took a voluntary plane trip, she had a damn good reason for it.

"A few days." Her eyes roamed the space, as if it were her first visit. "Just long enough to have a couple of meetings with this Savannah girl."

The hair on the back of Blake's neck stood up. "Thought you two were holding video conferences about the gala."

"We have been, and we've gotten lots done. She's sharp, and she's not just talk. She makes things happen."

Blake crossed one leg over the other. "Sounds like the arrangement is working. So why the surprise trip?"

"What, you didn't miss your mama?"

"I did." Blake leaned on the armrest. "But you haven't answered my question. Why make a special trip just to meet with Savannah?"

His mother shifted in her chair, brushing imaginary crumbs from her summery floral skirt. "Technology is great, but it doesn't replace sitting across the table from someone and getting a good read on them."

"And why do you suddenly need a better read on Savannah?"

She folded her arms. "A little birdie told me her car was here all weekend."

"We had one heck of a storm. The bridge was closed, and she lives on the other side of the river. She obviously got stuck on this side."

"And *where* do you suppose she spent all that time?"

"Why are you asking me?" Blake composed an email to Savannah, warning her of his mother's suspicions.

"Tread carefully, son." Iris flashed her you-ain't-fooling-me smirk. "I saw the video of you bringing her back to her car on Monday afternoon."

*Damn blabbermouth security guards.*

"What if I did?" He shrugged. "She's new to the area. Didn't know it's prone to flooding. I wanted to make sure she was all right. What's wrong with that?"

His mother hiked one brow. "You still haven't answered my question. Where did she spend that long weekend? In your bed?"

"Just so we're clear, that question will *never* be okay." His cheeks flooded with heat. "Who I sleep with—or don't—is my business."

"Except when it threatens *our* business."

"You're being melodramatic, Mother."

"Am I?" She folded her arms. "You remember how ugly things got when Parker made a mess of things with his secretary?"

Blake groaned, recalling how angry the woman had been when Parker broke it off.

"This situation isn't the same."

"So you *are* sleeping with her."

He wasn't a good liar, which was why he preferred to

take the it's-none-of-your-business approach. But his mother never had trouble getting to the truth.

Still, what happened between him and Savannah wasn't up for family discussion.

"Blake, you were the one son I could count on to not break the rules. What happened? Did she seduce you?"

"I'm a grown man. Nothing happened I didn't want to happen. Let's leave it at that."

She folded her arms, pouting.

"I need you to promise me something, Mama." He moved to sit beside her.

"And what is that?"

"Don't mention this to Savannah."

"Now you want to dictate what I can say to her? This is why I made the rule in the first place, son. Can't you see the problems this is causing already?"

"Do this for me. Please."

"Fine." She stood, flipping her wrist to check the time. "I won't say anything—"

"To anyone," he added.

"For now." She leaned down and kissed him. "Come by for dinner tonight. I promise you and your little girlfriend won't be the topic of discussion."

"I'll be there around six."

Blake groaned in relief as his mother left.

His weekend with Savannah made him realize that his feelings for her were deeper than he'd imagined. Savannah evidently had feelings for him, too. Yet she was hesitant to explore them.

If she found out what his mother knew, it would only spook her. She'd pull away again.

Blake returned to his desk and discarded the email to Savannah. He could handle his mother, and what Savannah didn't know wouldn't hurt her.

# Fourteen

Savannah pulled her car into Blake's garage and parked, as he'd requested. She'd spent the previous weekend at his place out of necessity. But this was a deliberate decision.

She'd crossed the line and the guilt bored a hole in her gut. Savannah could only imagine what Laney would say, if she knew.

Her sister would be gravely disappointed in her.

But she hadn't slept with Blake as part of some grand scheme to elicit information from him. What had happened was precipitated by the very real feelings that had been developing between them.

But didn't that make what she was doing worse?

She was giving him hope. Making him believe something could come of the game they were playing. Only Blake had no idea he was playing a game.

Savannah got out of her car, her hands shaking.

*This was a mistake. I should go.*

Blake stepped into the garage, a dish towel thrown over one shoulder. He seemed to know she was grappling with the decision to come inside.

His welcoming smile assured her everything would be okay.

"Hey." He took her bag and kissed her cheek.

"Hey." She slipped her hand into his and let him lead her inside. The house smelled like roasted vegetables and baked goods. "Are you sure this is a good idea? Your sister or one of your brothers could pop by at any—"

Blake set the bag on the floor and pulled her into a kiss that ended her objections. Her heart raced and warmth filled her body.

She forgot all the reasons she shouldn't be there as she

tumbled into a morass of feelings she might never be able to escape.

A buzzer sounded in the kitchen. Blake reluctantly suspended their kiss.

"We'll finish this later." He gave her a lingering kiss before removing a pie from the oven.

"Smells delicious. What kind of pie is it?"

"Strawberry rhubarb." He removed his oven mitts. "Hope you like it."

*He remembered.*

"You made it?"

"It's my first one." He grinned. "So I want you to be brutally honest. If it tastes like crap, don't pull any punches. It's the only way I'll learn to make it the way you like it."

"You did this for me?"

"Why else?" Blake tugged her against him and kissed her again.

It was just a silly little pie. So why was she so moved by the gesture?

Because Blake cared about what she wanted. About what was important to her.

And all she cared about was getting revenge for her grandfather and hurting his family in the process.

She pulled away, tears burning her eyes.

Blake cupped her cheek. "Did I do something wrong?"

"No." Savannah's neck and face tingled with heat. She swiped away warm tears and forced a smile. "Anyone ever tell you you're a little too perfect?"

"No." He chuckled, then kissed her again. "Certainly not any of my siblings."

"Brothers and sisters are there to rein us in when we get a little too big for our britches."

"At that, they excel." Blake grinned. "But they're also there when I need someone to help me get my head back on straight. Or to remind me that things aren't as bad as they seem." He moved to the counter and uncovered the steaks. "I imagine you and your sister do that for each other, too."

"Laney does her best to keep me on the straight and narrow. Doesn't always work, but she tries."

"And what about you?"

"I'm the pit bull." Savannah sat at the counter, watching him prep the steaks. "Even when our parents were still alive, it was my job to protect my sister." She swallowed past the thickness in her throat. "It still is. Even when it requires me to make difficult choices."

"Like what?" He held her gaze.

Savannah's heart felt heavy. It was a lead weight pulling her beneath the sea of guilt washing over her. Blake's reaction to learning the truth flashed in her head. Would he be hurt or angry? Probably both.

He'd regret the day he laid eyes on her.

She'd always anticipated that the day she finally vindicated her grandfather would be the happiest day of her life. Now she could only envision heartbreak and pain.

She'd have to explain to Blake why she'd misled him about her reasons for coming to King's Finest. Her only comfort was knowing she hadn't lied to him. Which meant she couldn't answer his question now.

Blake put the steaks in a skillet and washed his hands. When he turned around, she handed him a towel.

"It's been a long week." She looped her arms around his waist, tugging his lower body against hers as she gazed up at him. "I'm not in the mood for talking or eating right now."

She guided Blake's lips to hers and kissed him.

Blake gripped her bottom, hauling her closer. She accommodated his silent request by grinding her body against his until he grew hard against her belly.

Savannah broke their kiss and whispered in his ear. "I want you, Blake. Now."

"What about dinner?" His voice was as rough as his

beard, which scraped against her skin as he trailed hot kisses up her neck.

"It'll be just as good if we have it later…in bed." She unfastened his belt and slid her hand beneath his waistband. Savannah took his steely length in her palm and stroked his warm flesh.

Blake groaned against her throat, his body tensing. He pulled away just long enough to turn off the broiler and put the steaks in the fridge. Then he grabbed her bag and followed her to his bedroom as quickly as their legs would carry them.

They stripped each other naked. Blake tried to lead her to his bed, but Savannah urged him into a brown leather chair.

Her gaze fused with his as she slowly sank to her knees. She swirled her tongue around the head of his thick erection before taking just the tip in her mouth.

Blake cursed and his thighs tensed. He gripped the arms of the chair, as if it took every ounce of self-control he could muster to refrain from palming the back of her head and urging her to take him deeper.

She gripped the base of his shaft and ran her tongue lazily along the underside before taking him in her mouth again. Until she could feel him at the back of her throat.

Blake swore under his breath. He loosely gathered a handful of her hair in his fist so it wouldn't obstruct his view of her taking him deep.

"Do you have any idea what you're doing to me, Savannah?"

She ran her tongue along a bulging vein. "I'd like to think so."

"That's not what I mean." His expression became serious. "It's been a really long time since I've cared for anyone the way I care for you."

Savannah froze, her heart racing. She'd done this to remind them both that this was only sex. They were mutually satisfying each other's needs.

She hadn't expected Blake to say she meant something to him. What did it matter if she felt the same? She couldn't say it back. It would only make it hurt more once he knew the truth.

"Blake…" Her mouth went dry and her chest ached. "I can't—"

"It's okay." He pressed a kiss to her mouth. "My mother always says I'm the kid that goes from zero to a hundred in sixty seconds flat." He sighed, then stood, pulling her to her feet. "Forget I said anything."

But she couldn't forget.

It was all she could think of as he took her into his arms and kissed her.

When he made love to her.

Fire and passion spread through her limbs. Her body spasmed with intense pleasure. Her heart was overwhelmed with the emotions that sparked between them.

Blake Abbott had turned her inside out. Made her feel there was nothing in the world he wanted more than her.

He'd left her wishing desperately that this was more than an illusion, born from deception and half-truths.

Unable to sleep, Savannah lay in Blake's arms after their late-night dinner, listening to him breathe as he slept. Blake Abbott had ruined her. Her life would never be the same without him.

If only she could reclaim her grandfather's legacy and have Blake Abbott, too.

# Fifteen

Blake straightened his tie and adjusted the cuffs of the suit jacket Savannah had helped him pick out for the jubilee gala. His jaw dropped as he surveyed the barn.

He'd witnessed the slow transformation of the structure as his brother Cole's construction crew renovated and painted it over the past month. He and the rest of the team had assisted with the execution of Savannah's party plans and decor over the past three days.

Still, he was floored by the remarkable beauty of what had once been a run-down building at the edge of his parents' property. His brother's company did excellent work. But this had all been Savannah's vision.

It was everything she'd promised when she'd pitched her idea. An upscale event with down-home roots. An event that honored their past while celebrating the future.

"The place is beautiful. I had no idea this old barn had so much potential." His mother suddenly appeared beside him, dabbing the corners of her eyes with a handkerchief. "Your Savannah is a genius."

"She isn't *my* Savannah, Mother. She's very much her own woman." Blake wasn't being evasive or ambiguous. He'd spent the past month trying to convince Savannah to formalize their affair. He cared deeply for her, but he was tired of being her dirty little secret.

He and Savannah had spent lazy weekends getting to know each other better. They cooked together, ate together and spent their nights making love.

Bit by bit, he was falling for her, diving headfirst into emotions he'd spent the past two years actively avoiding.

"Women who maintain a sense of self make the best

mates." Iris squeezed his hand reassuringly. "Ask your father."

They both chuckled and the tension in his shoulders eased. He squeezed his mother's hand back, appreciative of her underlying message. She wouldn't stand in the way of him being with Savannah.

Now if only he could convince Savannah it was time to take the next step.

"Can you believe this place?" Zora's eyes danced with glee as she approached. "It's incredible, and I've been dying for a good reason to dress up."

Not many occasions in Magnolia Lake called for elegant attire. The typical town event required a well-worn pair of jeans and a sturdy pair of boots.

"Will Dallas be here tonight?" Iris elbowed Zora.

"Said he wouldn't miss it for the world."

Zora's eyes sparkled when she talked about Dallas Hamilton—her best friend since kindergarten. Though Dallas still had a home in Magnolia Lake, he and Zora didn't see each other much.

Dallas's hobby of building stunning handmade furniture pieces in his family's run-down work shed had exploded into a multimillion-dollar business. He was frequently overseas attending trade shows, visiting with vendors and presiding over the setup of new retail stores in some of the world's most glamorous cities.

Sometimes Blake envied the guy. He was a self-made millionaire who'd built an empire out of nothing with a vision and hard work.

"Make sure Dallas comes to see me as soon as he gets here." Iris beamed. "There's a spot in the entry hall just begging for one of his custom pieces."

"Dal is here as our guest, Mother. Not to work. Let him enjoy himself, please," Zora pleaded.

"That means she plans to keep Dallas to herself all

night," Iris whispered to Blake loudly, fully aware Zora could hear her.

His attention shifted to Savannah as she flitted about the space. Tonight she was simply stunning.

She wore a black one-shoulder blouse and a high-waisted, long, flowing gray skirt with a bow tie at the back of her waist.

He loved her enticing curves. Had memorized them. But tonight, the cut of the blouse emphasized her bustline. Not that he was complaining. The generous flow of the skirt made her curvy bottom seem fuller, too.

Her hair, swept to one side, fell on her creamy, bare shoulder in loose curls. Blake's hand clenched at his side, his body tensing with the memory of combing his fingers through those soft curls as she lay naked in his bed.

"Seems your brother is more impressed with Ms. Carlisle than with what she's done here tonight."

Blake's cheeks warmed. He shifted his gaze back to his mother and sister. Zora giggled, likely glad their mother was temporarily distracted from her attempts to pair her and Dallas.

"I'm monitoring how she handles herself under pressure." Blake congratulated himself on his quick recovery. "Maybe you two haven't noticed who Savannah is talking to."

His mother and sister carefully assessed the tall, dark-haired man who hovered over Savannah.

"Wait a minute. Is that—"

"It's Dade Willis," Zora squealed. "I knew a couple B-and C-list Tennessee celebs had RSVP'd. I had no idea Dade Frickin' Willis would be here."

A tinge of jealousy gnawed at Blake as the man flirted with Savannah. The Tennessee native was country music's latest phenom. His single had topped the country charts for the past ten weeks. That didn't mean Blake wouldn't rearrange his pretty, surgically-enhanced face if he didn't back off Savannah.

"I'd better go greet our guest." His mother hurried toward Dade.

"Not without me you aren't." Zora caught up to their mother.

Blake went to the bar to check on their stock for the event. As Savannah rushed past him holding a clipboard, Blake stopped her with a discreet hand on her hip.

"Everything looks great, Savannah. You've done well. Take a breath and relax."

"I forgot to bring Dade's badge. He was a last-minute addition, so I made it in my office this morning."

"Not a big deal. Send one of the guys to get it."

"I need everyone here. There's still so much to do. The first band is already late and guests will arrive shortly." The words rushed from her mouth.

"Then I'll get it." Blake fought the urge to kiss her. He held out an open palm. "Give me the key to your office."

Savannah dropped her keys in his hand, her eyes filled with gratitude. "There's a small crate on the edge of my desk. My cell phone is in there, too. Thanks, Blake."

"Anything for you, babe." He lowered his voice so only she could hear him. "Now stop being such a perfectionist, or you won't get a chance to enjoy your own damn party."

Savannah seemed surprised he'd called it *her* party. She smiled gratefully, then made a beeline for the caterer.

Blake's gaze followed the sway of Savannah's hips as she crossed the room. He turned in the opposite direction when someone squeezed his shoulder.

"Gramps." Blake gave his grandfather a bear hug. "I wondered when you'd get here." He gestured around the room. "So what do you think?"

"It's remarkable." The old man removed his thick glasses and wiped them on a hankie he produced from his inside pocket. The corners of his eyes were wet with tears. "I didn't expect all this."

"But you deserve it, Gramps." Blake draped an arm

around his shoulders. "We wanted to show you what you and King's Finest mean to us and to the community. And this is only the beginning."

His grandfather's eyes widened. "What do you mean?"

"This gala kicks off a yearlong international celebration of our brand. The entire thing was envisioned by the new events manager we hired a couple of months ago—Miss Savannah Carlisle." Blake nodded in her direction.

"Oh, I see." His grandfather chuckled. "The pretty little thing you were cozied up with here at the bar. The one you couldn't take your eyes off when she walked away."

Blake didn't bother denying it, but refused to throw any more logs on the fire.

"We were discussing a small problem, which I promised to handle." Blake's gaze met Savannah's. Her mouth pinched and her eyes narrowed. "But first, let me introduce you to the woman behind all of this."

Blake walked his grandfather toward Savannah and she met them halfway, forcing a smile as she got closer.

"Don't worry—I'm headed out to take care of that errand in just a minute," Blake said quickly. "But my grandfather arrived, and I know you've been dying to meet him."

"For longer than you know." Savannah's smile was tight and her shoulders stiff. Her hand trembled slightly when she placed it in his grandfather's palm.

His grandfather clasped her hand in both of his and smiled broadly. "My grandson tells me I have you to thank for all of this. Can't begin to explain how much it means to me."

"The look on your face when everything's said and done… That's all the thanks I'll ever need." Savannah's attention turned to members of the band finally arriving. "I look forward to chatting with you at length later, but right now I need to show the musicians where to set up. Excuse me."

They both watched as she approached the band and guided them to the stage.

"I see why you're so taken with her, son." The old man chuckled. "You go on and take care of whatever it is you need to." His grandfather smiled at Zora, who was walking toward them. "My granddaughter will keep me company until you return."

Blake drove the short distance to the distillery. He retrieved the small crate from Savannah's desk and checked to make sure the badge and her phone were there.

Her phone buzzed, indicating a text message. The message scrolled across the screen, capturing his attention.

It's been two months. Give up and come home. I feel icky lying to Gramps. Giving you one week. Won't do it anymore.

Blake scanned the screen quickly before the message disappeared. It was from Savannah's sister, Laney.

A rock formed in Blake's gut.

What did Laney want Savannah to give up? Her job at the distillery? Her relationship with Blake? And why was Savannah asking her sister to lie to their grandfather?

Uneasiness skittered along his spine.

Blake couldn't ignore the text. His feelings aside, if there was a risk of Savannah leaving them in the lurch, he needed to know. They'd scheduled a year's worth of events to celebrate the King's Finest jubilee. Savannah was the point person on every one of them.

What if there was a simple, harmless explanation?

Savannah would be furious he'd read her private text message. Even if he'd done so inadvertently.

Blake had been burned before by getting involved with someone who wasn't as committed to the relationship as he was. Perhaps Savannah's reluctance to take their relationship public went beyond worries over her career.

And then there was the day she'd been in his home office, ostensibly to find a pen. Could there have been another reason?

Blake groaned.

He was being paranoid. Admittedly, her sister's text message didn't look good. But it wasn't as if Savannah had initiated a relationship with him. Or even wanted to come back to his house that night. Both had been his idea.

Blake grabbed the crate and returned to his truck. Whatever the truth was, he'd find a way to get to the bottom of it.

# Sixteen

Savannah sat down at the bar for a moment and ordered an energy drink.

Most of the night's pomp and circumstance had already played out. The Abbott family had taken the stage and thanked everyone—including the town of Magnolia Lake—for its support for the past half century. A handful of celebs, business executives and longtime employees had shared anecdotes about King's Finest bourbon.

A few other big names circulated throughout the crowd. They mixed it up with employees, townsfolk, distributors and the numerous reporters she'd invited.

Savannah had been moving at warp speed for the past seventy-two hours. It wasn't surprising she was tired. But tonight, she was unusually exhausted. And she'd felt slightly nauseous all day.

She finished her energy drink. Then she ordered a ginger ale to allay the queasiness.

"Everything okay?" Blake sat beside her.

There was something going on with him. He'd been slightly aloof since he brought the crate to her.

She'd tried to create distance between them in their public dealings. But there was something about Blake's sudden indifference that made her feel she was standing naked in a blizzard, desperate to come in from the cold.

Blake wore the expensive sand-colored suit and navy-and-white gingham-check shirt she'd selected for him during a recent visit to Nashville. It suited the man and the occasion. Serious and elegant with a bit of playfulness beneath the refined surface.

"Everything is fine. It's just been a really long couple of days. I'm a little run-down."

"Anything else wrong?" He turned slowly on the bar stool to face her. For the first time, he was sizing her up.

Judging her.

A chill ran down Savannah's spine. She wasn't imagining it. Something was wrong. Had she left an incriminating note on her desk?

*Impossible.*

She didn't handwrite notes about the Abbotts or the distillery. She captured digital notes in her phone.

*My phone.*

It'd been in the box Blake delivered to her. Had he gone through it and found her notes?

Savannah forced a smile. No point in panicking without good reason. That would only make her seem guilty.

"Everything is good. Nearly everyone who RSVP'd made it. All of the staff and musical acts showed up. Things are running smoothly." As she spoke, Savannah inwardly ticked off possible reasons for Blake's change in attitude. "People seem to be enjoying themselves, especially your grandfather."

"Haven't seen him that emotional since my grandmother died ten years ago." Blake's stony expression softened. His eyes met hers. "I can't thank you enough for giving him all this."

Savannah's spine was as stiff as her smile. When she'd proposed this event, she'd hoped it would be the night she humiliated the Abbotts. The night when she pulled back the curtain and revealed the ugly truth that they were cruel, heartless liars and thieves who'd taken credit for her grandfather's work.

"My pleasure." Savannah finished her ginger ale and stood. "I have to go powder my nose." Her bladder was clearly unable to keep up with the amount of liquids she'd consumed throughout the day. "See you later."

Blake caught her hand in his and pulled her closer. He

searched her eyes, as if seeking an answer to some burning question.

"What is it, Blake?" Savannah glanced around, her cheeks hot. She ignored the bartender's sly grin. "There's obviously something you want to say."

He averted his gaze. "Wrong place. Wrong time." He nodded toward the restrooms. "We can talk later."

Savannah made a beeline for the bathroom. But she couldn't help thinking that whatever it was Blake wanted to ask her would be the beginning of the end.

As Savannah exited the restroom, a hand reached out from the doorway of the back office and pulled her inside. She immediately recognized the scent and the hard body pressed against her.

"What on earth is going on?" Savannah whispered angrily. Blake had nearly given her a heart attack.

"We need to talk, and I'd rather do it without my mother and sister staring at us."

"Why would they be staring at us? Wait… Does your mother suspect, too?"

Blake didn't respond.

"That's why she's been looking at me like that all night. Why didn't you tell me?"

"That's not the pressing issue right now." Blake was agitated.

Her heart beat faster. "What is?"

"What's happening between us… It isn't a game for me. And regardless of what you say, this isn't just about sex for you, either." He took a deep breath. "So I want you to tell me the truth. Is there something you're keeping from me?"

Savannah's blood ran cold, and her throat was dry.

"What are you asking me, Blake?"

"Are you unhappy at King's Finest?" He frowned.

"Of course not. I told you, I belong here. I've never had a job I enjoyed more."

"Are you entertaining another job offer?"

Savannah felt a sense of relief. "How could you ask me that? Hasn't tonight's gala proven how important this company is to me?"

"It would appear so. Still—"

"Still…what?" Savannah wouldn't blink first. If Blake thought he knew something, he'd have to ask her directly. She wouldn't volunteer information unnecessarily and compromise the mission. Not when she finally had a chance to question Joseph Abbott.

Blake gripped her shoulder, his fingers warm against her skin. His eyes demanded the truth. Something she couldn't give him.

Not yet.

"Savannah, it's been a long time since I cared this much for anyone. So if this doesn't mean the same to you, tell me now. Before I get in deeper."

Her hands trembled. Blake's expression was so sincere. It reminded her of all the things she adored about him.

Why did she have to hurt him?

"I… I…" She swallowed what felt like a lump of coal. "I can't answer that right now. Please, give me some time. This relationship is still new. What's the rush?"

"Is that what this is, Savannah? A relationship?"

"Yes." She nodded, pushing her hair behind her ear. "And it's all I can offer right now. Please, just be patient."

Blake palmed her bottom and pulled her closer. His mouth crashed against hers in a searing kiss that took her breath away.

Her body filled with heat. The hardened tips of her breasts were hypersensitive as they grazed his rock-solid chest.

"Blake…" Her objection died on his lips.

He turned her around, jerking her against him. His erection was pinned between them. Blake squeezed her full breasts. They felt tender, almost sore. Yet she craved more of his touch.

"I've never wanted anyone the way I want you, Savannah." His voice was thick as he trailed kisses along her shoulder. His beard sensitized her skin.

He kissed the back of her neck, his hand lightly gripping her throat. Blake hiked her skirt and glided his hand up her inner thigh. He palmed the drenched space between her thighs.

She moaned with pleasure as he ran firm fingers back and forth over the silky material that shielded her sex.

When Blake kissed her ear, Savannah nearly lost all control. Her knees quivered as Blake slipped his hand inside the fabric. Her flesh was so sensitive she could barely stand it.

"Blake, yes. Please."

She needed him inside her. Her mind was so clouded with lust, she didn't care about the risk they were both taking.

She only cared about Blake Abbott making love to her. Making her feel as only he could. As if there was no one in the world but the two of them.

Blake unfastened his pants and freed himself. She lifted her skirt higher to accommodate him as he shifted her panties aside and pressed his thick head to her slick entrance.

Savannah nearly lost it when he massaged her clit.

She pressed back against him, needing him inside her.

"You sure about this, baby?" Blake breathed the words in her ear.

She nodded, wanting desperately to bear down on his thick length. She hadn't missed a single day of her birth control since the storm.

With one hand still moving over her sensitive flesh, he grabbed the base of his shaft with the other. He pressed himself inside her.

They both groaned with pleasure.

Whatever happened between them later, they would always have moments like this.

Moments in which she couldn't deny how much she cared for him. That she was falling in love with him. And maybe he was falling in love with her, too.

Savannah braced herself against a cabinet as Blake brought her closer to the edge. His hand moved over her slick flesh as he thrust inside her. Taking them both higher.

Her legs trembled and her whimpers grew louder. Blake clamped a hand over her mouth, muffling her cries as he whispered in her ear, telling her all of the deliciously dirty things he wanted to do to her once he got her back to his place.

The sounds of people laughing and talking outside the door didn't deter either of them from their singular goal: to bring each other pleasure.

Savannah was floating higher. Dizzy with her desire for him. Finally, pleasure exploded in her core. She shuddered, weak and trembling, muttering his name against his rough palm still pressed to her lips.

Soon afterward, Blake stiffened, cursing and moaning. He held her in his arms, their chests heaving and their breath ragged. Both of them seemed reluctant to be separated from the other's warmth.

He'd made her feel incredible. Yet she was quickly overcome by a wave of sadness. Tears burned the backs of her eyelids.

Would this be the last time he'd hold her, make love to her?

"I'll leave first," he said after they'd made themselves presentable. "Wait a few minutes before you come out."

Blake reached for the doorknob. He paused and turned back to her. "Are you sure you don't need to tell me anything?"

She shook her head, her heart breaking. "Nothing at all."

It was a lie from which they would never recover.

Eyebrows drawn together and lips pursed, he turned

and slipped out of the door, leaving her alone with the bitter tears that spilled down her cheeks.

When she got back to the party, Savannah hid in the shadows near the back of the room, trying to regain her composure and make sense of the change in Blake's mood. Her skin prickled and her breasts still throbbed from her encounter with Blake.

"This is quite the affair you've orchestrated, young lady."

Savannah nearly dropped her clipboard and cell phone. "Mr. Abbott."

Joseph Abbott stood beside Savannah as she surveyed the crowd, the smell of bourbon heavy on his breath. "My granddaughter tells me that even the decision to renovate this old barn was your idea."

Savannah's fists clenched so tightly she wouldn't have been surprised if blood dripped from her palms. Her throat seized, rendering her mute. She swallowed hard, forced herself to smile in the face of the devil who'd been the catalyst for every devastating thing that had happened in their lives.

"Yes, sir. It was. I'm thrilled you're pleased." Once the muscles of her larynx relaxed enough for her to speak, she oozed warmth. Like honey. Sticky and sweet. Because she was more apt to catch a fly with honey than vinegar. "I must admit, I'm obsessed with the story of how you started King's Finest all those years ago with nothing more than your father's bourbon recipe and his moonshine stills."

There was a flash of something across the old man's face. Sorrow? Regret? Whatever it was, for an instant, he looked every bit of his seventy-plus years.

"It's not that simple, I'm afraid. Nothing worthwhile ever is. I had the support of my family. Of people who helped me make this happen."

Savannah turned to the man. Her heart racing. "Like who?"

His gaze didn't meet hers. There was a far-off look in his eyes. One that would've made her feel sorry for the old man, if he hadn't destroyed her family's lives.

He didn't answer her, and for a moment they both stood in silence.

"My father died in a car accident when I was young. I wanted to revive his moonshine business, but I didn't know much about it. I partnered with someone who could teach me the ropes."

Savannah's stomach churned. Her fingers and toes tingled. Time seemed to slow.

She was finally going to get her proof from the mouth of Joseph Abbott himself. Savannah turned on the recording app on her phone.

"There's no mention of a partner in the company story on the website." Or anywhere else she'd looked.

"We dissolved the partnership before I incorporated King's Finest."

That explained why Savannah hadn't been able to find proof that her grandfather was a partner in the distillery.

But if Joseph Abbott had used her grandfather's recipe, wouldn't that still give him claim to part of the company's profits?

"Who was your partner, Mr. Abbott?"

The seconds of silence between them seemed to stretch for an eternity.

Joseph Abbott rubbed his forehead, finally raising his gaze to hers.

"Forgive me, Miss Carlisle. I'm afraid this lovely affair has been a bit too much excitement for an old man like me after my travels yesterday."

"But, Mr. Abbott—"

"Please, excuse me." The old man nodded his goodbye, then made his way across the room to where Duke and Iris stood.

Savannah's belly clenched and her hands shook. She'd

been so close to learning the truth. To getting the information she needed to change her family's fortune.

She'd pushed too hard and spooked the old man. Now he'd never tell her the truth. Worse, there was a wary look in his eye before he'd fled. As if he'd seen her intentions.

Joseph Abbott wouldn't tell her anything more.

Savannah wiped away the hot tears that leaked from her eyes. Giving up wasn't an option. Not when she was this close. She'd find another way.

Her phone buzzed. It was a text message from Laney.

Did you get my previous text?

Laney knew how important the gala was to her. She'd obviously forgotten this was the night of the event. Otherwise, she wouldn't have expected a timely reply.

Savannah scrolled up the message chain.

It's been two months. Give up and come home. I feel icky lying to Gramps. Giving you one week. Won't do it anymore.

If her grandfather learned what she'd been doing, he'd insist that she stop putting herself at risk by working in what he referred to as "a den of hyenas."

Just when she was so close to finding answers.

Savannah quickly typed a reply.

Please think about what you'll be doing, Laney. I'm so close. Nearly got Joseph Abbott to admit everything just moments ago.

Savannah stared at her phone, as if that would make Laney's response come any faster.

Another alert came.

Two weeks. No more.

Savannah huffed. That didn't give her much time, but two weeks was better than one.

It was time to beat the Abbotts at their own game. She'd have the same level of callous disregard for them as Joseph Abbott had for her grandfather. She'd be as ruthless as Duke Abbott had been when he'd acquired Kayleigh Jemison's family property for a song.

She'd do whatever it took to resolve the issue once and for all.

Even if the truth would hurt Blake.

# Seventeen

Blake stood at the window in his office, watching as a gentle breeze stirred the water on the lake. He shut his eyes for a moment, but it made no difference.

Eyes wide open or tightly shut, Savannah Carlisle had taken up residence in his head.

Blake groaned and returned to his chair. He finished his third cup of coffee and scrolled through his emails.

He'd made a couple of phone calls and answered a few emails. Otherwise, he'd gotten very little done. Instead, he'd been rehashing Laney's text message to Savannah. He imagined a dozen different scenarios her message could have alluded to. None of them good.

Blake picked up his desk phone to call Savannah. She'd been avoiding him since the night of the gala, more than a week before. And she'd made every excuse imaginable for why she couldn't come to his place.

Regardless of the consequences, they had to have this conversation. He'd confess to reading the text message and demand an explanation.

The door to his office burst open.

Blake hung up the phone. "Parker, don't you ever knock?"

His brother slipped into a chair on the other side of his desk, not acknowledging his complaint. "We need to talk."

"About what?"

"About whom," Parker corrected him. "Savannah."

Blake's spine stiffened and the muscles in his back tensed. He took another gulp of his coffee and shrugged. "What about her?"

"I'm concerned."

"About?"

Parker leaned forward, his voice lowered. "She's been asking a lot of questions."

"She's inquisitive. That's her nature." Blake had expected Parker to let him have it with both barrels over his affair with Savannah. "I'd say it's served us well."

Parker stood and paced. "It has when she's used it for us, not against us."

Blake sat on the edge of his desk. "What are you talking about?"

"She's been asking a lot of questions about our company. About how it got started and whether Gramps ever had a partner. Why is she suddenly so interested?"

"She works here." An uneasy feeling crawled up Blake's spine. Still, he folded his arms and shrugged. "That information could be useful as she prepares for the remaining jubilee events and news coverage."

"But why is she so fixated on some nonexistent business partner of Granddad's?" Parker shoved a finger in his direction.

That was odd. If she wanted to know, why hadn't she just asked him? It was one more thing they needed to discuss.

"I'll get to the bottom of it, Parker. Don't worry. Besides, it's not as if we have anything to hide." Blake studied his brother's face. "Do we?"

"No, but I still don't like it. Feels like she's got her own agenda. One that isn't aligned with ours." Parker sank into his chair again.

"Then why come to me? Dad's CEO of the company, and she reports directly to Max." Blake's eyes didn't meet his brother's.

"You hired Savannah, and I know…" Parker ratcheted down the judgment in his voice. "I know how fond you are of her."

Blake's jaw tensed. "I'd never jeopardize this company. Nor will I allow anyone else to. So if you think we have reason to be wary of Savannah…"

"That's not what I'm saying." Parker crossed an ankle over his knee.

"Then what are you saying?" Blake pressed his brother. If he was going to make an accusation against Savannah, he'd damn sure better be clear about it.

Parker tapped on the arm of the chair. "One of us needs to find out exactly what she's trying to uncover and why."

"Are you willing to possibly burn this bridge?" It was the same question he'd been forced to decide where he and Savannah were concerned.

"Dammit, Blake, none of us wants to lose her." Parker sighed heavily. "She's been good for us. Made a major impact in a short period of time. But our first job is to protect this distillery, and to protect the family. Even if that means losing Savannah."

Blake nodded. "Let's talk to Max about this when he returns from Philly tomorrow. Then we'll decide how to approach it."

The situation between him and Savannah had just become exponentially more complicated. If he gave her an ultimatum on their relationship, and she turned him down, the company's inquiry into her behavior would seem like retaliation.

That would be devastating to their reputation. Something he'd never allow.

# Eighteen

"I'm going on my dinner break now. Do you think I'll be able to clean your office when I return?" Maureen stood in the doorway in her housekeeping uniform, doing her best not to look annoyed.

"I'll try to finish up for the night before you come back." Savannah smiled at the woman, and she turned and left.

When the elevator doors closed, Savannah rushed to Maureen's cleaning cart.

Savannah had worked late every night since the gala, looking for her opportunity to search the archived files that predated the company's use of computers.

It was her last hope of finding something useful before her sister's looming two-week deadline.

Savannah retrieved the large key ring from Maureen's cart and made her way down to the file room. She tried nearly every key before she found the right one.

She slipped inside the large, windowless space and switched on her flashlight. The room smelled stale and dust floated in the air. Steel file cabinets lined the brick walls in the first portion of the room. Antique wooden furniture was pushed up against the back wall.

Savannah checked her watch. She had little more than half an hour. She moved to the file cabinet marked with the earliest dates and pulled out a drawer stuffed with yellowed files. Most of the papers were typed. Some were handwritten.

By his own admission, Joseph Abbott had dumped her grandfather as his partner before starting the company. Maybe the files contained information about the origin of the company's recipes and procedures.

Savannah checked her watch again and cursed under her breath. Fifteen minutes left.

She was dirty, sweaty, and had gotten several paper cuts during her frantic search through the files. She finally found a pad with notes written in familiar longhand.

Her grandfather's.

She removed the notebook and continued sifting through the files. Savannah opened an envelope marked "Old Photos." She recognized her grandfather in one of them. "Joe and Marty" was scribbled on the back.

Savannah froze at the sound of voices in the hall.

*Someone's coming.*

She quietly closed the drawer and hid in the shadows, crouching between a tall bookcase and a large antique bureau desk. She clutched her grandfather's notebook and the photo of her grandfather and Joseph Abbott.

Keys jangled in the door, and then the hinges creaked.

"Switch on the light. I just walked into a spiderweb."

Savannah's blood ran cold.

*What's Parker doing here?*

He'd never been her biggest fan, but lately he'd been grumpier and questioned everything she did.

Had he followed her down here?

The light switched on.

"So where's this stuff Mom just had to have tonight?"

*Max.* He'd left hours ago. Why had he returned? And what were they searching for?

Had her conversation with Joseph Abbott prompted them to destroy evidence of their theft?

"Mom had a few of the guys set the pieces she wants aside in the back."

*Blake.*

"Wait—do you guys smell that?" Blake sniffed, then glanced around the room. "Someone's been in here, and I know that scent."

Savannah pressed a hand to her mouth to muffle her

gasp. She was wearing the perfume Blake had bought her. Her heart beat furiously as footsteps crept closer.

Blake made his way through the maze of furniture until he was standing in front of her.

"Savannah, what are you doing in here? And why are you hiding?"

Her knees shook so badly she could barely stand. Blake didn't offer to help her up, so she braced herself on the wall and climbed to her feet.

"Blake, I'm so sorry." She could hardly get enough air into her lungs to say the words.

All three brothers stood in front of her.

"I knew something was going on with her." Parker's nostrils flared. His entire face had turned crimson. She got a chill from his arctic stare. "You aren't authorized to be down here. You're trespassing. You'd better have a damn good explanation for being here or I'm calling the sheriff."

Max almost looked amused. "Don't tell me this is how you've been spending all those late nights."

"I've never been down here before tonight. I swear."

"Why should we believe anything you say?" Parker demanded. "And where'd you get these keys?"

"From Maureen's cart. I recognize her key ring." The heartbreak in Blake's voice and the pained look in his eyes were unbearable.

Blake didn't deserve this. And nothing she could say would fix it.

"What's that you're holding?" Max asked.

"They're mine." She clutched the photo and notebook, her hands shaking.

"Hand them over." Blake held out his hand, his voice jagged.

Savannah released a long, agonizing breath. She had no choice. There were three of them and one of her. They weren't going to let her leave with the notebook and photo. She handed both items to Blake, who handed them to Max.

"That's it. I'm calling the sheriff. We'll have them search her. Who knows why she was down here or what else she might be hiding." Parker gestured wildly.

"Calm down, Park. Why don't we ask her what she's doing down here?" Max kept his voice calm. "Maybe Savannah has a logical explanation."

The three brothers turned to her.

Savannah stared at each of them, her gaze lingering on Blake's face. Tears stung her eyes and rolled down her cheeks.

"I was… I was looking for…" Savannah stammered.

She couldn't tell the Abbotts the truth. Not until she was sure she had solid documentation to support her grandfather's claim. Once they learned her reason for being there, they'd surely destroy any potential evidence.

The truth wasn't an option.

She'd tell them she was looking for info to use in the yearlong celebration of the company's inception.

"I came down here because…" Savannah snapped her mouth shut, stopped cold by the pain and disappointment in Blake's eyes.

She couldn't tell Blake the truth, but she wouldn't lie to him, either. Which left her out of options.

Savannah turned her attention to Parker. She held out the keys. "If you're going to call the sheriff, call him. I don't have anything else to say."

"Gladly." Parker pulled out his phone.

"Don't." Blake took the phone from him.

"Why not? We caught her stealing irreplaceable archival documents. Who knows what else she's taken since she's been here? She's obviously a thief." A vein twitched in Parker's forehead. "Likely a corporate spy. She was probably sent here by one of the Kentucky distilleries."

"Blake's right, Park. We don't need the bad publicity. It'll counter all the positive press we're getting now." Max clapped a hand on Parker's shoulder. "Most of it thanks to her."

"All right." Parker snatched the key ring from her open palm. "But I'm filing a complaint with the sheriff. So don't think of skipping town until everything has been accounted for."

"Of course." Savannah extricated herself from the small space, unable to bring herself to meet Blake's wounded gaze.

"Where do you think you're going?" Parker held up a hand, his large body blocking her exit. "A member of the security team will escort you to clean out your desk. It should go without saying that you're fired."

"Is that really necessary?" Blake turned to his brother.

"Very. Who knows what else she'll try to take on the way out," Parker insisted.

"No." Blake made it clear the topic wasn't up for debate. "We're not causing a scene. I'll walk her to her office, then to her car."

"Good idea." Max stuck his hand out. "Give me the key to your truck. Parker and I will load those tables and lamps Mama wanted for the barn."

Blake handed Max the truck key and took Maureen's keys from Parker. He gripped Savannah's arm and led her out the door to the elevator.

"Blake, I can't tell you how sorry I am."

"Then don't." He wouldn't look at her. The tone of his voice was icier than Parker's eyes had been moments earlier. Shivers ran down her spine.

When they got on the elevator, she plastered her back against the wall.

"I never meant to hurt you, Blake, I swear. This isn't what it seems."

"Then what is it, Savannah? Do you have a reasonable explanation for stealing the housekeeper's key, breaking into our archives and cowering in the corner? If so, I'd love to hear it."

Her eyes met his, tears spilling down her cheeks. Her answer caught in her throat.

She'd imagined the misery of the day when Blake would learn she was a fraud. But the pain in his eyes and the pain exploding in her chest were so much worse.

For an instant, she wished she'd never come to Magnolia Lake. But if she hadn't, she wouldn't have uncovered the hand-scribbled notes and photo that proved her grandfather had worked closely with Joseph Abbott.

"I wish I could tell you everything…but I can't. Not yet."

"You lied to me. Made a fool of me."

She'd misled Blake. Taken him off guard. But he wasn't the fool. She was. Because she'd fallen for him. Hard.

"I had no choice. Believe me."

"I wish I could." He stepped off the elevator and led the way to her office.

"Blake, what are you doing here?" Maureen looked up from searching her cart.

"I had to retrieve something from the archives. I forgot my key." He held out her key ring. "Hope you don't mind— I borrowed yours."

Savannah's breath hitched.

Blake was protecting her, even now. Allowing her to save face with Maureen.

"Of course not." Maureen grinned as she accepted the keys from Blake and dropped them into the pocket of her smock. "I was afraid I'd lost them some—" Maureen paused, her head tilted. She'd noticed Savannah had been crying.

"Savannah isn't feeling very well." Blake spoke up before Maureen could inquire. "We'll be ten or fifteen minutes. Then we'll be out of your way."

"Hope you feel better, Savannah." Maureen nodded and rolled her cart away.

Blake closed the door and shoved his hands in his pockets. He leaned against the wall, maintaining maximum distance between them.

"I'll help you carry your things down." His voice was stripped of the warmth and affection she'd come to adore. He was looking through her. Past her. Probably wondering what it was he'd ever seen in her.

The wave of nausea she'd been feeling for the past week rose. Savannah grabbed a half-full bottle of ginger ale from her desk and chugged it.

She dropped her planner, phone and a few other items from her desk into her bag and grabbed her purse. She held it up. "This is everything. Do you need to check it?"

Blake sighed, as if repulsed by, then resigned to, the idea of needing to search her.

He did a cursory search through the two bags she held open. Then he patted her pockets while she held her arms out wide and turned her back to him.

"One more thing." Savannah pulled a small package from her desk drawer and handed it to Blake. "I've been meaning to give this to you. It's one of those calming shirts for Benny, so he doesn't freak out during the next thunderstorm. Unfortunately, they didn't have one in my size."

Her crushed heart inflated the slightest bit when a small smile curled the edge of Blake's sensuous mouth.

The same mouth that had kissed hers. That was acquainted with her most intimate parts.

"Why didn't I see this coming?" Blake laughed bitterly as he scanned her office. "Your office is as nondescript as your apartment. No family photos. Nothing personal. You never intended to put down roots here. You used me, and I was such a fool that I begged you to do it."

Tears stung her eyes again and her nose burned. But Savannah bit her lower lip, refusing to let the tears fall. She had no right to cry. In this, she'd been the one who was heartless and cruel. Blake had been innocent.

And she'd hurt him. Just as his ex had. Only Savannah

was worse. She'd always known this was inevitable. That they would both be hurt.

It was a sacrifice she'd been willing to make for her family.

As Blake's eyes searched hers, demanding an answer, her conviction that the sacrifice was worthwhile wavered.

"I know you don't believe me, but I honestly didn't intend to hurt you. I swear." She swiped angrily at her eyes and sniffed.

"Say I'm crazy enough to believe that's true." His voice vibrated with pain and anger. "Then tell me why you did this. What did you hope to gain?"

Savannah lowered her head, unable to answer him. She'd betrayed Blake and lost the best man she'd ever known. And without the notepad and photo, she didn't have a single thing to show for it.

# Nineteen

Savannah pulled the covers over her head, blocking out the sunshine spilling through the curtains. It was nearly noon and she'd spent the entire morning in bed for the second day in a row.

She was stressed, scared, miserable and missing Blake. Her body wasn't handling the wave of emotions well. It rebelled.

She'd made countless trips to the bathroom and felt so tired and weak she could barely get out of bed. All of which was out of character for her. She prided herself on being able to endure just about anything. After watching their rattrap apartment burn to the ground with her parents inside, there was little else that could faze her.

*Until now.*

The attachment she felt to Blake Abbott was powerful. Unlike anything she'd experienced before.

She'd been in a handful of relationships. She'd even imagined herself to be in love once or twice before. But the end of those relationships hadn't shaken her to her core, the way losing Blake had.

She missed his intense, dark eyes, mischievous grin and sense of humor. She missed the comfort she felt in his presence—even if all they were doing was watching a movie together in silence.

Savannah clutched at the hollowed-out emptiness in her belly. She'd lost Blake and a job she actually loved. And she'd gained nothing. Except possibly an arrest record if Parker Abbott had his way.

She made another trip to the bathroom. After more retching, she rinsed her mouth and splashed cool water on her face, sure there was nothing left for her body to reject.

Savannah crawled back into bed and dialed her sister.

"Thought you weren't talking to me anymore." There was a smile in Laney's voice when she answered the phone.

Savannah was about to make a smart remark in reply, but the instant she heard her sister's voice, tears welled in her eyes. She whimpered softly.

"Savannah? What is it? What's wrong?"

Savannah told her sister about everything, including her relationship with Blake and how she'd hurt him.

"You're in love with him, aren't you?"

Savannah cried harder, unable to answer the question.

"Vanna, why would you do something so risky?"

"I only had two weeks to make something happen, so I switched to a more aggressive approach."

"Will the Abbotts press charges?"

"I don't know. Blake and Max won out against Parker that night. But in a full family meeting, I don't know if the two of them will be enough. If they don't take legal action, it'll only be because they don't want the bad publicity."

Her chest ached with the pain of letting down her family and losing Blake.

*Why does it hurt so badly when he was never really mine?*

Savannah hated herself for descending into a weepy, hot mess. She was the one who'd always taken care of Laney. Like she'd promised her father when she was a girl.

"What did Blake say when you told him about Granddad's claim?"

"I didn't tell him." Savannah dabbed her face with a tissue. "It would blow any chance of us getting proof down the road."

"What did you tell him?"

"Nothing. I couldn't look in his face and lie."

"You pleaded the fifth?" Laney groaned. "No wonder you nearly ended up in jail."

"And I still might."

"I'm sorry, Savannah. I know you'd hoped for a different outcome, but at least this is over and you can come back home. Harper and I miss you."

"Yeah." Savannah's response was flat. She hadn't expected to fall in love with Magnolia Lake and its town full of quirky people. But she'd begun to enjoy her life there. "Miss you, too."

"Wait... You haven't just fallen for Blake. You actually like living there, don't you? And I know you loved your job. No wonder you're miserable."

"And sick as a dog. Plus, I promised not to leave town until I get the okay from Parker and the sheriff."

Laney was silent for a few beats. "You're sick how?"

"A virus maybe. I've been run-down and exhausted. Nauseous. Haven't been able to keep my breakfast down the last couple of days." Savannah burrowed under the covers again. She felt nauseous just talking about it.

"Sweetie, you aren't late, are you?"

"For work? You do realize they fired me?"

"Not that kind of late."

"Oh!" Savannah bolted upright in bed when Laney's meaning sank in. "I can't be. We used protection and I'm on the pill."

"Protection isn't foolproof. Nor are the people who use it. Besides, if you slept with him that weekend you got trapped there by the storm...well, did you suddenly start carrying your birth control around with you?"

Savannah's forehead broke into a cold sweat. They both knew the answer to that question. She hadn't had her pills with her that weekend. And then there was that night they'd fallen asleep with the condom on.

"Shit."

"What is it?"

"I need to make a trip to the pharmacy."

"So there is a chance you might be pregnant."

"Can you at least *pretend* not to be excited about the

prospect?" Savannah paced the floor. "This entire situation is already a disaster. How on earth would I explain this to Blake?"

"Tell him the truth."

"Everything?" The thought made Savannah nauseous again. "Once he learns the truth, he'll never believe I didn't plan this."

"It's your only play here."

Savannah's chin trembled and tears flowed down her face. "Blake will never forgive me for what I've done. For how I hurt him."

"Calm down, honey. It isn't good for the baby if you're stressed out."

"Pump your brakes, sister." Savannah stopped pacing. "We don't know there is a baby."

The grin returned to Delaney's voice. "Well, it's time you find out."

"Did the lessons on knocking before entering begin and end with me?" Blake looked up from his computer as his brother Max slid into the seat on the other side of his desk.

"I need to tell you something, and it couldn't wait." Max's brows drew together with concern.

It had to be about Savannah.

"Did Mom and Dad decide whether to press charges?"

"Not yet, but I discovered something and I wanted to tell you before I tell the rest of the family."

"What is it?" Blake's heart thumped against his rib cage.

"Since Savannah wouldn't tell us why she was in the archives or why she wanted that photo and notepad, I did some digging."

"And?"

"The photo was of Gramps and a man named Martin McDowell. The notepad was his, too. Did she ever mention the name to you?"

"No." Blake shrugged. "Who is he, and why would she want his old stuff?"

"This is only a copy." Max handed him a file. "But I'm sure Gramps has the original locked away somewhere safe."

Blake quickly scanned the document, reading it three times. It felt like a cannonball had been launched into his chest. Blake fell back against his chair, speechless.

"Marty McDowell was Granddad's partner in the moonshine business. *Before* he opened the distillery," Max said.

"I had no idea he had a partner." Blake rubbed the back of his neck. "But that still doesn't explain why Savannah would want the guy's old stuff."

"I couldn't explain it, either, so I looked at her employee file. Take a close look at her birth certificate." Max indicated the file folder he'd given Blake earlier.

Blake studied the birth certificate carefully.

"Her mother's maiden name was McDowell." His heart thundered in his chest. "She's Martin McDowell's granddaughter."

Blake dragged a hand across his forehead. He really had been a fool. Savannah Carlisle wasn't interested in him in the least. She'd used him to get information about the distillery and their processes. And to gain access to his grandfather—the company's founder. She'd talked to him the night of the gala.

"McDowell must've sent her here to spy on us." Max leaned forward, his elbows on his knees.

"But why? What did they hope to gain?" Blake racked his brain for a reason.

"Sabotage?"

Blake rubbed at his throbbing temples. Savannah was clever and resourceful. If she'd come to work for them with a plan to sabotage the distillery and its reputation, there were any number of ways she could've done it. Yet she hadn't. Why?

"If sabotage was their aim, they're playing the long game. Because everything Savannah has done since she's been working for us has boosted our sales and gotten us good press."

"Hmm...that's difficult to explain." Max leaned back in his chair and perched his chin on his fist. "Guess there's only one way to find out exactly why she came here."

"You want me to talk to Savannah?"

"If you can't handle it...no problem." Max shrugged nonchalantly. "I'm sure Parker would be happy to do it."

"No." Blake shot to his feet, then cursed silently when Max chuckled. He sighed. "You knew I wouldn't let Parker do it."

"You care for Savannah, and she obviously cares for you. Maybe you can turn up that charm you think you have and get some straight answers from her."

Blake sank into his chair again and blew out a long, slow breath. He'd spent the past two days trying to scrub every happy memory of Savannah Carlisle from his brain.

It was an abysmal failure.

Her laugh and broad smile crept into his daydreams. At night, he'd been tormented by memories of her body—naked, in all its glory. Her gentle touch. The sound she made when she was close. The way she'd called his name.

Blake had cared deeply for Savannah. He'd been willing to break the rules for her. But she'd used him and was ready to toss him aside, while he'd been prepared to give her his heart.

"Look, I don't know what's been going on with you two." Max's voice stirred Blake from his thoughts. "Frankly, I don't need to know. But if talking to Savannah would be too difficult for you, it's okay. I'll talk to her."

"No." Blake's objection was much softer this time. "I'll try to get the truth out of her."

"Sorry things didn't work out." Max clapped a hand on his shoulder. "We all liked Savannah. Even Parker, in his own way. That's why he's so angry."

"Thanks, Max. I'll let you know what I find out."

When Max left, Blake loosened his top button and heaved a sigh. He was ready to face Savannah again. Only this time, he was the one who held all the cards.

# Twenty

Savannah sat on the edge of the tub, rooted to the same spot she'd been in for the past ten minutes. She'd taken three different pregnancy tests. Each had given her the same answer.

*I'm pregnant.*

Savannah got up and stood in front of the mirror, staring at her image. Red, puffy eyes. Hair pulled into a frizzy, low ponytail.

She looked a hot mess, had no job and had let down everyone who cared about her. Her grandfather, Laney, Harper and Blake.

Now she was growing a human being inside of her. A tiny little person for whom she'd be responsible.

Savannah braced her hands against the sink, her head throbbing and her knees unsteady.

*I'm going to be a mother.*

Being a parent wasn't something Savannah had ever really considered. Not the way Laney had. Yet the moment she'd seen the word *Pregnant* on that third test, she knew instantly she wanted this baby.

Suddenly, nothing was more important than her child. And there was one thing Savannah knew for sure. She'd never use this child as leverage against Blake and his family.

She'd tell Blake about the baby, because he deserved to know. But only once a doctor had confirmed the test results.

She owed Blake the truth. And she owed her child the chance to know its father—if that was what Blake wanted.

After Savannah called her sister to relay the news, she stared at the phone in her hand. She wished she could call Blake and tell him they were going to be parents. And that he'd be genuinely happy about it.

She decided to call her grandfather instead. She wouldn't

tell him where she'd really been or about the baby. Not until she was 100 percent sure. But she needed the comfort of hearing his voice.

Still, she couldn't help thinking about her grandfather's reaction when he learned the identity of his great-grand-child's father.

*How do I explain this to him?*

Savannah screwed her eyes shut. Her grandfather would be hurt and angry. Of all the men in the world, she'd chosen to make a child with an Abbott.

His mortal enemies.

Savannah wiped angrily at the tears that wouldn't stop falling. No matter how much the truth would hurt her grand-father, she wouldn't lie.

She was exhausted by deception. Weary from trying to walk the line between truth and an outright lie.

When she returned to West Virginia, she'd tell her grand-father everything.

Before she could dial his number, there was a knock at the door.

*Kayleigh.*

Savannah hadn't moved her car or left the apartment in two days. Until this morning, when she'd made her run to the pharmacy looking a disheveled mess. Kayleigh would have noticed and been worried.

Plus, it was Magnolia Lake. News of her firing was prob-ably all over town by now.

Savannah counted to three and opened the door.

"Blake?" Her heart nearly stopped.

He was as handsome as ever in a pair of gray dress pants and a baby blue checkered shirt. Yet there was something in his face and eyes. He looked tired and as miserable as she felt.

"What are you doing here? Did your family decide to—"

"Nothing's been decided yet." His response was curt. "That's why we need to talk. Now."

Savannah let him in. "Have a seat."

"No, thank you. I won't be long."

Another wave of nausea rolled over her. She sat on the sofa, her legs folded beneath her as Blake paced the floor.

Finally, he turned and glared at her.

"I'm so angry with you, Savannah. I don't know where to begin."

She chewed on her lower lip. "Then let me start by saying I am truly sorry. I honestly never meant to hurt you. Even before I knew—"

"How easily you could manipulate me?"

That hurt.

"Before I knew what an incredible man you are. That you'd never purposely hurt anyone. I was wrong about you."

"Not as wrong as I was about you." He dropped into the chair across from her, as if his legs had buckled from the weight of the animosity he was carrying.

"I deserve that."

"You're damn right you do." His eyes blazed. "You're not the first corporate spy we've encountered. But none of them seemed willing to take things as far as you did."

"I didn't intend to get involved with you. I came here to do a job. And maybe in the beginning, I didn't care who got hurt. But then I got to know you. All of you. Suddenly, things weren't so simple."

"Not that you let that stop you."

"There was too much at stake. I couldn't let my feelings for you get in the way."

His steely gaze cut through her. "You still haven't told me why you did this. What was your endgame?"

"You wouldn't understand." Savannah went to the kitchen and poured herself a glass of ginger ale.

He stood, too, and turned to her, his arms folded. "Try me."

"Why does it matter?" She put the glass down roughly.

"What I did was wrong, but I swear to you, I did it for an honorable reason."

They stared at each other in silence. They were playing a game of chicken and waiting for the other person to blink.

Savannah walked around Blake, back toward the couch.

"How's your grandfather?"

She froze, then glanced over her shoulder at him. The hair stood on the back of her neck and her hands trembled. He wasn't making a friendly inquiry about her family.

Blake knew who she really was.

Still, she wouldn't blink first. "I was about to call him before you arrived."

"Why? To tell him his little spy got pinched?" Blake shook his head. "What kind of man would send his granddaughter to do his dirty work for him?"

"My grandfather didn't send me." She folded her arms over her chest. "He'd never have allowed me to put myself in jeopardy this way."

"You expect me to believe Martin McDowell didn't send you here? That he was oblivious to your little plan?"

"It's the truth."

Blake stepped closer. "Your word doesn't hold water around here anymore."

Savannah lowered her gaze. Her voice was softer. "Grandpa didn't know, I swear."

"Maybe we're going after the wrong person." Blake folded his arms and rocked back on his heels. "The marionette instead of the puppet master."

"No, please…my grandfather didn't have anything to do with this. It was all me. My sister can testify to that."

"And was she involved, too?"

"Laney never wanted me to come here, and she's been begging me to give up and come home."

Blake rubbed his chin. "You want to keep them out of this? Then tell me the truth. Why did you come here? What does Martin McDowell have against our family?"

Savannah fought back tears. If she showed her hand to the Abbotts, she'd lose the element of surprise and jeopardize any chance of making a claim against them. If she didn't, her sister and grandfather would be pulled into the mess she'd made.

"Tell me the truth, Savannah, or I swear I'll do whatever it takes to make your grandfather pay for this."

"It isn't my grandfather who needs to pay for his sins." She blinked back the tears that made Blake a blur. "It's yours."

# Twenty-One

"What are you talking about?" Blake returned Savannah's defiant gaze. Her expression had morphed from fear and concern to righteous indignation.

"I'm talking about how he betrayed my grandfather. Cheated him. Is stealing from him even now."

Now Blake was furious. He knew his grandfather well, had worked beside him as long as he could remember, learning the business of making premium bourbon. He had so much affection for the old man. Joseph Abbott was a generous and loving man, and a pillar in his adopted community of Magnolia Lake, where he'd raised his children and grandchildren.

"How dare you accuse my grandfather of being—"

"A thief."

"That's a lie. My grandfather didn't steal anything from anyone. Why would he need to? He's a wealthy man. He can buy whatever he wants."

"He's a wealthy man *because* he's a thief." Savannah stepped closer. "Why don't you ask him where he got that recipe for his world-renowned bourbon?"

"That's what you were looking for? The recipe for our bourbon."

"Unlike most distilleries from here to Kentucky, you've taken great pains to conceal your grain bill." Her tone was accusatory.

"Even if you had our mash bill, that's only part of the recipe. There's the water source, our proprietary yeast strain and so many other factors."

"Then why is it so top secret, Blake? Ask yourself, and really, truly allow yourself to consider the answer. No matter where it leads you."

"No." Blake ran a hand through his hair. "Gramps would never do that. He'd never steal someone else's work. If you knew anything about him, about his work ethic, you'd know that's not possible."

"Let's forget about your grandfather for a minute. Tell me how your father acquired the land you expanded on."

Blake narrowed his gaze. "The Calhouns' old place?"

"How'd your father acquire the property?" She repeated the question.

"Ownership fell to Mae Jemison—Kayleigh's mother. She was the last of the Calhouns still living around here. She sold the place to my father."

"You mean your father swindled her out of it. Paid her pennies on the dollar because Kayleigh's father was dying, and her mother needed the money to help her girls finish college."

"Who told you—" The question answered itself when he remembered he was standing in the middle of an apartment owned by Kayleigh Jemison.

That explained why Kayleigh had been so cold toward his family since she'd returned to town a few years earlier. Not that she'd had any great love for them before. She and Parker had bumped heads for as long as he could remember.

Still, he had no idea Kayleigh harbored such ill will against them. Especially since they'd barely broken even at the time of the purchase, with the amount they'd had to invest in it.

"That property was an overgrown mess. It was littered with rusted, broken-down machinery and a couple of run-down shacks. Large tanks had been leaking fuel onto the property for years. It cost us a fortune to clean it up and make it usable again."

"Of course you'd say that." Savannah folded her arms.

The move framed her breasts, which looked fuller than he remembered. Or maybe it was his brain playing tricks on him. Making him want her even when he knew he shouldn't.

"It's true."

"Why would Kayleigh lie about it?"

He shrugged. "Maybe that's what her parents told her. Or maybe that's just what she chooses to believe. I don't know, but I do know my father. And he wouldn't have cheated them."

"You're just blind where your family is concerned." Savannah propped her hands on her hips. "The mighty Abbotts can do no wrong."

"Never said that. No one is perfect, and we've all made our fair share of mistakes."

He narrowed his gaze at her, chastising himself. Even now, what he regretted most was that he couldn't be with her.

"Maybe you should talk to your grandfather and father before you dismiss what I'm saying. Find out what they have to say to these accusations. You might not like what you hear."

Savannah turned around and bumped into the table, knocking her glass onto the floor, where it shattered.

She stood there, her hands shaking.

"Where do you keep the broom and dustpan?"

Savannah shook her head, as if she were coming out of a daze. She stooped to clean up the mess. "I've got it."

"You're in your bare feet." He gestured toward her. "You're going to—"

"Ouch." She lifted her bleeding foot; a shard of glass was embedded in it.

"Sit down," he instructed, glad she complied without further argument. "There must be a first-aid kit around here. Where is it?"

"In the linen closet in the hall." She drew her foot onto her lap and examined it.

Blake went to the hallway and opened the closet. He spotted the white metal box with red lettering on the top shelf. He pulled it down and looked inside. There were bandages, gauze, alcohol wipes and a few other items. He grabbed a clean washcloth and went to the bathroom to wet it. When he wrung it out, he knocked something to the floor.

Blake froze, his eyes focused on the white-and-blue stick.

*A pregnancy test.*

His heart thudded against his rib cage. He retrieved it from the floor and read the word on the screen over and over. As if it would change if he read it one more time.

*Savannah is pregnant.*

Blake swallowed hard, his mouth dry. Was that the whole point of this game? For Savannah to bear an Abbott heir?

His head was in a dense fog and the room was spinning. He returned to the living room, his steps leaden.

He handed her the first-aid kit and washcloth. "You still haven't told me. What was your objective in coming here?"

Savannah seemed to sense the anger vibrating off him. She pulled a set of tweezers from the first-aid kit and tugged the piece of glass from her foot.

"To restore my grandfather's legacy and get what's owed to him."

"Money. That's what this is all about." He'd encountered lots of women whose only interest in him had been his family's fortune and name. Until now, he'd never imagined Savannah Carlisle was one of them. "That's all it's ever been about for you."

Her chin dropped to her chest and her eyes—already red and puffy—looked wet.

"Don't look at me as if I'm some moneygrubbing gold digger. I'm not here for a handout. I only want what's owed to my grandfather."

"You want King's Finest." His gut churned as the realization dawned on him. "That's why you've worked so hard to grow the company's sales. You hope to acquire it."

"Only the half that belongs to my grandfather." She sat taller, meeting his gaze. "We don't want anything we didn't earn."

"And how exactly is it that you *earned* half of King's Finest?"

"By providing your grandfather with the recipe he's used to build his fortune." She narrowed her gaze at him. "And I think I'm being generous in saying we're only entitled to half the company. A jury might make the argument that all of the profits should go to our family."

"Bullshit." Blake's face was hot and his heart beat like a war drum. "If you thought you had a legitimate claim, why not take it to court? Why all of the cloak-and-dagger corporate espionage?"

"My grandfather doesn't have any proof."

"If the recipe is his, it should be easy enough to prove." He gestured angrily. "Take a bottle of King's Finest to a chemist to see if his recipe and ours are the same."

"It isn't that simple." Savannah lowered her gaze, focusing on cleaning her wound and opening a bandage. "He no longer has the recipe. It got lost in the fire at our apartment."

"Why would your grandfather have entrusted something so important to someone else?"

Her cheeks reddened. "I... I don't know."

"Then how did you intend to prove that our bourbon recipe is his?" He stepped closer.

She bit her lower lip and avoided his gaze.

"Remember our deal? Tell me the truth, in its entirety. Or we'll go after your grandfather and sister, too."

Savannah repositioned herself on the sofa. "I hoped to find evidence that would corroborate Granddad's story."

"That's why you were in the archives that night. Looking for proof of your grandfather's involvement in creating the original recipe." Her expression confirmed his theory. "And did you find anything besides the photo and notepad?"

"No, but maybe if I'd had more time to search the files or to talk to more people—"

"Like my grandfather." Blake swallowed hard, remembering that his grandfather had looked perturbed and had gone home soon after his conversation with Savannah.

"What did my grandfather tell you?" Blake had an unsettling feeling in his gut.

"That he did have a partner in the moonshine business before he started King's Finest. I was *this* close to getting him to name my grandfather as the partner he left behind."

"I don't know what role your grandfather played, but my grandfather inherited that moonshine business from his father. And he kept his father's recipe."

"Your grandfather knew nothing about the business when his father died. He was too young. My grandfather taught him the business and tweaked the recipe."

"Even if that was true, you just said he helped tweak my great-grandfather's recipe. That still makes it *our* recipe."

Savannah blinked rapidly. It seemed she hadn't considered that before. "The courts will determine that."

"If you've known about this story all your life, why wait until now to try and get proof?"

"My grandfather is gravely ill." Her eyes filled with tears. "I couldn't bear the thought of him never realizing his dream. Never getting the recognition he deserved."

Blake sighed. For all he knew, they were a family of grifters who'd pulled this stunt on other wealthy families.

He could hear his mother's voice in his head. *And that's why we don't date employees, son.*

Savannah shoved her feet into a pair of shoes and got a broom and dustpan to clean up the glass.

She stooped to the floor, her short shorts providing an excellent view of her firm, round bottom.

He had zero self-control, which was exactly how he'd ended up in this mess in the first place.

*She's a liar and a user. Best not forget that.*

"Anything else you need to tell me?"

Savannah's shoulders stiffened. She shook her head and finished sweeping up the glass before returning to the sofa.

Blake's heart contracted in his chest. His limbs felt heavy.

He was desperate to believe some part of Savannah's story. To believe she'd been sincere in their moments of intimacy, which had evidently led to the conception of a child.

His child.

He wanted a reason to believe their relationship hadn't been part of Martin McDowell's calculated effort to swindle his family out of half their fortune.

But even now, when she'd agreed to put all her cards on the table and level with him, she wasn't capable of telling the complete truth.

Blake pulled the blue-and-white indicator from his back pocket. The one that declared the truth in a single, devastating word.

"Then how the hell do you explain this?"

Savannah gasped, her fingers pressed to her lips. "What are you doing with that?"

He ignored the question, asking one of his own. "Is it mine?"

Her head jerked, as if she'd been slapped. "Of course."

"You say that like I can just believe you, no questions asked." The pained look in his eye hurt even more than his question had. "How do I know this isn't part of the sick game you're playing?"

She felt the tears rising. "I'd never lie to you about this… about our child."

"You just did. I asked if there was anything else you needed to tell me and you said no. I'm pretty sure the fact that I might be a father qualifies as something I'd need to know."

"I wanted to be sure."

"There were two more of these in the garbage." His voice boomed, making her jump. "That wasn't confirmation enough?"

"I wanted indisputable confirmation from a doctor. I

didn't think you'd believe me otherwise. I was afraid you would think—"

"That this was your backup plan all along?"

Hot tears burned a trail down her face. She wiped at them angrily. "You don't honestly believe I'm capable of that."

Blake huffed, sinking onto the sofa beside her. "A few days ago, I wouldn't have believed you were capable of any of this. I was stupid enough to think you actually cared for me."

"Oh, Blake, I do." Savannah placed a hand on his arm, but pulled it away when he glared at her. "I never intended to get involved with you. But there you were. Handsome and funny. Sweet. Persistent." She wrapped her arms around herself, an inadvertent smile playing on her lips. "I honestly couldn't help falling in love with you."

She'd admitted she'd fallen in love with him, and he hadn't so much as blinked.

"Did you know about the baby the night we found you in the archives?"

"No." Her voice was barely a whisper. "I only found out this afternoon. I have the receipt from the drugstore across the street, if you don't believe me."

"I can't believe anything you've said, since the moment we met." Blake shot to his feet and paced.

"Everything I've told you is true. About my grandfather and parents. About my sister. Even my résumé. All of it's true. Check."

"Believe me, I will." He tossed the pregnancy test on the table in front of her and left, slamming the door behind him.

# Twenty-Two

Blake left a trail of burned rubber in his wake as he exited the parking lot behind Savannah's apartment.

He was a complete idiot.

Savannah Carlisle had played him like a fiddle from the moment she'd first sashayed into his office.

She'd been smart and confident with just the right amount of Southern sass. She'd flirted with him, then feigned a lack of interest, posing a challenge he simply couldn't resist.

Then the storm had given him the opportunity to ride in like the hero on a white horse and save her.

*She didn't ask to be rescued. You insisted on it.*

A little voice in the back of Blake's head refused to let go of the belief that, on some level, what he and Savannah shared had been real. He was hurt by what she'd done. Furious that she and her grandfather had taken aim at their company. And still, something deep inside of him couldn't accept that she'd purposely used him as a pawn.

Martin McDowell had obviously filled his granddaughter's head with lies her entire life. Built up some crazy fantasy that they were the rightful owners of King's Finest.

Maybe Savannah really hadn't intended to get involved with Blake. But once she had…how could she allow things to escalate, knowing how he felt about her?

How could the woman he thought he knew use him that way?

Blake pulled into the drive of his grandfather's log cabin by the lake and knocked at the door.

"Well, this is a surprise." The old man chuckled. "Didn't expect to…" He shoved his glasses up the bridge of his nose. "What's wrong, son? You look like you've lost your best friend."

"We need to talk, Granddad." Blake followed his grandfather into the house and sat beside him on the plaid sofa in the den.

"About what?"

Blake was embarrassed to relate Savannah's accusations. Afraid there may actually be some truth to them.

"Blake, whatever you need to tell me…it isn't the end of the world." His grandfather gave him a faint smile. "So just say it. We'll get through it."

"You already know what happened with Savannah."

"Yes." His grandfather nodded gravely as he rubbed his whiskered chin. "Shame. I liked the young lady quite a lot. Seems you did, too."

*Is there anyone who doesn't know what a fool I was?*

"Max did some digging. He discovered that Savannah is the granddaughter of Martin McDowell."

The man's mouth fell open, his large eyes widening. He seemed to be staring into the past. "There was something familiar about her. Couldn't put a finger on it then, but now… now it all makes sense. She has her grandfather's nose and eyes. His boldness and spirit. But she has more business acumen than Marty ever had."

A knot clenched in Blake's belly. "I thought you inherited the business from your father when he died in his accident. When did you have a partner?"

"I was quite young when your great-grandfather died. Barely even a teen. Papa had wanted to teach me the business, but Mama wouldn't hear of it. White lightning was the reason she was so unhappy, despite the money and comforts we had. Eventually, it was the reason my father died."

"He'd been drinking." Why hadn't he realized that before?

"Wrapped his car around a tree coming home from a juke joint in the wee hours of the morning." His grandfather groaned. "Not the kind of thing I was proud to talk about."

"So you learned the business from Martin McDowell."

"He was a bit older than me, but he'd worked with my father. A couple years after my father died, we were just about broke. I found Martin, and I made a deal with him for a sixty/forty partnership split if he taught me everything he knew...everything my father had taught him. He was the muscle and he negotiated deals for us. Together we tinkered a bit with Papa's recipes."

Blake could barely hear over the sound of blood rushing in his ears. "Granddad, Martin is claiming that our bourbon recipe is his. That you stole it."

"That's a goddamned lie." His grandfather shot to his feet, his forehead and cheeks turning bright red. "That was Papa's recipe."

"But you just said..."

"I said we tinkered with the recipe while he was my partner. But I kept perfecting it, even after I bought him out."

"You bought him out as your partner?"

"Still got the paperwork in my safe-deposit box at the bank."

"That's good. You have proof." Blake heaved a sigh of relief.

"Why do I need it?" His grandfather raised a wiry, white brow.

"Because Martin's got it in his head that half of King's Finest should be his. That's why Savannah came to work for us. To find proof that her family should be part owners."

The old man averted his eyes and grimaced.

"What is it, Granddad?" Blake gripped his grandfather's wrist and the old man shifted his gaze to him. "Like you said, whatever it is, we'll get through it. We always do."

Joseph Abbott groaned and sank down on the sofa again. He dragged a hand across his forehead.

"By the time I was twenty-one, I got tired of Martin trying to boss me around. The business had belonged to my father, and I wanted it back."

"So you bought him out."

His grandfather nodded. "Even as a kid, I dreamed big. But Marty wanted to stick to what we'd always done. I wanted to start a proper distillery. Become a respectable citizen with no need to dodge the law. Martin had no interest in doing that."

"If you bought him out fair and square, he has no claim," Blake pointed out.

"True." His grandfather's voice lacked conviction. "But I wasn't very fair to him, either." He lowered his gaze. "He was a heavy gambler, and I knew he'd go for a lump-sum payout, despite it being less than half of what was probably fair at the time."

His grandfather ran a hand over the smooth skin of his head. "Always felt bad about that. Especially after he gambled most of it away. Got in debt to some pretty shady characters. He and his wife left town in the dead of the night. Haven't heard from him since."

"If you felt so bad, why'd you…?" Blake stopped short of using the word *cheat*. "Why'd you shortchange him?"

"Didn't have enough saved to buy him out at a fair price. Not if I was going to buy my building, get new equipment and hire workers. I used his vice against him. It's not one of my prouder moments, son."

"So Martin was aware you wanted to start a legal distillery?"

"Like I said, he didn't have the vision his granddaughter has. Martin thought it was a terrible idea. He expected the venture to go up in flames, as it had for a few other moonshiners who'd tried to take their business legit."

"So he made a choice." Blake needed to believe his grandfather was the upstanding man he'd always thought him to be. That he hadn't wronged Savannah's grandfather. Joseph Abbott had always been his hero. Even more than his own father.

"He did. And when he signed the contract, he relinquished everything. Including the right to take up a similar business in the state for at least fifty years."

The answer to the question he'd posed to Savannah earlier. Why now?

"So legally, he has no claim to King's Finest."

"No. Got myself a damn good lawyer to draw up that contract." His grandfather's voice was faint and there was a faraway look in his eye. "It's airtight."

"But?"

"But I do feel I owe him something. I was a young man making gobs of money. I got a little bit full of myself, and I wasn't as fair as I should've been to Marty after everything he'd done for me." His grandfather rubbed his chin. "We certainly wouldn't be what we are today without him."

"But technically, Martin sold all of the recipes, all of the processes to you."

"Legally, yes." His grandfather nodded. "Morally... I've always felt like I gave the guy a raw deal."

"There's something else you need to know." Blake sighed. "Savannah...she... I mean, we..."

"Go on, son." His grandfather prodded. "At this rate, I'll be called home before you get the first sentence out."

"She's pregnant."

"And you're the father, I assume."

"Yes." The word was a harsh whisper.

"Sounds like we both need a drink." His grandfather moved to the bar and poured two glasses of their top-shelf bourbon. The same drink Blake had shared with Savannah the night of the storm. Joseph handed him a glass and returned to the sofa.

"Congratulations are in order, I suppose." His grandfather sipped his bourbon.

"It hasn't sunk in yet." Blake sipped from his glass.

"So you didn't know who Savannah was or why she was here?"

Blake shook his head. "I only learned the truth today."

His grandfather stared into his glass for a moment before meeting his gaze. "Do you love her, son?"

"I think I do. At least, I did before I realized it was never about me. It was about the money and restoring her grandfather's legacy."

"Can't it be about both?"

"Sir?"

"Maybe she did come here with the sole purpose of getting what she felt her family was owed...a noble thing, in my mind. But that doesn't mean she didn't fall for you along the way."

"What makes you believe that, Granddad?"

"Explains the tortured look in her eyes the night we met. When she was grilling me about the history of the company. Now I understand what I saw in her eyes. She probably hated me. Wanted revenge. But then there were her feelings for you. Must've been a mighty struggle for her."

Blake didn't directly address his grandfather's conjecture. "Do you think Martin McDowell is the kind of man who would've sent her here, hoping that one of us would get her pregnant? It'd be a slam-dunk way to ensure their family got a stake in the company."

"Never. In fact, I'm shocked he would've agreed to her coming here at all. He was too proud a man to let his granddaughter fight his battle."

Blake sighed in relief. "She claims he doesn't know she's here or what she's been up to."

"Does Savannah seem to you like the kind of person who'd trick you into getting her pregnant?" His grandfather took another sip of his drink.

"No." Blake finished his bourbon and put the glass down. "Then again, I wouldn't have thought her a spy. So what do I know?"

"You know you care about the girl and that she, like it or not, is carrying the first of the next generation of Abbotts." His grandfather's mouth curled in a reserved smile.

Blake's head spun. Not from the bourbon, but from the idea that he would be a father. It certainly wasn't under the circumstances he would've wished, but still…he was going to be a father.

He poured himself another glass and topped off his grandfather's drink before settling on the sofa again. He studied the ceiling, his mind spinning.

"The question is, is it possible for you two to get past this? If you really care for this girl, maybe you can salvage it," his grandfather said. "If not, you still need to have an amicable relationship for the sake of the child."

"I don't know if I can get past what Savannah did. I know she felt she had good reason, but how can I ever trust her again?"

"Only you can answer that, son." His grandfather's voice was filled with regret. "I'm sure Marty will probably always distrust me, too."

"What are you going to do?"

"Not sure. I find it best to sleep on decisions like this." Joe tapped a finger on his glass. "But call your parents, brothers and sister. Tomorrow morning, we need to have a family meeting."

# Twenty-Three

Savannah was going stir-crazy.

It'd been nearly a week since Blake had learned of her pregnancy. Two days of silence since she'd left him a message informing him a doctor had confirmed the test results. And still no word as to whether they planned to press charges.

There was a knock at her door and she answered it.

"Got a surprise for you." Kayleigh beamed, opening the signature pink box from the local bakery. "Sticky buns."

"My favorite. Thank you. C'mon in and I'll make you a cup of coffee. I can't eat these all by myself."

Savannah gave the woman whom she'd fast become friends with a grateful smile. She'd told Kayleigh the truth about why she'd come to Magnolia Lake and about the Abbotts discovering her plot. But she hadn't told Kayleigh about her and Blake. Or about the baby.

"I've gotta get downstairs and open the shop, but I brought you some company. That's the other surprise."

Kayleigh stepped aside to reveal her sister and niece in the doorway.

"Auntie Vanna!"

"Harper!" Savannah stooped to hug and kiss her niece. Then she stood and wrapped her sister in a hug. "Laney! I can't believe you guys came all this way."

Savannah's eyes filled with tears. She'd desperately missed her sister's face, so similar to her own. Laney's hair was styled in an adorable pixie cut, top-heavy with shiny, dark curls.

After turning the television to a kids' channel for Harper and setting the little girl up with her favorite snacks, Laney slid onto the couch beside Savannah.

"You ready for this?" She indicated Harper, singing along with her favorite educational show.

"I will be." Savannah's hand drifted to her belly and tears stung her eyes.

"Aww, honey, don't cry." Laney squeezed her hand. "Everything's going to be all right."

"Everything is *not* all right. I really screwed up." Savannah shot to her feet and paced the floor. "I still don't have anything to support Gramps's claim. I'm apparently the worst burglar in the history of burglars. There is still the very real possibility the Abbotts could send me to jail. Then let's not forget that I'm unemployed and pregnant... by an Abbott."

She dropped onto the sofa again, cradling her face in her hands. Her heart squeezed in her chest as she remembered Blake's face. How hurt he'd been to learn the truth. The tears started again.

"And my baby's father hates me. He doesn't want anything to do with either of us." Savannah wiped away tears.

"Did Blake tell you that?"

"No. But I got the hint from his radio silence." Savannah sighed. "I honestly don't believe things can get any worse."

A soft smile played on Laney's lips. "Then they can only get better."

Savannah loved how her sister saw the good in people and had an optimistic view of the world. But in the midst of her personal hell, with the world crumbling around her, she had no desire to pretend everything would be okay.

"Laney, maybe you missed some of what I just said." Savannah swiped a sticky bun from the box, took a bite and murmured with pleasure. "So far, the only upside to this has been that I can eat whatever I want without an ounce of guilt."

Her sister's smile grew wider. She stood and extended a hand to her. "You've been cooped up in this apartment too long. You need some fresh air. Let's go for a ride."

"I'm not supposed to leave town, and believe me, Magnolia Lake is so small that by the time we start the car, we'll already be out of it."

"I made an appeal to the sheriff. Got permission to take you on a little field trip." Laney pulled Savannah off the couch and steered her toward the bedroom. "Now take a shower and put on something nice. We'll take a little ride and get something to eat. You'll feel better. I promise."

Savannah shoved her sunglasses on top of her head and returned her seat to the upright position as Laney pulled her rental car into the parking lot of a medical center in Knoxville.

"Why are we coming here?" Savannah turned to Laney. "Are you all right? Is Harper?"

"We're both fine." A wide grin spread across her sister's face. "As for why we're here…you'll see. C'mon."

Savannah and Harper waited in a sitting area while Laney spoke to the attendant at the front desk. Then they had their pictures taken for temporary badges and rode the elevator to the fourth floor.

Laney tapped on a partially open door.

"Yes?"

Savannah's heart nearly stopped when she heard the familiar voice. She turned to her sister.

Laney nodded and smiled, taking Harper from her arms. "You two need to talk. Harper and I will be in the cafeteria."

Savannah burst through the door. "Grandpa, what on earth are you doing in Knoxville? And why were you admitted here? Is everything okay?"

"You won't believe me when I tell you." He chuckled, raising his arms to her. "Come here and give me a hug."

Savannah gave him a bear hug, hesitant to let him go. Delaying what she needed to do next.

*Come clean and tell him everything.*

She sat beside his bed, gripping his hand. "I have so much to tell you."

"It'll have to wait." He sighed as he rubbed his beard. "Because there are a few things I'd better tell you first."

"Like what?"

"Your sister told me why you came to Magnolia Lake, Vanna." He squeezed her hand, halting her objection. "Don't be mad at Laney. She did the right thing by telling me. If you should be upset with anyone, it's me."

"Why?"

"Because I left out an important piece of the story." His shoulders hunched and his chin dropped to his chest. "Joseph Abbott bought me out as a partner."

"You mean he already paid you?"

Her grandfather nodded. "A lump-sum payout to dissolve the partnership and secure full ownership of any recipes I helped develop."

"That changes everything, Grandpa. How could you not tell me that?" Savannah stood, her hand to her mouth. No wonder Blake thought they were crooks, trying to get one over on his family. "What happened to the money?"

His eyes didn't meet hers. "I had terrible drinking and gambling habits back then. Within a year, I'd gone through it all."

Savannah dropped into the seat again, too weak to stand. She'd risked everything based on a lie. A lie that led her to a man and a career she loved, but then had cruelly snatched them away.

"How could you let me believe all this time that you'd been cheated by the Abbotts?" Her body vibrated with anger.

"I may not have told you the entire truth, Vanna. But I did feel I'd been cheated. Joe didn't pay me my fair share. Then when he went on to make a fortune off formulas I helped create…" He sighed and shook his head.

Savannah was furious with her grandfather. And miserable over losing Blake.

"Do you have any idea what I've done to try and make things right for you? How much I've lost?"

"Laney told me." Her grandfather's eyes were shiny. He clutched her hand. "And I'm so sorry, dumplin'. To you and to the Abbotts. It was easier to blame them than to admit I'd chosen unwisely. That I'd only thought in the short term when I accepted that lump sum from Joe rather than being patient."

Savannah cradled her forehead in her palm, her lips pressed together to repress the scream building inside.

"I had no idea you'd take my words to heart, Savannah. That you'd act on them. You and your sister and little Harper... You mean everything to me. I couldn't protect your mama, but I've done everything I could to look after the two of you. I didn't want you to see me as a horrible failure. A man that never amounted to much of nothing."

"I never thought that, Grandpa. If it wasn't for you taking us in...who knows what might've become of Laney and me?"

"Still, what I done wasn't right, and I'm ashamed."

They were both silent for a moment. Savannah narrowed her gaze at her grandfather. "You still haven't explained what you're doing here in Knoxville."

"Joe Abbott."

"You talked to him?"

"He came to West Virginia to see me, a few days ago. Told me everything about you, about his grandson...and about the baby."

"You know about the baby?"

"I do. And I'm sorry about the split between you and the Abbott boy."

"Why? You always said not to trust an Abbott any farther than I can throw one." She folded her hands. "If Joe

Abbott cheated you out of a fair price for your share of the partnership, that only proves you were right."

"We both made mistakes back then, but I've compounded them by misleading you." Martin ran his free hand over his head. "And maybe Joe wasn't fair then, but he's making it up to me...to all of us, Savannah."

"What do you mean?"

A slow smiled curved the edge of his mouth. "I mean you did it, honey. Joseph Abbott and his family are giving us a stake in King's Finest. Not half, of course. But he's giving me a five percent stake in the company and he wrote me a check outright."

"For what?" Savannah couldn't believe what she was hearing. Surely it was a dream.

Her grandfather dug a piece of paper out of his wallet and handed it to her. She unfolded it and read it twice. It was a check for $1.5 million.

"Is this real?"

"Yes." He smiled, tears in his eyes as he cradled either side of her face and kissed her forehead. "I can't believe the chance you took for me. Or Joe's generosity. He brought me here on his dime to see if I'd be a good candidate for the therapy program they're conducting."

"That's incredible, Grandpa. I'm really happy for you." Savannah handed him back the check. She forced a smile, but tears brimmed, spilling down her cheeks.

She'd gotten everything she wanted for her grandfather and lost everything she never knew she wanted for herself. Her job with the Abbotts, her relationship with Blake, a chance for them to be a family.

"I'm glad Joseph Abbott is a decent man after all." Savannah wiped away the tears.

"I don't think that's why he did this at all." He folded the check and returned it to his wallet.

"Then why?"

"He did it for your beau, Blake. And for you." A smile softened her grandfather's face.

"Me? We only met once. Why would he care about doing anything for me?"

"He was impressed with you. With what you were willing to do for me. And what you've already done for his company. Not to mention the fact that you're carrying the first Abbott great-grandchild." Her grandfather's smile widened. "And my second."

Savannah forced a smile in return, determined not to shed any more tears.

"Then they won't press charges against me?"

Something Blake hadn't bothered to tell her. Just as he hadn't bothered to return the message she'd left confirming her pregnancy. A clear indication he wanted nothing to do with her or their child. It was a reality she needed to accept.

"Don't worry about that anymore. As soon as I'm out of here, we can go back home to West Virginia, if that's what you want."

"Of course it is." Pain stabbed her chest. Memories of the nights spent in Blake's bed played in her head.

He nodded sadly. "All right then, Vanna. You go on home. Get some rest now that you know everything is okay. Come back and see me tomorrow, if you have time."

She had nothing but time.

"See you tomorrow, Granddad." She kissed the old man's whiskered cheek before making her way to the cafeteria to find her sister.

*I honestly, truly did it.*

So why was she more miserable than she'd ever been?

Because Blake wouldn't answer her calls or return her messages. But she wouldn't leave town without thanking him and Joseph Abbott for what they'd done.

# Twenty-Four

"Can I talk to you, son?" Iris Abbott stuck her head in Blake's office.

"Sure. Come in." He finished typing an email to a group of distributors before giving her his full attention. "What can I do for you, Mama?"

She fiddled with her scarf, her expression apologetic.

"Whatever it is, Mother, just spit it out." He sat on the edge of his desk.

She paced the floor. "It's about Savannah."

"What about her? Is something wrong with her or the baby?"

"No, it's nothing like that."

Blake was still furious with Savannah. She'd lied to him. Gotten involved with him under false pretenses. Hid her pregnancy. Yet he couldn't stop thinking of her. Wanting her.

"What is it, then?"

"Let's just say she did too good of a job around here." His mother sighed. "I'm plumb exhausted from trying to pick up where she left off."

"I see." Blake returned to his seat. "Ask Max to run the event manager ad again. Hopefully, we can find a replacement before you get too swamped. In the meantime, Zora and I will help however we can."

"I suppose that's one way to go."

Blake put down his pen and cocked his head. "You're not suggesting that we—"

"Who better to carry out these plans than the brilliant mind that devised them?" his mother interrupted. "Besides, the distributors liked working with her. I didn't dare tell them she wasn't here anymore. I said she was out for a few weeks on personal leave."

"How could you even suggest we bring Savannah back?"

"Because she did exactly what we hired her to do and more. Did you know she'd already booked several corporate events and weddings at the old barn?" Iris wagged a finger. "We'll need to hire permanent event staff out there just to keep up."

The storage room at the barn. That was the last time he'd been with Savannah. His body hummed with electricity at the erotic memory.

He tried to push the sights and sounds of that night from his brain.

"So we'll hire permanent staff for the space. But that doesn't justify bringing back someone we can't trust."

"But I do trust her, honey. You're right—she should've told us the truth. But she had free rein while she worked here. If she'd wanted to harm our company or sell our secrets, she could've. But she didn't, because that was never her intention."

"She's a liar with a heart of gold, is that it?"

"Something like that." His mother smiled sadly. "Did I ever tell you that when I was about ten years old a man came to town and swindled my daddy out of a good portion of his savings?"

"No." Blake had learned more about his family's financial past in the last week than he had in more than three decades.

"It nearly broke him, and to be honest, he was never quite the same after that. He felt he'd failed us. I guess in some ways he had, going for a get-rich-quick scheme like that."

"Must've been tough for Grandpa Gus."

"It was tough for all of us. Especially for my mom. She'd never trusted the man to begin with and she'd begged my daddy not to invest with him."

"Did Grandpa Gus ever get his money back?"

"No. And I used to dream about tracking down that man and making him pay for what he did to my father. And to us." She leaned back in her chair, her eyes steely. "I'd have done just about anything to bring him peace again."

"I can't believe you and Gramps admire what Savannah did, as if she's some modern-day Robin Hood. Don't forget that would make us the villains in this story."

"I do admire her. Look, honey, I know this isn't what you want to hear. She deceived us and she hurt you, even if she didn't intend to. But from what I hear, she's hurting, too. You know Grandpa Joe already gave Martin his money and his stake in the company. If that's all Savannah cared about, would she still be walking around looking miserable?"

"How do you know that?"

"It's Magnolia Lake, darlin'," his mother said matter-of-factly. "I know everything that goes on around here."

"Maybe she should've considered that before she put herself in this position. Before she put us all in a compromising position."

"Maybe so. But let me ask you a question. And I want you to be completely honest, if not with me, then at least with yourself."

"Shoot."

"If the shoe had been on the other foot, how far would you have gone to get justice for your grandpa Joe?"

Blake's attention snapped to hers. His mother knew how much he loved and admired his grandfather. He would've gone to hell and back to protect the old man, if he believed someone had wronged him.

Apparently, Savannah had the same level of love and affection for her grandfather. Unfortunately, he hadn't told her the whole truth. But then again, neither had his.

"What does Parker think about giving Savannah her job back?"

When their family had met to discuss the situation, they'd all been angry at first. But when his grandfather explained the history between him and Martin McDowell, most of them had softened their stance. Only Parker had objected to giving McDowell a stake in the company.

Surely, Parker would be Blake's one ally.

"Your brother says that if you can deal with Savannah coming back here, he can, too." A slow smile lit his mother's eyes. "Parker says that for him, it's about the bottom line. And she's certainly proven she's good for that."

"It would be awkward, us working together and having a child together, but not actually being together."

"It's important that you two get along. There's my grandchild to consider, after all. So perhaps this is a good way to force your hand." Her voice softened. "Of course, there is another option."

Blake raised an eyebrow. "Which is?"

"Things wouldn't be so awkward if you two were actually together."

"Mother…"

"I know you love her, son. You're just being stubborn, because your feelings and your pride were hurt."

"You make it sound as if I'm being unreasonable. Aren't you the one who always told us that honesty is the very least we should expect in a relationship?"

"True." She nodded gravely. "But then I also told you that we sometimes do the wrong thing for all the right reasons. Can't you see that's what Savannah has done?"

"I appreciate what you're doing, Mother, but it's not that simple." Blake tapped his thumb lightly on the desk. "Parker is right, though. This is about the bottom line. Savannah's impact in her short time with the company is undeniable. I'll consider it, I promise."

Blake loved Savannah. He honestly did. But he didn't know if he'd ever be able to trust her again.

· He ruminated on the question for the rest of the day. It was still spinning in his head when he approached his driveway and found Savannah, parked there, waiting for him.

* * *

Savannah climbed out of her car as Blake pulled into the drive. She'd been parked there for an hour, determined not to leave until she'd said what she came to say.

"Hello, Blake." She was undeterred by his frown.

"Savannah." The iciness of his tone made her shudder. "Surprised you're still in town. After all, you got everything you came for."

His words sawed through her like a jagged blade.

"I needed to thank you and Mr. Abbott for everything you've done for my grandfather." Her mouth was dry and there was a fluttering in her belly. "You couldn't possibly know how much what you've done means to him and to our family."

"It means you won. Perhaps deservedly so," Blake acknowledged as he swiped the dogs' leashes from their hook on the wall. He opened the door and Sam and Benny raced toward her.

"Sam! Benny!"

The larger dog jumped on her, nearly knocking her backward. Blake was suddenly there with his arms around her, ensuring she didn't fall.

Her heart raced as her gaze met his.

Blake held her in his arms, his chest heaving. Sam poked her leg with his wet nose and Benny barked. Yet, in Blake's arms, it felt as if the world had stopped. It was only the two of them and the baby they'd made growing inside her.

"Thank you, Blake."

Blake released her without response. He grabbed the leashes he'd dropped, clamping one on Benny and the other on Sam.

"I missed you two." She showered the dogs with hugs and kisses. Their tales wagged and Benny licked her face. Savannah stood, meeting Blake's gaze. She swallowed the lump in her throat. "I've missed you, too, Blake."

Hurt and disappointment were etched between his

furrowed brows. Yet there was a hint of affection in his dark eyes.

If she could peel away the layers of pain and distrust, maybe they could salvage the warmth and affection buried beneath. Grow it alongside the love she felt for him and for their child. Nurture it until it turned into something beautiful and lasting.

He didn't acknowledge her admission. Instead, he gestured toward the path by the lake. "I have to walk Benny and Sam."

"Blake, I... I love you." The words stumbled from her lips.

"I would've given anything to hear you say that a couple of weeks ago." He sighed. "Now, how can I trust that it's not just another ploy to manipulate me?"

"I never used what happened between us to manipulate you. Everything I said to you...everything we did... For me, it was real. All of it." She bit back the tears that stung her eyes. "I never intended to fall for you. But I couldn't help wanting to be with you."

Benny and Sam started to whine.

"Walk with us?"

She fell in step beside them.

"If you feel...the way you say you do...why didn't you tell me before?"

"I felt guilty because of the secrets I was keeping. Making one confession without the other wouldn't have been fair to you."

"So what was the plan? To string me along until you found something?"

"There was no 'plan' where you were concerned." She wrapped her arms around herself as they stopped for the dogs.

"Then why did you get involved with me?" He studied her.

"It wasn't a choice." She couldn't help the involuntary

smile or the tears that leaked from her eyes. "How could I not fall for you? You're the most amazing man I've ever known."

"But you couldn't trust me with the truth?"

"I was torn between what I felt for you and doing right by my family. After I lost my parents, I promised myself I'd never stand by and do nothing again. I was determined to protect my family at all costs. Even if that meant losing what I wanted most. You."

"So you used me to get what you wanted, and I played right into your hands." Blake turned on his heels and headed back toward the house.

"I wasn't trying to use you, Blake." She scrambled to keep up with his long strides. "You were just...this vortex that pulled me in. I couldn't resist, and after a while, I didn't want to because you were incredible. And you made me feel special in a way I never had before. You made me want things I never wanted before."

He stopped and turned to her. "Like a baby?"

"Yes." Her mouth curved in a soft smile. She wiped away tears. "I didn't plan this baby, but the instant I knew, there wasn't a question in my mind about what I should do. I was given the most amazing gift. A piece of you. *Our* baby."

His gaze dropped to her hand on her belly. He swallowed hard, neither of them saying anything for a moment.

Blake walked away without a word.

Savannah wanted to dissolve into tears, but she had no right to expect forgiveness. All she could do was hope that someday he'd want to be part of their child's life.

Blake took the dogs inside. Savannah's words pierced the hardened shell that had formed around his heart. Reminded him of the incredible moments they'd shared.

During the past week, he'd been forced to question every moment. Every kiss. Wondering if any of it was real.

Something deep inside him believed it had been, and that

she truly did love him. He wanted to forgive her and to be excited about the child they were having.

But could he ever trust her again?

Blake stepped out into the garage again as Savannah opened her car door. The sight of her leaving triggered something in him. Maybe he didn't know for sure how things would end between them, but he knew he couldn't let her walk away.

"Where are you going?" He approached her.

"Back to my apartment, for now. Back to West Virginia once Grandpa is done with his treatments."

"Just like that…you're walking away?"

Savannah blinked, her brows scrunched in confusion. She shut the car door and walked toward him.

"You obviously don't want me here, and I don't want to make things worse. I just want you to know that you're welcome to be as involved in this child's life as you choose. I'd never stand in the way of that."

Blake took a few steps closer and swallowed the lump in his throat, unable to speak.

It was fear, plain and simple.

He wanted to be with Savannah. To raise their baby together. It would be difficult to get past this. To trust her implicitly. But it couldn't be worse than the torment that seized him as he watched her turn and walk toward her car again.

"Does that mean you don't want your job back?"

She turned toward him, eyes wide. "Your family would trust me to work for you again?"

Blake rubbed the back of his neck. "My mother, Max, Zora…even Parker… They all want you back. You're good for King's Finest. There's no disputing that."

"And what about you, Blake? What do you want?" She stepped closer and studied him. "As much as I love working with your family at King's Finest, I won't come back if it'll be too painful for you. I couldn't do that to you. I've already hurt you so much. I won't do it again."

Tightness gripped his chest as he stared into her lovely eyes, glistening with tears. His throat was raw with emotion.

Blake could see the love in her eyes. Hear it in her voice. He'd been right all along. Her feelings for him were real. Now that there were no more secrets between them, what remained was the love and friendship they'd been building. It ran deep, and it was as sweet and clear as the waters of King's Lake.

"What I want, Savannah, more than anything, is to be with you and our baby." He slipped his arms around her waist. "Because I love you, too."

He kissed her. Savored the taste of her sweet lips and salty tears. Then he took her inside, determined to make up for lost time. To make love to her and get reacquainted with every inch of her glowing skin.

Later, as they lay sleeping, he cradled Savannah in his arms, his hands perched protectively over her belly. His heart overflowed with the love he felt for her and for the child she carried.

Their child.

He pulled her closer, determined to never let them go.

# Epilogue

*Eleven months later*

The old barn had become a popular wedding venue, and it had never looked more elegant than it did now.

Blake surveyed the crowd of people who'd assembled in their Sunday best to help him and Savannah celebrate their special day. Family, friends, employees and townsfolk. Most of whom he'd known his entire life.

Blake's hands were shaking. His breath was ragged and labored. A stone lodged in the pit of his stomach.

But he didn't have an ounce of doubt about marrying Savannah Carlisle. Aside from the day little Davis was born, it was the happiest day of his life.

So why was he so nervous?

Maybe he was afraid Savannah would come to her senses, turn tail and run. That she'd decide she didn't want to be part of this big, noisy, opinionated family.

Blake clenched his hands together in front of him and released a slow breath.

He was letting his nerves get the better of him.

Savannah loved him and their son. With a love he felt in every fiber of his soul.

He'd seen that love, true and deep, in Savannah's hazel eyes each morning. Felt its warmth as they played with their child.

Was rocked by its power when he made love to her. Felt it surround him as they fell asleep in each other's arms each night.

No, he didn't question the authenticity of her love for him.

And unlike the feelings he'd once had for Gavrilla, what

he shared with Savannah wasn't contained within the small unit they formed. It encompassed both of their families.

"You ready for this?" Max, his best man, stood beside him.

"Never been more ready for anything in my life." Blake smiled at Davis, who waved his arms at him as his great-grandfather bounced him on his knee.

As the ceremony began, Blake's pulse raced. He watched their family and friends march down the aisle. His mother, Daisy, arm in arm with his cousin Benji. His brother Cole and his cousin Delia. Dallas Hamilton and Zora. Kayleigh Jemison and Parker—who had managed to be civil to each other through most of the proceedings. Then Savannah's sister, Laney.

His grandfather carried little Davis—the honorary ring bearer—down the aisle.

Laney's three-year-old daughter, Harper, scattered rose petals onto the white, custom aisle runner printed with his and Savannah's names and the words *Always and Forever*.

When the music changed and everyone stood, his heart felt as if it would burst. Savannah stood at the head of the aisle on her grandfather's arm.

The love of his life was an incredible vision to behold in an off-shoulder, antique white lace wedding gown. The mermaid silhouette hugged the curves that had mesmerized him the moment he laid eyes on them.

Savannah's hair was pulled into a tousled, messy bun low over one shoulder. A spray of flowers was intertwined in her hair.

She floated down the aisle toward him. All eyes were on her, but her gaze was locked with his. As if only the two of them were there in that old barn.

Savannah turned and kissed her grandfather's cheek, and Blake shook the old man's hand. Mr. McDowell was grateful he'd lived to see his granddaughter get married, and that he had the health and strength to walk her down the aisle.

Blake extended his palm and Savannah placed her delicate hand in his.

"You ready for this, baby?" he whispered as they turned and stepped onto the stage.

Savannah grinned, her eyes glistening with tears. "Blake Abbott, I can't wait to become your wife."

They stood before the magistrate in a room filled to capacity with the people they loved most, and she did just that.

* * * * *